TENNESSEE
Dreams

STACY BRADY

Stacy Dare Brady
Stacypdxbrady@gmail.com
www.tennesseedreams.net
https://fb.me/MyTennesseeDreams

To my family and friends for your inspiration and support.
Mom and Dad, please skip past all the sex scenes.

CHAPTER ONE

Sadie was desperate to get inside and out of the heat and humidity. Sweat trickled down her neck and ran between her breasts. She had spent the last fifteen minutes walking from her hotel in the heart of downtown Nashville to a brewpub that she had researched right after booking her business trip several months ago.

Business.

It made Sadie giggle like a child with a secret.

She had spent more time researching bars, restaurants and live music venues than reading the itinerary for the conference. She had never been to Nashville before, so when the opportunity came around to mix business with pleasure, Sadie figured why not. No one would ever know and who would care?

Sadie plotted her strategy. She realized that between the Tennessee State History Museum, the Country Music Hall of Fame, and the General Jackson River Boat Cruise, she would maybe attend two or three sessions at most during the two-and-a-half-day conference.

The welcome dinner later was definitely a no-go. Those dog and pony shows were never Sadie's cup of tea. She wouldn't be on his arm tonight and being on her own felt foreign now after all these years. Sadie liked to think that she was outgoing, perhaps when she was younger, but she had lost her confidence amongst strangers and felt shy and timid deep inside.

The cool air enveloped her body as she pushed open the door of the brewpub and walked inside. It was happy hour, and the bar was packed. Sadie was quite pleased with herself. It looked just like the pictures on the website, and she stood in the entryway craning her neck around for a full look.

The room before her was large with an L shaped oak bar at the back, rows of square tables towards the middle of the room, and along the perimeter sat a maze of comfy chairs and sofas. The patio was empty. No one was foolish enough to sit outside in the heat of the day, but Sadie could tell that it would be the heart of the brewpub after the sun had set. The windows along the patio resembled garage doors that rolled up, and there were tables and chairs around several gas firepits with a small strip of grass to the side that housed two cornhole sets and a small stage for music.

In Sadie's research of Nashville, she discovered that almost every bar and restaurant had some form of live music, mostly bluegrass, and country. She couldn't wait to enjoy everything that Nashville had to offer.

Sadie planned to sit in one of the comfy chairs or couches and decompress for a bit. She longed to sip on a cold beer and clear her head. She wasn't hungry yet, but she would need to eat before the show started. Sadie was free, and she felt giddy. In her purse was a single ticket to the Ryman Auditorium for the 7 p.m. Grand Ole Opry show.

As Sadie wandered through the perimeter of the bar, she quickly realized that the comfy chairs and couches were all taken. A big *Reserved For A Private Party* sign in one whole section.

"Great!" Sadie mumbled under her breath.

She didn't want to sit at a table in the middle of the room *alone*, so she turned her attention to the bar. There had to be at least twenty barstools, and they were all taken except for one – most likely, its occupant taking a quick bathroom break.

Sadie took a deep breath and clutched her black leather tote close to her side. It was worth a shot, otherwise… she'd be forced to pull her phone out and go searching for the address of her second choice. Sadie couldn't face walking around again outside in the heat of the day.

She cleared her throat and stood behind the empty bar stool. There were no napkins or glasses on the bar, so Sadie was hopeful. She was tired and ready to sit. The early morning flight into Nashville meant her day had started before the sun came up, and Sadie had already walked over 10,000 steps. The heat and humidity had turned her normally coifed A-line bob into an untamed wavy mess, and she was reasonably certain that her makeup had slid off her face after walking two blocks in the Tennessee sun.

"Is this seat taken?"

He abruptly turned, and her smile took his breath away. She wasn't from around here... he knew that in an instant as he let out a sigh and grinned back at her.

"It is now."

Sadie was instantly relieved. She retrieved her phone and reading glasses from her tote and threw it at her feet as she hoisted herself up on to the stool. It was at that moment when she felt settled that she realized he hadn't taken his eyes off her.

With a smile still on her face, Sadie lifted her chin and turned her head towards her seatmate and realized that he was utterly and unmistakably handsome. Rugged and strong looking, but certainly not model gorgeous. No one feature made him attractive, although his smoky hazel eyes came close.

People often speak of the color of one's eyes as if that were of great relevance, yet his would be gorgeous in any color. From them came an intensity, a kindness... a gentleness. Perhaps this was what was meant by a gentleman, not one of fragility or usual politeness, but one of a great spirit and virtuous ways.

Sadie had no doubt that she was sitting next to a true southern gentleman, and he smiled broadly as he extended his hand to her.

"I'm Beau. It's a pleasure to meet *you*…"

He held the upward inflection hoping he wouldn't scare her off and that she would return his greeting and provide him with, at the very least, her name.

Sadie quickly held out her left hand. Her fingers were long and slender, and her nails were lacquered with a bright pink polish and weighted down with a vintage gold toned interwoven ring which took up half of her index finger. There was no visible wedding ring in sight.

"It's a pleasure to meet you, Beau. I'm Sadie."

His eyes looked her up and down as she nervously brushed her honey highlighted bangs from her eyes with her right hand, slowly turning her upper body towards him.

"You're not from around here… are you?"

There was a slight twang to his deep voice, but with an intelligent tone. Beau looked like a guy that enjoyed the outdoors. His skin was tanned – his short brown hair sun-kissed with blond highlights. As he spoke to her, Sadie noted his prominent cheekbones and a well-defined chin and slender nose. He was dressed impeccably in a long-sleeved light-blue shirt and jeans – simple brown cowboy boots on his feet. Sadie liked what she saw.

"Is it that obvious?" Sadie chuckled nervously and then fidgeted a bit in her seat.

She had overdone it. Although Sadie's fashion choices never made her stand out in a crowd, she suddenly felt very out of place. She thought about her bulging suitcase and what she had packed for the three-and-a-half-day trip. Sadie had packed enough clothes for a week or longer and nothing remotely country. Sadie didn't own any cowboy boots. It wasn't her style.

Sadie knew the weather would be brutally hot, so in anticipation, she spent weeks on-line shopping and updating her wardrobe. She bought several summer dresses and a fancy black pencil skirt with ruffles around the bottom, just in case she hit a honkytonk or two. Sadie was encouraged to dress chic and classic at all times, but the new clothes in her suitcase reflected her need to escape and spend the next few days finding herself again.

When she dressed at dawn, her main goal was airplane comfort. Sadie threw on a comfy black V-neck maxi dress and her black wedge summer sandals. Underneath the ensemble was a new black lace bra and thong. The dress fit her like a glove and accentuated her curves. She quickly realized that it was probably a bit too low-cut and a bit sexy for the characteristics of a true southern woman. Sadie did not lack in the breast department, and she always seemed to fight them like two unwanted house guests – ever demanding and always in the way.

Beau's comments made Sadie immediately self-conscious, and she realized that she probably stuck out like a sore thumb. She looked down and ran her hand down the front of her dress and let out a heavy sigh as she watched Beau lift his beer glass to his lips and shake his head.

"You look like New York or South Beach," Beau said with a wide grin.

Sadie didn't want to blush. She knew the self-tanner she'd been using on her face would turn her into a ripe tomato if she got too embarrassed. She leaned forward, elbows on the bar.

"Gosh, no! I'm from Seattle."

She turned to face him, and their eyes locked. Before she could look away, Beau continued the conversation.

"It rains a lot there, right?"

Sadie let out a laugh and shook her head from side to side. People think of laughing as a sound that comes from the mouth, but when Sadie laughed or giggled, it was nothing like that. Her laugh was in her big brown eyes and in the way her face changed into a vision of relaxed happiness and unrestrained mirth. Yet truly, it wasn't in her face either. Sadie's laugh came from deep within her heart and soul. Just the sound of Sadie's laughter was enough to transport Beau far, far away from his current worries and the tension in his life.

There was no doubt that Beau was flirting with Sadie, but it had been a while since Sadie had flirted with a man. In an instant, she turned her entire body towards him and caught his sincere gaze. Beau was a man that Sadie wanted to know more than she'd ever felt before. It was almost instinctual, and before she could turn away with shyness, a genuine grin spread across her face. In that moment, Sadie knew that she could do it. That she would do it. Why not? To keep it locked up and hidden… unappreciated, no longer seemed fair. Truth be told, Sadie hadn't felt sexy in years… felt desired by a man. She was cold and lonely, and at that moment, she felt her entire body flush warm.

"Sorry. What can I get you?"

The red-faced bartender, a trickle of sweat rolling off his brow, appeared before her and Sadie instantly turned her attention and her body away from Beau.

"Jesus, Mac! It's about time you showed up. Can't you see this pretty girl is thirsty?"

Mac gave Beau a dirty look and filled a glass with ice and water and placed it on a coaster in front of Sadie. It was too hot for wine, Sadie's go-to beverage, so a beer would have to do.

"Um… have you got a pale ale… something local, or at the very least from Tennessee?" Sadie asked as she put on her reading glasses and quickly glanced at the beer list.

Mac nodded. "Be right back," he exclaimed as he turned and disappeared again to the other end of the bar – over 50 beer taps at his back.

People often confused Sadie's super thick, dark-rimmed reading glasses with fakes. Something trendy wannabe hipsters liked to wear. She wished. They only made her appear older than she felt. Unfortunately, her glasses were authentic and very needed, and she could feel Beau's eyes still on her.

"So, Sadie… business or pleasure?"

Sadie composed herself and took off her glasses and let out a sigh. She realized that just the sound of his voice made her heart beat faster.

"Oh, I guess business… with enough pleasure as I can squeeze in."

Sadie felt something deep inside her gut. She felt the memories of her youth flooding back to her. It was like riding a bicycle.

Beau loved the curve of her lips. The gentle softness in her voice. There was a shyness to her, a hesitation in her movements. She was the most intriguing woman he had ever met.

There is beauty in being a good listener, someone who seeks to make connections and joy and sees things in new perspectives, and they spent the next half an hour sipping on their beers and talking. Sadie was light and easy to talk with, and Beau loved how her voice quickened when she became excited about something.

"What do you do for a living, Beau?"

Sadie felt good. The beer was starting to make her feel relaxed, and she knew that she had all of Beau's attention. Aside from a watch on his right wrist, Beau's style was plain. He didn't have a wedding band, and although that didn't always mean a man was necessarily single, Sadie was betting that a married man might not take the time to flirt with a woman like her. It didn't appear that he was waiting for someone, and the person sitting next to him had left. Sadie had Beau all to herself.

"I'm an environmental architect. Right now, I am concentrating on urban planning. There is a lot of that going on right now in Nashville. One of the jobs I am leading is a park and garden around a major business development on the other side of the Cumberland River."

"Ummmm… you look like someone who works outdoors."

Beau laughed at her comment, and Sadie was mesmerized by the way one side of his mouth turned up when he smiled. It was sexy and playful and slightly naughty.

"I wish I worked outdoors more than I do. I guess to oversee the project, but I spend most of my days chained to a desk."

"I hear you," Sadie responded and then smiled back at him, holding his gaze.

"What about you, Sadie? What pays the bills?"

Sadie took another sip of her beer and tucked a loose strand of hair behind her right ear. She tended to bite the edge of her lip when she became self-conscious, a vain attempt to keep her bulging smile at bay.

"I'm a real estate appraiser. I specialize in commercial properties, and I am getting my feet wet with land. My conference here in Nashville this week is sponsored by the Appraisal Qualifications Board."

Sadie had safe eyes. Perhaps that was the best way to describe her. She had a beauty that made those magazine cover models… those waif-like reality TV stars look like phony paper dolls. Sadie was robust and real – her ordinariness was stunning. Something radiated from within that rendered her irresistible, even though she was not beautiful in a classical way.

Mac came back around, looking even more disheveled if that was even possible. His dark black unruly curls were sticking out from a backward baseball cap.

"Hungry?" Mac asked.

"Um… yes… may I please see a menu?" Sadie asked, and Mac tore off again to the opposite end of the bar.

"No! Don't eat here. I have a better idea. Can I take you out to dinner, Sadie?"

She wasn't sure if she should grab her tote and run for the door or take Beau's hand and have him lead her away someplace. Sadie would love to get lost in Nashville for the night with a handsome stranger.

"Oh, thank you, Beau. What a lovely thought, but..."

Sadie was distracted once again by Mac, who reappeared and laid a menu at the bar. As Sadie glanced at it, Beau threw Mac a look and gave his head a quick tilt. Mac took the hint and disappeared again.

"I don't normally... I mean... meet men in bars that want to take me to dinner. You are seriously charming, but... hey, so was Ted Bundy."

Beau was glad that he had already swallowed his beer, otherwise his gregarious laugh may have doused Sadie in flat ale.

"Hey, Mac!" Beau shouted. "How long have you known me?"

Mac turned around, nearly dropping a stack of beer glasses as he galloped back towards Beau.

"Um... second grade... Miss Landrum's class... so what, that's about 32 years."

Beau turned to Sadie and raised his eyebrow as she did the math quickly in her head. Beau was close to 40 years of age – nearly ten years younger than her.

Oh my god... that makes me a cougar!

"Was I not in your wedding party... three years ago... March? I would have been his best man if it weren't for his derelict brother." Mac laughed at Beau's comment and took off again.

Sadie was still reeling from the thought that a younger man... a much younger man was still flirting with her and had just asked her out... on a date!

"Look, if that's not convincing enough, here is my last text message chain, with my mama. It was her birthday today, and she was thanking me for sending her flowers. Read it right there..."

Beau quickly turned his phone to Sadie as she scrambled for her reading glasses and focused on the last few text messages.

Thank you, Beau - for the beautiful flowers! You are my favorite son.

I love you, Mama. Happy Birthday. See you next weekend. XXOO

Love you too!

"And by the way... I happen to be her *only* son. I do have a younger sister, Presley. Mama loved Elvis."

Sadie instantly thought of the velvet Elvis painting that hung in her living room growing up. She shook her head as she silently chuckled at the memory.

"Okay, Beau... so maybe the Ted Bundy thing was a little farfetched, but I do have other plans. I have a ticket to the Ryman for tonight's show. Kind of like a bucket list item for Nashville."

Beau couldn't hide the disappointment in his eyes that quickly. He picked up his beer and finished it off. Beau hadn't been out on a real date in almost a year. He hadn't met a woman he even wanted to strike up a conversation with, let alone ask out after only knowing less than an hour.

"Do you take rainchecks... here in Nashville, Beau... say for tomorrow night?" Sadie couldn't believe what she had just potentially agreed to. Dinner with a man. *A date!*

Suddenly it felt like someone had turned off the air conditioning. Sadie felt a warmth travel from the bottoms of her feet up the base of her neck. She lifted her hand and placed it around her neck and smoothed her hair down. The humidity was turning her hair wavier, and it was scratching her neck.

"Yes, Sadie... we do have rainchecks in Nashville, and I would love to take you out to dinner tomorrow night."

Her smile was the prettiest thing he had seen in a while. It was the kind of smile that made you feel glad to be alive, and just a little bit more human.

Sadie's conference itinerary mentioned something about a cocktail reception tomorrow night, and she made a mental note to scratch that off the list when she had the chance.

"So… tell me… this Nashville bucket list. What else is on your list, Sadie?" Beau asked as he watched her lips curl around her beer glass. Sadie swiftly tipped her head back and finished the last drop.

"So… I am not really looking forward to spending two and a half days inside a hotel conference room. I think I am going to skip out on some of the seminars. I'd love to see the Tennessee State History Museum maybe the Country Music Hall of Fame." Beau watched her talk… completely mesmerized.

"Oh, I absolutely have to eat some barbecue. Wrap my lips around some juicy ribs," Sadie said with a devilish laugh. "Oh, and grits. I've never had them before. I would love some shrimp and grits. That's what people eat around here, right?"

Beau watched her close her eyes deep in thought. Sadie's face was pure and innocent, like a small child.

"Beau, promise you won't tell anyone… you know letting the pleasure take over the business," she said with a wink. The lashes on her big brown doe eye quickly fluttered at him, and his heart skipped a beat.

"You are a bad girl, Sadie… but your secret is safe with me. I won't tell a soul."

Beau comically made a gesture with his fingers like he was locking up his mouth and throwing away the key. He then laughed deeply, which made Sadie laugh deeply. She leaned forward, closer to him… so close that she caught his scent… spicy and clean… like cinnamon and fresh laundry that had been left outside all day to dry in the summer sun.

"Can I please buy you another beer, Sadie?"

As much as Sadie wanted to sit next to Beau all night and talk, she realized that she should finish up and head down closer to the Ryman, but something pulled her back. She glanced at her phone and then looked into his eyes.

"Oh… alright. One more, and then I'd better be on my way."

At a quarter past 6:00, Sadie rechecked the time. "Beau, I should really make my way down to the Ryman. I should grab a quick bite to eat someplace since you've indicated that the food pretty much sucks here. I don't want to miss the start of the show."

Beau chuckled and watched Sadie place some money underneath her empty beer glass.

"Please don't tell Mac… what I said about the food," Beau pleaded. He ended his question with a wink, and Sadie melted right into the floor.

"So, Sadie… my loft is very close to the Ryman. I'm heading home to finish up some work, but would you consider meeting me somewhere for a nightcap after the show? The Tuesday night show typically lasts about two hours."

Millions of thoughts were swirling around Sadie's head, and as tempting as it sounded, Sadie was scared. The thrill and the excitement and the beer were making it hard to concentrate on anything other than Beau's sexy and mysterious eyes and the way he smiled at her when he talked.

"Oh, I'm not sure… a nightcap? I've been up since before dawn and traveled more than halfway across the country. I am afraid that I might fall asleep during the show… maybe get kicked out for snoring."

Sadie was honest. She wasn't sure if she would make it to nine o'clock tonight between the travel, the heat, and the beer.

"Okay, so if you won't let me treat you to a nightcap, then at least agree to let me walk you back to your hotel after the show. No woman should be walking the streets of Nashville alone after dark. I know that may sound a bit old-fashioned, but my mama would tan my hide if she found out that I let a pretty lady walk home alone."

Sadie wanted to cry. It had been a while since a man had put her first and extended that kind of gesture to her. Sadie could get used to this southern hospitality thing.

"Oh, Beau… that is so sweet of you."

Sadie reached out and placed her hand on his as he reached into his back pocket for his phone. Her hand was warm, and her skin soft. Her touch made his groin start to twitch.

"Sadie… may I have your telephone number?"

This was happening. This was going down. It hadn't been all politeness and courtesy. Beau wanted more of Sadie.

"Yes, Beau."

Her voice was barely a whisper as she rattled off her phone number and grabbed her phone, as Beau returned the favor.

"Look, text me after the show ends… or maybe I should text you to make sure that you are awake before some security guard has to wake you up and escort you from the building."

"Very funny, Beau," Sadie said. She flashed him that smile, like a naughty child caught with their hand in the cookie jar.

"If you change your mind, I'll understand, but seriously… Nashville is pretty safe and all, but I would feel better if I could walk you back to your hotel, okay?"

"Okay, Beau. Thank you."

Sadie leaped off the barstool, and Beau followed her cautiously, placing his hand gently in the middle of her back. Sadie felt her knees go weak at his touch.

"After you, Miss Sadie."

She was taken aback by his height as he stood behind her. Even with her almost two-inch sandals, Sadie came to Beau's chin. He opened the front door of the brewpub, and the hostess bid them a good night, and they awkwardly stood to the side of the entrance.

"So, let's walk up to Broadway together, okay and then you'll be headed in the right direction."

Sadie was relieved that she didn't have to pull out her phone and bring up Google Maps like some directionally challenged tourist.

When they got to the street corner, Beau hit the opposite crosswalk button to change the light and pointed his hand down Broadway.

"It's about half a mile… or five blocks… probably take you 10-15 minutes to walk… in those shoes."

Beau looked down at Sadie's feet slowly. She was fairly certain he took his time looking down the entire length of her body.

"Honestly, you can't miss it. The entrance is right off 5th and Broadway."

Sadie looked down the street and then back at Beau. His light had changed, but he remained standing next to her.

"I'm this direction, but I'll see you later, okay?"

Beau quickly reached down and squeezed Sadie's hand before crossing the street and disappearing.

CHAPTER TWO

Sadie recognized him immediately as he stood on the opposite side of the street. The light had not yet changed, and as soon as Beau picked her out in the crowd, he took his hand out of his pocket and gave her a friendly wave – the streetlights illuminating his pearly white grin. Beau had changed from what he was wearing in the bar into a dark black t-shirt, which was untucked and stretched tight over his body. He had kicked off his cowboy boots and threw on a pair of charcoal Cole Haan sneakers. His hair was still wet from the cold shower he quickly took after Sadie texted him that she would love for him to walk her home.

Sadie hadn't gotten a real good look at his physique until he stood to escort her from the brewpub earlier in the evening. He had a beautiful shape to him but didn't look like a bodybuilder or a workout junkie. She prayed her ass looked good in her tight t-shirt dress, for she felt his gaze so strong on her body that she turned her head and peered over her shoulder to look at him before they reached the front door of the brewpub. He never caught her eyes, for he was staring elsewhere.

Sadie thought this was crazy but also incredibly sweet. A man walking a woman home was innocent enough. He didn't appear to be a lunatic, and there was a substantial crowd from the Ryman milling about.

The light changed, and she hesitated. Sadie didn't want to seem too eager. She carefully stepped off the curb and made her way across the street, looking down at her feet to ensure that she didn't take a header into a pothole.

As Beau watched her walk, it was like she was coming to him in slow motion. She had the posture of a ballet dancer... strong and graceful, but Sadie was a tight little petite package that he desperately wanted to unwrap. He'd spent the last three hours in his loft trying to finish up a project, unable to erase her from his mind.

Most of the crowd in the crosswalk turned left towards the music clubs down Broadway, and Sadie could hear music and laughter spilling out from down the street. There were only a handful of people headed in the direction of her hotel. Maybe Beau was right. She instantly felt relieved that someone was with her.

"How was the show?" Beau asked. He could see the excitement in Sadie's eyes as he reached out for her and ran his hand up and down her bare arm. She leaned into him as her mouth opened, and the description of her night ran out of her like a runaway train.

"Let's head in this direction, okay?" Beau said, nodding his head.

Sadie had lost her way. She had no idea which direction her hotel was, but she was comfortable in his presence, and her arm still tingled from his touch as she described every singer and every song from the Grand Ole Opry performance.

"Um... so I know you said that you weren't sure about a night-cap, but I make a mean chamomile tea." Beau suddenly stopped and stood in front of Sadie, halting her in her tracks.

"I've been patiently waiting the last three hours to see you again, Sadie... and your hotel is five more blocks away, and I don't want to say good night." Sadie's smile radiated from within, and Beau knew that he had her.

"I took you down this street, because... well. This is my building... my loft."

Sadie gazed over Beau's shoulder and up at the old brick building. Although the neighborhood was mostly re-built, some derelict buildings remained. With just the two of them on the sidewalk, the neighborhood felt like a ghost town.

Beau's loft was in a refurbished six-story textile house. When he found it a year ago, the surrounding area was in even worse shape. Still, this part of Nashville was becoming hip, and several of the abandoned buildings were already turning into luxury hotels, condos, and apartments.

Sadie reached for his hand. "I'd love a cup of tea."

Beau practically danced towards the front door, pulling his passkey from his back pocket and holding open the door of the lobby to let Sadie pass through.

"I should have told you something, Sadie," Beau said in a low voice.

She felt her stomach tighten. Suddenly she wasn't sure if this was a good idea. Heading up to a stranger's apartment in a city she was unfamiliar with. She felt the side of her bag for her phone.

The conversation with Mac and text message chain with his mother… his southern charm and hospitality were sweet, but Sadie still felt leery. A surge of tiredness hit her body like a rogue wave. A few sips of tea and Sadie promised herself that she would be telling Beau goodnight and asking him to finish taking her home.

"I have a roommate… um… he was asleep when I left, but I am fairly certain that when he hears you, he's going to wake up."

Sadie knew that sometimes she had a cackle to her laugh and a pitch to her voice, not to mention that her ears were still plugged up from the flight. She leaned closer to Beau in the elevator.

"Oh, I'm sorry. I can be quiet. We can whisper if we have too."

Beau just laughed as the elevator doors opened on the third floor.

"Well… it's not just that. He's probably going to smell you."

Beau had walked ahead of her, down a hallway, and he turned around and smiled. He could see the confused look on Sadie's face. It had been a long day, but before she texted Beau and left the Ryman Auditorium, Sadie did her best to freshen up in the bathroom.

"My roommate is a six-year-old English bulldog named George."

Sadie's confusion vanished as Beau stopped outside his front door.

"Listen… Sadie, this is embarrassing, but George gets pretty excited when he meets new people. In fact, he's going to get so excited meeting you that he will most likely pee on the floor."

Sadie threw her hand up to her mouth to try and squelch her laughter.

"Oh, no… that's not the best part. See… after he finishes peeing… he's going to follow you around and then sit at your feet and stare at you… and then… oh, dear Lord, I can't believe I am saying this out loud, but I think you should be prepared. Sadie, George is going to sit at your feet and gaze up at your pretty face… and get an erection."

Beau could hear Sadie saying *oh my god* even though her hand was still firmly over her mouth.

"Let me in, Beau. I absolutely have to meet your dog."

Beau's back was leaned up against his door as if to allow Sadie to back out. She took a step closer to Beau and placed her hand on the door handle and looked up at him.

"Shall we go inside, Beau?"

The loft condominium had windows that would no doubt let in every ounce of sunlight during the day. There was only one big great room with a small patio that had a long wooden table and a large market umbrella. The kitchen was the heart of the loft and had enough appliances to make Sadie wonder if Beau did some moonlighting on the side as a personal chef. Next to the front door was a small downstairs bathroom with a shower, sink, toilet, and laundry.

The color scheme of the loft was autumnal, the reddish-brown of the wooden floor echoed in the old brick walls. The vintage industrial windowpanes were thick and ornate and ran the length of the walls by the patio. The loft was small, but it was perfection in miniature… everything a person could need without walking more than ten paces in any direction. Off the kitchen was a staircase that led to the bedroom and master bath, and Sadie could just barely see Beau's bed… an industrial-looking steampunk metal bed frame with a thick off-white quilt folded neatly on top. The downstairs was rounded out by a small breakfast nook with a four-top table and a workspace by the patio door with a stand-up computer desk, a whiteboard, and rolls of architectural plans. Sadie gathered that Beau likely spent a lot of time working from home.

Right on cue, George leaped up from his bed near the foot of the staircase and lumbered over to Sadie. His head was large and spherical and his muzzle short, giving his face a flattened appearance. His eyes were dark and wide, his skin loose and pendant with heavy wrinkles. He was the most adorable dog that Sadie had ever seen. Having a nub for a tail, it was not at all hard to tell that George was excited. His entire back half shook from side to side as he drew near Sadie – a trail of drool spilling from his mouth being drug across the wood floor.

"Oh, boy! Behave yourself, George," Beau cautiously remarked as Sadie looked over at him. Beau had made his way into the kitchen and was standing in front of the stove, a kettle in his hand. Sadie knelt to George and placed her hands around his face as he let out a loud breath and began to dribble a bit of pee.

"Great! Buddy, you are so busted. This is so embarrassing." Beau appeared at the dog's side with a wad of paper towels.

"It's not like I didn't just take him outside, like five minutes before I texted you. Geez."

Sadie gave George a quick pat on the head as Beau walked back to the kitchen.

It was at that moment that something caught her eye – a light underneath the staircase. Sadie slowly began to scan the rest of Beau's loft casually. As a real estate appraiser, Sadie always found herself assessing and appraising people's homes – she found it hard not to. She could instantly tell that Beau loved music, a few framed festival posters lined the entry wall, and, in the corner, by the fireplace, an acoustic guitar sat in a stand. The light by the stairs caught her attention again, and it held her gaze. Under the stairs, a tiny bedroom had been carved out… a single bed adorned with a Batman bedspread – a stuffed animal tucked inside the bed covers waiting on the pillow for its master to return for a cuddle. On top of a bookshelf, which was overflowing with children's books, toys, and games… a light blue lamp shade with a yellow dump truck held Sadie's attention.

"Sadie…"

She turned her head as Beau walked around the end of the kitchen counter, his hands in his pockets and a sheepish look on his face. He could tell by the look on Sadie's face that she was shocked and confused, but there was no doubt that she had discovered the child's nook.

"Can you come here, please?"

Beau gestured for her to come over to him with his indexed finger and then pulled out a stool for her at the kitchen bar. He walked back through the kitchen and over to his workspace and emerged with a couple of framed photographs.

"This is my son, Patrick. He's four… well, almost five. See that calendar on the refrigerator with the black x's." Beau quickly turned and pointed to the kitchen. "Well, that is the countdown to his birthday. A month from tomorrow." Sadie reached out for the picture. There was no doubt that the little boy was Beau's… he was the spitting image of his father with long eyelashes and sandy brown hair, and the same mischievous smile.

"That's my mama in the photo. Lady Jane, everyone calls her. Runner-up, Miss Georgia, 1975." Sadie let out a chuckle, and Beau felt like he could breathe again.

"This was taken about a month ago... Mother's Day weekend. She came up from Atlanta for a visit."

Beau's mother was beautiful, and Sadie wondered if she would approve of her son flirting with an older woman.

The other photograph was of the small child with a beautiful blond-haired girl. At first, Sadie thought that it might be Patrick's mother, and she almost felt sick to her stomach, but she looked again closely and realized that the girl in the photo had the same facial features as Beau.

"Is this your sister?" Sadie quietly asked. She was instantly relieved when she saw Beau nod his head.

"She's my best friend... so witty and smart. She's an ER nurse in Atlanta." Beau looked at Sadie's face as she studied the pictures.

"Look, Sadie... I really like you, but I will be honest. I don't ask women over... that often, I mean... never actually." Beau's face reddened with the comment.

"Gosh, what I am trying to say is that... this is all new to me."

Sadie placed the photographs back on the kitchen bar just as the kettle started to whistle. Beau ran around the counter and pulled the kettle off the stove and filled two mugs with boiling water. She watched him turn and open up a cupboard and pull out a bottle of Remy Martin from the top shelf along with a box of teabags.

"Sadie... don't you think for one minute that I invited you up here for anything other than a cup of organic, caffeine-free chamomile tea, but I did mention that I make a mean cup." Beau held the bottle of cognac above her mug, and Sadie lifted her hand in front of her face and pinched her fingers together.

"Just a splash, okay," she replied.

"Okay, then," Beau quickly responded as he topped off each mug with a splash of liquor.

"So... your ex-wife, then... if I am safe to assume that you do have an ex."

Sadie smiled at the end of her question. She wanted to sound light and not like she was ready to aim and fire. All of a sudden, the thought that Beau might be married crossed her mind. He didn't seem like the type, but then again... Sadie didn't have much of a track record in dating.

Beau exited the kitchen and took a seat next to Sadie at the bar setting the hot mugs of tea in front of them.

"Patrick's mother, Hannah, and I... um... were never married. We met at a ribbon-cutting ceremony for a project we were both working on for different companies. We had been emailing back and forth for months, and we finally met face to face at the wrap-up party. We became inseparable. Six weeks later, I moved into her apartment, down in Atlanta... our hometown... well, my hometown... Hannah's originally from Boston." Beau smiled. "I am a Georgia boy, born and raised."

Sadie picked up her mug and brought it to her lips to blow on it, slowly processing the information Beau was giving her.

"So, things were going along great. We were in love, and she started immediately talking about having a baby. I was almost 35. I figured, why not. I felt like I was ready to be a parent. I lost my father when I was 20, so I felt like the clock was ticking, right? Men get that too, I think?" Sadie shook her head as if she knew, when in fact, she had no clue.

"Not four months later, and Hannah was pregnant... and here we go, right! Headfirst... full steam ahead into parenthood. I did what every good, responsible man does and bought this ring and got down on one knee and proposed and... she turned me down." Sadie blinked her eyes, taking in Beau's story.

"I guess I should have known right then... that something wasn't right, but she had a great excuse. She didn't want to walk down the aisle, pregnant – I didn't blame her. We moved on past it, still in love, and preparing for our baby. Then... Patrick was born, and it was the most incredible thing I've ever witnessed or experienced in my life. Shit... it was crazy!" Sadie watched Beau, lost in his story. She saw the joy in his face talking about his son.

"We had no clue. I mean, I babysat Presley when she was little. My mama was a big help, but it was completely insane. Hannah is an only child... very messed up family, so it was just her and I figuring it out as we went along. The entire first year was intense. I kept asking, though... about her wearing the ring... getting engaged and possibly married. She claimed that she still had baby weight to lose, that last 20 pounds was driving her crazy. The ring didn't fit anymore. It was just one excuse on top of another excuse. God, I must sound like an idiot." Sadie reached out for him, tapped his thigh with her hand and shook her head. The touch made Beau catch his breath.

"Um... Hannah told me she wanted to go back to work when Patrick turned one... so that was an adjustment. We just kept moving forward, or so I thought. I just didn't want to believe that something wasn't right. By this time... our sex life was a joke. Another clue hitting me right in the face." Sadie almost choked on her tea. If only he knew her frustrations.

"Patrick slept in our bed most nights, or one of us was up with him in the night. She was tired, and I was tired. Hannah started working on a project out of town, right before Patrick turned three... or so I thought she was working on a project out of town. Come to find out... she was working on someone else."

"Oh shit, Beau... I am so sorry." Sadie reached out and placed her hand on top of his, and he looked over at her and shook his head in embarrassment.

"She came home one night from a business trip and basically told me that she met someone else. She didn't mean to hurt me, but she was moving out over the weekend and taking my son with her." Sadie's eyes flew open wider. She could hear the pain in Beau's voice.

"Oh, wait… it gets even better. Hannah wanted to not only take my son from the only home he had ever known, but she wanted to take him to Nashville. Yup, that's right… the love of her life, Ryan… was taking a job in Nashville, and she and Patrick would be moving from Atlanta to Nashville as soon as possible."

"Oh, Beau! What did you do?" Sadie's mouth was hanging open. Beau's story rivaled her favorite soap opera storyline.

"I watched her pack a couple of bags and take off with my son. I thought I was going to die… I was so afraid that I would never see him again. I called my mama. I knew she would know a good lawyer, and as I soon discovered… I had rights, but they are tough to determine and enforce… even if your name is on the birth certificate. I knew for certain that I had to keep my anger and hatred in check. If it got ugly, the only person who would suffer would be Patrick."

Sadie watched as Beau composed himself… running his hands through his hair before looking over at her sipping on her tea.

"What happened? Did she leave the state right away?"

Beau leaned over the kitchen counter and grabbed the bottle of cognac, and Sadie shook her head up and down as Beau poured another splash into her mug.

"Yes… she left, and so every other week for almost a year, I drove or flew to Nashville to see my son so that he wouldn't call another man, daddy. I soon realized that I couldn't be apart from him like that… and so I quit my dream job and moved to Nashville. I actually won that round because my current job is ten times better." Beau smiled at his perceived victory.

"I found this loft and finally moved here. It was a year ago last week… right after we hashed out the final custody agreement. Perfect timing! The happy couple had their dream wedding, and Hannah was finally a June bride."

Silence settled over the loft.

"Ouch!" Sadie wrinkled her nose at Beau and stuck her mug up in the air. "Cheers, Beau!"

"I'm sorry, Sadie. Maybe I shouldn't have spilled my guts all out like that, but you did ask… I mean, about my situation and Hannah… and I just felt like I really wanted to set the record straight. I saw it in your eyes when you saw Patrick's space. I didn't want you going off with the wrong impression." Sadie took a deep breath and tucked her hair behind her ears.

"Oh, Beau… I am so glad that you did… honestly. Thank you for sharing that. I know that it must have hurt you deeply. I've been there too… totally different situation, but I know what it's like to get your heart broken, and it sucks."

Sadie looked away. She wasn't about to counter his story with any of her own, not now. Her current sad and pathetic situation didn't need to be exposed. George sensed a change in the vibe and got up from the floor next to Sadie's chair, where he had been sitting, and retreated to his dog bed.

"At least I got to keep the dog," Beau said with a hearty laugh.

Silence enveloped the room again. Sadie was enjoying her time with Beau, but she was finishing her tea, and it was getting late.

So, Sadie, what do you like to do for fun?"

Beau watched Sadie look down towards the floor deep in thought, but with a somewhat pained expression on her face.

"Fun? Hmmm… I guess I try to do what brings me joy… fills up, my soul… whenever I can."

Beau could tell that she was struggling with his question. As if fun was an unobtainable goal, a finish line that she wanted to cross, but couldn't make it.

Sadie let out a deep breath and looked Beau right in the eyes. She couldn't remember the last time she had fun. Something that wasn't forced on her. Never her idea or her desire. She let her mind fill with her happy thoughts. The things she long remembered that took her to a place away from the loneliness and uncertainty of her current situation.

"I love to sit outside around sunset and wait for the sky to turn my favorite shade of blue and then practically hold my breath until the first star appears in the sky."

Beau watched as Sadie's face and body language changed. She stared out past him, and he watched her eyes glaze over with a mist.

"I love long drives with no destinations, especially getting lost on old country roads. I enjoy a perfectly cooked steak with a nice glass of red wine. Oh, and seafood. I like lots of fresh seafood. You'll find me most nights snuggling in my favorite pajamas in front of a roaring fire. I love candles and twinkle lights and long hot baths."

Sadie was on a roll. Beau took a sip of tea, but he never let his eyes leave her.

"Do you like the sound of the rain, Beau?" Sadie asked. Her voice was husky and seductive as she spoke. He shook his head up and down as her eyes found his again.

"Well, I love to lie in bed on a Sunday morning and listen to the rainfall... knowing that I don't have anywhere to go."

Beau looked away before his mind was consumed in thoughts of Sadie naked under her covers.

"I enjoy cooking for my friends and family and entertaining. I make a music playlist for just about every occasion. Ummmm... let's see... I don't get to enjoy one often, but I love an outdoor bonfire and roasting marshmallows... the more burnt, the better!"

Beau laughed, thinking back to his childhood summers roasting marshmallows on Lake McIntosh, always striving to make the perfectly toasted marshmallow.

"I love to dance, but I can't carry a tune, so don't ask me to sing you anything."

"Okay, I'll try and remember that," Beau said as they both began to laugh.

"I love farmer's markets. I've been known to drive around in search of a good one. In the summer, I love to pick up bouquets of sunflowers. They are my favorite… and when in season, I love fresh peaches picked right off the tree, sliced and served with homemade vanilla ice cream." Sadie let out a deep breath and smiled.

"Oh, and don't even get me started on Christmas," she concluded as her eyes lit up like a child on Christmas morning. Beau quickly thought he'd better leave that one alone.

"Wow… Sadie, that's… hearing about you like that… thank you." Beau felt something deep inside him, looking at her. She had opened up a part of herself that he thought that many people didn't know or appreciate, and he wasn't sure why.

"Well, it might not be someone's traditional description of what they do for fun, but that's just who I am. Fun to me is enjoying the simple things in life. I don't need anything fancy to have a good time. I just like to appreciate good things… good people… everyday life, I guess," Sadie said. She picked up her tea and took her last sip.

Beau set his mug down and turned towards her. As if she knew what was coming next, Sadie followed suit.

"Sadie… would it be okay if I kissed you?"

Beau leaned over to her and grabbed her face with his strong hands staring intently into her big brown eyes.

"I thought you'd never ask."

Sadie could have sworn she heard a crack of thunder and felt a bolt of lightning through her body when Beau brushed his lips against hers. His breath was hot, and his lips tasted sweet, and Sadie parted her mouth for him, but he backed away. Beau intended for their first kiss to be innocent and gentle. It was hard restraining himself, but he didn't want to come on too strong and scare her away. To Beau, Sadie felt like a flower, and he wanted to hold, caress, and preserve her delicate petals.

"Hey. I just noticed… you shaved."

Beau was missing his five o'clock shadow and a small patch of hair that sat just below his lower lip. Sadie ran her hands over his smooth face and smiled. She wasn't sure about that little patch of hair anyway, and she was glad that it was gone. Beau's face was beautiful, and it made his eyes light up free of all that facial hair.

"Were you planning on kissing me this whole time, Beau?" Sadie asked, laughing.

He shook his head up and down as he got up from his stool. "Wait here… okay?"

Beau padded through the kitchen and turned off the lights, flicking the switch on the outside patio lights casting a warm glow over the living room.

Beau approached Sadie slowly from behind and gently put his arms around her waist, lightly kissing her neck. It took Sadie's breath away, and she giggled. Beau let go, walked in front of her, grabbed her hand, and brought it slowly to his lips, looking deep into her eyes.

Sadie rose from her stool, and Beau embraced her, pulling her close. He whispered in her ear. "Is this okay?"

Beau wanted to be certain that Sadie was comfortable. She felt so good in his arms. Sadie didn't answer him… instead, she stood on her tippy toes and kissed him hard and deep as he let his hands explore her back, moving slowly over her hips and ass. Beau dove his tongue inside her mouth, and Sadie let out a moan and returned the favor. Her mouth was warm and wet, and he tasted the liquor that she had just consumed. When they finally pulled apart, Sadie's lips were ruby red and engorged like two ripe strawberries. Her deep brown eyes begging him to continue.

Beau took Sadie's hand and led her to the leather couch, and they sat down. He gently pulled her towards him as he leaned back against a mound of throw pillows. Sadie could feel him hard against her thigh – the lights from the patio setting his face aglow.

Without speaking, Beau reached under Sadie's dress and ran his hands along her outer thighs and around to the bare cheeks of her ass, making him gasp. He played with the soft lace on her thong with the tips of his fingers before letting out a deep breath and laughing.

"What?" Sadie asked as she pulled away, staring longingly into his eyes. Beau simply grabbed her ass and pulled her closer to him, letting his lips find hers once again.

Sadie sat up and repositioned herself. Beau's kisses, once gentle, turned demanding, and Sadie let her hands go exploring. She stroked up his thighs and around his back, pausing quickly when her hand caught on a small metal object. Beau looked down as Sadie pulled out a bright yellow Matchbox car wedged between his sofa cushions.

"Whew!" Sadie exclaimed, rolling the truck up Beau's arm. "I'm gonna keep this in case I get bored."

Beau let out a husky laugh as he watched Sadie lean into him. He knew that once she started kissing his neck that his resistance would crumble. She went straight for Beau's ear, tenderly kissing and sucking his lobe – his erection growing as her soft moans of desire filled his head. After just a few delicate touches of her warm lips on his neck, he was all hers. There was one wish and one craving, and he knew that it was just a matter of time before it happened.

Just as Beau was about to lay Sadie back down on the couch, she began to squirm and laugh on his lap. It aroused him even more, feeling her movements on top of him. He brought his arms around her and gently began to lift her off his lap, but Sadie continued to squirm and giggle, and Beau struggled to get a firm grip on her.

"Sadie-girl… what's so funny?"

Sadie leaned into Beau's neck and whispered into his ear. "George is licking my toes." She squirmed once more and fell off Beau's lap, lying on her back on the couch, laughing like a little girl.

"Man... George... really? Can't you see it's me she wants and not you? Go to bed, buddy... let us be."

Beau leaned over Sadie and grabbed her by the waist, pushing her body further up the couch, cautiously running his hand between her legs to part them. He leaned down and kissed the inside of each thigh, brushing his tongue slowly up her leg. Sadie immediately began to shudder and moan. Beau inched his fingers slowly upwards, catching her smile and the gentle nod of her head encouraging him to proceed.

Sadie felt out of breath from excitement as Beau lowered his face, running his chin hard between her legs before gently lifting her dress above her hips to kiss her belly button.

Before Beau's fingertips reached up to search for Sadie's breasts, George waddled to the front door and let out a loud bark.

"Seriously..." Beau bellowed. He lifted up to stare down the dog, letting out a deep sigh. Sadie reached out for Beau... urging him to continue, but he just shook his head as George let out another deep bark.

"I'm so sorry, Sadie."

Beau pulled himself up off the couch, and Sadie scrambled to pull down her dress... embarrassed to be caught up so suddenly with lust.

"The only reason that George barks like that is when he needs to take a crap. I seriously can't believe this, but I have to take him out." Beau reached down and pulled Sadie up off the couch and gently kissed her cheek.

"Listen, I'll be... five minutes. There is a little alleyway across the street. Don't you dare move."

Beau scampered to the front door, bending over to latch George's leash to his collar. When he turned around, Sadie was right behind him... hopping into her sandals and grabbing her black leather tote.

"Sadie... you don't have to go with us... seriously, we will be five minutes, I promise."

George howled again, shaking his hind end in anticipation of Beau opening up the front door.

"No... Beau, actually George's timing is perfect. It's a nice excuse to have you both walk me back to the hotel. It's getting late."

Beau looked at Sadie and pouted. He was anticipating seeing her bare breasts, and possibly so much more. Now all he had to look forward too was George's foul-smelling poop.

"Sadie... no. You and I were just getting to the good parts."

The look in Beau's eyes melted her heart, but she was resigned. It was getting late, and she didn't want Beau getting the wrong idea even if she knew that she was prepared to let him take her right there on his couch just moments ago.

"Okay." Beau let out a sigh and opened the front door as George galloped ahead and into the elevator. Once inside, Beau reached out and grabbed Sadie by the waist and pulled her close... George whimpering at her side until she reached down and stroked the top of his head.

"I'm so sorry that we got... um... interrupted, Sadie."

Beau's lips were soft and wet, and he pulled Sadie into a kiss, grabbing her ass. It made her momentarily lose her mind. When the elevator hit the first floor, George pulled Beau out towards the street, and their kiss ended.

"Buddy... cool it."

Beau tried to tighten George's leash, but he was halfway across the street before Sadie made it out the lobby door, and he did his business quickly, just as Beau had predicted.

Beau scooped up George's deposit in a small green plastic bag as Sadie stood nearby with a packet of antibacterial wipes in her hand, pulling out a moist wet-one to hand to Beau.

"Thank you." Beau grinned at Sadie. He wanted to kiss her, but first…
he handed her George's leash and dashed across the street to throw the
trash in the can. Sadie watched George strut around near the grass before
handing Beau back the leash. They quickly stole a couple of quick kisses on
the sidewalk. Beau's lips were hungry, and he let out a soft groan of frustration before taking Sadie's hand and turning for her hotel.

"Let's go, buddy."

George trotted ahead, almost regally making Sadie chuckle as Beau
clutched onto her hand. He brushed her fingertips against his lips, and
Sadie instantly regretted her decision. If she had played her cards right and
stayed on Beau's couch, his mouth would be on her left breast right about
now. Shit… maybe the right. Did it matter?

"So, tomorrow?"

Beau's question brought Sadie back to reality. She shook the thought
of Beau's wet mouth sucking her tit escape her mind.

"Um… my conference starts at 1:00. So, I have my morning free."
Sadie couldn't believe what she had just said. She sounded desperate.
She knew that Beau had rain checked dinner. He hadn't rain checked the
whole day.

"So, about that bucket list. Listen, Sadie. I am a pretty good tour
guide. This is what I am thinking. I pick you up at eight in the morning. We
go get a good breakfast… see a few sights… hit the museum, which opens
at ten o'clock, I promise to have you back for the start of your conference.
Then we grab dinner… or not?"

The light had not yet changed green, and both George and Beau were
anxiously awaiting her reply.

"Wow. Don't you have a project… or work tomorrow?"

Sadie looked down first at George, who was panting and then at
Beau… his slate-gray eyes glimmered from the lights of the nearby hotel.

"Come on! This is a once in a lifetime opportunity, Sadie-girl."

Beau's dazzling smile warmed her soul like hot molten caramel sauce drizzled slowly over a bowl of ice cream.

The light changed green, and George galloped ahead as Sadie contemplated Beau's offer. On the sidewalk outside the entrance of the hotel, Sadie stepped ahead of George and knelt in front of him.

"Listen, buddy. I think this is the end of the line for you tonight. I don't think the JW Marriott allows dogs into the hotel and certainly not into room 716… so, I think this is where you and I say good night… for now."

716…716.

Beau shook his head. Had he heard Sadie correctly? Would there be any reason for her to mention her room number? He watched her place her hands on George's face as she gave him a quick kiss.

"Thanks, boys… for walking me home. It really meant a lot to me."

Beau stood his ground and repeated Sadie's room number over and over again in his head. This woman was driving him insane. Her voice radiated in his head.

716…716.

"As for you… I will see you *later*?"

Beau caught the slight inflection in her voice and saw the desire in her eyes. He couldn't be sure, but he thought he caught her tipping her head to the side as if he were supposed to respond in some way to her question.

Beau didn't know the protocol… the dating etiquette. If he guessed wrong, he might offend her and scare her away, and if he guessed right… then he had a feeling that it might be one of the best nights of his life.

Before he knew it, Sadie's arms were around him, and she reached up and kissed Beau's lips and like a breeze she turned and headed through the revolving doors leaving Beau and George on the sidewalk.

Sadie rushed upstairs and flew through the door of her hotel room. If she calculated correctly even if Beau and George ran, it would take him at least 15 minutes to get back. She had just enough time for a five-minute shower, a quick brush and floss of her teeth, and any other last-minute beauty details she thought might make a difference. She grabbed her floral spaghetti strap negligée and headed for the bathroom.

Sadie let the warm water splash over her skin and then quickly toweled off and pulled the negligée over her head. She used a makeup wipe and took off her foundation, then re-curled her eyelashes and applied a thin layer of lip balm to her lips. She had just slathered lavender and vanilla body lotion on her legs when a faint knock sounded at her door.

Beau.

Sadie peered through the peephole and smiled before opening up the door.

"Just so you know. I gave my dog away to a homeless guy down near Broadway," Beau said, slightly out of breath. "If I get back in two hours, I can buy him back for $25."

Sadie stepped out of the way, and Beau cautiously stepped forward and into the entryway of her suite.

"If not?"

Beau watched as Sadie closed the door behind her, taking in how her skintight negligée clung to her body.

"He was a pain in the ass anyway."

"Beau!" Sadie shouted. He laughed as he grabbed Sadie's shoulders and pushed her up against the door.

"He's tucked in tight at home. I ran like the wind to get back here. I figured the room number was a clue." Beau chuckled. "God, I love puzzles, Sadie-girl."

"New York Times? Sunday puzzle?" she asked. Beau's smile was broad as he nodded.

"Um… if I have Patrick, the Sunday takes all day. I do not have the luxury of lying in bed and listening to the rain, just so you know."

Beau still had Sadie tight up against the door of the hotel room. She couldn't get over the fact that he was looking her over... up and down, focusing intently on her breasts, her hard nipples poking out through the thin material in her negligée.

Sadie smiled as Beau reached around her taking both her arms at the wrist and pulling her into him. She made the most glorious sounds as he slid his tongue down her neck. He released his grip, and Sadie reached down and grabbed his hand, and led him into her suite, turning the lights off with a flick of her finger.

When they reached the bed, Sadie let go of Beau's hand, and he sat on the edge of the king-sized bed, and watched Sadie walk to the window pulling the thin curtain closed – the lights of downtown Nashville filling the room with a kaleidoscope of muted colors. Sadie turned from the window and walked to the nightstand and tapped the button on the clock radio, the Bluetooth on her phone syncing to her Nashville playlist. She reached up and rolled the button on the wall sconce up. It wasn't a roaring fire, but it was just enough warm light that Sadie felt comfortable.

Beau couldn't take his eyes off her. The way she moved, the sway of her hips and the bounce of her breasts. It made Beau come alive.

"Hello."

Sadie's voice was barely a whisper as she stood before Beau at the end of the bed.

"God... you are so beautiful," Beau responded.

Sadie shook her head side to side and looked away as Beau reached out for her and ran his hands under her negligée and up the backs of her thighs.

"Beau... listen... um, things... I mean, they used to be... better, um... smoother and tighter... and I am really trying to work out more. What I mean to say is that my body... isn't all that great. God... I'm sorry. I must be a huge disappointment."

Sadie suddenly did not think that she could continue. The idea of becoming naked in front of Beau made her feel slightly sick to her stomach.

"Listen, Sadie… you've been turning me on since you took that seat at the bar tonight… and I don't mean just your body. It's everything about you. You have nothing to worry about. No one is perfect… and I am not looking for that. You are beautiful in so many ways."

Beau squeezed Sadie's ass, and she was pleased… for at the moment, it was the firmest part of her body. The squats she had been doing daily for the past six weeks were paying off. The trainers at the Hustle Hut were getting a thank you card when Sadie got back to Seattle.

"Jesus, Sadie… do you know what's running through my head right now? I wished I'd gone to the gym more in the last few months," Beau chuckled. "Running after my son… that's kind of my current exercise routine. I'm seriously contemplating going into your bathroom and doing a few sit-ups… just saying." They both laughed, and Sadie instantly felt at ease.

Beau stood and placed his hands on her shoulders, looking deep into her eyes. He turned Sadie around and eased her down on the bed, slowly sliding her negligée up and over her head. Beau smiled down at her before he let his mouth kiss and suck every inch of her body, pausing slowly to admire everything with his eyes. Beau teased Sadie's nipples until they shone wet with his saliva, and each stood at his attention.

When he knew that she was ready, Beau took his hands and moved them down between her legs, spreading her apart. Sadie took in a sharp breath as he swirled his fingers around her forbidden zone. He watched the expression on her face change as Sadie's eyes widened in excitement.

Beau had barely touched her before she was gasping for air, his fingers searching for that one spot. It felt so good that Sadie wanted to let herself go, and Beau knew it. He quickly removed his hand and let his fingertips dance along her inner thighs, allowing her breathing to return to normal.

"Are you alright?" Beau asked as Sadie slowly sat up and reached for him, scooting herself forward and pushing her face close to his, hungrily searching for his mouth.

"I have never felt better," she whispered.

Sadie ran her hands down Beau's chest and pulled his t-shirt off, her mouth brushing up against his nipples – her soft kisses planted deliberately across his chest.

Aching tension built between them as they locked eyes. Beau brushed his thumbs against Sadie's already plump and swollen nipples, tugging at one and rolling it between his thumb and index finger. In response, Sadie tossed her head back and arched her body, opening her mouth to let out a groan.

Beau's movements became urgent as he grabbed her at the waist and forcefully pushed Sadie back onto the bed again, pressing himself between her thighs… his tongue dipping and swirling inside Sadie's mouth. Beau quickly reached one hand around to the small of Sadie's back and pulled her closer, the other hand fumbling with his belt. With an infectious giggle, Sadie reached out to run her hands down the front of Beau's jeans, unzipping his fly and then pausing briefly before sliding her fingers inside.

"These have got to come off."

Beau struggled free of his jeans, engulfed with emotion, and entranced by her most recent touch. He brushed his fingers along Sadie's mouth, and she parted her lips and wet them. He quickly returned his fingers between her legs and slowly slid one finger inside her. Delighted with her excitement, Beau withdrew and glided two fingers inside her, enthralling her with his touch. With a come-hither motion, he turned her previously quiet moans into long and deep cries, her breath turning into a deep pant. He withdrew his fingers, not wanting to take her to ecstasy too soon, and when he did, she gave him a husky laugh.

"You like that, don't you?"

Sadie shook her head up and down as Beau pulled away, inviting Sadie to wrap her legs around his waist as he carefully pulled her close to him, her body surging toward his.

"There are condoms and lube on the bathroom counter," Sadie panted as she pulled away breathlessly, searching his face for a reaction. It had been an impulsive buy in the hotel lobby sundry, but Sadie had been reasonably sure that he would come back to her.

Beau nodded and jumped up from the bed in a sprint for the bathroom, knocking Sadie off his lap and onto the floor. She landed with a thud next to the bed.

"Jesus… Sadie… fuck, I am so sorry." Sadie couldn't contain her laughter as Beau sat down next to her.

"Beau, I love your enthusiasm… this is going to be a lot of fun."

Beau grabbed Sadie's hand and pulled her up, gently kissing her lips before heading for the bathroom.

"I'll be right back."

Sadie suddenly was not sure what to do. Should she sit on the end of the bed or crawl underneath the covers? She sat down on the bed with her legs crossed, arms folded over her chest and laughed at herself.

I hope you know what you are doing.

When Beau returned, he came to her, and Sadie took the silver bottle from him and pumped a small amount of lube in her hand. He was taller than most men she had ever been with as he stood before her, his erection at eye level.

Sadie was nervous, but it was all coming back to her. The fun, the excitement, and the release. She reached out to circle his hard length and felt him pulsating in her hands. Beau had already put a condom on, so she knew that he was ready, but Beau was content to play with Sadie, in no hurry to finish his pleasure before her. His voice was breathless as Sadie moved her hand faster and faster up and down his shaft.

"God, that feels so good."

Focused totally on her, Beau pushed Sadie back down onto the bed, and she parted her legs, and he gently and quickly slipped inside her.

Beau laid perfectly still and watched her smile back at him, placing his hand on the side of her head, gently brushing the hair away from her face. He slowly began to rock back and forth inside her, and Sadie opened her mouth to let an almost silent moan escape. Beau felt like no one she had ever been with before.

"You feel so incredible," Sadie moaned. Her voice was low and raspy, and Beau propped himself up on his elbows and lifted his body away from her, placing his hands under her ass as Sadie arched her back.

She was a delicate instrument, and as he found their rhythm and played her just right, she made the most amazing sounds – pure and intense and primal. A song that Beau had never heard before. He slowly pulled her into him, taking him deeper inside her each time.

"Oh God… Sadie."

Beau shuttered against her, and he could feel Sadie's legs trembling as he continued to push and pull, driving into her and taking them right to the brink before he withdrew from her and watched the shocked expression on her face.

"Beau… oh, Jesus… no, please don't stop."

Beau gently laid Sadie back down on the bed and felt the wetness between her legs… his fingertips traced her outline. "What are you doing to me, Beau?"

He loved her smile and hearing her breathless pleas. Her hair was a jumbled mess, and her eyes blazed. He felt her body melt against his exploring hand, and he knew it was time to resume.

"We need to go slow, okay?" Beau begged, and Sadie nodded at him, understanding that he wanted to last for her.

Beau quickly entered her again to a chorus of sighs and winded praise. He pulled her around him faster and harder than before, and he waited until she was calling for him and repeating his name over and over again, inviting him to join her in shared pleasure, before he withdrew again completely... a mischievous laugh escaping his mouth.

"No... no... no... Beau, please. Why are you doing this? God... I want to come so bad... Beau, please."

The smile faded from Sadie's mouth as he leaned down and kissed her lips. Beau darted his tongue in and out of her mouth until he felt her smile.

"Sadie-girl... are you begging me?"

Beau let out a sigh and looked down at her with that grin on his face. The one where only one side of his mouth curved up. Sadie wiggled under his weight, and he pinned her leg down with his knee pushing her legs wider apart.

Sadie reached up and let her finger trace his mouth as if she somehow wanted to remember this exact moment for all of eternity.

"Is that what you want, Beau? Do you want me to beg you?"

Sadie's voice was barely a whisper, and she drew her leg up along the side of Beau's hip, slowly rubbing it back and forth, waiting for his answer.

"Tell me what *you* want, Sadie." Beau overemphasized the word you, and she let out a tiny laugh.

"Okay, then.... I'll tell you what I want. I want you, Beau. Now... will you please... finish fucking me?"

CHAPTER THREE

Sadie didn't mean to doze off, but she could feel her body relax in Beau's arms as he softly caressed her back and shoulders. Every few minutes, he would let out a small hum and brush his lips across her forehead. Sadie felt as if they were levitating above the bed.

"Ummmm... you know, I don't even know your last name," Beau asked. His voice was quiet, almost a whisper, and Sadie giggled and pulled herself closer to him, resting her chin on his bare chest.

"Isn't that a country song... Attwood, somebody?"

"Underwood... Carrie Underwood," Beau responded.

"Underwood. That's it."

Sadie was silent for a moment, collecting her thoughts. She'd heard the song before maybe even seen the music video.

"I'm just Sadie.... you know, like Adele... Beyoncé... Madonna."

Sadie let out a long sigh and raised her eyes to him, but Beau was silent. She could feel him lessening his grip around her middle... his limbs stiffening. He raised his hand to his head and threaded his fingers through his hair.

"Sadie..."

Beau wiggled away from her and turned to prop himself up on his elbow. Sadie slid off his chest like a melted piece of cheese. She threw her head back on the pillow, pulled the thin sheet around her exposed nipples, and quickly put her hands to her side.

"It's complicated, Beau. My life is... well... complicated. Honest to god. I never expected this to happen tonight. To meet you and to feel so connected to another person... a man like you... ever again. It's been so long."

Sadie turned and reached her hand out to run her fingers along Beau's chest, circling the small patch of hair in the middle of his broad chest. He drew her close and breathed her in, and Sadie could feel him getting hard.

"Sadie... I don't want to be another complication... trust me, as you've heard tonight... I've sort of got my hands full. It's just that... I don't do this... it's never really been my thing. Picking up women in bars. I only go into that brewpub because Mac works there a few nights a week, and it's close to the loft. I needed a break tonight to clear my head. I was doing my own thing, up until you sat down."

Sadie pulled away and looked deep into his eyes. He had a blank expression on his face, and as tempting as it was for Sadie to open up, she erased those thoughts from her head.

"I don't do this either, Beau... honest." Sadie reached up and ran her hand down the side of his face, brushing her thumb against his lips.

"My middle name is Mae... short for Maeve. It was my grandmother's name. So, I'm Sadie Mae. That's going to have to be enough for now."

Beau let out a big sigh and nodded his head up and down, but Sadie sensed that this would keep the wolves away from the door for only so long.

After he had taken her again and they had untangled themselves from the hotel bed sheets, Beau reached out for her hand and held onto it tight as they both caught their breath.

"You didn't answer my question, earlier... about the tour tomorrow?" Sadie realized that she could get lost in a man like Beau. Lost in his voice, his eyes and the touch of his skin.

"Are you sure, Beau? I mean, I can find my way?"

"I'll be here at 7 a.m."

Beau quickly leaned over and kissed Sadie's forehead with a smile on his face.

"Um... wait a second. I thought you said eight o'clock. Didn't you say eight, earlier?"

Sadie pulled away and propped herself up on her elbow, waiting for his explanation.

"Yes, well... my tour of your sexy body starts at seven o'clock. I need an hour to complete all my pre-tour requirements." Sadie giggled as Beau pulled her into yet another toe-curling kiss.

"Okay, then. I guess I'd better get my beauty sleep. You should probably leave before I start to snore and ruin the whole fairy tale for you."

Beau honestly didn't want to leave Sadie, but he knew that she must be exhausted. He felt her doze off in his arms several times as they lay basking in their orgasms. George would need a bathroom break at dawn, anyway.

He watched as she laid her head back on the pillow and closed her eyes, and then he quietly slipped out of bed and dressed, never taking his eyes off her.

"Beau..."

He blew her a kiss as Sadie sat up in bed.

"Go back to sleep, Sadie Mae," Beau ordered. He watched as she laid her body back down on the bed.

"Okay. There is an extra room key by the TV in case I am still out in the morning."

Sadie was nearly asleep by the time Beau left the hotel room. She prayed that he would come back in the morning, but she had just about convinced herself he would not, by the time she fell into a deep sleep.

* * *

"I smell coffee."

Sadie rolled over in bed and caught sight of Beau entering the room. A *New York Times* in one hand and a Starbucks coffee in the other. He looked even better in the early morning light of day. He had on a pair of faded tight jeans and a light blue t-shirt that set off his eyes. He was clean-shaven, and his hair was damp. A spicy and musky man scent filled her hotel room, making Sadie giggle.

"I figured a girl from Seattle would appreciate a taste of home."

Sadie sat up in bed and tucked the sheet in tight around her as if she had forgotten all that she had already shown him.

"Be still my heart," she said.

Beau delivered her coffee along with a deep kiss. Sadie looked like an angel, her light brown hair cascading around her face – her natural radiance free of any embellishments. Sadie looked pure like freshly fallen snow on a carpet of pinecones.

"Hey… you taste minty," Beau said as he pulled away. Sadie took a long sip of her coffee and shook her head up and down.

"I got up and brushed my teeth, but I could use a quick shower."

If only Beau knew. Sadie had been up since first light, and not only washed her face but also layered her body in moisturizer and rubbed on a bit of deodorant.

"Not so fast, Sadie Mae."

Sadie watched as Beau kicked off his shoes and stripped the clothes from his body… quickly crawling into her warm sheets.

"Good morning, Beau!"

"Yes, it's about to be a very good one."

Sadie laughed as Beau's hands began to explore her in ways that she never imagined. As last night's moves were intense and fiery… this morning, Beau wanted to be smooth and satisfying. His desire was to take his time as if he didn't believe that Sadie was real.

* * *

"You know we need to stick to our schedule."

Sadie groaned at Beau's request. He had been trying to tempt her out of bed for the past hour. They had taken their time together, but the morning was moving along.

"Anyway, I'm starving, and I know a great place for biscuits with applewood smoked bacon. Come on, Sadie Mae."

Sadie peeked out from under the covers. Beau had partially dressed and was reading the paper in an oversized leather chair by the window. He had opened the curtains to let the full light of the new day fill the hotel room.

Sadie had no clue where her negligée from last night was… but she spied Beau's blue t-shirt not far away. The bathroom was quite a walk, and Sadie didn't want Beau watching her back-end jiggle as she made her way to the bathroom.

Oh, fuck it.

The hotel room was bathed in a hot white light, and Sadie was sure that Beau had now seen every inch of her body… top to bottom and front to back. The thought made her laugh out loud.

"Good Lord, woman. What's going on over there?"

Sadie peeled the covers back and stood at the side of the bed, closest to Beau. He lifted his eyes from his newspaper, cataloging every firm curve before him.

"Wow!" Beau exclaimed as Sadie drew closer to him. She watched him take her in, and when she was satisfied with his reaction, she turned and allowed herself to walk her naked body all the way into the bathroom.

"Thanks for the coffee. Give me 20 minutes."

As Sadie neared the bathroom, she heard Beau take in a deep breath and exhale.

* * *

"You're sure you don't mind walking?"

Beau grabbed Sadie's hand as they exited the hotel lobby. A light breeze blew her hair around, making it fall in kinky waves around her face as she pulled her sunglasses from her tote bag. Sadie hadn't wanted to take too much time getting ready. She partially blew her hair dry and skipped most of her morning skin routine, opting for a generous layer of tinted sunscreen and a dusting of bronzer. Adding a few swipes of lash lengthening mascara, Sadie announced she was ready for their adventure to begin.

Beau couldn't get over how amazing Sadie looked. She pulled a tight navy blue and white striped racerback sundress out of her suitcase, just perfect for their morning together. After she showered, Sadie dressed, and Beau caught her reflection from the bathroom in the hallway mirror. Her bronzed creamy skin set off her strapless white lace bra and panties. He silently watched her putting on her makeup, completely mesmerized as she stood balancing her foot against the inside of her opposite leg like she was doing yoga.

As they walked down the street together hand in hand, Beau felt like the luckiest man in Nashville. Being in Sadie's presence was an out-of-body experience.

"I actually prefer to walk. I do a fair amount of walking at home and for work. It's the best way to explore a new city," Sadie said, feeling Beau's large hand squeeze hers tighter.

"More clouds today. It's gonna be humid. Just wait for tonight, Sadie… storms for sure."

Tonight.

Beau alluded to a day and night that Sadie wouldn't forget as she casually stole quick glances at him – his beautiful profile accentuated by gold-rimmed aviator style sunglasses.

True to his word, Beau took her to one of his favorite breakfast spots, an outdoor patio café at the Bobby Hotel just off Printers Alley in downtown Nashville.

"I love this spot, Beau. It reminds me of New Orleans."

Sadie immediately buried that thought. She wanted to rid the memory of him, that place and that trip in her mind. She had dreamed of coming back to Seattle engaged, but their trip was nothing more than an antique art tour and ended with Sadie getting food poisoning and him leaving her behind a day to head back to Seattle for a business meeting.

"Iced Americano?" Beau asked. He peered over the top of his menu as Sadie shook her head up and down. Beau placed their drink order as Sadie continued to peruse the menu. Beau then ordered applewood smoked bacon, fried eggs, red potatoes, and an extra biscuit, and Sadie went for something southern – a pimento cheese and bacon omelet with a side of fruit. She skipped the biscuit. She felt the need to stick to some form of dieting if she planned on getting naked with Beau again.

"I'm not giving you a bite, Sadie Mae. You had your chance for one of the best biscuits in Nashville. You're going to be sorry."

Sadie stuck out her tongue at Beau and laughed. "Maybe just one little bite?"

It was the way that Sadie said it and pursed her lips together in a pout, her big doe eyes fluttering that almost made him lose all control. Beau had not felt this way about a woman in a very long time, if ever. Whatever love he felt for Hannah was long gone and as hot and intense as it had once been, it was a long-forgotten memory down a painful heartache road. Beau just shook his head and reached across the table for Sadie's hand, giving it a gentle squeeze.

Stacy Brady

After breakfast, they walked east along James Robertson Parkway through the Bicentennial Capitol Mall, under the shadow of the Tennessee state capitol.

"These are all native trees and plants. That 200-foot granite wall right there is a map of the state, and over there is a World War II memorial. That's the Tennessee State History Museum ahead."

"Oh, my father, James… he would really love this. He loves anything to do with history, especially World War II." A lump caught in Sadie's throat as she thought about him.

After a 90-minute tour through the museum, Beau led Sadie next door to the Nashville Farmer's Market.

"Two sweet teas, please," Beau requested. The young waitress brought the iced cold beverages quickly, and they found a perfect table on the patio, an ideal place to people watch.

"Almost as good as Mama makes," Beau said after taking his first sip.

Sadie let out a long sigh as she kicked off her shoes and wiggled her toes under the table. She didn't want to tell Beau, but she was exhausted. Tired from last night and this morning, but in the most satisfying way possible. If anything, it was her feet that hurt from all the walking.

"So… you mentioned your dad. What's he like? I'm just curious. God, I miss my dad so much." Sadie could hear the pain in Beau's voice.

"He's got a great sense of humor, but he's tough. Very stubborn and a hard worker. He was a finish carpenter. He loves to work with his hands. He basically raised me. It was just the two of us."

"Your mom… did she pass away?"

Beau looked at Sadie with deep empathy in his eyes.

"No, I mean… I don't really know."

Sadie took a big sip of her tea, and something in the way Beau was looking at her made her feel safe to continue.

"My mom was an original flower child from the sixties. My father thought he could tame her. I guess he did, for a while. They got married and had me, but she was restless. She wrote poetry and songs... played the guitar in beatnik coffee shops in Pioneer Square in downtown Seattle, well ahead of Starbucks. She hung out with the wrong crowd and started using drugs. She would disappear... sometimes days... sometimes weeks. She would always come back around. I remember her begging my father to take her back. She'd try... to get clean and be a good mom. She would do the laundry, have dinner ready at 5:30, be there to walk me to school... and then, one day, she'd be gone again. I'd come home, and the house would be empty, and my dad would find me next door at the neighbors. The last time she left was the day before my tenth birthday. My dad just had enough. He packed up our tiny apartment, and we left. We never saw her again."

Sadie's story ended abruptly as Beau reached across the patio table and grabbed her hand. A small squeeze and Sadie felt like continuing.

"My aunt, my mom's younger sister, would check in from time to time. Mom managed to keep in touch with her. She never thought much to keep in touch with her husband or daughter. We heard she got as far as Santa Fe. She's been in and out of jail... drug possession... prostitution." Sadie snapped back to reality, flushed with embarrassment.

"God, Beau. I'm so sorry. Like you wanted to hear all that this morning."

Sadie couldn't look up at him. She swallowed hard and fought to hold the tears back.

"Don't you ever apologize for sharing something so personal... a part of you. Sadie... it means a lot to me that you would share that with me." She turned and met his eyes.

"I told you last night... about Hannah and me... my son. Damn... that's still like an open wound, so... I get it... I get you, Sadie."

For the first time in her life, she felt like someone did. Sadie knew that Beau could relate in some way.

"You ready to continue the tour?"

Sadie grabbed her tote, slipped back into her white Ked mules, and took Beau's hand.

"Yes! Lead the way."

* * *

Beau's gait slowed as they got closer to Sadie's hotel. Her conference was due to start in a few minutes, and Beau needed to get to work and finish up a project, but he didn't want to say goodbye to her.

"Listen to me, young lady. No skipping out on any sessions, okay?"

Beau stopped and turned towards her, cupping Sadie's face in his strong hands. She was so tempted... to blow her conference off and invite Beau upstairs for a long nap - the kind where very little sleeping occurs.

"We are just pushing pause on this tour for a bit." Sadie nodded her head as Beau leaned in for a goodbye kiss.

"I'll meet you in the lobby bar around 5:45. I'll text you if I am running late."

"Sounds perfect, Beau. Thank you for a wonderful morning. I can't wait for tonight."

It was pretty obvious what Sadie meant, so Beau kissed her back a little bit harder and squeezed the cheeks of her ass.

Sadie breathlessly pulled away, and he watched her walk through the revolving door of the hotel lobby before he turned and headed out towards his office.

* * *

"Well! If it isn't Beau Walker... in the flesh. We all thought you'd fallen off the face of the earth. Is your son okay?"

Mia.

She leaned over Beau's cubical, flashing him a generous amount of cleavage and smiling at him like a butcher's dog. She tossed her long blond hair back over her shoulder and stood up straight, having not received the greeting she was expecting.

"You got the latest draft, I see. I got your notes. Did you really review this at 2:30 this morning, Mia?"

"I couldn't sleep. What about you? Are you having trouble sleeping, Beau? Wanna grab dinner tonight?"

Beau was used to Mia's aggression. In the beginning, it was one of the things he thought was so hot about her. Now, it felt claustrophobic.

"No. I've got my son."

Beau wasn't sure why he lied to Mia, but he didn't want to piss her off. It was dangerous sleeping with a co-worker, but Beau knew that it had run its course, and he'd been giving her subtle hints the last few weeks. Mia was slow to catch on.

"Okay, then. You gonna be here for the three o'clock meeting? I guess I'll see you around."

Beau kept his head down, staring at his computer, and Mia turned, let out a small huff and walked down the hallway.

"Dodged a bullet there, buddy."

"Tell me about it."

Beau laughed at Sebastian, his office cubical mate, seated on the other side of Beau's desk at the drafting table, obviously eavesdropping.

"You good, Beau? I haven't seen you around much this week," Sebastian asked.

Most of Beau's office worked remotely several times a week. They had a very open work environment. Sebastian was married with three small children and used the office as his escape. He seldom worked from home.

"Everything is wonderful. It couldn't be better. I met someone. She's amazing." Beau lit up when he thought about Sadie.

"Dude... congratulations! Don't tell Mia, okay. She'll throw herself off the roof."

Beau laughed. He realized he should probably let Mia know that he was seeing someone. Then again, they hadn't slept together in over a month, and to be honest, it was never really anything other than an occasional dinner and sex at her place. No strings. Netflix and chill.

And then it dawned on him... like he honestly hadn't thought about it before.

Sadie would be heading back to Seattle the day after tomorrow.

* * *

At five minutes to five, Sadie flew out of the hotel ballroom and hurried up to her room. She had just enough time for a quick shower and to change her clothes before meeting Beau downstairs. Suddenly, Sadie was thrilled that she still had several items of clothing to choose from. She quickly pulled out the black pencil skirt, a black halter top with red roses and black lingerie. She slipped into her black strappy sandals and texted Beau that she was on her way downstairs at 5:30.

Sitting on one of the small couches in the lobby, Beau quickly stood when Sadie walked into the room. She took his breath away. He held out his arms, enveloping her as he greeted her with a kiss on one of her tanned bare shoulders. Sadie heard him take in a deep breath as he reached behind her neck and pulled her close to him, letting his lips finally find hers.

"I've missed you."

Beau's confession made Sadie weak in the knees as a broad smile swept across her face.

"Wow... you look incredible, Sadie Mae. You ready to get outta here?"

Sadie shook her head as she took his hand and let Beau lead her out the hotel and towards Broadway.

"You're staring. Do I look okay? I know… not very Nashville, but very new Sadie."

Beau couldn't take his eyes off her. The short black skirt hugged her hips and made her legs look long. Her bare shoulders would make the evening more distracting.

"New Sadie? Wait a second. I liked the old Sadie." Beau stopped and clutched her hand.

"No. This is me, I promise. I just feel so good… so different being here with you."

Sadie couldn't explain it to herself, let alone explain it to Beau, but it was time. It was time that Sadie started to put herself first again.

"I'm sorry… I know it's bad manners to stare, but I just can't help myself," Beau confessed.

Sadie chuckled and then blushed. She was having a hard time keeping her eyes off Beau as well. He had on a pair of jeans so black and pristine that Sadie wondered if he had gone shopping earlier in the day. He paired them with a slim fit untucked midnight gingham oxford shirt and steel gray cowboy boots. They looked like Nashville's hottest couple as the hit lower Broadway.

"Sadie Mae… are you a fly by the seat of your pants, girl… or should I tell you every item on the evening tour?" Sadie laughed. She was so used to being controlled and having everything planned out for her that she wasn't sure what spontaneity was anymore. The thought of it thrilled her.

"Beau… I trust you and since you did so well this morning… I am good to just fly by the seat of my pants. I'll let you know if I need anything… food… drinks… sex." Sadie wasn't sure who she was anymore with that kind of statement flying out of her mouth.

"Oh, all three are on the itinerary, don't you worry," Beau said as he turned and winked at her. Sadie felt her whole body tingle.

They could hear the music spilling out of the clubs as they neared lower Broadway, and Sadie spotted the Ryman Auditorium and realized exactly where she was. It was just 24 hours ago that she was floating towards the Ryman, having just met Beau.

"First stop is Tootsie's Orchid Lounge. I love the roof-top bar," Beau said as he took Sadie's hand and led her up the long staircase.

"This place is a Nashville legend. A woman named Tootsie Bess bought the bar in 1960, and she credited a painter with the name. Apparently, she came in one day to find that he had painted the walls orchid, thus the name Tootsie's Orchid Lounge," Beau said with a chuckle.

They stopped at the top of the stairs, and Beau pointed out pictures and memorabilia.

"Rumor has it that the great Charlie Pride gave Tootsie a jeweled hatpin that she used on unruly patrons and that Roger Miller wrote, "Dang Me," sitting at that bar," Beau said, pointing to the long bar at the back of the room. "A group of us were in here one night, and Kris Kristofferson walked in the back door, jumped up on stage, and played an impromptu set. It was incredible."

They found a perfect table outside, and Sadie peeked over the edge and couldn't get over the crowds milling about Broadway. There were dozens of clubs and honkytonks, block after block.

"Might be hard to find you a glass of wine here… next stop, though… okay, baby?

Baby.

Sadie loved it, and there was no denying that Beau felt like calling her that. She shook it off that perhaps it was just more of his southern charm coming out. Maybe he called all his women, baby. Sadie decided that she didn't care. She was content to be Beau's baby for the rest of her time in Nashville.

They both loved the band at Tootsie's and stayed for one whole set, watching people dance and sing along. The breeze on the roof-top cooled the heavy air as Beau leaned over and kissed Sadie's cheek, whispering in her ear that she was the most beautiful woman in the room.

"Are we ready to head to spot number two?" Beau asked, taking Sadie's hand, and leading her down the stairs and out onto busy Broadway.

They walked a few blocks down the street to Acme Feed and Seed, a unique four-story bar and restaurant and a bit of a more up-scale honky-tonk with arguably one of the best views on Broadway from their roof-top bar. Established in 1890, the building was first used as a grocery store, and in 1943, it became the home for Acme Feed and Hatchery, known as Acme Farm Supply. Beau told Sadie that a few years ago, a local restauranteur and several locals, including country music singer Alan Jackson leased the building and had turned it into one of Broadway's best restaurants and music venues.

"Okay, promise you won't laugh." Beau pulled out a seat for Sadie, and she gazed out upon the Cumberland River. "So... this restaurant partners with Sanctuary for Yoga and they do this power lunch yoga daily from noon to one. Sometimes my work buddy, Sebastian, and I come down here for yoga."

Sadie tried not to snicker. "Beau... you do yoga? That's so great. I love yoga. I'm not very good at it, but it's great for stress and muscle strength. I'm seriously impressed."

The waitress set a glass of chardonnay in front of Sadie and a honey blond ale in front of Beau. Sadie thought back to this morning, and Beau's strong and flexible moves in bed. It no doubt had to be from the yoga.

"Cheers!"

Sadie's face hurt already from smiling so much. She wanted time to stand still and for this night to never end. Each place that Beau had taken her was hand-picked, his favorite places in Nashville.

"I don't get down here… to the clubs at all unless Presley comes to town. She usually brings a girlfriend, or else all the boys think she's with me. I stay in the back in the shadows… sip on coffee and chaperone. Kind of like a bodyguard."

Sadie loved that Beau took care of his sister like that… her safety and well-being. It was clear that Beau liked to put others first.

"I'm having the best night, Beau… thank you." Sadie's comment made him squeeze her hand tighter. She realized that Beau hadn't let go of her the whole night. He was always touching her, praising her, and filling her soul with compliments. It was about time she returned the favor.

"You are so welcome, but the night is still young, Sadie Mae. We haven't even got to the good parts yet."

Beau ran his fingers down Sadie's arm and a shiver up her spine. She was lost momentarily in his beautiful eyes, and the way his hand quickly found her thigh.

"Dinner is next. I hope you are hungry!" Beau said as Sadie took another sip of her wine and nodded her head.

* * *

There was a line out the door and down half a block at Martin's Barbecue. Beau took Sadie by the hand and around the alley, cutting through the crowd.

"Hidden secret."

Beau flashed Sadie a devilish grin as he clutched her hand tight and led her up the back steps to the upstairs.

"Everyone waits in line and then sits cafeteria-style downstairs. None of the tourists even know this garden bar exists. It's basically for locals."

Sadie looked around the beer garden, as they called it. It was quaint and charming with dozens of picnic tables under a patio filled with twinkle lights and a long bar near the far back wall.

"Sorry... no air conditioning. I think the rain will hold off through dinner... hopefully," Beau said with a bit of doubt. He realized that his perfect date night might completely fall apart if the rains started before dinner. Beau gently placed his hand in the middle of Sadie's back and escorted her to a small picnic table in the middle of the garden.

"Would you like a wine?" Beau asked.

Sadie shook her head. "I think barbecue requires an ice-cold beer."

Beau's smile widened. "That's my girl!"

Sadie emphatically nodded. She definitely wanted to be Beau's girl in so many ways.

"What's good?" Sadie's eyes were wide as she scanned the menu. She was grateful for the large print as she couldn't bear to pull out her reading glasses on their date. "Oh, my God... I want to order one of everything."

Beau loved Sadie's mannerisms and her zest for life. He was staring at her again. He couldn't help himself. Beau kept one eye on the menu as the other took in her beautiful features.

"Just so you know, I think this is the best barbecue in Nashville. Can I throw in my two cents? A barbecue tray is the way to go... you get more options. I think we should get a tray and a third slab of ribs and then share everything." Beau finished and set his menu down.

"Wow! That sounds fantastic!"

Sadie did a little happy dance at the table and giggled. Beau loved how her eyes twinkled, and a little dimple appeared to the left of her mouth whenever she smiled.

"God... you are so cute... you know that? So easy to be around... talk with. Hanging out with you, Sadie Mae is like a dream."

Sadie's face turned a bright shade of pink. She loved hearing it, but she had a hard time believing it.

"No... come on," Sadie barked out her rebuttal. Beau reached out and grabbed her hand and laced his fingers with hers. She kept her head down, looking at the menu, but she could feel Beau's eyes on her.

"I meant what I said, girl. You are something amazing."

It was the way that Beau was looking at her at that moment when she felt something change between the two of them. Sadie looked up at him as their eyes locked, and the silence stretched on.

"Okay... six ounces of brisket... six ounces of smoked chicken... ribs. What else would you like, baby?" Beau asked. Sadie lowered her head and went back to the menu.

"Ummmm... I think I need some hushpuppies, Beau."

"Yes, of course, you do. What about maple baked beans?"

Sadie laughed uncontrollably and then caught her breath. "You want to eat beans on our first date, Beau? I think you'll be sleeping with George tonight if that's the case."

Beau let out a raucous laugh, that he could not stop, and the two of them fought to gain control. Beau's laugh made Sadie laugh even more. When the waitress brought their cold beers, even she got caught up in their laughter.

"Mac and cheese, okay then?" Sadie quickly shook her head up and down, unable to compose herself to continue speaking.

Beau had never seen such a tiny thing put away so much food. He was extremely jealous of the ribs and the way she licked the meat off the bone and then moaned. Beau wondered if he could do anything to Sadie that would make her moan the way she did when she had barbecue in her mouth.

"I'm gonna need to take you out the back and hose you off," Beau stated with a broad grin on his face. "Come here, baby. You've got sauce on your cute little chin here."

Sadie lifted her sticky fingers and wiggled them in the air as Beau grabbed his napkin and dabbed the sauce off her face.

"I think I can die a happy woman now, Beau. Thank you. That was amazing."

In all honesty, since they shared the platter and ribs, it wasn't a lot of food, and Sadie hadn't eaten since breakfast. She excused herself to freshen up in the bathroom when she heard the first clap of thunder. Her eyes were wide when she came back to the table to meet Beau.

"I just saw the sky light up. We'd better get moving," Beau said as he took Sadie by the waist, and they headed out the side entrance door and back towards Broadway.

* * *

Layla's Honkytonk was a genuine Nashville original and one of the best places on Broadway to hear bluegrass and Americana music.

Beau and Sadie walked in the front door just as a loud clap of thunder shook the sky overhead. Vintage license plates lined the ceiling of the lively, intimate bar, and Beau took Sadie to the back of the room where they took a seat at the bar. Not a minute later, Mac came staggering from the backroom, his t-shirt drenched in sweat carrying far too many six-packs and a box of liquor bottles – a lemon and a lime wedged under his chin.

"Jesus, Mac! You suck at bartending. We've been waiting forever for a drink." Beau winked at Sadie, and Mac dropped his haul and extended his hand out to Beau. Instead of shaking Beau's hand, he just gave him the middle finger.

"Hey, Sadie Mae. Nice to see you again," Mac exclaimed while wiping the sweat from his brow.

"Hey, Mac. Beau didn't tell me you work here too."

"Yup, but just on Wednesday nights. Trying to pay off my final year of law school… and we're pregnant. Baby is due in October."

Mac had a charming smile. Despite his bantering with Beau, it was pretty apparent that they were very close.

"Cry me a river man. Hey, if it's not too much trouble, can you get Sadie Mae a white Russian and I'd like a Maker's Mark on ice… please?"

"Sure thing. I'm just behind. Re-stocking the bar. Man, there is a real estate appraiser conference in town. Shit…. what a bunch of drunks."

Beau looked at Sadie, and they both laughed. About that time, Mick's Bluegrass Band started playing, and Beau and Sadie turned around on their barstools to listen and watch the band as a torrential rain began to fall outside.

* * *

"So… here I go thinking again, but I was wondering… if you are free tomorrow night, can I make you some shrimp and grits? It's my mama's recipe, but it's the best. We can have a quiet night at the loft. You can stay the night if you want. I'd really like it if you did?"

Beau was as adorable as a small child and quite the negotiator. The look in his eyes stole Sadie's heart.

The storm had finally passed, and after several slow dances at Layla's, holding Sadie tight in his arms, Beau was finally ready to take her back to her hotel and to bed. They quickly walked back, the thunder and lightning well off in the distance.

"Yes, Beau. I would like that very much."

The smell of the barbecue, the booze, and the sweat were too much for Sadie. She sexily stripped out of her clothes, coaxing Beau into a hot shower. They dangerously lathered each other up and quickly rinsed off, Beau wrapping Sadie tightly in a bath towel.

He carried her to the king-sized bed and laid her down, but it was Sadie who took the lead, letting her mouth go over every inch of Beau's body, making him writhe and beg as he had done to her the night before. When they were finished with each other's bodies, Sadie curled against him, and Beau held her tight.

"Will you stay... all night?" Sadie pleaded.

"Yes, absolutely, Sadie Mae. There is no place on earth I'd rather be, okay."

"Me, either."

Sadie had no doubt that Beau meant every word.

CHAPTER FOUR

B eau opened his eyes and reached for her, but Sadie wasn't in bed next to him. He sat up and let out a gruff as Sadie peeked her head out from the bathroom.

"Hey, sleepyhead. It's about time you woke up."

Sadie walked over to the edge of the bed. She had dressed in smart work clothes, and Beau chuckled. She looked the part of a real estate appraiser, her dark-rimmed glasses accentuating her smoothed polished hair – gone were the wavy curls framing her face. She wore a crisp white button-down blouse accentuating her breasts and a slim pair of black pants, making her hips and ass look luscious. Sadie's make-up looked fresh, and her face sun-kissed. Her lips shimmered wet with gloss.

Sadie looked nothing like she did after they had sex last night, their bodies dripping in sweat, her nipples and lips engorged and rosy pink. Beau's hips and legs spent. It wasn't like any work out he'd ever had in a gym or with any other woman, that was for sure. What Sadie had done to Beau last night was like nothing a woman had ever done to him before. She was adventurous and erotic, but with grace and tenderness.

This morning Beau wanted to start all over again. As she stood before him, Sadie was absolutely ravishing.

"Don't go getting any ideas. I know that look in your eyes. I have to go. I've missed breakfast, and my conference starts in five minutes. I put myself together without the assistance of coffee." Her smile first thing in the morning was sexy as hell.

Sadie reached out for his hand. She wanted to reach out for more than that, but she didn't dare.

"When this corner of your mouth turns up and not the other, I know I am in trouble." Sadie's fingers traced his upper lip, and she bent over and gave him a quick kiss, anything else, and she knew her clothes would be in a pile on the floor.

"You wanna grab a quick lunch?" Beau asked, looking up at her with anticipation in his eyes. He ran his hands through his short hair and rested them on the back of his neck. Beau let one leg fall over the side of the bed. His thigh was taut, and tan and Sadie backed away.

"Yes! I'm done this morning at about 11:30. Do you want to meet someplace?"

Sadie stood with her back to Beau, packing her leather tote when he quickly jumped out of bed and came at her from behind. She instantly turned around, and he buried his head in her neck.

"I don't want to mess you up. You just look so fucking hot." Sadie giggled, the stubble on Beau's face tickling her neck.

"Feel free to take a shower. From the looks of things, I'd say a long cold one might be in order."

Sadie couldn't take her eyes off him, and it just turned him on even more. Beau groaned as she finally pulled away from him.

"I'll pick you up in my Jeep at 11:45."

Sadie nodded her head, grabbed her tote, and quickly left the hotel room.

* * *

"Turkey and swiss or roast beef and cheddar?"

Stacy Brady

Beau's midnight blue Jeep Grand Cherokee was idling in the round-about at the hotel entrance as Sadie climbed in.

"They had these bagged lunches for us to take today, and so I snagged us two."

"Well done, Sadie Mae. I've got someplace to take you, and now we will have the time."

Beau drove east, out of the city and over the Cumberland River. The June sun was shining down through the sunroof with downtown Nashville in the rearview mirror.

"God, I wish I could see more of Tennessee. I'd love to get lost here for a while."

Sadie loved the idea of the open road. No plans. Exploring new places. The idea that she and Beau could just keep going… just keep driving… not looking back, made her eyes well up with tears.

"I'd love that, baby… I really would… to get lost with you." Beau reached out for her hand and let out a sigh.

He didn't want to think about it, and he certainly didn't want to say it. He started to last night in bed when her legs were intertwined with his. He could hear her trying to catch her breath as he ran his fingertips over her shoulders and back… his post-coital moment of clarity, smacking him in the face before he addressed her.

"Sadie Mae. What are we doing here?" He felt her tense up in his arms as she shrugged her shoulders in response.

"I'm not sure what you mean, but I think that was the best sex of my life," Sadie laughed, but Beau did not return the favor. Sadie was more than just sex to Beau, yet he didn't quite know how to tell her.

"I'm not sure that I am going to want to let you go," Beau responded as Sadie pulled away and sat up in bed.

"You thirsty? I could use some water. I think I drank too much... beer... wine... beer... a white Russian." Sadie pulled the covers back, and Beau grabbed for her hand.

"Baby..."

Sadie wasn't going to be able to avoid it much longer, but there were just some things that were better left unsaid.

"Beau, I'm right here with you... right now is all I've got. Don't skip ahead to the end just yet, okay? We've got to live in the moment. Absolutely nothing is promised to us tomorrow... so we have to enjoy right here... right now."

Sadie leaned over and kissed Beau's lips before she got them both a cold bottle of water. He let it go and didn't say anything more, but he knew their conversation wasn't over.

Beau pulled the Jeep into the finished parking lot of the construction site and reached in the backseat for the blueprint tube. The building in front of them was a jungle of steel and glass, slowly growing out of a giant slab of concrete. Right now, the building looked to Sadie like nothing more than an ugly deformed monster. A tall chain-link fence surrounded the site, and a big sign read: ALL VISITORS REPORT FIRST TO THE SITE OFFICE.

"Wait here a sec," Beau shouted as he ran inside a long prefab building. He came out a minute later with two bright orange hard hats, handing one to Sadie. "Let's grab the lunches. I want to show you around."

Sadie retrieved the brown bags with the sandwiches and followed Beau through the fence.

The site was surrounded by a swarm of men in construction hard hats... bulldozers, cement mixers, and a huge yellow crane. Sadie could feel dozens of eyes on her and heard a few catcalls and a whistle. Beau looked at her, embarrassed as he grabbed her hand. Now everyone would know that she was his.

"I want to take you over to the other side… sorry, we have to walk through this. No way to drive over."

"It's perfectly fine. I'm appraising the shit out of this place right now," she enthusiastically shouted.

Sadie's eyes were all over the site… the land and the building. It was as much of Beau's domain as it was hers.

Beau took Sadie around the back of the building and pointed out to where soon, another building would be started. There was a little wooden bench that looked very out of place with a tall Coors Light can – top ripped off to use as an ashtray.

"Sorry, not the most glamourous of lunch spots, but I wanted to show you this."

Beau looked outward and raised his hands, pointing towards a mound of dirt. His animated movements caused Sadie to snicker.

"Hey, smartass… I'm not finished."

Beau swatted Sadie's ass and invited her to take a seat on the bench, and he sat next to her and opened the end of the blueprint tube.

"I'm very proud of this. It's the first time that I have taken the lead on a project. Kind of a big deal. I just thought that my girl might want to see all that I am capable of."

Sadie was his girl. She felt it. Those were not just words to Beau. Sadie knew that words from a man like Beau went much deeper. As much as she had brushed him off last night… spouted all that bullshit about living in the moment, she wanted nothing more than to be held tight in his arms every night for the rest of her life. She constantly kept playing the last two days in her head. It seemed like two months. How can you grow so close to someone in less than 48 hours? Sadie fought back the fear and wondered how in the fuck she was going to get on that plane tomorrow night.

"I'm very proud of you, Beau and I know all that you are capable of. I am so honored that you wanted to share your project with me."

Beau looked over at her and smiled, and his heart exploded in his chest.

"I brought the plans. I can't wait to show you."

Beau excitedly pulled the blueprints out of the tube and began to unroll them. At the top of the architectural drawing was a pink sticky note with a big heart drawn in a red pen.

Dinner tonight? XXOO Mia.

"Shit!" Beau yelled out, ripping the sticky note off the plans. He quickly crumpled the note in his hand and threw it into the beer can.

"Sadie... I... nothing is going on... anymore... with Mia."

Sadie was silent as she turned her attention away from Beau's plans. She felt like a fool. Someone like Beau had to have a string of women. She foolishly realized she was probably one of many. Sadie realized at that moment that it didn't matter. She would be out of sight in a matter of days, and she was grateful that she hadn't told him her real feelings. If Beau didn't want to have dinner with Mia tonight, he would undoubtedly have the opportunity after Sadie got on the plane for Seattle.

"Beau... really, I mean you don't have to explain. I understand."

"Um... no, I don't think you do. Mia and I work together, and well... we hang out sometimes... or we did, but not anymore. Not for a while now. I am not interested in Mia." Beau stood and turned to Sadie, pleading his case.

"Well... apparently, she's pretty interested in dinner tonight," Sadie said, reaching into the lunch bag to pull out a bottled water.

"Fuck, Sadie! I don't want to have dinner with Mia. I don't want to have dinner with anyone... kiss anyone... and certainly not sleep with any-one... other than you. That's the God's honest truth."

Sadie's blank expression and silence said it all. She continued to stare straight ahead, out at Beau's unfinished project. He turned and retook a seat next to her.

"Beau, I think you should take me back to the hotel. Let's get back. Traffic might be bad, and I have work stuff this afternoon." Sadie stood, and Beau grabbed her hand.

"Baby..."

"Let's go, okay."

Beau could see the pain in her eyes as he dropped her hand. The realization that this... this thing between them was a vast chasm that neither one of them knew how to navigate slapped him in the face.

The drive back into downtown Nashville was agonizingly quiet. Neither Beau nor Sadie said much. Beau picked out a few things on the trip back that he thought might be of some interest to her, and Sadie managed to grunt a few responses. As Beau pulled into the hotel, Sadie quickly undid her seatbelt, clutching the door handle.

"Thanks... Beau. I had a really nice time with you... honestly. You are a great guy. It's just that..." Sadie choked on her words, and she felt tears stinging the backs of her eyes. She couldn't look at him, but she could feel his gaze on her.

"You're gonna be sorry... missing out on my mama's shrimp and grits."

Sadie turned to see one corner of Beau's mouth turned up.

"What was all that crap you were dishing out to me last night? Huh? What was that... Seattle hogwash bullshit, anyway? All that talk about living in the moment. Fuck... that was good. You were good. I kinda believed it." Beau couldn't hide the venom in his voice. He turned his head back and stared straight ahead – hands gripping the steering wheel.

"It wasn't bullshit. It was the truth. I meant it." Sadie pouted out her response and turned her head towards him.

"Well, baby... words are cheap. You can say all you want, but you have to show it."

Sadie let out a deep sigh... Beau's words stinging her eyes with tears.

"Sadie, we have 24 hours to make the most of this… whatever this is. I intend to spend as many of those 24 hours with you as possible. I want that more than anything. Do you want that too?"

Beau had pleaded his case, and he leaned across the console of the car, awaiting her response. His mouth was inches from her ear, and Sadie could feel his hot breath on her neck.

"I know you want those grits, baby."

Sadie turned her head and let Beau kiss her. She melted when he gently cupped her face, and his tongue briefly danced with hers. Sadie knew at that moment that it had gone too far, and she had let her heart fall. She was falling deeper and deeper at every turn, with every touch and with each wink and kiss Beau stole. He had taken her heart. Sadie was finally able to admit it to herself and let the floodgates to her heart open.

"I'll text you this afternoon… when I am finished with my sessions," Sadie said breathlessly.

Beau brushed his nose against hers and watched her hop out of the car. She turned abruptly and waved as Beau pulled away from the hotel.

"What the fuck am I going to do?" Beau mumbled under his breath as he steered his car down Demonbreun Street towards his office.

* * *

"You're back! Derek called. He said he saw you at the site, but you took off before he could get you the updated survey."

Mia tried to keep up with Beau, stride for stride as he flew through the front door of his office building, down a long hallway and over to his desk. Sebastian wasn't around, so Beau threw the blueprint tube on his desk and turned to face her.

"Listen, Mia… about that note."

She walked closer to him, pinning him inside his cubicle.

"Good! I am glad you got it. What time are you coming over?"

Mia was a pretty girl, no doubt about it, but there wasn't anything about her that he found remotely attractive anymore. Nothing that he wanted to pursue. It had run its course.

"I'm not... listen. You are a great girl and one hell of an architect, but I am seeing someone. It's not appropriate for you and me to see one another... like that... outside of the office. I hope you understand."

Beau wasn't sure of the look in Mia's eyes, but she pursed her lips together and nodded.

"Derek said that you had someone with you," she said, dropping her arms to her side in apparent defeat. "Suit yourself, Beau... and take care."

Beau watched Mia turn and walk back to her side of the office.

He then let out a huge sigh, booted up his laptop, and got to work.

* * *

Beau hadn't heard from Sadie since he dropped her off at the hotel, but he dashed out of work late afternoon and went back to the Nashville Farmer's Market to pick up a few items for dinner along with a bottle of wine.

Sending Sadie a text when he got home, Beau started prepping their meal... asking her if she wanted him and George to come and get her, either on foot or in the Jeep... and still no response.

For Sadie, the afternoon stretched on, and she found herself fixated on that pink sticky note. She knew she had no right to be jealous and no right to Beau. She hadn't been entirely honest with him about her complicated situation, and she wasn't about to go opening up a can of worms. In 24 hours, Sadie would be gone, and this week would be nothing more than a very sweet memory.

The afternoon speakers couldn't hold her attention, so Sadie ducked out a bit early and went back to her hotel room. The sheets had been changed, and the room had been made up, but she could still smell Beau's scent. She sat on the edge of the bed, deep in thought when his text message popped up.

As far as Sadie saw it, she had two choices. She could hide in her room, make up some excuse and hope that Beau wouldn't come to her or she could put on the last summer dress that she packed and spend her last night in Nashville with a man she was falling in love with.

* * *

"Sadie Mae!" Beau answered his intercom and buzzed her in.

He was waiting on the third floor outside the elevator when the doors opened. Beau reached out for her in a pair of retro straight-legged faded Wrangler blue jeans and an ultra-soft charcoal gray V-neck t-shirt. He looked her up and down as she slowly came into his arms. Sadie had contemplated not wearing the dress. It was way too sexy, and she wasn't even sure why she bought it. It suited her once… a long time ago. She didn't want to appear obvious, but she had officially run out of clothes except for what she would wear home on the plane tomorrow.

Sadie's dress was a floral print wrap dress in a deep shade of burgundy. It had a tight bodice with short sleeves and tied at the waist above a flowing skirt that cut her at the knee. Sadie knew she had to be careful. One tug of the tie at the waist and the dress fell open. The walk over to Beau's was challenging, and she had to clutch the dress closed in her brisk pace.

"I picked up a bottle of wine. I hope I'm not too early?"

Beau wrapped his arms around her tight and kissed her, letting his hand fall to caress her ass. It was an apology kiss, that was for sure. Sadie could feel it and see it when she pulled away and looked into his eyes.

"Wow! You look sexy as hell, baby! I'm not going to be able to keep my hands off you tonight, okay?"

Sadie embarrassingly nodded and stepped inside the loft as she handed Beau the wine and set her tote down next to the sofa. She didn't want Beau to see that she had packed her tote pretty full, planning for a potential overnight stay. She folded up her pants and worktop, clean undies, mini-hairdryer, and a few toiletries. He had asked her to stay, so Sadie told herself to quit worrying. That was before the pink sticky note.

"Make yourself at home. I'm just about done here in the kitchen, and I'll join you on the patio. Do you like Motown?"

Sadie nodded to Beau as he turned the volume up on the wireless music system. Sadie heard Marvin Gaye on the patio speakers outside. The air was still and warm, but not as hot as the last few days.

"Um… Beau… where is George?" Sadie asked, looking around the loft. The dog was nowhere to be found.

"WAG… dog walking service. I had too much stuff to do in the kitchen, and so I booked him in for a nice long walk. No interruptions tonight," Beau said, winking at Sadie as he brought her a cold glass of chardonnay in a vintage-looking goblet.

"That dog is not coming back into this loft until he has pooped and peed… twice!"

Sadie laughed as she clinked her glass against Beau's beer bottle, and he leaned in for yet another smoldering kiss.

"Something smells amazing. I hope you didn't go to any trouble."

Beau pulled out Sadie's chair, and she took a seat on the patio. He took his time peering over her shoulder, staring down at her chest. He loved the way the lace of her bra lay smoothly over the tops of her breasts.

"Are you hungry? I've planned a slow three-course meal tonight," Beau asked.

Sadie turned and caught his eye, realizing that he was ogling her chest. She shook her head up and down and felt her cheeks flush.

"Yes! I didn't eat lunch," Sadie blurted out.

The memory of their lunch date was etched in her mind. She immediately wanted to take back what she said. She didn't want to dwell over the other woman. What was the point?

"Yeah... about that, Sadie... listen..."

"No, Beau... you don't have to explain."

If Sadie expected Beau to explain, then she would have some explaining of her own to do. Sadie's gut clenched with guilt.

"But I want to."

Beau pulled out a chair and took a seat on the patio opposite Sadie and reached for her hands.

"I saw Mia when I got back into the office today, and I told her it's over and that it was wrong for her to put that note on my plans. I mean... honestly... it's been over for 6 weeks. Listen... Sadie..." Beau was interrupted by the sound of his intercom buzzing. "Shit... sorry... it's WAG. Guess who's back?"

Beau sprinted to his front door and collected George, who then made a beeline for Sadie on the patio, snorting as he licked her ankles.

"Oh, Georgie... stop that!" Sadie exclaimed. She got up and started to dance away from him – swaying her hips to Beau's Motown mix. Sadie grabbed George's chew rope and played with him as he jumped around her.

Beau was mesmerized as he approached the patio to join them, watching Sadie dance to the Temptations. She twirled around in her dress... that fucking sexy dress she was wearing – her tan legs shimmering in the sunlight.

Beau laughed at her, trying to teach George how to spin around her. As Beau watched her move, he was aroused in a way that he had never been before. It wasn't raw sexual energy that was pulsating through his body. It was something far more intense. A million thoughts went through his mind, but it was a deep feeling of contentment that came over him. Something that he wanted to hang onto and never let go of.

"Come here, baby... dance with me and not that dog," Beau said, grabbing Sadie and pulling her close, causing the tie at her waist to unravel. Her dress fell open, exposing her upper thigh... all the way up to her cream push up bra. Beau didn't need an invitation, his hand immediately found that spot that he knew she loved. His thumb slid over her wet panties until he heard her faint moan.

"God, I love your dress."

His mouth was hungry for her. Sadie could feel it immediately, and it took her breath away. He stopped and looked into her eyes, and without saying a word, he picked her up and carried her into his bedroom.

* * *

"Voila, mademoiselle. Your appetizers are served."

Beau carried a tray upstairs piled high with Marcona almonds, pimento cheese stuffed large green olives, and fresh figs that had been grilled and wrapped in prosciutto.

"We didn't ruin the grits... did we?"

Beau pulled the covers back and crawled into bed, shaking his head as he set the tray down between them.

"Not a chance. Remember I told you that this was going to be a slow evening. Open up, beautiful," Beau commanded as he seductively popped an olive into Sadie's mouth, kissing the olive juice that had dribbled down her chin and neck.

The appetizers didn't stand a chance, and they were gobbled up before Sadie even had a chance to finish her wine. Beau sweetly retrieved the goblet from the patio and then plopped in an ice cube all before delivering the appetizer platter... completing all tasks in the buff.

"What time does your conference start in the morning?"

"Um... well, 9:15... I guess 8:30 if I want coffee and breakfast."

Sadie began to wonder if Beau had genuinely intended for her to spend the night. Maybe he was looking for a way out.

"Perfect! I've got coffee and breakfast covered. You like scrambled eggs and sourdough toast?" Beau asked.

How could Sadie do anything but emphatically shake her head up and down?

"By my calculations, Sadie Mae... that gives us... thirteen... fourteen hours in bed," Beau said, letting out a loud whoop, which caused George to bark downstairs.

"You are something else, Beau."

Sadie cupped the sides of his face in her hands and looked into his mesmerizing eyes.

"Awe... but let's go back outside. Sit on the patio, okay? It's such a beautiful night. I know it's hours from sunset... but, well... the forecast in Seattle calls for rain when I get home."

It was as if someone had completely sucked all the air out of the room. Sadie immediately wanted to take her words back. Just hearing the word Seattle and she felt the appetizers roll around in the pit of her stomach. What she couldn't escape was the look on Beau's face... the sadness in his dark gray eyes. He just stared at her. There were no words. Sadie could not think of one thing to say to make it all better.

She wanted to go back. Go back to Tuesday night and not walk up to the bar. She wished she had walked out and found her second choice. Why in the fuck did she walk up and take a seat next to him? Why did this have to happen to her now?

Beau looked away and smiled, shaking his head. He then complied with her request to leave his bed, even when he knew he wanted to take her again. Listen to her breathing quicken and feel her body tremble culminating in her cry of release. He knew that he would never be able to get enough of her.

Beau stood from the bed and pulled on his briefs and jeans before taking her hand. It was at that moment that he finally and fully understood, just how fucked he was.

* * *

"You want to pick up that plate and lick it clean… don't you?" Beau asked.

Sadie's wide-eyed smile was dazzling. The candles flickering on the patio table made her look like an angel… an angel in Beau's retro Atlanta Hawks t-shirt and her panties.

"That's what I call a clean plater!" Beau said as he grabbed Sadie's empty plate and his own and walked them into the kitchen. His three-cheese grits and grilled shrimp were just about the best thing that Sadie had ever eaten.

"Outstanding job, chef! You know if this whole architect thing doesn't pan out, you could open up a restaurant."

Sadie giggled and pulled Beau's t-shirt down over her thighs. She let her mind wander to more nights like this. Making love after work and sharing Beau's kitchen. An image popped into her mind of setting a plate of mac and cheese with a hot dog in front of a toe-headed boy.

"Let me top off your wine."

Beau watched her face and set his hand upon her shoulder. He knew he had caught her lost in thought.

"A penny for your thoughts?" he asked.

"Beau, are you trying to get me drunk… take advantage of me?" Sadie was honestly starting to feel pretty buzzed. She giggled as she brought the wine glass to her lips. If there was one thing that he loved the most about Sadie, it was her sense of humor and her infectious giggle.

"Ummmm… already happened. Did you forget already?"

Sadie simply shook her head. There was no way that she would ever forget the frenzied race to fulfillment and euphoric aftermath in Beau's bed. What he did to her should be illegal, and she was reasonably certain that in some states, it probably was.

He emptied the rest of the wine into his glass, looking overhead at the evening sky. The sun was just about ready to set, bringing with it the night... their last night together. The sky was a fire of orange and red as Sadie watched him. Beau's lips bore the semblance of a smile, just enough to show that he was enjoying his thoughts, whatever... she wondered they might be. She watched him saunter to the patio railing and look west towards the setting sun.

Sadie stood up and moved to him so that he could feel her presence at that moment, yet not uttering a word, allowing him to stay lost in the moment a while longer, while they both looked out at the sunset. He laced his arms around her and held her close, breathing in her scent.

"As soon as you see your first star, that's when dessert is served," Beau said, grabbing her hand and giving it a quick squeeze. He wanted to tell her, right then, and at that moment... but he let the moment pass, although Beau was certain that she felt it too.

He saw the tears in her eyes when he served her the shallow bowl of peaches with vanilla ice cream. He was doing his best to tick off every item on Sadie's fun list. He wanted to know her by heart and give her the joy that he knew she was missing.

"They are from Georgia and pretty fresh. I picked them up at the Farmer's Market this afternoon. I hope you like them."

"What's not to like?" Sadie said through a beaming smile.

"I drizzled them with a bit of honey. I'd have pulled down the ice cream maker and made the ice cream from scratch, but the inside needs to be in the freezer overnight. I had to settle for Häagen-Dazs."

Sadie set her empty bowl down on the table and came to him quickly, pulling up her t-shirt and straddling him in the patio chair. Her lips were sticky and sweet, and her kiss had an intensity that Beau had never felt from her before. He brushed the hair back from her face and felt the tears wet on her cheeks.

"Oh, Beau..."

Sadie fell hard into Beau's chest, and she reached around him and held onto him tight.

"We'll figure it out."

Beau let out a big sigh and let Sadie continue to kiss him as the June sky filled up with twinkling stars.

* * *

"Sadie Mae! Your eggs are ready."

Sadie galloped down the stairs, stuffing last night's dress into her tote. It was already nine o'clock.

"I'm going to be late. You're late... shit! Beau, I am so sorry."

"Baby, the pleasure was all mine," Beau said with a laugh. He quickly scooped scrambled eggs onto a plate and grabbed the toast from the toaster.

He had left her in bed with a kiss on the cheek and walked George at dawn before returning to the loft. Her smoldering eyes drew him in again, and Beau felt the urgent need build inside him quickly. After they had finished, he wrapped his arms around Sadie and savored her as she fell back asleep in his arms. When she finally heard the shower running, she couldn't help but follow him.

"I was just trying to conserve water," she said with a wink, slathering butter on her toast. Their joint shower cost them another hour.

"So... your conference ends at 12:30 and your flight..."

"Late this afternoon."

Sadie instantly felt claustrophobic. She didn't want to talk about it or bring it up. She wanted to run back into Beau's bed and bury her head under the pillows.

In the light of a new day was an ending and nothing Sadie said or did was going to change that. She knew that she couldn't run. It was time to stand and face the music.

"Perfect! I'll pick you up. We can grab a bite to eat. Get a drink or something before..."

Even Beau couldn't say it. He couldn't believe it. This was not happening. It was as if he knew that she really wouldn't leave... get on that plane. How could she? The thought that Sadie was leaving was something that he could not acknowledge.

Sadie wiped her mouth with her napkin and jumped off the kitchen stool.

"I gotta run."

"No, let me drive you," he pleaded.

"Beau, by the time you get the car out of the garage, I'll be halfway back to the hotel. You better get going... off to work."

Sadie hesitated and then walked over to George and knelt. It was at that moment that she realized this was their last goodbye.

"Take good care of him, Georgie."

The bulldog let out a low growl as his back end shook from side to side. When Sadie stood, Beau was right beside her.

"I'll see you in a few hours, okay?" Beau said, managing a weak smile as he took her in his arms.

"Yeah... sure. I'll see you soon," she responded, and when they pulled apart, Sadie could see the sadness in his eyes.

She cried all the way back to her hotel, but she knew that her decision was final.

* * *

Sadie sat on the edge of her hotel bed and went over her options once again.

It was for the best. The best way to handle things. She could see no point in dragging it out any longer. The memories of last night... one of the best nights of her life, not counting the previous two nights with Beau, made her decision agonizing.

Sadie hit download on her phone and installed the delay text app for $0.99. She then typed out her message to Beau before taking one last look around the hotel room, running her hand over the edge of the bed and smiling. By the time Beau got her text, Sadie would already be on her way to the airport… checked in and through security. Sadie would be gone. She wheeled her suitcase out of the hotel entrance and spotted her Uber.

"Good afternoon. Are you Sadie?"

"Yes."

"Heading to the airport?"

"Yes, thanks."

Sadie laid her head back against the seat, watching downtown Nashville fade from view.

CHAPTER FIVE

The ride to the airport didn't take as long as Sadie thought. The Uber driver had asked about her trip and what she thought of Nashville. Sadie responded with one-word answers. His questions just kept coming, and she didn't want to be rude, but all she wanted to do was close her eyes. When she shut them tight, she only saw Beau.

In those moments in the backseat, a flash of anger protected Sadie from the pain. She hated herself. She understood now what it meant to set love free. It had to be free for it to live on in some other form... perhaps in Sadie's life again, but she doubted it. Nausea swirled in her empty stomach, and her head swam in deep regrets. When her phone started vibrating, she knew. Sadie's text had been delivered and read. She stared out the window and fought back the tears. Even the bright colors of the summer day were drab and lifeless like a silent songbird. She looked at her phone and started reading Beau's responses to her text before throwing her phone to the bottom of her tote.

Her heartache was like a red-hot poker being pushed deep into her chest. Sadie had a hard time breathing. Her mind filled with their last conversation – their last kiss haunting her. She tried desperately to push it all from her mind as they neared the airport.

"Well, I hope you had a nice time in Nashville."

Sadie had been lost in thought when the driver put the car in park outside the terminal.

"I'll help you with your suitcase."

Sadie thanked the driver and paused for a moment as he pulled away. She let the summer breeze tousle her hair. It carried with it a fragrance of the earth, and she took in Nashville one last time before heading into the air-conditioned terminal.

Sadie hadn't counted on the long check-in line, and she cursed herself for even needing to check in a bag. She fidgeted as the line moved at a snail's pace. She finally reached the kiosk and typed in her flight number and printed off her baggage receipt. Sadie had just handed her checked bag to the ticket agent at the counter when she heard his voice.

"Sadie!"

Beau shouted from halfway across the airport. The desperation in his voice was alarming. Sadie kept her eyes locked on the ticket agent.

Beau had scanned all departing flights to Seattle on the departures board and narrowed it down to two airlines with flights leaving in the next three hours. He spent fifteen minutes running down the concourse and scouring the lines frantic to find her.

"Thank you," Sadie replied to the agent, who peered over his reading glasses as he handed over her passport and boarding pass. He looked down the concourse to see Beau running towards them at full speed, continually shouting Sadie's name.

"Miss…?" Sadie just shook her head, and the agent continued.

"Gate B9. Boarding begins in two hours."

"Sadie!" Beau appeared at her side, slightly out of breath.

"Thank you again," Sadie said, acknowledging the ticket agent. She stuffed her travel documents into her black tote and turned from the counter, completely ignoring Beau.

"Sadie! What the fuck is going on? Why did you take off from the hotel like that? I told you that I would drive you to the airport." Beau placed his hand in the middle of her back to maneuver her away from the ticket counter, and Sadie stiffened.

"Beau, why did you come? I told you not to. I know you read my text. You shouldn't have come."

Sadie kept walking as quickly as she could towards the TSA security line, Beau running alongside her.

"I thought we had an understanding... last night... about us."

Sadie went back to last night and replayed the evening over and over again in her head. She let the wine and the peaches with the honey... Beau making love to her, cloud her judgment. It was love between them that she felt last night... in his bed, and there was nothing she could do but run as far away from Nashville as possible.

"Sadie Mae... please stop. Look at me."

Sadie kept walking, and Beau kept pleading. He stopped as she continued to walk ahead.

"Please, girl... don't. Please don't do this to me." Sadie halted. His voice sliced her in two, but she couldn't look at him. She knew if she looked into his eyes, it would all be over. Sadie could not resist him, and it was taking everything she had to not run into his arms. She bowed her head and stared down at the airport concourse carpet.

"Sadie... please."

Beau took two steps towards her and reached down for her hand, and he immediately felt it. A large single solitary diamond ring on the fourth finger of her left hand.

"Fuck!" Beau cried out. He dropped her hand like it was on fire. "I can't fucking believe this." Beau stumbled backward, running his hands through his hair.

"Beau, please..."

He mumbled something under his breath and took several steps back, finally letting his hands rest over his mouth as if to trap his words permanently.

"It's not what you think. Shit! I didn't want to do this. I told you... it was complicated."

Beau kept backing away, and Sadie tried reaching out for him, but he increased his distance.

"Don't you dare fucking walk away from me now. If you leave... you'll be making a big mistake, Beau. Fuck! You have to let me explain now. I didn't want it to come to this, but you've left me no choice."

Sadie walked over to a row of chairs and took a seat, but Beau did not move. He was frozen. He kept looking down at his feet as if willing them to go to her.

"Beau... please."

Sadie's voice was hushed. She reached out her right hand, but he didn't dare take it. Beau shuffled his feet over to her and stood in front of her, his head bowed.

"Will you please sit here with me?" Sadie tentatively asked. She tried to look up at him and catch his gaze. She could tell that Beau was in pain. His whole demeanor had changed so dramatically that she felt her heart break open.

"I'm not engaged. The ring... I don't know what it means. He gave it to me years ago. He bought it at auction and then ceremoniously placed it on my finger like it meant something. It only symbolized another possession. I took it off when I arrived in Nashville. Don't ask me why? Maybe I knew. Would you have honestly struck up a conversation with me at the brewpub if you saw this ring on my finger?"

Beau remained frozen with his head bowed in silence. Sadie willed him to look up and look into her eyes, but he remained distant.

"I hate this ring. I try not to wear it, but he questions everything that I do. I figured that if I put it back on, that it would make me feel different... accept my situation... help me ease back into my life, but it only made me hurt more. Beau, I don't want another man looking at me or talking to me... or flirting with me ever again... other than you."

Beau raised his chin to look at her, but he didn't smile. He took two steps towards the row of chairs, turned quickly, and sat next to her, never uttering a word.

"Beau, I want to be honest with you. I should have been honest with you from the beginning. There is someone else, but it's over. God, it's been over for so long. I want to think that there was love between us... so long ago, though... I can't remember what it felt like. I no longer love him, not in a romantic way. He's been good to me, but I know he doesn't love me either, not like a man should love a woman."

Sadie felt a tear slide down her cheek, landing on her hands folded gently in her lap.

"We remain together, but we live very separate lives. Shit! I didn't want to tell you this. It sounds so fucking pathetic. My life... my situation. I only stay because of my father. He's sick."

Beau leaned forward and placed his elbows on his thighs. Sadie heard him take in a deep breath and exhale, trying to make sense of her confession.

"I met him about 15 years ago. His name is Joel. He's older than me, by 13 years. At first, I didn't notice. He was so worldly. I was always a bit naïve when it came to love, and I was overwhelmed by all the attention he gave me. I was trying to finish school, and I was just starting out as an apprentice appraiser. I didn't make much money. I didn't come from any money. Joel swept me off my feet. He took me to concerts and fancy parties. Trips all over the world. He travels a lot as an international banker. He showered me with things I could never have afforded." Sadie wiped another tear that had escaped her eye, not wanting to cry in front of Beau.

"I guess I got swept up in all that. I thought we'd get married, maybe have children. I don't know why I ever believed that. He had been married a long time ago and was never much into children. It was pretty apparent in the beginning that Joel was looking for a companion. I became more like an escort. Someone he could take to all his events. I was bored and lonely. I guess you could add stupid to that list," Sadie said with a slight chuckle. She felt weak and pathetic. Having received no positive reinforcements from Beau, Sadie bowed her head and continued.

"Joel asked me to move in a few years after we started dating. I suppose it was kind of like we were married, but then the years started to go by, and I realized I was stuck. I became more complacent. I started to focus on my job, and then things began to change even more. I realized that we would never have children... maybe never be married. I thought he'd change his mind, but that was foolish on my part. What we had was an arrangement and nothing more."

Beau remained silent – his eyes staring down at his feet. Sadie cleared her throat. She just wanted to finish and run away. The pain was too much to bear.

"Not long after I moved in, Joel moved into a separate bedroom, and our sex life deteriorated. I was just so confused that I didn't know what to do. We still enjoyed each other's company... I guess. He has a lot of social commitments, and I am always expected to be by his side. As the years went by, he dictated what I wore and how I styled my hair. God, this is so hard to explain. I was happy but incredibly sad and so *lonely*. There were so many times I wanted to walk away... and then my dad got sick."

Beau heard Sadie's voice break, and he leaned back and turned towards her, reaching for her hand.

"It started about six years ago... with little things. He was forgetful. He'd repeat himself. We would make plans, and he would forget. It just got worse from there. He got angry... really angry, and then the next day, my dad would call me, and he would be crying. This went on for well over a year, but he continued to work, and he would have weeks… months even with clarity. He was seeing a lady… a really nice gal, but she couldn't handle the situation as it worsened. I didn't blame her. At least she finally convinced him to see a doctor, and that's when they diagnosed him with Alzheimer's Disease."

"Oh, Sadie. I am so sorry." When Beau finally spoke, his eyes were soft and kind, and Sadie let big tears roll down her cheeks.

"I started looking… for places, but there are waiting lists, and they are so expensive. We didn't have that kind of money. My dad had a modest pension, but…"

Beau interrupted. A lightbulb going off over his head. "Joel. He had the money. You've stayed with him all these years for your father."

Beau took in a deep breath. It all made sense to him… Sadie's complicated life.

"Yes…"

Sadie put her head in her hands and wept.

"I feel so ashamed. I gave up my life so that my dad could have the care he needs. Joel arranged it all. He said it would work out better to have my father live with us… at least while his condition is somewhat manageable. The house is certainly adequate. Medicare covers a great deal, plus my dad's social security and Joel… well, he takes care of the rest. He has a full-time nurse and an aid, plus a doctor anytime he needs one… 24/7. My dad spends his days in the garden and when he isn't tending to his roses or birdwatching, he's building model airplanes or birdhouses. The tough part is that my dad is healthy as a horse, but his mind is slipping away. Oh, Beau… sometimes he doesn't know who I am and recently he calls me by my mother's name, Elenore. We haven't seen my mother in over 40 years."

Sadie blew her nose and dabbed her eyes, and Beau felt his heart break inside.

"Complicated," Beau said as he turned to her, and Sadie nodded.

"Beau, I have to go. I need to get back to Seattle. I don't have a choice. Joel isn't stupid. Leaving him is not an option. He can be difficult, and I don't want to upset him… upset the situation." Sadie stood, and Beau reached for her hand.

"Does he hurt you? Has he ever? Fuck, Sadie! I swear to you. I'll kill him with my bare hands if he has ever physically hurt you."

Sadie shook her head. There was no point in telling Beau that it wasn't the physical pain that Sadie was afraid of. Joel's words cut Sadie the deepest when she disappointed him, which was more often than not.

"No, it's not like that. I promise." Sadie's smile was weak, and Beau wasn't sure if he believed her or not.

"I can help you. We can do this together, Sadie Mae. I am falling in love with you. You know that, right?"

Sadie jumped up and grabbed her tote as Beau squeezed her hand tighter.

"I can't… um… I have to go, Beau."

"Did you just hear what I said? I love you! Sadie… listen to me. Don't get on that plane."

Beau side-stepped in front of her, and Sadie felt panic rise up inside her.

"Come with me… right now. In 90 minutes, you and I will be up in Cheatham in a little cabin along the Cumberland River. I'll build us a bonfire and then take you inside and make love to you until you beg me to stop, and then I'll wrap you up in a blanket and take you outside and show you every star in the Tennessee sky. I'll even burn your marshmallows if you want me too."

Sadie laughed, and Beau brushed a stray tear that had fallen from her eye with his thumb.

"Come with me, Sadie Mae."

Sadie lowered her eyes and shook her head. The dream was tempting.

"Beau... I can't, and you know I can't."

"Just stay through the weekend. Let's talk this through. I have some ideas. I can fix this."

Sadie could hear the excitement in Beau's voice, and she immediately sensed his analytical skills kicking in.

"You're just talking crazy, Beau. God... you have to just let me go. Let me walk away. Pretend you never met me. Go get Patrick and in a few days... I'll be a distant memory."

Beau let out a loud chortle. "You honestly believe that bullshit. No way. If you didn't hear me the last time... I love you!" Beau shouted at the top of his lungs, turning heads in the airport as Sadie's face blushed bright pink.

"I have to go. The security line is long, and my plane boards soon. You take care now, Beau."

Sadie clutched her bag tight and turned and walked away, biting the inside of her mouth.

"Sadie..."

She stopped dead in her tracks and then turned to face him.

"Please, Beau! Don't make this any harder than it has to be, okay? God, I had the best time. You gave me something these last 72 hours that I haven't had in a very... very long time. I will take that with me. I will take *you* with me for the rest of my life."

Sadie tried to be convincing, but she knew that she probably gave it away in her eyes.

"You don't understand. I can take care of you, baby. I have the money and I can give you... give us the kind of life that we deserve. I can love you... the way a man should love you, and I can see that your father is well taken care of."

Sadie stepped back and shook her head. She swallowed her anger, clenching her fists hard at her side.

"No! Don't fucking say that… fuck you! I don't want your goddam money, Beau. I don't need you. Why can't you just accept it? Let it be what it was. Two lonely people having sex."

Her words tore at his gut, but Beau knew. Sadie couldn't look him in the eye.

Beau slowly walked toward her, and she let him come to her one final time. He reached up, placed his hand behind her head, raised his other hand, and tucked a stray strand of her hair behind her ear. He could feel her breathing quicken and her body tense. Beau brought his lips to her ear and whispered.

"I want to hear you say it, Sadie Mae. I want to hear you tell me that you don't love me."

His breath in her ear made her want him like she had never wanted another human being. Beau took his left arm and wrapped it tight around her waist and pulled her closer to him. Sadie began to tremble in his arms.

"Say it… goddamit, and I'll walk away." Beau pulled away slightly and looked at her, but Sadie wouldn't make eye contact with him.

"You look me in the eyes right now and say it," Beau said through gritted teeth. Sadie wiggled from his arms and stepped back and looked into his eyes.

"I don't love you, Beau."

Her matter-of-fact admission tore through his gut. Only someone, all the way inside a heart, could shatter it with just a few words.

"Fuck you! You're lying to me," Beau shouted.

Sadie quickly turned away from him and slumped over as gasps flew from her throat. Beau slowly walked in front of her and grabbed her by the shoulders, giving her a gentle shake until she looked him in the eyes once again.

"You want to try that again?" Beau cautiously asked as Sadie shook her head from side to side. "I'm not going to forget you… stop loving you,

Sadie… not today and not tomorrow and not next week, but I'll walk out that door, and I'll let you go. If that's what you really want. I'm scared too, baby. I've got a lot to lose as well. You just have to trust me."

"I… I… can't. Please try and understand. Fuck, Beau… I'm ten years older than you. What the fuck do you want with a woman like me anyway?"

"Is that it? Is that what this is all about… you being older than me? Jesus Christ, woman. You think I care? I mean, come on. I think I figured that out about a minute after you sat down on that bar stool. You are beautiful to me. I don't care how old you are. I love you."

Beau had that child-like look in his eyes that Sadie found irresistible. One side of his mouth turned up on cue.

"I've always kind of had a thing for older women anyway." Sadie looked deeper into his eyes, and they both chuckled. "Shit, my mother was six years older than my dad. She loved him until the day he took his last breath, and it never made a difference to either one of them." Sadie continued to stare at Beau. Her expression turning blank once again.

"Sadie, I've connected to a part of you that others have never felt. I saw a part of your soul… touched something inside you that is beautiful and raw. This time with you has been more real than the blood pulsing through my body." Beau searched her face again, and she let her gaze fall away.

"You have to let me go… please," Sadie pleaded once again as Beau dropped his hands to his side and watched her turn and walk away.

"This isn't over, Sadie… not by a long shot," Beau yelled out as Sadie dug into her bag and grabbed her passport and her boarding pass. She swiftly entered the security checkpoint. The line snaked around, and Beau waited on the other side of the line until she came back around to him.

"I love you, Sadie Mae. I'm not giving you up. I'm going to fight for you… fight for us. You and me. You'll see. I'm going to take care of everything."

Sadie turned and hissed at him. "Beau... please! You're making a scene."

She shuffled forward in line, and when she had made her way back over to where he was standing, he leaned over the rope and whispered in her ear.

"I don't give a shit."

His bravado made Sadie laugh, although she fought hard to hold it in.

"They'll arrest you. You know that, right? You'll spend the weekend in jail if you don't turn and leave right now," Sadie stated, folding her arms defiantly across her chest. Beau turned to the lady standing behind Sadie and smiled.

"Why don't you pass through, ma'am. We've got some unfinished business here," Beau said with a wink. The woman clutched the grip on her roller bag and quickly passed between them, a broad smile on her face.

Sadie was a dozen people away from the TSA officer. She looked straight ahead and opened her passport and smoothed out her boarding pass.

"I'm going to book myself out on the next flight to Seattle... tonight."

Sadie immediately snapped her neck around as panic filled her eyes.

"Beau... no! I forbid it... besides, you have your son this weekend. Think of Patrick."

Beau just smiled at her. "I don't have Patrick until noon on Sunday. That gives me plenty of time to get to Seattle and back."

Sadie looked at the line behind her, and she stepped out and let a group pass by her. She needed to try and talk some sense into him.

"And then what... huh? You'll never find me. You don't even know my last name." Sadie's smile made him cringe. "Beau, please! I am begging you. Let me go!" Sadie shouted as Beau just shook his head.

"Sadie Mae… I am never going to give you up."

Suddenly, Sadie leaned across the ropes and placed her palms flat against Beau's chest. Her mouth crushed against his as she kissed him hard, breathing into his mouth and dragging her hands up his chest and into his hair. Her tote fell off her shoulder and crashed to the ground as Beau reached out and pulled her into him. It was as if he wanted to melt into her. Sadie's hands went crazy… up and down his back… oblivious to everyone and everything around her.

"I love you. Oh Beau. I love you so much," Sadie whispered breathlessly.

He quickly pulled away, and Sadie could see the tears forming in his eyes.

"Okay, then… now we're talking."

Beau smiled at her, and they stood in silence for a moment… forehead to forehead – Beau gently cupping Sadie's ass in his hands.

"Now what, baby?"

Sadie pulled away. She didn't have a clue, and she began to regret her admission. She played her hand, and telling Beau she loved him might have been a huge mistake. Right now, in her mind… it still didn't make a difference.

"I don't know exactly. You have to let me figure it out, okay? Just give me some space… and time. I mean it, Beau." Sadie reached out and cupped his face. "But… I do love you. I really do."

Sadie immediately felt guilty as she looked into his eyes. She didn't want to hurt him. She did love him as crazy as it sounded in her head, but she knew she had to walk away for now. She picked up her tote, passport, and boarding pass and resumed her place in line. Their admission to one another hadn't changed anything. It had only made it worse.

"I'll see you… *soon*?" Beau's comment came out more like a question, and Sadie ignored it as she took in a deep breath.

"Sadie?"

In silence, Sadie handed the TSA agent her passport and boarding pass. She knew she couldn't turn around... look into his eyes again. If she did, she would be in his Jeep... bare feet on his dash... heading up to that magical cabin in the woods, he told her about. She could see it all in her mind... making love in front of the fire... Beau nibbling sweet and sticky marshmallows off her lips and Sadie pointing to the stars in the sky like Galileo's daughter.

The TSA agent handed her back her passport and document, and she passed through the line. He couldn't touch her, kiss her, and once she rounded the corner, he would never see her again.

"I'll always love you, Beau... goodbye."

The words tumbled out of her mouth as he watched her put her passport into her tote. Sadie never turned around. She put her head down and shuffled forward in line. She knew in her heart it would never work, and whatever plan he had could never be executed. This was all for the best.

"Sadie! No, Sadie... wait!"

Beau's shouts reverberated through the airport. She could still hear him even after she placed her tote on the conveyer belt and walked through the metal detector.

Sadie replayed the ending in her head... over and over again as she walked towards her gate. She let the tears and snot trickle down her face. Sadie didn't care. She had done it. She had broken her heart and also Beau's, and she would never forgive herself.

Beau would never be able to find her. She was careful. No credit card receipts when they were out, although Beau paid for most everything. She paid cash only when necessary. She knew the hotel would not give out her information. The conference was over, and the participants scattered. Beau didn't know where she worked or even her last name. Sadie was untraceable.

She cleaned herself up in the bathroom before finding her gate. She could feel her phone vibrating in her bag... no doubt Beau calling or texting her. She dug around until she found it and quickly switched it off. She closed her eyes and took a deep breath. In five hours, Sadie would be back in Seattle. Her heart ached, but she knew that it was for the best. Joel would never understand, and her dad would suffer. Sadie closed her eyes and took a deep breath and waited for the boarding announcement.

* * *

Beau quickly walked back to his car in the airport parking lot and slammed the door to his Jeep closed. He struck his fist against the steering wheel, but Beau had a grin on his face from ear to ear.

He reached into his front pocket and felt the thin cardboard name tag that he had ripped off Sadie's suitcase Thursday morning while she was in the shower. He pulled it out of his pocket and stared at it again.

Sadie M. Morgan. 287 West Magnolia Way, Seattle, WA 98199.

CHAPTER SIX

"Welcome home, darling. How was your flight?"

Sadie rolled her bag through the front door and tossed her tote next to it, glancing into the study. Joel was sitting behind his desk, reading his *Wall Street Journal*. He didn't even glance up as he addressed her.

"I'm sorry I couldn't pick you up. Did you have trouble finding the car service I arranged? I knew you would understand... what with the gallery opening and cocktail reception this evening."

Sadie couldn't relate to Joel anymore, it had started long before Nashville, but walking through the front door solidified her feelings. He was almost a stranger to her as she looked over at him. He rose from his desk and quickly took a seat in his royal blue wingback chair. Joel looked uncomfortable in his crisp white button-down shirt – his gray slacks perfectly creased. Why he didn't find a comfortable pair of lounging pants was beyond comprehension.

Joel was an attractive man of average height. He was aging well... no doubt from the serums and oils that he slathered on his face, although his eyes bore deep crow's feet. His hair was greying, and he was losing hair at his temples, more and more each year. Joel's face was tanned, and his body trim. He worked out religiously, although he gave up running years ago after several orthoscopic knee surgeries. These days, Joel enjoyed tennis at the club twice a week, golfing with clients, and riding a stationary bicycle in the basement that cost him a fortune.

Nobody liked Joel Lewis much, yet no one really disliked him. He was a bit forward and a little intrusive, but it was clear that his mannerisms were due to financial status and self-made privilege and not to any intent to be objectionable. He worked hard to get where he was, including working connections to be put up at the club... several of them, including the Rainier Club and the Sandy Point Country Club. Joel would never overstep his privileges.

In the boardroom, Joel was the finest diplomat anyone had ever seen. He put everyone at ease, drew them into liking him and wanting him to like them, before delivering the critical thing he needed them to agree to. He was a master manipulator, and he always seemed to get everything he wanted... everything he needed. Once the ink was dry on his latest deal, and the assets tied up, all the promises he made died in the wind. An honest man would feel bad, but to Joel, it was a game. It was a thrill for him. He did the same to his women. No one is his life was indispensable to him, and everyone in his life fulfilled a purpose. In the fifteen years he was with Sadie, she never saw a genuine emotion other than greed, but he did profess his love for her as she was loyal... and nothing else. In return, she was rewarded with a place to live, access to his excesses, and care for her father.

"Fritz and Abigail send their regards. Everyone missed you tonight. You would have loved the art. It was absolutely dreadful. Modernism mixed with recycled materials. No accounting for taste these days."

Sadie hated how he belittled her. It always left a sour taste in her mouth.

"Do you know what I like the most about you, Sadie Mae?" She could hear his southern Georgia drawl in her head as she tried to push Joel's toxic words away.

"Everything!"

She could almost feel Beau plunging his tongue into her mouth. It always felt like the first time when he kissed her. His touch and his taste. She remembered what it felt like when he moved inside her. She could feel his sheets in her balled-up fists and remembered what it felt like to barely catch her breath after their climax. Sadie blinked her eyes and returned to her life.

"Abigail suggested dinner at the club next week."

Sadie wondered how Fritz and Abigail would handle sticky ribs at Martin's… sauce dribbling down their chins and all sloshed back with a cold Music City pale ale.

"Thank you for arranging the car. I hope you gave everyone my regards and apologies."

Joel nodded his head and shook his paper out in front of him, folding over another page. It was Sadie's cue to leave, and she silently turned towards the study entrance.

"My darling… please forgive me. I've missed you. How about a cognac?"

Sadie's blood ran cold. There was no possible way Joel could have known. He folded his newspaper and jumped up, dashing to the liquor cart in the corner. Sadie hardly ever drank hard alcohol, and Joel rarely offered a taste of his private collection. His evenings in his study were spent alone listening to Vivaldi or the opera. When his door was shut, Sadie knew that he was not to be disturbed.

"A cognac?" Sadie thought back to Tuesday night. The taste of the liquor on Beau's lips. Beau's lips on her nipples. Beau's luscious mouth between her legs.

"Sadie… to help you sleep. You must be exhausted. I know just how excruciating those conferences can be. I barely heard from you, and you've barely spoken two words since you walked in the door. Please, take a seat and tell me all about it."

Sadie was tempted. Rip the band-aid off.

Why yes, Joel... my trip to Nashville, you ask? Mind-blowing sex with the most amazing man I've ever met. Oh, and by the way... I am in love with him, and he is in love with me.

Sadie had read and re-read Beau's text messages since landing in Seattle... and they kept coming. The last few made Sadie laugh. Beau had freely admitted that he had been drinking, and she was mad at herself for not staying. What she did to him when she passed through security was wrong, but Sadie was terrified and needed time to think things through. Beau's messages were sweet and supportive... and sad. Sadie ached all over for him, and she knew that she could not let him go.

Beau had asked her to come back to him... come back to Nashville whenever she was ready. He offered to buy her a plane ticket, and he would put her up in a hotel if she didn't want to stay at the loft, but he told her he really wanted her to stay with him. He told her he wanted to make love to her all over the loft again... on the patio table... on the bathroom counter... in the shower... tangled up in the sheets on his bed... over and over and over again. If Beau ever gave up being an environmental architect, he could definitely find a job writing erotic literature.

Joel swirled the cognac in front of Sadie's face as she took a seat in the oversized wing-backed chair opposite his. The gas fireplace was on, and it made the room feel stuffy. Sadie couldn't believe the contrasting weather. Near 90 in Nashville and barely 60 in Seattle in late June.

"I'm sorry... my mind is elsewhere. How's my father?"

Sadie let the liquor warm the inside of her mouth. She wanted to get this homecoming over with quickly and call Beau before he passed out. She needed to apologize and set the record straight.

"He's well. Philomena said he had a good day. The Amazon order came with the model airplanes you ordered. You got him the B-24 Liberator. He was very excited."

Sadie was pleased. Her father's life was so small now. He took pleasure in working with his hands, which seemed to make him more alert. Sadie gave the airplanes and the birdhouses away when he was finished and had moved on to something else. He never missed them.

"I thought we'd all take a walk in the morning... through Discovery Park, and then you can head out to the market if you'd like. We have the charity benefit tomorrow night. Please remember that it is black tie and be ready to leave at six o'clock. Also, I think you should book yourself into the hairdresser." Sadie reached up to smooth her hair down as she took the final sip of her drink.

Rip the fucking band-aid off, girl.

"Well, then I guess I should be off to bed. I'm tired. Good night." Joel barely looked up. He didn't bother to kiss her or escort her upstairs. His face was buried in his phone.

"Good night, darling."

Sadie grabbed her bags and silently climbed the stairs to her bedroom.

* * *

"Baby? Oh God... Sadie, is that you?" Sadie giggled. The phone barely rang before Beau answered. His drawl was quite pronounced. His tongue thick from booze. Sadie sat in her bathroom with the door shut and bathwater running. She didn't want Joel to wander up the stairs and hear her talking.

"Beau, you should not be drinking. You're going to have one big headache in the morning."

"You betcha... to go along with my big heartache. I needed some heartache medication, baby. Fuck, I thought I was never going to hear from you again."

Beau still had the luggage name tag in his hand. He hadn't let go of it all night.

Beau busted through the door of the loft after getting home from the airport, and by the time Sadie's flight reached 10,000 feet, Beau had amassed a complete dossier on Sadie Mae Morgan. From Facebook to Instagram to LinkedIn, Beau knew where Sadie lived and where she worked. He knew her gym and where she liked to go to yoga… even her favorite coffee shop. He found out her best friend was named Juliette, and he saw dozens of pictures of them and also pictures of Sadie and her dad. It was the pictures of her and Joel that made him grab the bottle of Jack Daniels. Despite what little details Sadie had confided in him if she wasn't in Beau's arms… he was going to be jealous.

"Beau, I just wanted to let you know that I got home okay."

Sadie had intended for their conversation to be short and amicable. She needed time to think and separate herself from the intense feelings of the past few days. She didn't want to lead Beau on, down some unknown path when she had no idea what path, if any, was possible.

"Your home, Sadie Mae, is here in Nashville with me. This is where you belong. I can give you and your dad a home."

Beau was balancing his laptop on his knee, phone in one hand and a beer in the other… staring at a picture he had blown up of Sadie and Joel. She didn't fool him. Beau knew that smile was phony. He shut his eyes and remembered the smile on her face when she convulsed with her orgasm.

"It's been a long day. I'm tired, okay. I'll give you a call soon."

Sadie felt the tears forming in her bloodshot eyes. She knew she should apologize and tell him what he meant to her, but he had been drinking, and she realized that it probably wasn't the best time for them to talk and hash things over.

"I love you, Sadie Mae. I'll wait for you, but you have to know something. I need to be honest with you, and you aren't going to like it."

Sadie heard Beau take in a deep breath and exhale. She suddenly felt her stomach drop.

"Okay, Beau. What is it?"

"I know. I know everything there is to know about you. I snatched your luggage tag off your suitcase when you were in the shower on Thursday morning. I know your last name is Morgan. I know where you live and where you work. I know Juliette is your best friend. I know where you love to get your morning coffee. I'm fucking staring at a picture of you and Joel right now… I went digging through your Instagram."

When he finished, Beau heard Sadie gasp.

"Sadie… Sadie Mae…?"

All Beau heard next was silence.

Sadie quickly hung up, turned her phone off, and threw it at the bottom of her tote.

Sadie knew that she was in big trouble.

* * *

"Tall iced nonfat vanilla latte, please."

Sadie moved forward in line at Starbucks, glancing over her shoulder. She fully expected to see Beau at any moment, even though she knew that would probably not happen. She contemplated finding another coffee place, and she was going to have to figure out how to turn off the GPS tracking on her phone. Sadie couldn't believe all the stuff Beau had found on her. How stupid was she?

It had been three days. Three long, endless days since Sadie had hung up on him. A weekend from hell! The day after she discovered that Beau had taken her luggage tag, Sadie left her phone at the bottom of her tote and went about her day. She walked the park with her dad and Joel and then drove north to Edmonds to walk through the weekend farmer's market… finishing up in the garden, watching her dad complete his latest model airplane. It wasn't until very late that night when she got home from the charity benefit that she retrieved her phone and turned it on.

Beau had left her dozens of voicemails and sent her numerous text messages. Sorry appeared to be the central theme. Sadness and deep remorse were a close second, followed by love. More than anything, Beau loved her, and he promised to never, ever fuck up again, but she had to call him... or, at the very least, text him.

Sadie was mad at first and then scared. Joel wasn't a fool, and he had already commented that Sadie was acting different since Nashville, which Sadie played off as jet lag and catching up with her dad. Sadie had to play her cards right, and Beau wasn't helping.

Joel's patience was wearing thin. He didn't like the dress she wore to the benefit, and Sadie had failed to pick up her dry cleaning and had nothing else suitable to wear. When she asked if they could leave early, as she was tired and had a headache, he sent her home in a cab... verbally abusing her by telling her what a disappointment she was. Sadie was the perfect companion the following night at the symphony, stroking Joel's ego with compliments and letting him kiss her cheek and hold her hand in front of his clients and friends. His lips on her flesh made her sick, but she smiled... that smile that she had practiced for years.

"Tall iced nonfat vanilla latte for Sadie." Sadie grabbed her drink and took a seat by the front windows. She was expecting Juliette, dragging Liam and Lola close behind at any moment. Her best friend was the perfect mother. Two kids, two dogs and a house overlooking Alki Beach. She had a husband that adored her. Not hard with a body like a super-model and a mind like an artist. Juliette was the best cook, best sister, best friend, and best sports photographer on the west coast. Sadie knew that she was bored, taking a break from work over the summer to spend time with the kids, aged ten and seven, and summer meant no school and endless activities. Juliette was anxiously awaiting a return to normalcy. Sundays at CenturyLink when the Seahawks season started in a few months.

Right on time, Juliette came jogging through the door, but she was kid free with a camera bag slung over her shoulder.

"Hey, Jules. Kids?"

Juliette reached out and hugged Sadie. In addition to Juliette's list of accomplishments, she was the best hugger.

"Don't tell Geoff. Please promise me that you won't mention this to Geoff. I got the day game today at T-Mobile Park. The Red Sox are in town. Shit, I'm going to be in trouble. I dumped my kids at a YMCA day camp," Juliette said, pulling her mahogany ponytail tight while smiling at Sadie. Juliette towered over her in a pair of painted-on white jeans, a pink V-neck Under Amour t-shirt, and a tan photographer's vest.

"Damn! You look good, Sadie. Did you do something different with your hair?"

Sadie chuckled. As Joel had requested, Sadie had gone to the hairdresser and asked for the same cut and blow-in that she'd been getting for the past 15 years.

"Um, not exactly," Sadie muttered, grinning from ear to ear.

"Nashville must have been great then. How was the Opry?"

"Jules... I met someone... in Nashville. His name is Beau. I've fallen in love. We are in love."

Juliette's mouth fell open, and Sadie smiled back at her while trying to gauge her best friend's reaction.

"And you're telling me this here... at Starbucks? Fuck, Sadie! I think I need a drink. Come on."

Juliette drove them from West Seattle to the Triangle Pub two blocks from T-Mobile Park for Bloody Mary's. The dive bar was a perfect place to confess one's sins. Juliette threw a $20 bill on the bar, and the bartender gave her a wicker basket with dozens of tiny pull tabs.

"Look, Sadie... Joel is probably my least favorite person on the planet, but are you really sure? I mean... most days, I want to kill, divorce, and fuck Geoff's brains out like at least three or four times. I thought you were happy?"

"Yeah... not so much apparently. Not after meeting Beau and realizing what I was missing. A real life... normal stuff... a partner... sex." Sadie looked up at Juliette and winked.

"Well, yes... sex is great and all. I mean, look at the two treasures I got out of it. Relationships are complicated, and what do you really know about this guy?"

Sadie knew that Juliette had a point, but she wasn't about to let her talk her out of it.

"I know I love him, and he loves me."

Juliette sucked the last of her Bloody Mary through her straw and handed her $3 in winning tabs to the bartender as a tip. She stood to hug Sadie goodbye, pausing as she placed her hands on her hips.

"Sadie... you just met him. You're in love with him? This sounds like a fucking *Hallmark* movie. No! A *Lifetime* movie. That's the channel with all the psycho stalkers. You said he left you a ton of texts... voice mails, too. Fuck! Get a new phone... get a new number... and while you are at it, get a vibrator. I'll text you a picture of mine." Juliette chuckled and then embraced Sadie in a strong hug.

"Jules, I'm serious. Look... look at him," Sadie exclaimed, reaching into her tote for her phone. Her and Beau had snapped a couple of selfies in the beer garden at Martin's Barbecue. Sadie had looked at the one of Beau... his lips brushing against her temple at least 20 times a day since she arrived back in Seattle.

Juliette let out a high-pitched wolf whistle as she grabbed Sadie's phone. "Damn, Sadie... were all the men in Nashville this fucking hot?"

"He's more than that, Jules. It's more. I don't know. I'm not sure how I can convince you. He's real, and he loves me. It wasn't just some random hook up."

"I'll put up a $20 bill that he ghosts you by the end of the week."

Sadie got tears in her eyes, and Juliette finally pulled her eyes away from the picture on Sadie's phone and leaned in to hug her again.

"He's got a son, Patrick. He turns five next month."

Juliette's mouth fell open as she pulled away, processing Sadie's next admission.

"Oh, fuck! He's got baggage too!"

"Jules... come on!"

Sadie grabbed her tote and stood up next to Juliette, her shoulders slumped forward from the weight of their talk.

"I'm sorry to bail on you. You sure you don't want to go to the game?" Juliette asked. Sadie shook her head. She felt defeated, having not received the acceptance from Juliette that she was hoping for.

"No. I'll grab the C line bus back to my car and finish up that appraisal in West Seattle, but thanks."

"Listen, I love you... be careful. You've got a lot on your plate right now. I understand. Some hot stud muffin flirting with you is fantastic. Just be real about all this, okay. Don't go throwing away this amazing life your living, even if it is with boring Joel... for some fantasy."

When Sadie got back to West Seattle, she drove down near the lighthouse and texted Beau. After his late Friday night/early Saturday morning barrage of texts and calls, it had been radio silence.

Hi, can we talk? If you have time...I am free all afternoon.
I miss the sound of your voice.

It took Beau precisely 15 seconds to ring Sadie's phone.

"Sadie Mae... baby? I am so glad you texted. I've been crazy. Fucking out of my head."

Beau had been working from home, having spent Saturday vowing never to drink again and Sunday chasing after and being nicely distracted by Patrick. After he dropped his son off at summer camp Monday morning, Beau couldn't face going into the office. He played hoops with Mac at the gym, spilling his guts about Sadie's departure and his detective work.

"Beau, I understand what you did. God, I'd probably have done the same thing. I should have told you everything. My last name... where I work... about Joel. Fuck! It all happened so fast. I fell for you so fast and so hard. I didn't handle myself the right way, I'm sorry. I never set out to deceive you. Honestly, Joel and I are over."

Sadie took a deep breath not knowing precisely what Beau might have been thinking the last three days.

"Sadie... if you never, ever wanted to hear from me again... fuck baby, I'd deserve it, honestly." Beau stared at the luggage tag, which he had taped to the edge of his home computer. There were times in the last three days when he felt it was all he had left of her.

"Listen, Beau... I think we have something... the start of something amazing. I want to come back to Nashville... soon, okay?"

Sadie swore she thought she heard Beau crying. "Beau... are you there?"

"Yes, Sadie Mae. I'm here."

"I haven't worked out all the details yet, but I think I know a way to come to Nashville for a few weeks. I'm thinking 20 days or so. First part of August. No pressure or anything. I just want to see if this is real. You and me. What do you say, Beau?"

* * *

"I don't even know your last name. My mama would be so ashamed. It's started out hey cutie where you from and then it turned into oh no what have I done... and I don't even know your last name!"

Sadie was rushing around her bedroom singing and dancing as she quickly got ready for work. Her Nashville music playlist conjuring up memories that still made her blush.

"Sadie, for crying out loud! I could hear you all the way across the house. It sounds like a drowning cat!"

Joel scared Sadie half to death. He had walked into her bedroom dressed in one of his navy-blue pinstriped suits, adjusting the cufflinks on his wrist. His salt and pepper hair was more pepper, lately... no doubt from the *Just For Men* hair dye she knew he used.

Sadie pulled the earbuds out of her ears and grabbed her robe. She felt dirty being in her bra and thong in front of Joel. He didn't bat an eyelash.

"Sorry... I'm... not sure what came over me," Sadie muttered, but she knew.

It was love.

A week after telling Beau that she wanted to come back to Nashville, she reluctantly agreed to let him book her ticket. She had been certifiably giddy since then, even though she knew Joel was going to take a bit of convincing.

* * *

"Darling! August is sailing regatta season. Have you forgotten? Do you have to be gone for most of the month?"

Joel stared across the dinner table at Sadie as she took in a deep breath. She had been practicing her speech for days... in the car... in the shower... face timing with Beau under the sheets every night.

Their nightly Facetime session were the only thing that got Sadie through her day. In the course of the last few weeks, Sadie and Beau had gotten to know one another on a whole different level. They shared thoughts on religion and politics... embarrassing stories, favorite books, movies and TV shows, holiday traditions, and biggest fears. They talked for hours in the evening and checked in three or four times a day. A sweet text here. A few words of encouragement in a phone call to start each day. They quickly became each other's best friend.

"But Joel, I really want to get my land certification. Texas has tons of land to appraise. I need 1,000 hours for my certificate. Who wants to go to Texas in August, right?"

Joel set his knife and fork down and took a sip of his cabernet, a 2003 from Napa that he picked up at a wine auction several summers ago. Sadie had wanted to drive into San Francisco… across the Golden Gate Bridge, perhaps take in a tour of Alcatraz or eat a bowl of seafood chowder down at Fishermen's Wharf, but Joel had organized a private tour of Chinese art in Chinatown, spending more on an ugly vase than Sadie made in six months. When she asked about riding on a cable car, he dismissed her suggestion, and they headed straight back to Napa.

"Oh, it might not take me the entire month of August, Joel."

But Sadie was lying. She had no intention of coming back to Seattle early. Beau booked her out on an early morning flight on August 5th and home on August 28th… three full weeks. Sadie took in a deep breath and continued with her tale.

"I talked with the last appraisal team who went to Texas. They told me that they were so far out in the sticks, they had to drive two hours just to get the Internet."

This part of the story always made Sadie laugh when she practiced it in the mirror. For Joel, she sounded very convincing.

"Darling… this trip sounds so barbaric. It's entirely unnecessary. I think you should tell your boss that you'd rather not go. I mean, what purpose does this certificate really hold for you? I've told you before that there is charity work that you'd be perfect for. More time at home with your father… and me."

Sadie cringed at the thought of being under Joel's thumb more than she was now.

"Chuck and Mitzi would love for us to go sailing in the San Juan Islands this year," Joel announced.

Sadie wanted to choke on her beef bourguignon. She was dying for some slow-cooked brisket and a cold one.

"I've also been asked to co-host the end of season luncheon and now... apparently, I'll be doing that alone."

Joel's glare said it all. He'd find a way to make her pay, she was sure of it. Sadie would have to volunteer for the club golf tournament, or god forbid... be the new fourth for ladies' bridge or canasta.

"My only concern is my father. I'll check in daily with Philomena and I'll drive into town if I have to in order to get decent phone and internet reception. Joel, I really must go. It's a big step in my career, and it is very important to me. My job is dependent upon this." Sadie knew her life was dependent on this. Her new life and a possible future with Beau.

"Alright, darling."

Sadie hid her smile, complained of a headache, and raced upstairs to call Beau to tell him the good news.

CHAPTER SEVEN

Sadie landed back in Nashville, one day short of five weeks from the day she first set foot in Tennessee. She had spent the night before her return trip at Geoff and Juliette's, lying to Joel once again. Juliette was flying out for a Seahawks pre-season football game, and Sadie told Joel that they would share a cab to the airport, so Sadie wouldn't need to disturb him. The car service he ordered asked too many questions and always required flight information. That was a risk Sadie wasn't willing to take.

She grabbed her tote and exited the plane, texting Beau the minute she landed. She knew very soon that his arms would be wrapped tight around her, and the butterflies in her stomach flew in delight. Would he still feel the same, or would their time together prove that their love was nothing but lust?

Dashing into the ladies' room, Sadie brushed her teeth, and touched up her make-up – her phone buzzing with another text from Beau asking where she was. Sadie quickly finished in the bathroom and then sprinted down the concourse.

His were the first eyes she saw on the other side of security. He looked better than she remembered and a tad thinner. His hair was freshly cut, and he was cleanly shaven. The white and gray checked button-down shirt that he wore matched his eyes perfectly, but it was his smile. Beau's broad grin. His eyes fixated on her brought tears to her eyes. He reached behind his back and produced a bouquet of sunflowers tied with a light blue ribbon and laid them in her waiting hands.

"Beauford Patrick Walker. It's a pleasure to meet you."

"Sadie Mae Morgan… and the pleasure is all mine."

Sadie flew into his arms, and Beau held her tightly, finally succumbing to her body, letting his hands fall to his favorite place.

"Oh… baby… I've missed you so much."

Beau's mouth enveloped her soft lips tenderly, and he pulled back and looked deep into her eyes once again.

"I need to take you home now… quickly."

Sadie giggled and shook her head up and down, and they headed towards baggage claim.

The plan was to take the next three weeks to see how they felt about one another with no plans beyond figuring out if what they had was worth holding onto. Sadie was going to work remotely on a couple of projects… otherwise, she was all Beau's. He expressed his desire for Sadie to meet Patrick and have her spend time observing their routine and his day-to-day life. Beau also bought them airline tickets to fly to Atlanta the weekend Patrick was with Hannah to meet his mama and Presley. The hot August sun streamed through Beau's Jeep as they made their way into downtown. Beau never let go of her hand, and neither one could wipe the smiles from their faces.

When they reached the loft, George was waiting at the front door. He let out a whimper and ran around in circles.

"You'd better go get some paper towels. I'll take your bags upstairs."

George wiggled around Sadie's legs and followed her into the kitchen, snorting until Sadie bent down to give him some love. He let out a snivel with snot and drool flying in all directions before dribbling a bit of pee onto the wood floor.

Sadie stood in the middle of Beau's loft and looked around. It felt like home, and she promised herself that she would savor every moment... hold onto every memory. She feared that it might be the only happiness she would be able to take for herself for a while.

"I made a place for your things. There is a drawer in the closet and plenty of space to hang up some clothes."

Sadie watched Beau walk down the loft steps, and he took her breath away. She had fantasized on the plane of launching herself into his arms and ripping the clothes off his body, but she thought she should pace herself.

"You wanna get settled while I pour some wine?"

Sadie couldn't resist him any longer, and she shook her head sideways as she sexily walked towards him. When she kissed him, he could feel her giving him her heart, and he pulled her into his arms just as George let out a loud bark.

"Goddam, dog! I'll be right back."

It worked out perfectly. With Beau and George gone, Sadie ran upstairs and found her suitcase in the back of Beau's bedroom closet, sitting on an old chair... the bottom drawer to his dresser open and empty. She looked up, and he had pushed his hanging shirts to one side, giving her ample space and a dozen empty hangers. A chivalrous act that made Sadie swoon.

She quickly pulled off her t-shirt and wiggled free of her drawstring skirt and left everything including, her bra and panties on the floor of the closet. Sadie was excited to grab her new maroon lace bra and panties as she skipped into the bathroom. Sadie stood in front of Beau's bathroom mirror, smiling at the view. In between working, issues with her dad, and keeping up appearances with Joel, Sadie had been working out like a dog, sometimes twice a day. Although her body was still not perfect and never would be, Sadie was three pounds under her goal weight, and her stomach was tighter and flatter than the last time she stood naked in front of Beau.

"Sadie... we're back!"

Beau unclipped George's leash, and the lovesick dog waddled to the bottom of the loft stairs, waiting patiently for Sadie's return.

"I'm upstairs. Down in a sec."

Sadie dabbed some perfume behind her ears and ran her fingers through her hair... walking to the top of the stairs in her new underwear.

Beau picked up George's empty bowl and began filling it with dog food when Sadie appeared at the top of the stairs. She walked two steps down and stopped when Beau saw her. As if in a trance, Beau kept filling George's bowl, dog food spilling down onto the hardwood floor. Excited to be overfed, George chased down every piece of extra kibble.

Beau simply couldn't take his eyes off her. He couldn't believe that Sadie had actually come home to him.

"Hi, Beau."

"Hi, Sadie Mae. Wow !"

Beau gave her a wolf whistle, and Sadie threw her hands up to her face to squelch her laughter as Beau put George's bowl down, not bothering to pick up the mess.

He walked towards her at a brisk pace, taking the stairs two at a time. When Beau reached her, he gently lifted Sadie into his arms and walked her back into the bedroom, placing her carefully on the bed.

"Um... I wanted to bathe this room in candles tonight. Make it special."

Beau's voice was husky, and he was out of breath. He ran his hands down the sides of her face and brushed his lips against her cheek.

"Beau, it won't be dark for hours, You want to wait?"

Sadie tried to wiggle free under his weight, but Beau was too strong, and she felt his weight fall on top of her.

"God… no… I don't want to wait, baby. It's just that… well, this is the first time that I'll be making love to you. I just want it to be good… special."

Beau crushed his mouth onto hers and let his tongue take back all that it had been missing.

"Oh, Beau. It will be. I love you."

Beau was suddenly lost in her as he made love to her for the very first time… twice.

* * *

Beau let his fingertips brush over Sadie's shoulders and down her back. She had been asleep for about thirty minutes. George was snoring at the bottom of the stairs, and Beau was the most satisfied man on the face of the earth. Sadie fluttered her long eyelashes and smiled.

"Hey… you're awake?" Beau exclaimed. He leaned over and kissed her shoulder as Sadie slowly woke up.

"Oh, did I doze off?"

"Mmmmm."

"How long?"

Her smile was the most beautiful thing Beau had seen… that and her tanned and toned body, but Sadie wasn't the only one who had been working out. She could feel the definition in Beau's stomach and back-end.

"About a half an hour."

"Did I snore?"

"Yup… and you drooled on my pillow."

Sadie quickly rolled over, wiping drool off her face that never existed then swatted Beau's bare behind.

You gettin' hungry?"

"Um… no… definitely a bit later. Whatcha thinking?" Sadie reached out for Beau, pulling herself closer to him and then breathing in his scent – musky from the sweat of their union.

"A walk… out and about… a bit later. Do you like Italian?"

Sadie shook her head emphatically. She could get used to this… all of this… all of Beau. She watched him watch her, and she suddenly felt like she couldn't get enough… wouldn't be able to get enough of him over the next few weeks.

"Um… baby, I have to tell you something," Beau stated. Sadie suddenly looked up and into his eyes. Something in the tone of his voice alarmed her, and she pulled away and tucked the sheet up around her. "It's nothing bad, I promise."

Beau pulled her hand free of the sheet, cradling it between his palms before bringing it to his mouth as he softly kissed the underside of Sadie's wrist.

Sadie let out a deep sigh as Beau leaned in to kiss her on the mouth. What was it about this man's lips on her lips, anywhere on her body, for that matter that brought her immediate comfort? She knew at that moment that whatever came out of his mouth, they would be okay.

"I know we said that we'd spend this time together… the next few weeks taking our time… making sure… about us and our future. Sadie, I love you. I don't need three weeks. I love you… so very much, baby. I know you are scared. I am scared too, but I want you to know… today just how strongly I feel about us."

Sadie felt her eyes well up with tears as she looked away.

"Sadie Mae… I want you to move to Nashville. Will you?"

Sadie took a deep breath and held it. Beau's question swirling around in her mind, along with his previous comments.

"Baby? Are you still breathing?"

Sadie blew out the air and laughed, shaking her head up and down.

"I know. I can see that look in your eyes, but I've got plans… big, big plans. It's all I have been thinking about the last 38 days… how we can make this work. Honest… you'll see. You don't have to give me your answer about moving today. I know you didn't want to talk about it tonight, but… well… as Patrick would say, I'm s'ited."

"I'm s'ited too, Beau… I am, but fuck! I am so scared. This is huge. It's overwhelming to even contemplate. Trust me, I've spent the last five weeks thinking about nothing but you and me and your son and my father… my job… and…" Sadie paused and looked away.

"Joel."

Beau hated the sound of that man's name on his lips, but he knew he needed to keep his jealousy in check.

"Yes… Joel. There is no way that I am going to move on without hurting him in some way. I'm not that kind of person, Beau. It's going to be incredibly hard. Like it or not, we have a history."

Beau knew Sadie loved him, and the thought of her loving another man was hard for him to imagine. Beau knew that he would have to tread lightly and let Sadie deal with Joel in her own way.

For tonight, and the next three weeks, he was content knowing that he had her all to himself. Beau was prepared to wait to hear Sadie's answer when she was ready.

* * *

"Everyone got their clothes on?" Beau called out as he reached over the side fence of the little house in the neighborhood called Music Row, within walking distance of Vanderbilt University and undid the latch to the garden gate. Sadie was holding on tight to George's leash, as she followed the boys into the back yard.

"Barely… oomph. I can't even get these overalls buttoned up anymore. Hey, y'all!"

Mazelle Mackenzie or Mazie, as everyone called Mac's wife, was standing on the back porch in a pair of stone-washed overalls. Her jet-black hair was French braided and lying just past her shoulders.

"Come on back. I got a cold beer for you, Beau," Mazie exclaimed. Sadie reached down to unclip George's leash, and Beau walked up onto the porch and patted Mazie's stomach.

"You're getting big."

"Two months to go."

Mazie tugged at the ballcap on Beau's head and then turned her attention to Sadie.

"Mazelle Maureen Mackenzie, I'd like to introduce you to Miss Sadie Mae Morgan."

Sadie let out an adorable giggle. Southern people were so formal. Mazie jumped off the porch and gave Sadie a big hug, practically knocking her over with her belly.

"Sorry. Tucker here has popped out this week. I can no longer see my feet."

Mazie was plain with not a stitch of make-up and stood a head taller than Sadie, who was wearing platform sandals.

"Well, I must say it's a pleasure to meet you, Sadie Mae."

What Mazie lacked in looks, she made up for in personality – a wide Cheshire cat grin and a dimple in the middle of her chin.

"You go on in and find Mac, Beau. Sadie and I are going to get acquainted," Mazie barked out the instructions like a woman in charge and took Sadie's hand and led her onto the back porch.

"Let's find you some wine. Beau said you like wine, and I got a lot of it. I swear, I told Mac to make sure and bring a bottle to the hospital because as soon as Tucker comes out, I'm pouring myself a glass. I know, right... Tucker Mackenzie. Mac says it sounds like a law firm. I say, why not? Nothing wrong with a little positive reinforcement, right?"

Sadie instantly felt welcome. Beau had done nothing but talk about Mac and Mazie since she arrived back in Nashville three nights ago, and Sadie had already met Mac twice. She felt like she was integrating into Beau's world nicely, and it felt natural.

They barely left the loft the first 24 hours, going out only to walk George and eat, having Grubhub deliver dinner, which they ate in bed, Tuesday night. Sadie lost track of how many times they made love, not able to quench their desire. They ravished each other's bodies all hours of the day and night as the thunder and lightning rolled overhead.

On Wednesday, Sadie had time alone to explore Beau's neighborhood. He left with George in the early afternoon to pick Patrick up from summer camp, then to Hannah and Ryan's for Wednesday dinner. Most Wednesdays, Beau ate dinner with Patrick, Hannah, Ryan, and George, and Beau and Hannah used the opportunity to co-parent Patrick together… talking over activities, attitudes, and schedules. Sadie was a hot topic, and Beau told her that when he got home. It seemed that Patrick wasn't the only one that was excited about Sadie's visit. Hannah was on board with everything and eager to meet Sadie on Sunday when she picked Patrick up from his weekend visit with Beau.

"So, Sadie… Beau was right. You are as cute as a bug's ear," Mazie proclaimed as she grabbed a bottle of wine from the back-porch refrigerator and poured Sadie a generous amount in a red solo cup. Sadie nervously ran her hands down the front of her dress before taking a seat in a chair on the back porch.

When Beau talked about a barbecue at Mac and Mazie's, Sadie debated about what to wear, and she finally opted for a white no-sleeved eyelet dress and her Nixie tan wedge sandals. Sadie had picked up a few new items to bring to Nashville that reflected her new personal sense of style.

"Sorry… the solo cup is a bit redneck." Mazie's face reddened as she handed Sadie a generous cup of wine, but not before holding it up to her nose and taking in its aroma.

"Gosh, that smells good. Let's just sit and talk, Sadie Mae."

Mac and Beau came out of the house, each with a beer in their hand, and Mac sauntered over to Sadie and gave her a quick peck on the cheek… one on the lips for Mazie.

"Nice to see you again, Sadie Mae."

The boys quickly headed to the back corner of the garden, where Mac had a cornhole game set up. Sadie watched as George galloped back and forth, chasing after the bean bags. The August air was stiff and humid, and Sadie had gotten used to letting her subtle waves frame her face.

"Mazie, something smells wonderful."

Sadie took a sip of wine and quickly glanced over at Beau, not surprised that he was looking at her… mouthing a quick, *I love you.*

"Um… Mac put the brisket on the smoker at the butt-crack of dawn. The collard greens have been on for hours, and I just took the cornbread out of the oven. Thank you so much for bringing the icebox cake. Beau told you that's my favorite, didn't he?"

Beau and Mac had been friends since the second grade, and when they started junior high together, they met Mazie's older brother Hank. Truth be told, Mazie had been in love with Beau since she set eyes on him in her backyard playing touch football with Mac and Hank, but she knew she wasn't his type and she was also four years younger. The little sister. The tag-along. It was Mac that finally caught her attention, but it took years for her to get old enough. She grew up right before his eyes, and when he finally came home from college and got an apartment in the city with Hank, Mac couldn't stay away from his sister.

"So… when do you meet Patrick?"

Mazie leaned forward in her chair. Her entire attention was focused on Sadie.

"Tomorrow night. Beau's bringing him home at 5:00."

Sadie let out a deep breath and smiled at Mazie.

"You are going to love that little boy. He's an angel. Nothing to worry about. Beau is the best dad. Just follow his lead, and you'll do just fine."

Easy for Mazie to say. She was an assistant principal and elementary school counselor... perfect mom-to-be material. It wasn't like Sadie hadn't been around kids. She'd taken care of Liam and Lola a time or two, but Sadie didn't feel motherhood instinctually. Perhaps it was her own mother's absence in her life that made her feel that way. When the opportunity to be a mom seemingly passed her by, Sadie never batted an eyelash.

"What else you two got planned while you are here?"

Mazie's eyes twinkled when she spoke, and Sadie instantly felt at ease.

"Well... next weekend, Beau and I are flying to Atlanta."

Mazie let out an ear-piercing scream causing George to bark and the boys to turn away from their cornhole game.

"Oh, my! Beau is taking you to Broadfield House... to meet his mama? Damn, girl!"

Sadie's faced reddened as she nodded her head, taking in Mazie's palpable excitement.

"Broadfield House? What's that?" Sadie asked, innocently sipping her wine as Mazie threw her hands over her mouth and danced in her chair. Beau hadn't mentioned that his mother lived in a facility. Broadfield House sounded like an old folks' home.

"You're joking, right? Lady Jane Broadfield... well, Walker, but Beau's a Broadfield too."

Sadie continued to stare at Mazie with a blank expression on her face.

"Broadfield House is Beau's homestead, probably one of the oldest homesteads in Fulton County." Mazie continued. "They have a chandelier hanging in the formal living room that survived the Civil War."

Sadie looked at Mazie, and her eyes widened.

"Oh, my goodness! You don't know, do you? I mean, how could you? Why would you?"

"I'm sorry, Mazie. I'm afraid I don't know much about Atlanta, Georgia. I've lived all my life in Seattle. Beau and I have talked about family. I know about his dad and a lot about Presley and his mom. I guess we are just taking it one day at a time."

Mazie leaned forward in her chair – her voice a hushed whisper.

"Well… Beauford Patrick Broadfield Walker comes from a fairly prestigious family. It's what we call old Georgia money."

Mazie's declaration made Sadie feel sick to her stomach.

"I mean Beau's father, Patrick Walker was a self-made man. Salt of the earth. A real hard worker and so smart and so handsome. The apple doesn't fall far from the tree, hey?"

Mazie stared past Sadie at Beau and Mac and gave them both a flamboyant wink.

"Beau's dad never gave a rat's ass about the money. He was forbidden to marry Lady Jane… practically got shot off the front porch by her daddy. Anyhoo… he died, so we know how that part of the story ended up. They got married before his body had a chance to cool in the earth."

Sadie took a big swig of her wine and let Mazie just keep talking. She wondered if she ever stopped for a breath.

"The money never really mattered to Beau either, but it did give him… opportunities, but he's humble and very nonchalant about it all. See… it was never supposed to go this way. Lady Jane's brother, Bingham, died. Things work kinda different here in the south, and when old drunk Bing wrapped his Porsche around that tree when he was 30, it threw the whole line of inheritance out-of-whack. It's the end of the line for the Broadfield's. I mean… Presley will marry and take a name. It's all going to go to them once Lady Jane passes. There isn't anyone left to stake a claim."

Sadie was dumbfounded and almost speechless. She would love Beau if he were penniless. She didn't want this to change them, and she wondered why on earth he hadn't mentioned it, and then it dawned on her. Beau knew all about her relationship with Joel. Sadie bit her lip. She didn't want to cry, but she was reasonably certain that Beau was just holding back... holding on... just in case Sadie was a gold digger.

"What do you know about Beau's mom, Mazie? Do people really call her Lady Jane for crying out loud?" Sadie took another swig of wine, draining her cup.

"Oh, hang on two ticks."

Sadie watched as Mazie jumped up from her chair and fetched the bottle of wine from the refrigerator, catching Beau's eye. He looked over at Sadie, slightly concerned by the look on her face, so she gave him a friendly wave, and he turned his attention back to Mac and their game.

"Lady Jane is a true southern lady, but she's got a great personality. Part Paula Dean... part Queen of England. Very progressive. Gosh... don't quote me on this, but I think she might be a democrat. Beau said she's got a lover," Mazie said with a giggle. "You're going to love her, Presley too."

Sadie suddenly realized that she was holding in her breath as she let Mazie's story swirl around in her head. This was a lot to take in and process.

"Dammit, Mac! Why did you get me knocked up, huh? Sadie Mae needs a drinking buddy."

Sadie sat back in her chair and laughed, trying hard to not let Mazie's stories cloud her judgment.

The rest of the afternoon and into the evening was the most fun Sadie had had in ages, and they gorged themselves on the Mackenzie's delicious food. Sadie could tell that Mac and Mazie were true friends. They were funny and down to earth and not snobby or pretentious, but Sadie couldn't get what Mazie had told her out of her head. It all made sense to her. What Beau had said about taking care of her... having money. It made her feel sick. This was the same pattern she always found herself in. Sadie felt like she was jumping from one situation to another very familiar situation, and it made her uneasy.

Back at the loft, Beau took George out for his nightly constitutional, and as Sadie prepared for bed, she opened up her laptop and googled Broadfield House. There was a ton of stuff on the family, but not much on Beau or Presley. Mostly it was references to the death of the Broadfield heir, Bingham Broadfield, in 1977. What Sadie found most interesting was the piece she found in *Architectural Digest* a few years back. It was a cover story on the house and the painstaking four-year renovation that had just been completed. The article showcased Lady Jane and Broadfield House… all eight bedrooms and six bathrooms on 14 acres along the Chattahoochee River.

"You've got to be fucking kidding me. Son of a bitch." Sadie's mouth flew open as she read the description of the home.

"Sadie Mae. Is everything okay?"

Sadie hadn't noticed that Beau was standing at the end of the bed. She shut her laptop, quickly and placed it under her side of the bed.

"Yes. Everything is fine. Just fine. It's work gossip stuff."

Sadie wanted to ask. She wanted to know why Beau hadn't mentioned any details about his family and their apparent wealth, but she didn't know how to bring it up. If he hadn't said anything about it before now, there must be a reason. Sadie was prepared to wait it out. At any rate, they would be at Broadfield house next weekend, and the cat would be out of the bag. There was no way that Beau could hide eight bedrooms and six bathrooms.

"So… tomorrow. Are you ready?" Beau asked.

Sadie took off her reading glasses and crawled to the end of the bed, where Beau was standing. By the time she got to where Beau was, she could see the definition growing through his tight jeans.

"Yes. I'm set. I'm working in the morning and Mazie is picking me up in the afternoon. I need to pick up a few things." Sadie's comments made Beau laugh.

"Like what... valium... earplugs?"

Sadie had already removed Beau's t-shirt, her hands and mouth roaming over his chest.

If Sadie was nervous about meeting Patrick, she hadn't mentioned anything to Beau; however, she kept the books Juliette had given her, *Your Five-Year-Old: Wild and Wonderful* as well as *Shitty Mom: The Parenting Guide For The Rest of Us* hidden deep in the bottom of her travel bag.

"Ummmm, Sadie... about tomorrow."

Sadie had already removed Beau's belt and slid his jeans from his hips.

"I should have told you sooner. I didn't know that you were planning on working. I was going to take you out for breakfast."

Sadie kissed Beau's stomach and drew a line with her tongue from his belly button to the top of his underwear. She couldn't stop herself, so she just kept going, sinking her nails into his ass, and pulling his black Calvin Klein briefs down his thighs.

"Oh, Beau. I should really get some work done. It's going to be a busy weekend, and I want to get something submitted this week. I want to get in some hours so that I don't have to take any more vacation... okay?"

Sadie leaned forward, teasing Beau with her tongue before wrapping her lips around him and taking him deep inside her mouth. Beau let out a growl and whispered her name before pushing Sadie back on the bed. She was wearing Beau's Cancun Spring Break 2001 t-shirt and nothing else, so Beau used his knee to separate her legs before his body surged into hers.

"Baby, I know I should have told you, but the house cleaner is coming tomorrow. She will be here at eight o'clock," Beau said with a groan. He rolled them over onto his back and put his arm over his face.

Stacy Brady

"Beau Walker. You didn't need to hire a house cleaner. I can clean the house in the morning. I can make it look nice for you and Patrick." Sadie stayed perfectly still straddling Beau's hips – leaning forward slightly while Beau took a firm hold of her ass.

"Fuck, Sadie Mae," Beau grunted out. "I did not ask you to come all the way from Seattle to clean my house. I'm not asking you to do my laundry or be my maid. I'm a boy-dad. We're messy."

Beau looked into her eyes and smiled. One corner of his mouth was upturned.

"Baby, she comes every Friday," Beau said breathlessly. He quickly sat up, wrapping his arms tight around Sadie's back, thrusting his hips upward.

"Will you take me for a biscuit?"

Sadie threw her head back, and Beau began devouring her neck. He let out a low moan as he nodded in response to her question and then rolled Sadie over again until her eyes slid shut in ecstasy.

* * *

"Okay… so George, Patrick and I will be back at five o'clock. Grilled hot dogs for dinner, okay?"

Sadie nodded her head. The answer was a no, but Sadie didn't want to deviate from Beau's plan, so she emphatically shook her head up and down and vowed to make sure she had a substantial lunch.

"God, Sadie. I hope you are ready for this?"

Beau was genuinely nervous, and although Sadie was a bit excited, she couldn't imagine that the recently turned five-year-old would be any more challenging than any other five-year-old she'd ever encountered.

As the day went on and Sadie thought about the situation, she grew more nervous. She finally called Juliette in a panic. Sadie paced around the back patio, her palms sweating.

"Sadie, just keep your expectations for the weekend low... okay? Crouch down. Talk to him on his level. Be polite. Demonstrate good manners. If he likes you, he'll copy everything you do and say so be careful. I've heard your mouth! A five-year-old is very egocentric. Just remember... everything about Beau is going to be about him and his son for the next 48 hours. Just stay out of their way. Remove yourself, if necessary and avoid over talking. You tend to over talk when you are nervous. Less is more, Sadie."

"Thanks, Jules."

"You did say that Beau has a liquor cabinet, right?"

Sadie heard George bark and she turned as the front door flew open.

"Shit! I've got to go. It's showtime. Thanks, Jules!"

Patrick un-hooked George's leash, and the dog galloped straight for Sadie. She had placed herself almost smack dab in the center of the loft on her knees.

"Hi, guys!" Sadie bellowed as Beau looked over at her and winked.

She remembered what he had told her about dogs and kids and that they both could smell fear. Sadie picked up George's Frisco rope with the squeaking ball, and George went nuts. Seeing Sadie play with Patrick's best friend made the little boy take a few steps forward.

"Let's take your backpack off, buddy. Go put this in your room, and I'll introduce you to Sadie."

Patrick ran over to his bed and tossed his backpack down on the floor and quickly ran back to his father's side.

"Patrick James Walker... I'd like you to meet Miss Sadie Mae Morgan. Son... Sadie is the friend I told you about that will be staying with us for a while."

Patrick extended his little hand out to Sadie, and she gently shook it.

"I didn't know your middle name was James. That's my dad's name. It's very nice to meet you, Patrick."

Silence filled the room, but Patrick kept his eyes on Sadie. He was curious about her interaction with George as the dog suddenly rolled over on his back. Sadie quickly leaned over to give him a few belly rubs, and the dog wiggled in joy.

"He likes his belly rubbed."

Patrick's face lit up as he fell on his knees next to Sadie and began to take over the belly rubbing duties.

"Who's ready for a cocktail?" Beau shouted from the kitchen as both Sadie and Patrick raised their hands and giggled.

"Patrick, would you like a purple stinger?"

"Yes, please!" Patrick shouted as he jumped up and ran for the kitchen. "I'll help!"

"Sadie Mae... would you like a purple stinger?" Beau asked.

"Um... yes, I think I would."

"Excellent choice, Sadie!" Patrick exclaimed as he retrieved his stepping stool, assisting Beau with the prep.

"Patrick, please get the glasses out and help Sadie Mae choose one," Beau instructed his son. Patrick filled his arms with plastic glasses and brought them over to Sadie and lined them all up on the living room floor.

"This one belongs to dad, Spiderman and this one is mine, Batman... but you can have any of the others," Patrick said with a serious look on his face.

"Son... I think you should let Sadie Mae pick out her own glass."

Patrick looked back over his shoulder at Beau, who was pouring lemonade, grape juice, and ice into the blender. He had the top off the jar of maraschino cherries and popped one in his mouth.

"Sadie, would you like to borrow my Batman glass?"

It was at that instant that Sadie fell deeply in love with Beau's son.

After dinner, and a riveting game of Candyland... Beau and Patrick were snuggled together on one side of the couch, watching a monster truck show that Sadie couldn't quite understand. She and George took up residence on the other side of the couch, totally engrossed in the fall Vogue. Sadie took Jules's advice and kept her distance. At 7:30, Beau gave the countdown to bedtime.

"Yes!" Sadie bellowed as she leaped off the couch and threw her hands up in the air. "I've been waiting all night. Don't move... Beau... Patrick... don't move. I'll be right back," Sadie continued as Beau and Patrick watched her dash up to the bedroom.

"Dad? What's going on?"

"You know, son... I'm not really sure."

Beau shook his head and watched Sadie fly down the stairs with shopping bags in her hands.

"Okay, so I was thinking since this is the first time that we are all spending the night together at the loft that we should have something special to remember this. All of us."

Sadie pulled a small square box out of a shopping bag and handed it to Patrick.

"You open up George's present first, Patrick." Beau sat up and intently looked at Sadie with a big smile on his face.

Patrick opened the box, and inside was a new dog collar, bright red to contrast George's snow-white fur with Super Dog written in big white letters across the seam.

"Cool!" Patrick yelled as George waddled over to him. Sadie helped unclip his old collar and put the new one on.

"Okay... you're next, Patrick. This box is for you."

The little boy's eyes were wide with excitement as he ran his hands over the white box.

"Is this a birthday present?" Patrick asked as he looked at Sadie.

"Kind of. Just open it up, okay. I've been waiting all day!"

Patrick tore open the box, ripping the tissue paper apart and pulling out a pair of Batman pajamas… a black short-sleeved top with the Batman logo emblazed on the front, and short bottoms with Batman and Robin in action poses… *ka-boom* and *pow*… written in numerous places.

"Wow! I got Batman pajamas, dad. Look… it says pow!"

Beau looked over at Sadie and shook his head, chuckling with laughter at the joy on both Sadie and Patrick's faces.

"Can I go put them on… now. Can I? Can I?"

"What do you say first, Patrick?"

Before Sadie had a chance to react, Patrick flew into her arms.

"Thank you, Sadie Mae."

Sadie scooped up the little boy in her arms as she saw Beau's eyes mist over.

"Okay… wait, Patrick. Your dad has to open his. Your next, Beau."

Sadie held Beau's box out to him, and he reluctantly took the box from her hands. Inside was a pair of long pajama bottoms decorated with Spiderman.

"Wow… dad. Those are way cool!"

"Thank you, Sadie Mae," Beau said. He gave her an innocent wink and thought about all the ways he would properly thank her later.

"No top for you. You've got plenty of t-shirts."

Sadie didn't want any more clothes to take off of Beau at bedtime anyway. She preferred him shirtless.

"Okay, I'm last but since I already know what it is… will you open it up for me, Patrick?"

Sadie handed over her box, and Patrick ripped it open. Her pajamas were boy cut style like Patrick's only decorated with Wonder Woman.

"Girl power!" Sadie exclaimed. "Too much boys stuff here. Girls have superpowers too!"

Sadie jumped up like a superhero, and Patrick giggled and rolled around on the floor.

"Okay, son. It's shower time and then pajamas and a story."

Patrick ran for the downstairs bathroom with his new pajamas clutched tight to his chest and George hot on his trail.

"You outdid yourself, baby."

Beau took two steps towards Sadie, who cautiously backed away and put her hand up to stop him.

"How long is shower and story time?"

Beau shook his head in confusion. It wasn't like Sadie to back away from him. He had missed her all evening and longed to hold her in his arms.

"Um... about 30 minutes."

"Perfect!"

Beau watched as Sadie grabbed her pajamas and quickly headed up to the bedroom.

* * *

"But I want Sadie to read me a story!" Patrick cried out.

Sadie had made herself scarce as the boys got ready for bed. As Beau tucked his son in and they cuddled together with a book, Sadie waiting patiently with George on the couch in their new pajamas.

Sadie Mae?" Beau called out.

Sadie rose from the couch and walked over to Patrick's bed. "What are we reading tonight?" Sadie inquired as Patrick handed her his book and patted a spot next to him.

"You sit here... and read *Dinosaurs Before Dark*."

Sadie snuggled up next to Patrick, opened up his book, and began reading.

After Patrick convinced Sadie to read him one more book, then fell asleep halfway through, Beau took George for a walk, and Sadie retreated up to the bedroom. She had just crawled into bed when she heard Beau shooing George into his dog bed and climbing the stairs.

Beau couldn't get over their evening with Patrick. He replayed it over and over again as George did his business across the street. As he rushed up the stairs, he wanted nothing more than to show Sadie just how much this evening meant to him and their future.

Sadie saw the look in Beau's eyes as he walked over to her side of the bed and slowly slid the pajama bottoms off his hips. Before Sadie had a chance to react, he lunged for her and tried to grab her by the waist. She quickly twisted away and rolled off the side of the bed, landing on the floor with a thud.

"Shhhh." Beau put his finger to his lips as they both listened to see if Patrick had stirred. They both giggled, and Sadie shook her finger at Beau and remained crouched on the floor on Beau's side of the bed.

"No! Beau Walker you march right in that bathroom and take a cold shower."

Sadie whispered her demands as Beau continued to shake his head, crawling around on the floor straight towards her. Before he reached her, she stood up and put her hands on her hips in a Wonder Woman pose, biting the outside of her lip after seeing the size of Beau's erection.

"I mean it, Beau. Absolutely no sex in this house with Patrick downstairs. I am serious."

Beau knew that Sadie meant business. She wasn't just playing hard to get. He remembered her hint downstairs when she backed away from him. Sadie relaxed a bit when Beau reached down and grabbed his pajama bottoms, and sat on the end of the bed.

"Baby, you can't be serious. You expect me to lie next to you in bed and keep my hands off you?" Sadie sat down next to him and placed her hands in her lap.

"Beau... your bedroom has no doors. Did you not tell me that Patrick still comes into your bed most nights for a cuddle? You think he's going to stop just because I am here? What if in the middle of you-know-what... we have a *visitor*? I am keeping my pajamas on and my hands to myself," Sadie exclaimed, folding her arms across her chest.

"Beau, tonight was wonderful... really special. I just can't. I don't feel comfortable making love to you while Patrick is within earshot. That's going to mean abstinence when your little boy is here. I'm sorry."

Beau let out a huff as the wheels in his head turned. He was an architect, and next week he would design a door and a way to close the bedroom off from the rest of the loft. Beau stood slowly and headed for the bathroom and let the cold water pound down on him. He waited for Sadie to join him, but he knew that would never happen, so he toweled off and put on his new pajamas. Sadie was lying on her back, covers up to her chin with her eyes closed as Beau flipped off the bedside lamp and crawled under the covers.

"Can I at least hold your hand?"

Sadie felt Beau's fingers brush the side of her leg, and she reached underneath the covers and took his hand.

They slept like that for hours until Sadie woke up with a jolt. Patrick was on her side of the bed, tapping his finger on her shoulder.

"Sadie... are you awake?" he whispered.

His face was literally two inches from hers, and she nodded her head and lifted the covers, and Patrick hopped into bed.

"I brought my bubby blankie and my monkey, Max. Can you give him a kiss, please? He had a bad dream, and I told him that Wonder Woman would make it all better."

Sadie brought Max to her lips and kissed him, then wrapped Patrick's blanket around him and pulled him close to her.

"Patrick... son... for Pete's sake. It's two o'clock in the morning. Come over here, boy... and let Sadie go back to sleep."

Sadie reached behind her and grabbed Beau's hand and squeezed it. He rolled over to her and reached out and patted his son's back.

"We're all good, Beau," Sadie confidently assured him as she kissed Patrick on the forehead, and they snuggled in for the rest of the night.

* * *

Sadie hadn't heard them both leave, but the bedroom was bathed in soft light. She looked over at the nightstand. It was 6:12 in the morning, and the smell of fresh brewed coffee filled the loft. Sadie threw the covers back and listened for a moment, but all she heard was silence. By the time she reached the bottom step, all three boys were coming back in through the front door.

"Good morning Sadie! Good morning!" Patrick squealed.

He ran over to her with George barking at his heels and threw his arms around her middle. Sadie ran her hand through his tousled hair and yawned.

"Coffee?" Beau asked. Patrick sat on the floor next to George, and Beau walked over to Sadie and gave her a kiss on the cheek.

"Hmmm," Sadie mumbled. She wrapped her robe around her and headed for the couch, watching as Patrick ran into his bedroom to retrieve a soft-sided container filled with Matchbox cars.

"Can we set up my racetrack, Sadie? I want to show you all my cars."

Patrick was still in his Batman pajamas, his hair sticking up wildly all over.

"Patrick, why don't you play quietly and let Sadie Mae have her coffee first."

Beau handed Sadie a steaming cup of coffee in her new Wonder Woman mug, trying to gauge whether the look in Sadie's eyes was mild irritation or if she hadn't quite woken up yet.

"I want coffee too!" Patrick shouted out as Sadie looked up at Beau, who returned her inquisitive glance with a wink.

"I fill his mug with chocolate milk. We pretend a lot around here," Beau said as he sauntered back into the kitchen for his coffee and Patrick's milk.

"Sadie, come down here. I set my track up behind the couch."

Patrick slid across the hardwood floor – Matchbox cars flying everywhere as Beau let out a long groan from the kitchen.

Sadie and Patrick spent about an hour setting up the track and playing with his cars – Beau content to read the paper and work on his crossword puzzle.

"Who's hungry?" Sadie yelled out. It was only 7:45, but Sadie was starving. Playing was hard work.

"Me... me... me," Patrick screamed. He jumped up and started running around the room... exciting George, who began to chase him around the loft. Sadie had never seen a kid with so much energy. Beau let out a huff, jumped from the couch, grabbed Patrick around the waist, and flipped him upside down over his shoulder.

"Sadie... you run along upstairs and throw some clothes on, and I'll get Patrick dressed, and we'll go out."

Sadie scrambled up off the floor and took her robe off.

"No way! I'm making waffles with my back-up cook, chef Patrick. You ready to roll, chef?" Sadie asked as Patrick and George followed her into the kitchen.

* * *

Beau was afraid to see what the kitchen looked like, but he didn't care. Sadie's voice was soft as she spoke to his son, teaching him measurements and cooking techniques with the patience of a saint. It filled Beau's heart with joy.

"Sadie Mae… these have to be some of the best waffles I've ever had." Beau was working on his third waffle, and Patrick cleaned his plate as well – sticky syrup all over his face and in his hair.

"When did you have time to do all this. Pick all this stuff up?"

"Mazie. She ran me over to the mall for the pajamas and the waffle iron. I do think this might be the only kitchen appliance you do not own, Beau Walker. Then we went to the Piggly Wiggly for groceries." The name of the store made Sadie laugh.

"Well, thank you, baby."

Sadie beamed at Beau's praise. This weekend was actually going better than she had expected thanks in part to Beau's excellent parenting and the fact that Patrick was cute as a button.

"Let me clean up," Beau responded, and Sadie leaped to her feet.

"Absolutely not! It's a war zone out there. I'm not really sure how I'm going to get that dried up batter off the floor."

"I'm sorry, Sadie," Patrick said. His little face filled with innocence.

"It's okay, Patrick. Remember what I said? Spills happen."

Sadie lifted her fork to her mouth and ate the last bite of her waffle with a smile.

"Patrick… time to pick up your toys. Let's take George out while Sadie gets ready, and then we will get your bike and head out."

Just as Sadie started in with the kitchen clean-up, Beau's cell phone rang.

"It's Hannah…" Beau quickly picked up his phone and slid his finger across his screen. "Good morning! Nope, we are fine. All is good. What's up?" Sadie listened to the one-sided conversation, but it sounded like the weekend plans had suddenly changed.

"Okay then, let me talk with Patrick, and I'll text you."

When the call was over, Beau set his phone down on the kitchen counter.

"So, son... that was your mama. She kind of messed up. Your school mate Zachary's birthday party is actually this afternoon from 2:00-4:00 at the bubble factory and not next weekend. So, would you like me to take you?"

Patrick jumped up and down, yelling yes at the top of his lungs, signaling his answer.

"Okay, everyone! New plans. We'll head to the park this morning once everyone is ready, and I'll run Patrick by his mother's later this afternoon to pick up Zachary's present and take him to the party. Are we good?"

Beau watched as Sadie nodded her head while loading up the dishwasher. Patrick ran into his bedroom to put away his Matchbox cars, and Beau took the opportunity to come up behind Sadie and grab her waist.

"Do you realize what this means Sadie Mae? That bubble factory is just down the road. I can drop him off and be back here in 10 minutes."

Beau kissed and sucked on the back of Sadie's neck until he heard a faint moan.

"We will have an hour in bed all to ourselves."

Beau's wicked laugh filled the kitchen as he continued to devour her.

"Excellent! Sadie exclaimed. "I'm exhausted. I'm going to need an hour nap if I am going to keep up with the two of you all weekend."

Sadie honestly hadn't felt her age since she met Beau, up until Patrick's arrival.

"Dad! Can you come help me wipe my butt?" Patrick yelled from the bathroom, and Beau let out a groan.

"Welcome to my crazy life, Sadie Mae."

Sadie watched as Beau ran to Patrick's aid, and she thought that Beau's crazy life seemed just about perfect to her.

CHAPTER EIGHT

"Not too far, Patrick. Keep an eye out for Mama, okay."

Beau took a seat next to Sadie and George on the park bench while Patrick went around in a loop on his pushbike.

"So, you're not mad that I have to get some work done this afternoon? It's just that... typically on Sunday afternoons, I have time to get caught up," Beau sheepishly asked.

Sadie turned to him and shook her head. All she could think about was a nap and some peace and quiet. Patrick crawled into bed at half-past three, tossed and turned for two hours, and finally woke up for good at 5:45. If Beau had to work at home this afternoon, Sadie was quite content to read a book upstairs and nap.

"I'll make it up to you later, I swear. I'll grill you a steak and open up a nice cabernet."

Sadie tucked her sunglasses up on the top of her head and leaned in for a peck on the lips.

She wanted to look good. Sadie hoped to make a good impression, but she wondered if she had overdone it. She put on a light lemon-yellow dress with ruffles down the V-neck, which accentuated her two best features. Sadie had dabbed the eye concealer on pretty thick when she put her make-up on. She was meeting Hannah for the first time, and she was more nervous than when Patrick bound through the door on Friday night.

"Hey, y'all?"

Hannah came up from behind the bench, and Sadie instantly saw that she was a giant. She had to be at least five foot nine and although she was not willowy, she was not as chunky as Sadie was hoping. Hannah had a face cut right from the pages of a fashion magazine with diamond-shaped emerald green eyes. She was the kind of girl that women loved to hate. So much for average with a bit of pudge around the middle. Her blond hair was pulled up loosely in a messy bun, and Sadie figured she was the kind of girl that could go two, maybe three days without brushing her hair and still look like she was ready to saunter down the streets of New York City. Hannah made the sleeveless t-shirt dress and flip flops she was wearing look like Gucci. She was, however, flat as a board. At least Sadie had her beat in that category.

"Hey!" Beau enthusiastically responded. He jumped up, and Sadie saw the look in both their eyes. There was love there. Respect and admiration. She was Patrick's mother for fuck sake. Sadie didn't want to be jealous, but she suddenly felt very small in Beau's world. She casually glanced over at him as he nervously put his hands in the front pockets of his tan cargo shorts.

"Sadie Mae... it's so nice to finally meet you. You're all Beau's been talking about for months."

Hannah didn't bother with the handshake and went straight for the hug. Even though Beau mentioned that she grew up in Boston, Hannah had spent the better part of the last 15 years living in the south. Southern people definitely did not have space issues.

"Hey, Patrick." Hannah looked over at her son on his bike, crazily going around in circles. "You gonna come give your mama a hug?"

"Hey... Han ...um ... we're gonna need to get him a proper bike. He's outgrowing that thing." Beau watched as Patrick laid his bike down on the grass and ran over to his mom. Hannah scooped him up, and he hugged her tight.

"Mama! Sadie and I made waffles... oh, and she bought me Batman pajamas, and she likes to play Matchbox cars!"

Sadie suddenly felt ten feet tall. No one was going to wipe the smile off her face today.

"Wow. You got spoiled something rotten this weekend," Hannah responded, and while she spoke the words to her son, the message was meant for Sadie. She felt cut down a peg or two as Hannah looked over at her and smiled.

"I've got grapes and kale for the ducks. Let's go on and head over to the other side of the park. Say your goodbyes and grab your bike."

Sadie watched as the exchange of their son began. Beau scooped Patrick up, as Hannah made a beeline for Sadie.

"So... it sounds like you and Patrick hit it off okay." Sadie wasn't sure if Hannah's words came out as a question or a comment.

"You and Beau are raising an incredible little boy. He's a handful, but he's lots of fun. I think we all did okay."

"Yep... Beau's a great dad... so is Ryan, my husband. I'm sure you'll meet him next time. I'm very fortunate to have two... no, make that three wonderful boys in my life."

Hannah had a sweet warmth to her like a cinnamon roll fresh out of the oven. Perhaps liking her wouldn't be as hard as Sadie had been thinking.

"So, Beau tells me that you are moving to Nashville."

Sadie froze in her tracks. She still hadn't officially given Beau her answer. She had only been back in Nashville for seven days. Sadie just shook her head up and down and smiled.

"We've got a lot to work out. It's probably going to take some time."

Sadie swore she caught a smirk on Hannah's upturned mouth, and she quickly turned her attention back to the boys.

Beau helped Patrick with his bike and whispered in his ear, and he came running over to Sadie, and she crouched down to her knees.

"Bye, Sadie Mae."

"Bye, Patrick James."

The little boy giggled as Sadie tickled his belly.

"Will you play with George for me?"

"Yes, every night, and I'll kiss Max good night and make sure he is tucked in."

Sadie felt her gut tighten when Patrick leaned in and wrapped his arms around her neck. The affection she had for the little boy was unmistaken.

"I'll see you Wednesday night, okay," Sadie said, watching as Patrick nodded his head in understanding. After family dinner on Wednesday, Patrick would be spending the night at the loft as he did every other week.

"Y'all have a wonderful rest of your weekend."

Sadie watched as Hannah grabbed for Patrick's hand, and walked down the park path and out of sight. She turned to Beau, who had lifted his hand to give them both a wave noticing a sadness in his eyes.

"You okay?" Sadie stood next to Beau. There was something about watching him watch his son walk away that tugged at her heart.

"Yeah, I'm good. Really good. That part is not always easy… for me. I mean, Patrick does great, but… I'm usually just left with George. Sundays can be pretty… well… lonely. I don't have that now. I've got you."

Beau turned to Sadie and reached for her hand. She knew she couldn't speak… even if she could form the words, they wouldn't come out the right way.

"Let's go home, Sadie Mae."

* * *

"So, I'm just dying to know. How was your weekend?" Beau turned to Sadie and asked.

Beau was fishing. Sadie couldn't imagine what must be going through his head. He was right. Patrick was a handful, but he made up a part of who Beau was, and Sadie didn't see that this would be an obstacle that she couldn't overcome. It would be something to build on together. Sadie saw before her, a family. Something she never knew she wanted. Now, it was all she thought about.

Both Patrick and Sadie got the most out of the Bubble Factory break on Saturday. Beau was right, they had precisely an hour together, and they took full advantage of the 60 minutes, knowing that it would be hands-off again Saturday night.

Beau made sure they enjoyed every second of their hour alone… taking Sadie to ecstasy twice. Once with his mouth on the couch not able to wait to take her up to the bedroom to finish making love to her.

Patrick came back to the house with funny stories, all told on a sugar high that rivaled a crack addict, and the day ended with time on the patio – Beau and Sadie cooking dinner together. Before the sun had set, they all walked up to the local ice cream parlor for kid cones – Patrick clutching Sadie's hand tight as they walked down the sidewalk.

When Beau and Sadie returned home Sunday, after dropping Patrick off in the park to be reunited with Hannah, they had the most perfect and lazy Sunday afternoon and evening. It was Sadie's most perfect day. Quiet and peaceful. A light breeze blew through the open patio door, and Sadie lugged George upstairs so he wouldn't pout and disturb Beau. The two of them snuggled under the covers with Sadie's novel.

When she ran the shower, just before five o'clock, she couldn't get the shampoo out of her hair before turning around to find a naked and aroused Beau behind her watching the water cascade over her body. As Beau and Sadie sat on the patio devouring their steaks, Beau couldn't wait for her answer to his question about the weekend. Sadie just smiled and nodded her head.

"Good. I think that was just about the most perfect weekend, ever." Sadie tipped her head back and looked skyward. "Still waiting on my stars," she said with a giggle and gave him that smile that would convince him of just about anything.

"So… my dog is in love with you. My friends are in love with you. You got my kid wrapped pretty tight around your finger. I'd say you were having a pretty good time here in Nashville."

Sadie nodded and took a sip of her wine. "What about you? You didn't mention how you are feeling?"

Beau had been fairly glassy-eyed all weekend. Beau's love meter was off the charts, and Sadie knew it.

"Baby, you know I love you but I'm gonna promise to tell you that every day, okay. I know that I can be a bit preoccupied when Patrick is around, but I could tell that you weren't bothered."

Sadie was going to send Jules the biggest bunch of flowers and a jug of Jack Daniels first thing in the morning.

"God, baby… I know you think that I don't notice, but I do. The way you tuck your hair behind your ear. Your adorable giggle… like at everything. I can't quite figure out why you stand like a flamingo when you put on your mascara, but… it's really cute. Sadie Mae, you are so strong… so independent. You can stand on your own two feet. That's what I love the most about you. I can't believe that you've been here a week, and you've already found a spin class. You're the farmer's market's best customer and Mazie's new best friend. Man… Hannah was so… insecure about everything. No matter how much I encouraged her, she never had the confidence. She never wanted to do anything without me. It was great in the beginning and then… fuck. I just wanted her to be more independent. I think it's one of the reasons she wanted the baby."

Sadie took a sip of her wine and gathered her thoughts. "Beau... everyone is insecure. I am insecure... like every time I get naked in front of you. Like this weekend with Patrick... meeting your friends. Shit... don't even get me started about going to Atlanta," Sadie quickly spoke and then sat back in her chair.

"Baby, you have something that not a lot of women have, and that's self-assurance. You know yourself. You know what you want and more than that, I don't think you really care about what other people think of you. Sadie, you are so grown up."

Sadie mouthed *thank you* to Beau. He had just given her more confidence than she could ever give herself.

"That's probably my age, Beau."

"Oh, Lord... don't start that again, okay?" Beau murmured as he threw his hands up in the air. He didn't see the issue, but he knew that it still bothered Sadie that she was nine years and six months older than him. Beau had done everything in his power to show her that the age difference didn't matter to him, yet she still subtly brought it up. He only wished that he hadn't blurted out that Hannah was only 34.

Beau realized that he still had a lot to learn when it came to women.

* * *

Beau and Sadie settled into a regular routine the next week, sharing Beau's office space at home, although he found Sadie wandering around in one of his old t-shirts, and nothing else... a bit distracting. On Wednesday night, when Beau went out for family dinner, Sadie and Mazie went for manicures, pedicures and Mazie's latest craving – Mexican food.

"Okie dokie... tell me the truth. What did you think of Hannah?"

Mazie moaned as she put her swollen ankles in the pedicure bath and turned the vibrating chair on so it only massaged her lower back.

"She's very sweet... and beautiful. Looks like a good mom." Sadie leaned back in her vibrating chair and thumbed through a travel magazine.

"Humph!" Mazie grunted out with a loud breath.

Sadie had not wanted to disrespect Patrick's mother. She had been very tight-lipped even to Beau about any of her thoughts about Hannah. There was nothing she could ever do about it. Hannah was Patrick's mother, and Sadie had hoped that they would all get along well for the sake of the child. After what Beau said about her confidence, she didn't dare tell him that she felt intimidated by Hannah and slightly jealous. It was entirely in her head.

"She broke him. Oh, Sadie, it was so gut-wrenching. What she did to him. It just wasn't right. Mac and I were so grateful that we were here for him. He stayed with us a few times when he came to Nashville to see Patrick." Sadie's eyes welled up with tears at Mazie's disclosure.

"She's gettin' what's coming to her, though... I mean... she and Ryan have been trying for a baby for well over a year. Beau says it's really break-ing her in two."

Sadie hoped that it didn't break her and Ryan in two. Opening up the door for a possible reunion with her baby daddy.

"I think he is healed. I mean look at him. He's falling in love with you, Sadie Mae."

Sadie smiled at Mazie. Just the thought that Beau Walker was falling madly in love with her was enough to ease her mind.

Sadie handed a bright pink polish to the young girl finishing up her pedicure and pushed thoughts of Hannah from her mind.

Tomorrow night they were flying to Atlanta for a long weekend with Lady Jane and Presley, and Sadie felt like it was her last initiation right.

CHAPTER NINE

Sadie kept the *Architectural Digest* tucked into the side of her tote. She asked Mazie if she could borrow her copy of the out of print magazine with the cover story on Broadfield House, and Mazie gladly gave it to her. Beau still hadn't mentioned anything about it, and Sadie was dying to find a way to bring it up.

She couldn't get the mischievous grin off her face when they sat down in the Delta lounge before their flight. Beau scurried over to grab them some snacks, a wine for Sadie, and a beer for him as they waited for their flight to board. He had been fidgety, nervous and on the verge of saying something to her all morning… only to shake his head… say nothing and go back to whatever he was doing.

When Beau returned to their seats with his hands full, Sadie had the magazine on her lap. The expression on Beau's face was priceless.

"Shit! Um… I've got this all worked out. Exactly everything I was going to say," Beau said, taking a swig of his beer and plopping down next to her. "How did you find out?"

Beau didn't let Sadie answer.

"Mazie!" He quickly responded, exhaling deeply and immediately realizing that Sadie had known about Broadfield House for some time.

"She told me at dinner last week."

For some reason, Sadie couldn't look Beau in the eyes. She stared down at the magazine and ran her hand over the glossy cover.

"You've known this whole time, and you didn't say anything?" Beau asked. Sadie finally looked up at him, unsure how to proceed.

"I was waiting for you to tell me, Beau. Exactly when did you think you were going to do that? Before or after we drove through the... let me find the description of the 14-acre grounds in the article so I can quote it correctly," she said with a chuckle.

Sadie thumbed through the magazine, watching out of the corner of her eye as Beau squirmed in his seat.

"Beau, I've been racking my brain trying to figure out why you didn't want to say anything. I think I know why. It's got something to do with me, right? My motives? I swear to you... I didn't know before I fell in love with you if that is what you are worried about. Other than the airline ticket from Seattle, which I will gladly pay you back for... I've never asked you for anything. So, what gives?"

Beau took another long swig of beer. He hadn't meant to not tell her, but he wasn't sure what to say. With his bottle almost empty, Beau had run out of time.

"Sadie, it's absolutely got nothing to do with you. I can't wait to introduce you to Mama and Prez. They are dying to meet you. That place... it's not a reflection of who I am," Beau said, pointing to the magazine cover.

"Notice only Mama appears in the article. She knew better than to ask me to pose for any magazine about that place. I take after my father. He never wanted it either. I never lived there growing up. This was my gram's house... my mama's mama. We lived in a modest neighborhood in north Atlanta, growing up. I'll show you. Mac's parents still live around the corner," Beau said. He sighed and then polished off his beer.

"It wasn't until gram died and my father got sick that they moved in there. He was too sick to fight her. I went off to college... Presley was 13.

Sadie, I didn't choose this, but I love my family.... Mama and Presley. The money is nothing. It means nothing to me. I do my own thing. I pay my own way and I'll raise Patrick to take care of himself."

Sadie could see the pride in Beau's eyes. This was obviously something that he had struggled with for years. It was a part of him, but he didn't let it define him. It was as if Beau was embarrassed by it.

"Baby, I know you don't care about the money. I was afraid to tell you because I didn't want you thinking I was like Joel. I'm not. All the bullshit that comes with money just isn't my thing, and I certainly know that it isn't yours."

Sadie exhaled deeply and smiled. Beau didn't think she was after anything other than his love, and he grabbed her hand as they headed towards their gate.

* * *

The Uber driver pulled up to the black iron gate in front of Broadfield House, and Beau rolled down his window in the back seat. He leaned out and keyed in the code, and the gate swung open. Sadie let out a deep breath. She hadn't meant too, but she felt the butterflies in her stomach, and she couldn't keep her nerves at bay. Beau leaned close to her and gripped her hand as the car inched forward along the long driveway, winding for nearly a quarter-mile up to the house.

Situated on the banks of the Chattahoochee River and surrounded by 14 acres of lush greenery sat an elegant Neoclassical-inspired home. Large floodlights lit up the front of Broadfield House, which loomed proudly flanked by rows of green-leafed trees, swaying gently in the late evening summer wind. At its threshold stood a marble fountain, water splashing out of the mouths of naked cherubs. The soft gurgling of the clear water was melodic, and it resonated in the surrounding silence of the backseat.

The car pulled around the large circular drive, and there on the front porch stood Lady Jane Broadfield Walker. She had a wide grin as she peered into the back of the car, spying Sadie and giving her a friendly wave. She was a tall woman with broad shoulders and a lean build, although Sadie noticed that she was wearing two-inch black patent leather heels. Lady Jane was elegantly dressed in a cream skirt belted at the waist with a black and cream floral top tucked in. A strand of long pearls hung loosely around her neck and was paired with simple drop pearl earrings. Her make-up was understated, her lipstick a pale pink with just a light dusting of blush. Her hair was gray and hung in a smooth and neat bob just below her chin. Sadie immediately noticed that Beau's eyes matched hers. Lady Jane didn't look 67, and Sadie hoped that she still looked this good at her age.

Beau quickly jumped out of the backseat and went around to the front porch to greet his mama.

"Welcome home, son," Lady Jane exclaimed as Beau embraced her tight.

Sadie quickly got out of the backseat, and Beau pulled away from Lady Jane and ran back to grab her hand and lead her up the steps.

"Sadie!"

Lady Jane took two strides towards her and pulled her into a big hug. She stepped away and grabbed both of Sadie's hands into her own.

"Lady Jane Walker... this is Sadie Mae Morgan," Beau said beaming. He stood behind Sadie with his hands on her shoulders as Lady Jane eyed the two of them.

"Well... I am so delighted to meet you, Sadie Mae. You are all Beau talks about these days, and I can see why. You are just adorable."

Sadie's smiled radiated. "Thank you, ma'am. I'm very excited to be here and meet you and Presley."

Sadie had laid awake the last few nights trying to figure out what to wear when she met Beau's mama. She didn't want to be too casual or too dressy or look like she was trying too hard. Sadie just wanted to be herself, and she realized that ever since she had met Beau that she was struggling with who she was. Sadie hated the prim, proper stuffy world of Joel, but over the years, Sadie had lost herself and her sense of style and her simple beauty. She was slowly morphing and coming out of her cocoon – flying free like a butterfly on a summer's day.

It was Mazie who spotted the black dress in the window of a shop called Luscious at the Arcade in Nashville and told Sadie that this was the perfect item for Atlanta. The dress had a pretty ruffle trim and intricate embroidery with ruffled cap sleeves and an elasticated waist. It was simple and classy and more than anything… it was comfortable. Sadie paired it with her dark indigo jeans jacket, black wedge sandals, and accented the ensemble with rose gold jewelry – bangles that hung from her ears, and a ropy bracelet.

Beau grabbed the luggage and set it just inside the front door as Sadie looked around the outside of Broadfield House and down the long driveway that they had just driven up. The house had a commanding presence from the driveway and a grand entrance featuring stairs up to a rocking chair front porch. Like many Neoclassical homes, it featured large Corinthian columns and a symmetrical façade.

Beau quickly ran back outside and took Sadie by the hand as he led her up to the front door.

"Sadie Mae, I've got something special chilling inside for you. You kids come in for the full tour and get settled," Lady Jane proclaimed as she turned and led the way.

The front door swung open, and Sadie stepped inside. A Persian rug laid elegantly over the marble entryway. To her left stood a white baby grand piano and overhead a lavish gold chandelier hung at the foyer. Sadie could just imagine Scarlett making her grand entrance down the sweeping stairwell, which split in two and led to a small landing where a white couch and two chairs sat in front of French doors. The screened porch on the second floor overlooked the back grounds – the perfect place for a glass of iced tea. The setting sun cast long shadows through the front doorway and splashed the room with an assortment of light and colors.

"Wow, ma'am. Your home is stunning," Sadie said with awe in her voice.

"I have always loved the timeless beauty and grandeur of classical architectural styles. They are dictated by history and so perfect in architectural structure and proportions. I am also a romantic sucker for the persona of the South," Lady Jane exclaimed. "Remodeling this home… reclaiming it, was a dream come true."

"Now I see where you get your love of architecture from Beau," Sadie said while nudging her shoulder against him.

To the left of the entryway was the formal living room with two dark cherry wood doors propped open – white stone pillars on either side of the doors, a sharp contrast. At the tops of the pillars were golden cherubs, and each base was lined with gold plating. In the middle of the living room hung another opulent chandelier. Sadie had remembered what Mazie told her and what she had read in the Architectural Digest article. This was the chandelier original to the homestead that had survived the Civil War. The room was decorated in taupe colored wing-backed chairs and couches, and a cream rug was centered over the dark hardwood floors. A small writing desk sat near the picture window, no doubt a place where Lady Jane wrote her formal thank you cards and opened her correspondence with a gold-plated letter opener.

Beau held on tight to Sadie's hand as Lady Jane led them from room to room. He cautiously watched Sadie's expression as her eyes darted around the downstairs of Broadfield house, knowing full well that she was in appraisal mode.

Directly opposite the living room was the formal dining room with a long wood table that sat 12, perfectly placed under yet another chandelier adorned with white crystals and quite plain, by chandelier standards.

Sadie gathered that the other furnishings in the dining room were most likely antiques and included a large china hutch and two sideboards. Another set of French doors led from the dining room and out to what the magazine called the smoking porch. Sadie peered her head inside the dining room and casually smiled over at Beau.

With opulent entertaining spaces, marble fireplace mantels, rich hardwood floors, and walls of windows that looked out amongst the grounds, it was hard to believe that the house felt warm and welcoming while still retaining sophistication and luxury.

"Let's go into the solarium, Beau… get you two a cold drink."

Lady Jane led Beau and Sadie down a narrow hall on the other side of the dining room and into the back portion of the first floor. They passed a room lined with bookshelves and a large desk with an oversized leather chair. In front of a fireplace sat a taupe couch similar to the ones in the formal living room. Beau stopped just outside the door.

"That was my father's study. Although, by the time they had finally moved in, he was too sick to use it much. He spent most of his time sitting in that big chair by the fireplace." Sadie caught the glisten in Beau's eyes and squeezed his hand.

"Come here and let me show you something."

Beau led Sadie out a door at the rear of the study, which opened into a round room with a vintage billiards table in the center. The handcrafted and carved table had a turn of the century styling with solid hardwood legs and leather pockets. The top of the table was a deep red felt.

"Wow… it's beautiful." Sadie ran her hand along the smoothed wood as Beau came up behind her.

"Can I tell you my fantasy, Sadie?"

Beau quickly grabbed her waist and pulled her tight against his groin as he whispered in her ear.

"I'd like to fuck you on top of this billiard table."

Beau let her go and casually walked away, turning when he reached the door – one side of his mouth upturned.

"Come on. Mama will think we got lost."

Sadie blushed and followed Beau back into the study with the image of the two of them on the table in the forefront of her mind.

They continued down a narrow hallway, and Sadie spotted two bedrooms with a large bathroom in between. At the end of the hallway at the back of the house stood the kitchen and solarium. Lady Jane stood in the middle of the kitchen in front of a silver bucket with a bottle of French champagne inside on ice.

"This room is so different."

Sadie could tell that the back of the residence was the heart of Broadfield House. It was entirely modern and very homey and was a polar opposite to the other rooms in the house. The great room encompassed the kitchen, casual living room, and the solarium, which overlooked the back gardens and swimming pool. The kitchen was an off-white cream with dark wood floors and an eat-in bar with shaker cabinets, stainless steel appliances and a large granite island with a hooded range, stovetop, and sink. Bright pink orchids in big white pots lined the kitchen window, and a wrought iron hanging rack dangling from the ceiling held numerous pots and pans. A small couch and two oversized chairs sat in front of a large sliding door that led out into the solarium. On the other side of the kitchen was the grand entrance to Lady Jane's bedroom suite.

"Son, you open the champagne, and I'll take Sadie into my boudoir," Lady Jane said with a chuckle. She clasped hold of Sadie's hand and led her into her suite.

The room was enormous and continued farther than Sadie could initially see. There was a formal sitting area with two floral pink and plum couches and an oversized chair, a small desk, and a television. Lady Jane's actual bedroom was on the other side of a walk-in closet, which lined both walls and also held a make-up table. They walked through the closet area and stood in the center of her bedroom. The room was decorated in various shades of light gray and purple. Her king-sized bed seemed dwarfed in the room with an upholstered headboard adorned with silver bangles that sparkled in the light of a vintage antique silver chandelier that hung in the middle of the room. To the left was the ensuite, smaller than Sadie imagined and highlighted by a silver brushed metal air-jet French bateau bathtub. Sadie wanted to weep and then beg Lady Jane if she could take her clothes off and jump in. Sensing her admiration for her tub, Lady Jane approached Sadie.

"There is one just like it upstairs that is all yours." Sadie turned towards her and let out a little giggle.

"Let's get back to Beauford."

* * *

"We've got a busy day tomorrow, kids. I think I'll turn in," Lady Jane said as she rose from the couch in the solarium. The three of them had spent the last two hours talking, and the girls polished off the champagne while Beau opted for two generous splashes of his mama's finest bourbon. It was fast approaching midnight.

"Let me show you two upstairs."

"I think I can manage, Mama." Beau helped Sadie up and rolled his eyes at Lady Jane.

"Oh… hush up now. I didn't show Sadie the upstairs."

Sadie followed Lady Jane out of the kitchen and to the bottom of the back stairs which led to the second level.

"This staircase goes right up to the bedrooms. Just head upstairs and then down to the end of the hallway." Lady Jane pointed up the staircase, and Sadie led the way ahead of her and Beau. Each hallway at Broadfield House seemed like it told a story, and Sadie couldn't get a handle of the convoluted configuration.

"Sadie Mae… your bedroom is to the right… last door. Beauford, your room is this first one… on the left."

Sadie walked ahead. She didn't dare turn around. Lady Jane had said her peace, and she and Beau would be in separate bedrooms. Why had she thought his southern belle mama would approve of them sleeping in the same bed? It was, after all, Lady Jane's domicile.

Sadie heard the snickering behind her, and when she got to her bedroom door, she turned to find Lady Jane doubled over in laughter and Beau with a shit-eating grin on his face.

"Sadie… baby, Mama is just kidding. You are here with me. This is *our* room," Beau said while opening up the door to their room. He folded his arms across his chest and waited for Sadie to re-join them.

"I told you, baby. She has a wicked sense of humor."

Beau opened his arms, and Sadie reluctantly fell against his chest, hiding the pink in her cheeks.

"I was only teasing, kids. I put you two all the way over here so you could cause a ruckus if you want," Lady Jane said, winking at Sadie. "I hope you are not offended, my dear."

Sadie let out a sigh of relief as Lady Jane gave her a quick embrace.

"Prez will be here by half-past seven. She just texted me that she is home from the hospital and going to bed, but she can't wait to meet Sadie Mae in the morning. Beauford, try and see that she gets at least a few hours' sleep, love… okay?"

Lady Jane embraced her son and blew a kiss to Sadie and then disappeared down the stairs.

"After you…"

Beau held the door open to the bedroom and swept his hand in front of Sadie as she walked inside.

The room was *Sex in the City* meets *Gone with the Wind*. Sadie walked towards the bed and then fell back onto it. The dark cherry wood four-poster bed had a four-inch-thick feather bed on top of a pillow top mattress that sunk under her weight. Sadie's hair cascaded in a halo around her face as Beau looked down upon her.

"What do you think of the mirror?" Beau asked.

Sadie glanced towards the head of the bed. A large oval antique mirror hung above the bed, angled in a way that made Sadie blush.

The color scheme of the room was rose with gold accents and dark wood antique furniture. The curtains reminded Sadie of a wedding dress, the way they hung so delicately – the crisp white fabric had a touch of lace at the edges. The moonlight was streaming through a gap in the French doors which led out onto a widow's walk. Sadie could smell the roses just outside. A smile spread across her face.

"You okay?" Beau asked as he leaned his back against one of the bedposts and smiled down at her.

"Yes, but it's a lot to take in. You should have told me sooner." Sadie tried to sit up, but she sank even further into the feather-like mattress.

"I know. I guess… well, I just think about my father. I don't see this the way other people see it. I see it the way he did. This isn't me, Sadie Mae. I'm not a part of this life. I'm sorry, I didn't tell you sooner. I guess I was unsure. I was embarrassed. Just like my father always was. It makes me uncomfortable," Beau said as he closed his eyes and let out a deep sigh.

There was so much that Sadie wanted to say, but she wanted to respect Beau's feelings and not risk alienating him.

"Beau, I think at some point in time you are going to have to come to terms with the fact that you will have to deal with all this… *your* wealth."

Beau looked into her eyes as he shook his head.

"Her wealth, but I hear what you are saying."

Beau turned and walked towards the end of the bed. It was apparent to Sadie that the conversation was finished, for now.

"There is an enormous tub in the bathroom," Beau said, pointing over his shoulder as Sadie fought to extricate herself from the bed.

"For now, it's the only thing that I can't get for you... on your fun list. You'd better enjoy it while you can."

Beau smiled at Sadie as she walked towards him and stopped to plant a smoldering kiss on his anxious lips. It was their first real kiss in hours, not counting Beau's attempt to run his hand inside her panties downstairs when Lady Jane excused herself to go to the powder room.

Sadie continued towards the bathroom and giggled as she opened the door and spied the tub. The entire bathroom was bigger than the tiny apartment she lived in growing up. Joel's world... his money, status, privilege, and friends paled in comparison to this type of wealth. Sadie couldn't begin to understand why Beau hadn't accepted who he was and all that he had. All she knew was that the ugly side of wealth would not control the life they would build together. At least Sadie hoped.

"Would you like to join me?"

Sadie slipped the black dress over her head as Beau watched her turn to run the bathwater.

* * *

"Wasn't he adorable?"

Beau heard the girls laughing all the way upstairs. He had slept in, and the bedside clock read 8:15 as he pulled on his jeans and grabbed his t-shirt, making his way downstairs. They had stayed up late... making love and talking... telling stories and laughing. After Sadie and Beau had finally finished soaking in the tub, Beau silently snuck them down the stairs to the billiards table and lived out his fantasy.

"I honestly can't tell if this is Beau or Patrick," Sadie said as she ran her hands over the picture. She couldn't quite believe it, but she actually missed Patrick and wished that he were there with the rest of the family.

"Oh, wait. Let me grab that book of Beau and Patrick... my Patrick... Patrick senior."

Sadie felt her heart tug a bit. She would have loved to have met Beau's father. She watched as Lady Jane rushed out of the kitchen to retrieve the photo album, and she wondered how different their lives may have been if Patrick were still alive.

"I'm so glad you and Beau are here, Sadie Mae," Presley exclaimed. Beau could hear Presley's voice as he entered the kitchen. "He's been beside himself waiting for you to get back to Nashville."

Presley looked up. Her smile was warm and bright upon seeing her older brother. Sadie turned her head and caught sight of him entering the room.

"Squirt!"

Beau waltzed through the kitchen and made a beeline for Presley.

"It's about time you got your lazy butt out of bed, Beaufart."

Presley giggled as she reached up to give Beau a big hug. Sadie's heart busted open when she heard Beau whisper in Presley's ear.

"What do you think of my girl?"

"I love her! You did good."

Beau patted the top of Presley's head before turning his attention towards Sadie.

"Hey, baby."

Beau came around to the kitchen stool, where Sadie was drinking her coffee and put his hands on her shoulders. She was in her Wonder Woman pajamas with no make-up. Her hair fell loose around her face, and her doe eyes were round and bright. Sadie was a take back home, girl. He leaned into her neck and smelled her scent, kissing her tenderly at the nape of her neck. Beau ached for her when he realized that she was not in bed with him when he woke... and then smiled to himself with the memory of Sadie's creamy skin against the billiard table's red felt.

"Where's Mama?" Beau asked as he poured himself a cup of coffee and took a seat next to Sadie.

"Looking for old photo albums to show Sadie. We are slow roasting you over hot coals this morning."

Presley had an adorable giggle. Sadie could tell that teasing her brother was a crucial part of their relationship. She was even more beautiful in person with light brown hair that was highlighted with thick blond streaks and hung loosely around her shoulders. She was of average height with bright blue eyes and an ass that Sadie would kill for. Presley had a powerhouse body, muscular and solid. She had spent time before Beau got up talking about her workout routine, which at the moment consisted of a circuit weight program and only because the trainer had asked her out on a date.

"Look what I found… yearbooks." Lady Jane reappeared with a stack of books and photo albums and set them down on the kitchen counter in front of Sadie.

"Well… look who's up," Lady Jane said while giving her son a wink.

"My ears were burning."

Beau's comments made all three girls' giggle. It was clear that Beau was used to being outnumbered.

"Well… we've got a big day planned," Lady Jane bellowed.

Beau glanced over at Sadie, who had a big but conciliated smile on her face.

"Mama is taking us to Marcel, that little French bistro in Lennox Heights," Presley exclaimed as she did a little dance in the kitchen.

"Yes! I love that place," Beau responded by raising his fists in the air.

"Well, son… see the thing is. You simply are not invited."

Beau smiled sheepishly at Lady Jane's admission.

"We know you want to work on that truck and throw a line in the water, besides… all the best shopping is in that neighborhood, and I want to treat the girls to something nice. We are having dinner at the club at seven o'clock tonight."

Beau's blood ran cold. He hadn't planned on dinner at the country club, and it made him feel like shit for not telling Sadie first. He remembered her late-night facetime stories before returning to Nashville of Joel and all his phony friends at the Rainier Club.

"Um… really… Mama… the club?" Beau said.

Presley turned and gave Beau the evil eye, and he gingerly ran his hands through his hair. He hadn't adequately prepared Sadie for the possibility that Lady Jane would want to take them to the Piedmont Country Club.

"Well, I hadn't really thought about that Mama, and so I didn't bring a dinner jacket. I guess we are going to have to go another time." Beau threw his hands up in the air and shot his mama that grin that normally fooled her every time.

"Nice try, son. Don't you worry about that. I'll take care of it. Since we are going to be out shopping today, I'll pick you up a little something. The governor and his wife will be dining with us. I want to show off my family."

And that was that. When Lady Jane made a request, everyone was to simply obey, and Beau knew that not another word would be spoken.

"Mama, I'm going to cook up some breakfast for Beaufart. Sadie Mae, you want something?"

Sadie shook her head sideways at Presley. "No… but let me help you."

Sadie and Presley worked together in the kitchen as Lady Jane excused herself to prepare for their day out.

"Girls… let's be ready to head out at 12:30. Our reservations are at 1:00."

Both Presley and Sadie quickly verbally confirmed as Lady Jane exited the room.

With his mama out of sight, Beau finally locked eyes with Sadie. Presley's head was in the refrigerator, pulling out breakfast meats and vegetables to make a scramble. Beau knew that Lady Jane had been up since dawn and already made a batch of biscuits. He mouthed *I'm sorry*, and Sadie shook her head and smiled.

Sadie could do the country club in her sleep. The governor and his wife didn't scare her. She felt the mechanism deep inside her gut switch on. This would be easy. It's all Sadie had known for the past 15 years.

"How on earth did you let her plan dinner at the club tonight?" Beau took a sip of coffee as he addressed Presley.

"Oh, come on now, fart face. It's Lady Jane Walker we are talking about. Her son is home with the love of his life... surely you knew that she would want to show your ass off."

Beau shrugged his shoulders at Presley's comments. All Sadie heard out of Presley's mouth were the words *love of his life*. Her belly warmed. She didn't dare look at Beau.

"Hey... at least you don't have to live in fear that you are going to run into your ex-boyfriend and his wife... oh... his pregnant wife... I keep forgetting to add that bit in." Presley went back to chopping vegetables, but Sadie could tell by the sound of her voice that the wound was still healing.

"Maybe Mama would let me bring her new boy toy as my escort?"

Presley's admission made Beau choke on his coffee.

"Oh, boy... she mentioned that she had taken on a new..." Beau couldn't form the words on his lips.

"What my stinky brother can't quite come to terms with is that our mama has taken on a series of... lovers. I think it's actually a brilliant idea. No strings. Just casual sex. They are all highly educated, and they absolutely worship her. She said she'd never fall in love again after daddy, but hey… the woman has needs."

Beau shook his head and placed his hands over his ears.

"Squirt… enough! Please do not use casual sex or needs when referring to the Saturday night habits of our mama."

Sadie just laughed. Lady Jane was a beautiful and vibrant woman, and she saw no reason why she shouldn't have a healthy sexual and social life. Given where Sadie had just come from, she knew deep in her heart that it was vital to her entire existence to have a man's arms wrapped tight around her, loving her deep down into her core.

"Prez… all jokes aside, I'm sorry about Andrew and the baby. Mama told me the last time she was in Nashville."

Sadie saw the tears in Presley's eyes and her hands shake.

"Goddam onions. Shit! I'll be right back. Sadie, can you take over?"

Sadie grabbed Presley's discarded knife and watched her open up the solarium doors and head for the pool. Ten seconds later, Beau and Sadie heard a big splash.

Beau had told Sadie about Andrew. He and Presley had grown up together and were high school sweethearts. A week after their father died, Presley came to Beau and confessed that Andrew had taken her virginity. They were each other's first, and she told Beau that Andrew would be her last. Presley hadn't counted on the distance when they went away to college. Her to Georgia Southern and Andrew to Tennessee, but they stayed together. When Andrew moved back home four years later, they talked about living together and getting married, only to be separated again by graduate and nursing school. They both promised to wait, and after another two years apart, they were finally ready to start their life together…and then Presley got the phone call.

Andrew tried to explain, but Presley couldn't hear anything other than pregnant, and I'm sorry. A month later, the shotgun wedding played out in the park just down the street from Broadfield House. Presley could hear the bridal march echoing off the magnolia trees as it wafted down the road and into the back garden. It didn't much matter a month later when Andrew called to tell her that they had miscarried. The damage was done, and he was married, although he tried, and Presley had a hard time staying away from him. The affair nearly cost Presley her mind. She had to finally let him go if she was ever going to move forward and so Andrew went back to his wife and vowed to be a good husband – the husband he wanted to be for Presley.

"Fuck. I'm a complete idiot. I'd better go grab her a towel," Beau said as he ran his fingers through his hair.

Sadie watched as Beau dashed out to the pool to check on Presley.

By the time Sadie saw Beau and Presley coming back to the kitchen, she had set the table, pouring orange juice into a tall glass pitcher. She placed the fresh-baked biscuits on a three-tier tray next to a small ramekin filled with peach preserves and finally had opened up a bottle of champagne that she saw chilling in the refrigerator. Beau and Presley walked into the kitchen, all smiles, and laughs.

"The vegetables are sautéed. Beau, do you want a scramble or an omelet?" Sadie sheepishly addressed Beau as Presley finished toweling off her hair and grabbed some champagne flutes out of the glass-fronted kitchen cabinet.

"What I think we need, Sadie Mae, is our first, of many… mimosas!" Presley squealed, grabbing the champagne and filling up their glasses.

"To Beau and Sadie. My amazing brother and his beautiful love."

"I'll second that," Beau said as he winked at Sadie.

"Cheers!"

Sadie took a sip of her champagne and let the contentment spread throughout her entire body.

* * *

"Beau... we're home. Are you up here?"

Sadie plopped down on the bed and let the shopping bags and boxes scattered around her. She heard the shower running and was tempted to join Beau, but they were due to leave for the Piedmont Country Club in an hour, and she wasn't sure if she would have time to re-do her hair and make-up.

"Beau... I'm back!" Sadie shouted out again when she heard the shower stop.

Beau threw open the bathroom door. He had a towel wrapped around his waist as he came to her. Between the bathroom and the bed, Beau discarded his towel.

"Sadie, are you in there somewhere? I can hear you breathing," Beau laughed as he moved in closer to her and pushed a bag away from her face.

"Hey, you. What have you been up too?" Sadie asked. She ran her hand down the side of Beau's face and her index finger over his lips.

"Went fishing... worked on my truck."

Sadie laughed and lifted up for a long deep kiss running her hands through Beau's damp hair.

"That sounds like a country song," she replied.

Sadie moved her hands over Beau's shoulders and down his back. "Beauford Walker... you're still wet. Get off me!"

Beau jumped off her and grabbed his towel, running it briskly over his head.

"Jesus... you did some shopping," Beau exclaimed.

Sadie was surrounded amongst bags and boxes with names like Dior, Saks 5th Avenue, Fendi, and Rigby & Peller.

"I see Mama took you to Tecovas."

Sadie rose and began removing her haul from the bed.

"I now own not one, but two pairs of cowboy boots."

Sadie's admission made Beau laugh.

"Mama loves to shop!"

"Beau, this is fucking obscene. I had to talk them out of the third pair of boots. Your mom and Presley insisted on ostrich leather for the second pair. They cost $400!"

Sadie ended her tirade with a smile, finally noticing that Beau was standing in front of her completely naked. His towel simply draped over his broad shoulders.

"Did you get anything for me?" Beau asked. Sadie had a mischievous grin on her face as she dug around until she found the bag from Rigby & Peller.

"The shopping was unreal, Beau. I've never seen anything like it. It's by appointment only. They gave us mimosas when we walked in the door."

Sadie dug through the bag until she found the red lace teddy and held it up for Beau.

"That's perfect. I love it. It's just what I wanted." A little white lie was okay. Beau honestly liked Sadie best in his old retro t-shirts and nothing else.

"Well, we aren't keeping it. This stuff... it's all going back, Beau. I can't even tell you how much all this stuff costs. I lost track in my head... and I'm good with numbers, you know that, right?" Sadie said, folding her arms across her chest. "Your mama and Presley got me liquored up on mimosas. Whew! The next thing I knew, I had my own personal shopper. Beau, her name was Adrianna and she just kept bringing me clothes to try on. Racks and racks of pants, skirts, and dresses. Presley and I did a little runway model thing outside our dressing rooms. If Lady Jane gave it a thumbs up, it went onto the sold rack. We lined three clothing racks. These boxes... oh, it's only what I could carry upstairs. There is more down there."

Sadie frantically pointed her finger in the direction of the bedroom door. Beau was slightly worried about her. She had a frenzied look in her eyes like an addict coming down off a crack high.

"Baby... Mama loves to spoil people she cares about. Did you have a good time, at least?"

Sadie smiled wide. "Yes!"

"Well... then that's all that matters."

"She's really looking forward to dinner at the club tonight," Sadie said as Beau quickly approached her and pushed her back on the bed.

"What are you looking forward to, baby?"

Sadie giggled as Beau slowly began undressing her.

* * *

Steam rose from the crack in the bathroom door at Broadfield House. Sadie had been soaking for over an hour, and Beau was starting to get worried.

"Sadie Mae.... you still alive?" Beau asked incredulously.

He knocked quietly on the partially open bathroom door and slowly pushed it open. Sadie was chin-deep in water that smelled like jasmine with flameless candles filling the bathroom in muted light.

"Yes, Beau. I'm alive."

"Baby... I'm lonely. Are you gonna stay in here all night?"

Sadie was finally relaxed. Dinner at the country club was nice, but she felt like she was on display all night, and it made her think about Joel and her father, and that made her anxious.

She excused herself from the dinner table as the band started playing and sent Joel a text. She hated the lies... hundreds of them by now. Sadie looked down at her cream lace dress and suddenly felt dirty.

She told him she was traveling all over south Texas and that her days were long, and her evenings were spent finding an internet connection to transfer her data and back up her reports. Joel's replies were short. He was busy with social commitments, but her father was good. It was all Sadie cared about.

"You're quiet. Everything okay, baby?"

Beau held her in his arms on the packed country club dancefloor. They had to be one of the youngest couples in the club that night, other than Presley's ex, Andrew, and his wife. Beau felt bad. He put Presley in an Uber just before dessert was served. She couldn't take Andrew and his wife one minute longer.

"I just texted Joel. I suddenly felt... I don't know. All of this just reminds me of home." Sadie quickly corrected herself. "I mean it makes me think of... Seattle." She quickly looked up, realizing her mistake. Beau's eyes were soft as his lips brushed over her forehead.

Beau wasn't sure what to say. This was no more of him than it was Sadie, but his mama was happy.

"I'm sorry, Sadie Mae. It's just that Lady Jane loves to show me off... you off, tonight. No one in this room can keep their eyes off you."

Sadie blushed as Beau twirled her around. The cream lace dress that Lady Jane had picked out for Sadie had sheer dotted mesh sleeves with a sweetheart silhouette and a low-cut back. The dress fit tight at the waist and shaped into a full skirt cut at the knee. It was lined with a layer of georgette and a touch of tulle-trimmed sateen.

"You charmed the pants off the president of Coca-Cola and the governor and his wife. Did I not hear you and Mama make lunch plans with the mayor's wife for the next time you are in Atlanta?"

Sadie shook her head up and down and smiled up at Beau as he pulled her in close to him and planted a soft kiss above her ear.

Beau thought about his father. He hated this shit, but he did it all for her. Beau would too. He knew he would do anything for Sadie, and he knew in his heart that her being here tonight, in a dress his mama had bought her was only because Sadie loved him just as much.

"Hey... I'm sorry. All of a sudden, I sound like I am complaining, and I'm not. It's just... this is so far removed from the Beau I know. I'm surprised... that's all."

Beau tightened his grip on Sadie's waist upon hearing her understanding words.

"You don't have to apologize, Sadie. I was just thinking about my father. He would've crawled over broken glass for her." Beau turned towards Lady Jane, who held court with a small group while admiring Beau and Sadie dancing.

"This isn't me, baby... and it doesn't have to be you anymore. If you want to take all those clothes back. If you want to go home right now, I'll take you. Let's get out of here," Beau said, pulling Sadie from the dancefloor.

"No! Beau... stop! We can't just leave Lady Jane. Presley has already left, and I know your mama was upset by her early departure. It's fine. I'm good. I just..." Sadie hesitated, then looked up at Beau, and he saw the tears in her eyes.

"Sadie... what is it?"

Sadie took in a long breath and exhaled. "Beau, I'm ready to give you my answer. I want to move to Nashville. Let's do this, okay? You and me. What do you say?"

The Piedmont Country Club had never heard a scream so loud, except when Pricilla Houghton accidentally fell into the foyer fountain, having had one too many martinis. Beau told his mama to finish her cocktail. He was ready to take Sadie Mae home.

Later, back at Broadfield House, Beau walked into the bathroom. The mirrors were fogged, and steam enveloped the room.

"Baby, are you in here?" Beau heard Sadie's faint laugh as he approached the tub.

"Did you apologize to your mama... for making a scene at the club?" Sadie asked. Beau knelt next to the tub and gently cupped her face.

"She understood. She's happy for me... for us."

Beau kissed Sadie hard, and when he pulled away, her eyes remained closed as she submerged herself back into the water.

"Beau, this isn't going to be easy. We've got some things to work through... plans. What about Patrick? How do you think he's going to feel?"

"Sadie Mae, he's five. He's going to be fine. He loves you," Beau exclaimed.

Sadie thought back to last Wednesday night. It was her side of the couch that Patrick wanted to be on. They worked on his writing in his green turtle workbook and snuggled under blankets leftover from the fort they built in the living room while Beau finished a work project. She laughed, thinking about how lonely Beau and George looked watching the motocross rally alone.

Sadie flicked the tub drain with her foot, and the water began to recede. Beau saw her brown nipples poking out through the depleted bubbles, and he reached into the water and gave the nipple closest to him a tug. Sadie's eyes opened wide, and Beau stood to retrieve her towel.

* * *

"So, this is the company website. It's called Angel Med Flight. Everyone on board is a licensed medical professional. They fly people in private fixed-wing aircraft when flying on a commercial airline or traveling by ground isn't an option. It's basically a flying ICU on a Lear jet," Beau eagerly spoke as he showed Sadie the website.

"We can have your dad here... on the ground in Nashville in seven hours. The plane makes one refueling stop in Colorado Springs."

Beau and Sadie had arrived back in Nashville, having left Atlanta at the crack of dawn Sunday morning so they could be back in time to pick Patrick up for a Sunday visit. Beau had been talking non-stop about planning, and Sadie realized that he had already given this whole process... her moving to Nashville a lot of thought even before she told him.

"Beau... this would be way too expensive."

Sadie had been conservative with her father's income. Living at Joel's had allowed her to save a bit of this monthly income in a high-yield savings account for the past few years. James paid for the extra costs associated with the full-time nursing that Medicare didn't cover, and Joel was generous with the rest. As a result, Sadie was able to save close to $50,000.

"See... I knew you were going to say that. We have the money."

Sadie put her head in her hands and walked away from the computer and stood by the patio door.

"No, Beau. You. You have the money. I can't ask you to do this. I'll figure it out, okay. Perhaps I should have spent down my dad's assets... put him on Medicaid. I just couldn't do it. He hated charity. He always paid his way. Those state facilities are horrible. I just don't think I could have done it."

Sadie knew that she would never be able to get her father on a commercial plane and get him to Nashville on her own, even if she had a nurse. He was prone to outbursts, and even on a good day, his behavior was fragile, and any change to his routine usually meant catastrophic results.

"I have another idea. This one is not as quick, but it's a MED coach. It's basically an RV with a nurse. They have fleets all over the country, so they re-supply, so to speak with a new driver and possibly a new nurse at various points along the trip. Your father would have a bathroom, a bed... they have a kitchen to prepare meals and the best part... you can ride along with him... if you want. The downside is that it takes 48 hours." Beau walked over to Sadie and put his arms around her shoulders.

"Can I show you the website?"

Sadie nodded her head as Beau went over all their options again.

Later in the week, Beau took a half-day off work, and they drove around to a few adult foster homes and memory care facilities. Some of them were small, private homes, but for one reason or another, Sadie didn't quite feel that it was the best fit for her father. The last place they went was to a large facility in the heart of the city. The only problem was that they had a six to eight month waiting list and they didn't have the outdoor space that she knew her father required.

"Thank you so much for your time. I appreciate you taking us around. The issue I see is that my dad loves the outdoors. He needs room to build things and to work on his airplanes and birdhouses. I am just not sure that this would be a good fit."

Sadie's head dropped. She felt defeated. Without a place for her father to live, the final piece of their Nashville puzzle would not be completed. Sadie feared that she would have to remain in Seattle, possibly through the winter, until they found the proper accommodations for him. With Patrick and the loft space, Sadie knew that James would never be able to live with them, even short term. It all seemed so hopeless. Sadie knew that the longer they spent apart, the harder it would be for her and Beau to stay together.

The assisted living director nodded her head and pulled open her desk drawer. "I had no idea that your father would thrive with more out-door space. I think I have just the place for you to consider...Tall Oaks Manor. It's about 35 minutes southwest of downtown Nashville... out in the country on three acres with plenty of outdoor space for the residents. The complex currently has one of the best memory care facilities in the state."

Sadie quickly grabbed the brochure out of the director's hands. "Wow... this place is beautiful. I think this might be more of what we are looking for. How would we go about scheduling a visit?" Sadie asked, and the director reached for her phone.

"Are you available this afternoon? The residential manager is my cousin, Maybelle Reed. I'll give her a quick call and let her know that you are on your way." Sadie looked at Beau and smiled.

"What do you think?"

"I say... let's go. This place has your dad's name written all over it," Beau said as he grabbed Sadie's hand, and they took off for Tall Oaks Manor.

* * *

Sadie couldn't believe the facility. Tall Oaks Manor was just that, a beautiful three-level building with majestic trees that lined the entrance. The front of the manor resembled a hotel in a park-like setting, with the top floor devoted entirely to memory care patients. As Sadie glanced at the brochure again, she rejoiced knowing that they had a room where residents could work on activities in groups or craft and build things, with supervision. It would be a perfect place for her father. The grounds resembled the park near their home in Seattle, and the bedrooms were large and comfortable. She knew that James didn't need much, and with his memory issues, a studio apartment would be perfect. Sadie's hopes were quickly dashed when Maybelle Reed sat down with them to go over availability.

"We have a 3-4 month waiting period for the level of care that your father requires. In all honesty, it will probably take that long to get his paperwork and financing arranged. You mentioned that he needs to move out here from the west coast."

Sadie nodded her head as she took in the director's words. "Yes, I guess I thought that we could move on this a bit faster," Sadie said, her voice laced with disappointment.

"Listen, let me print off all the information you need, and you can complete the forms and get them back to me before you head back to Seattle. You mentioned that you are leaving next Wednesday. Is that right?"

Sadie didn't want to say yes, and she thought about all the ways she would never have to go back to Seattle and see Joel again. Then she thought about her father.

* * *

"Sadie... that place looks perfect. Just think, your father could be here before Christmas?" Beau's voice contained the optimism Sadie needed. She looked over at him as they drove back to the loft from Tall Oaks Manor. His face was beaming. This was the one piece of the puzzle that Sadie was desperate to get finalized before she left town. Beau knew that if Sadie found a place where her father would be safe and happy, then she was his. She would tell Joel and pack her bags, and Sadie would be in Nashville in no time.

"Beau, this paperwork says his room would start at $4,800 and go up. With all the added care he needs, it's going to be pushing $6,000. His social security and pension are just under $3,000 a month. I'm going to need to get a job so I can help... otherwise, with his relocation costs, he's going to be out of money in just a few years. I just don't think..."

Sadie cut her words short as tears flooded her eyes. Beau quickly pulled over along the side of the road and threw his arm around her shoulder.

"Baby... please. I got this, okay. I don't want you worrying about anything other than taking one step in front of the other. We are going to get it all worked out. I promise you."

Sadie nodded her head, but her tears didn't stop. "Beau, I can't accept anything other than a loan. Promise? If I need your help. If I accept your help... I'll pay it back with interest, okay," Sadie pleaded and watched as Beau simply nodded.

"I like where this is going, Sadie. I think we can work something out... some form of re-payment," Beau snickered. Sadie wiped her tears and managed to laugh.

"Be serious, okay. I'm not sure what form of re-payment you're thinking in that head of yours, but something tells me it's not what I was referring to."

Beau gently kissed Sadie's cheek and ran his hand down the length of her arm. His touch still made her quiver.

"Let's go get some barbecue and strategize, baby."

Sadie nodded her head and dried her tears. She realized that it was going to be impossible for her to do this on her own. She was going to have to accept Beau's generosity and financial support, or coming to Nashville would be just a beautiful Tennessee dream.

* * *

Sadie hadn't slept all night, so when Patrick crawled into bed at 2:30, it was a welcomed relief. Even Beau didn't stir when Patrick asked Sadie to kiss Max's booboo. Patrick's stuffed monkey had been found in George's dog bed after a family outing to the Nashville zoo on Sunday. George, no doubt, pissed off to be left at home all afternoon.

Sadie laid in bed and listened to her boy's sleeping as a constant stream of tears slid from her eyes. Today Sadie would start her goodbyes. The first to Patrick, and she hadn't counted on the emotions that seemed to be taking over. Her days in Nashville were quickly coming to an end, and Sadie was beginning to dread going back to Seattle.

At dawn, she kissed the back of Beau's neck, and he turned to her. Patrick was still sound asleep next to her, but they laid together and stared into each other's eyes, never uttering a word. Beau knew how hard today would be on all of them.

* * *

"Patrick… get your shoes on, son. We need to leave in a few minutes."

Beau was getting Patrick's backpack organized, and Sadie was in the kitchen finishing up lunches. She used a large star cookie cutter to cut the crust off Patrick's peanut butter and jelly sandwich and filled two bags with purple grapes and animal crackers. She put a scoop of chicken salad on a bed of salad greens in a plastic container for Beau and also gave him a bag filled with grapes. Inside Beau's bag, she folded up a love note that simply read, *I love you, forever.* Inside Patrick's bag was a note filled with hearts and smiley faces. Her hands shook as she folded the tops down on the insulated lunch totes and watched Patrick put on his shoes.

"Here, let me help you." Sadie knelt and ran her hand over Patrick's hair and smoothed out a piece that was sticking out.

"Will you be back in time to see my new school?" Patrick looked into Sadie's eyes as she shook her head side to side. The little boy talked non-stop about starting Kindergarten in two weeks. He was looking forward to being able to ride his new bike to school most mornings.

"I don't think so, but I'll see it when I get back, okay."

"When are you coming back, Sadie Mae?" Sadie bit her lip. She didn't have an answer for herself, let alone Patrick.

"Soon, okay, but I need you to help me with something." Sadie took Patrick by the shoulders as Beau looked on from his office space.

"I need you to make sure to give George lots of belly rubs while I am gone." Patrick shook his head up and down. "I also need you to look after your dad for me… give him extra hugs and kisses for me, okay? I am going to be lonely in Seattle without the two of you, so I need to make sure that you take care of each other every day."

Patrick's face was solemn as he listened to Sadie. He turned quickly and ran back to his bed as Sadie stood up. She turned her head towards Beau and smiled, wiping a stray tear with her finger. This was going to be harder than she thought. As she turned back around, Patrick came running towards her with Max in his arms. He held the monkey out for Sadie to take.

"I don't want you to be lonely in Seattle... so I want you to take Max with you to keep you company."

Sadie fell to her knees and began to weep as Patrick wrapped his tiny arms around her shoulders and gave her a big hug.

"Thank you so much, Patrick. I know how much Max is going to miss you, so I promise that I will keep him safe, and we will be back home soon, okay." Sadie didn't think she would be able to let him go but having Max in her hands gave her immediate strength.

"Bye, Sadie Mae. I love you!"

Seemingly unfazed, Patrick ran towards Beau, who helped his son with his backpack as Sadie handed them both their lunches.

"You boys have a good day, okay." Sadie fought back the tears as she lifted Max's fluffy arm and waved goodbye to Beau and Patrick, blowing them each a kiss.

"I'll see you later, okay. I'll work from home this afternoon," Beau said.

He lifted his hand to return her blowing kiss and led Patrick out of the door. Beau wanted to carve out as much time with Sadie as possible. Aside from a goodbye lunch with Mazie, it was going to be Beau and Sadie 24/7 until he took her to the airport. All they both cared about was spending as much quality time together as possible.

Sadie turned as the front door closed and burst into tears.

* * *

Beau had never held her this tight before. Sadie could barely breathe, but she didn't want him to loosen his grip. They were standing in the Nashville airport exactly where they had stood at the end of June when Beau first told Sadie he loved her.

"I'm not going to let you go," Beau whispered.

"The sooner I leave Nashville, the sooner I'll be back, okay," Sadie said, nuzzling into Beau's neck, giving him sweet tiny kisses.

Beau and Sadie had planned everything out. They had prepared like two generals in a bunker during a war. If everything worked out and Sadie could hold on… keep up the charade with Joel and get her ducks in a row, she would be back in Nashville before the holidays.

"I'll call you as soon as I land. Joel's away. He doesn't get back from the San Juan Islands until tomorrow. It's going to make my reclamation so much easier." Sadie could hear Beau's low growl in her ear.

"You be careful. Take care of you. I don't want you doing anything that makes you feel uncomfortable. We have other options, Sadie Mae. You can be back here in Nashville tomorrow. You know that, right?" Beau said as he pulled away and looked into her eyes.

Sadie had been steadfast in doing this her way, gradually ripping off the band-aid. She would try to reason with Joel that it was time for them to move on and separate amicably… praying that Tall Oaks Manor would come through with a room sooner rather than later.

"Kiss me, and then I want you to go, okay. I don't want Patrick having to wait at camp any longer than necessary. You guys need to get to the park and get to Hannah's for dinner."

Beau took ahold of Sadie's hands and stepped back, looking deep into her eyes, then slowly scanning the rest of her face. He then let his eyes take in the rest of her body as if he wanted to remember her, as she stood before him in case he never laid eyes on her again.

"I love you, Beau Walker, and I'm coming home to you," Sadie exclaimed. Beau nodded, pulling her in close to him once again.

"I love you too, baby."

After a quick embrace, Beau let his arms drop to his side, and Sadie quickly turned and walked towards the TSA line.

As she weaved her way through the line, she looked over her shoulder once more and scanned the crowd, but Beau was already gone.

CHAPTER TEN

Sadie had dozens of encouraging text messages from Beau and an adorable voice mail from Patrick as soon as she landed back in Seattle. Sadie quickly realized that the message was for Max and not her. Max had already proven to be an exciting traveling companion. He assisted the flight attendants with the meal service, and Sadie managed to snap a Max selfie with the pilot when she deboarded.

As she waited in baggage claim for her suitcase, she was lonely, scared and missed her boys. Suddenly their plan sounded like complete crap, and Sadie had begun to re-think her Nashville timeline. She was desperate to talk with Beau. She had drawn up a new battle plan on the plane ride home, and they had some new ideas to ponder.

Sadie had told Joel days ago not to bother with a car service. There was no way she could give him accurate information since she wasn't returning from Texas but from Tennessee. She told him that it didn't really matter, considering that he was away. Sadie's only goal was to get home quickly and possibly eat a late dinner with her father if he was up for it.

Sadie called Beau's phone three times, and it went straight to voice-mail, and he didn't respond to her text messages. She figured since it was close to bedtime in Nashville that Beau had his hands full. She also wondered if Patrick's first night without Max might result in a quick video chat so Patrick could blow kisses to his monkey before bed.

The sun was starting to dip close to the Olympic mountains as Sadie made her way from the airport to Magnolia. Seattle had been her home for all of her 50 years, but it didn't feel like her home anymore. She hit the button on her armrest and rolled the window partially down in the backseat of the cab. The air was crisp and smelled salty. There was no doubt that she would miss the pacific northwest, but her soul now craved Tennessee and Beau.

Sadie had decided on the five-hour plane ride that her time in Seattle was over. She knew that she couldn't face months apart from Beau and Patrick, keeping up some farce with Joel. If Beau was generously offering, then Sadie was going to accept willingly. She cursed herself for getting him to agree to her plan and was suddenly afraid that he might doubt her feelings. As soon as Joel returned home, Sadie was prepared to tell him the truth and let the chips fall where they may. She was ready for her new life to begin tomorrow, and she was prepared to pack up her life in Seattle, say her goodbyes and go home. The only question mark being what to do about her father. Still, Sadie was confident that they would find a temporary option.

The sun sank below the mountains, just as the cab pulled up in front of the house, and Sadie quickly exited. She retrieved her suitcase from the trunk and pulled it towards her, thanking the driver. As she turned to head up the walkway, she was shocked to see Joel's car in the driveway. His plans must have changed, although the house looked dark – the upstairs curtains drawn closed. Sadie realized that perhaps Joel caught a ride with another club member or took a cab to the ferry. It would be foolish for him to have taken his car to San Juan Island at the end of August. Relief washed over her. She wasn't looking forward to seeing Joel tonight, and she just wanted a good night's sleep. Sadie would be at work, bright and early in the morning, and was prepared to tell Joel face to face that their life together was over before the sun set tomorrow night.

Sadie put her key in the door and turned the handle, letting the door slowly fall inward as she pulled her bag inside. The house was eerily quiet and dark. The only light filtering in was the muted orange hues of the sunset.

"Hello, Philomena! I'm home," Sadie called up from the bottom of the staircase. As she turned to set her tote down, Joel appeared behind her, having silently walked out into the foyer from his study.

"Sadie, welcome home. Tell me, how was your time in... um, Texas?"

Sadie turned abruptly to the sound of his voice. Joel's eyes were dark, and he looked disheveled, his cufflinks were missing, and the sleeves on his white button-down shirt were haphazardly rolled up.

"Joel? You startled me. I didn't expect you to be home." Sadie watched him lift a glass filled with a generous amount of scotch to his lips. Joel was drunk. Sadie let out her held breath and steadied herself.

"You didn't answer my question, Sadie." Joel abruptly turned and walked back into his study, stopping off at his bar cart to refill his glass – his pour missing sloppily.

"Oh, Texas was fine. Very busy, you know... with work."

Sadie thought she heard Joel snicker as she watched him turn around to face her.

"Texas... yes, right. Your land appraisal certificate."

Joel took another sip of scotch and then slammed his glass down on the side table next to his wingback chair, causing Sadie to jump. Her knees became weak, and she took a step back.

It was at that moment when their eyes met that she knew. Sadie had been caught.

"Joel, I'm exhausted. It's been a long trip, and I'd like to see my father."

Sadie turned to leave the study just as Joel picked up the crystal glass and hurled it at her. It struck the study doorframe, shattering into a million pieces narrowly missing Sadie's head.

"And what makes you think that your father would have anything to do with a slut like you?"

Sadie's legs wouldn't move. She could hear Joel breathing heavily. She wanted to run for the front door, but she was frozen in place. Where would she run to anyway? She suddenly remembered that her car was at Juliette's, and there was her dad to think about. She couldn't just leave him behind. Sadie slowly turned to face Joel.

"Listen to me, Joel. I don't think you understand. I just needed a break. I made some friends in Nashville in June. I knew you wouldn't understand, but they invited me back, and I wanted to go. I needed some space and some time away from my father. You must know how hard these last few years have been on me... on us."

Sadie's pleas fell on deaf ears. Joel threaded his hands through his slick hair and let out a loud laugh.

"You are a fucking liar. All you wanted to do was spread your legs for some dimwitted little cowboy."

Joel had certainly done is homework. Sadie didn't know how much he knew, but he had found out about Beau.

"If I knew that was all you wanted, Sadie... to make you happy... I could have arranged for something much closer to home."

Sadie watched as Joel stumbled to the bar, grabbed a fresh crystal glass, and poured himself another generous scotch.

"Please... Joel. I didn't want it to come to this. We've been through so much. Spent so many wonderful times together. It's just that... it's over, and you have to accept that. We need to go our separate ways."

Joel slowly approached her, and Sadie could smell the liquor on his breath and see the hatred in his eyes.

"You are not going anywhere until I say so, you fucking whore."

Before Sadie could react, Joel lunged at her, gripping her arm. Pain shot up through her shoulder, and she struggled to break free.

"Joel, please!" Sadie screamed. "Philomena and my father will hear you. They will be scared! Let go of me and let's talk like two civilized adults."

With Sadie's words, Joel's grip only appeared to get stronger. He leaned his face into hers as if he were about to kiss her, and Sadie couldn't pull away any further without Joel pulling her shoulder out of its socket.

"You are not very smart, Sadie. No one can hear us because no one is here. Philomena is gone. She was relieved of her duties yesterday."

The shock of Joel's words made Sadie tense up all over. Joel's grip made her aching arm begin to go numb.

"Why? I don't understand. Who is upstairs with my father? What have you done, Joel?"

Joel immediately let go of Sadie's arm and gave her a push backward. Sadie couldn't catch her balance in time and fell into the solid oak bookshelf whacking the side of her head. She put her hand up to her brow bone and felt it split and immediately swell.

"James is gone. I have removed him and his belongings from this residence as of yesterday morning."

Sadie let out a loud gasp and tried to steady herself. "Where is my father? Where have you taken him? You had no right... no right at all to take him from his home without my permission." Tears stung her eyes as Sadie pulled herself up off the study floor.

"You see, Sadie. I have every right. This is my home. I am simply protecting myself and saving your father from his daughter's poor choices. Like, mother... like daughter, right?" Joel's venomous words cut through Sadie's core.

"You fucking bastard. I can't believe that you would remove a sick and defenseless man from his home. Where is my father?" Sadie shouted at the top of her lungs, making her throat burn.

Joel began to toy with her, moving slowly behind his desk to grab the decanter and pour himself more scotch.

"Would you like a drink, Sadie?"

"Fuck you. Tell me where my father is."

Sadie trembled with fear and anger as she positioned herself close to the entrance of the study in case Joel came at her again. She reached up and wiped a trickle of blood that had inched down her eyelid.

"I received a phone call a few nights ago from our good friends, Rupert and Annabelle… you remember them? Annabelle rang me and let me in on a little gossip. Come to find out… the gossip involved you, of all people."

Joel swirled his scotch and then drained his glass in one long gulp.

"It seems her sister, Francesca is throwing a party for the autumnal equinox. The whole affair sounds dreadfully boring, considering it's being held at the Piedmont Country Club in Atlanta, Georgia. Thank god I won't get an invite to that… but I bet you will, won't you?"

Sadie was quickly putting the pieces of the puzzle together.

"Apparently, the club was all a buzz a couple of weeks ago with the arrival of a very charming woman from Seattle, on the arm of the only son of one of Georgia's wealthiest women. I do believe you have met her, Lady Jane Broadfield Walker?" Sadie nodded her head. She couldn't fucking believe it.

"Well done, Sadie… excuse me, I mean Sadie Mae. That is how you prefer to be addressed now, isn't it?"

Sadie folded her arms across her chest. Joel had an agenda, and Sadie would stand her ground and let him finish. It was her only shot at finding out where her father was.

"Annabelle was just beside herself. I mean, when Francesca told her sister that a Sadie Mae Morgan from Seattle had caught the eye of Beauford Walker… I mean, she felt compelled to phone me and see how I was doing. She had no idea that you and I had parted ways. Why she was shocked considering that you and I had been at their charity ball only a month ago."

"Joel..."

"You shut your fucking mouth. Don't speak to me. You have embarrassed and humiliated me. I am now the laughingstock of not only Seattle but some country club in podunk Georgia."

Joel came at Sadie again, but he was slowed by the scotch and lost his balance, falling into the edge of his desk and ripping the side of his trousers.

Sadie went for Joel, where it would hurt him the most. She approached the table with the 17th century Chinese Qing Dynasty rose porcelain vase and grabbed it in both of her hands, holding it high above her head. Sadie knew what he paid for it at auction in San Francisco.

"You've touched this vase more that you have touched me, Joel... in years. Let me go. Tell me where my father is," Sadie screamed. Joel just shook his head and let out a demonic laugh. "You tell me where my father is, or I'll shatter this vase into a million pieces." Sadie clutched the vase higher over her head, willing herself the courage to proceed.

"If you do that, you'll never see your father again, you fucking slut."

Sadie hurled the vase onto the hardwood floor with a smirk on her face. Before she had time to savor what she had done, Joel lunged at her, grabbing both her arms and pushing her hard against the study doorframe. The edge caught her square in the back and knocked the wind out of her. Joel gripped her arms tighter and continued to shake Sadie, her head hitting the doorframe repeatedly. She could see his lips moving, but his voice was muffled by the sounds of her heartbeat in her ears.

All of a sudden, Joel stopped. His eyes shot past her as he turned his head quickly. Sadie faintly heard a voice. His voice.

"You take your hands off her right this minute."

Joel let go of Sadie, and she fell to the floor in a heap. Beau took two strides and grabbed Joel by the throat with one hand, pushing him back into the study and against his desk.

"Don't you ever touch her again, you hear me. I swear if you ever lay a hand on her again, I'll kill you."

Sadie grabbed the back of her head and staggered to her feet. She thought she was hallucinating, and that Joel had knocked her out. There was absolutely no way that Beau was in this room... in Seattle with her. She blinked her eyes to bring them into focus, but double vision clouded her sight.

Beau released his grip on Joel and backed away. He kept his eyes on him, watching him recover. Joel was doubled over coughing and sputtering, giving Beau time to reach around and pull Sadie into his arms.

"Baby... Sadie... look at me. Are you okay?" Sadie nodded her head, and Beau ran his hand along the side of her face.

"Fuck, there is blood on your face. What did he do to you?"

Sadie couldn't speak. Her head was pounding, and she felt like she was dreaming. She blinked her eyes again and registered a faint smile.

"Are you really here? Am I dreaming, Beau... what's going on?"

"Listen, I'll explain everything later. Right now, I need you to go upstairs and get your dad. Can you do that for me, baby?" Sadie's eyes filled with tears as she shook her head.

"No... Beau, I can't."

"Shhhh... listen to me. This is all over. This ends here tonight. Is there someone upstairs that can help you get James ready?"

Beau caught Joel's movements out of the corner of his eye. He had pulled himself away from his desk and crept over to his bar cart to refresh his glass.

"Sadie's father has been... relocated," Joel responded with a raspy voice.

"What's he talking about?" Beau asked, turning back towards Sadie.

"My dad is gone. Joel fired the nurse and moved him. He's gone, Beau." Sadie burst into tears, and Beau pulled her into his chest... tenderly soothing her.

"Oh, for fuck sake Sadie, would you get out of my fucking house before I call the police and have your lamebrain cowpoke arrested for assault."

"Grow up, Joel," Sadie shouted. "Why don't you for once start acting like a real man." Sadie could instantly see that she had struck a nerve.

"I told you to keep your fucking mouth shut, you little cunt," Joel spat his words out and then lifted his glass to his lips and took another long gulp.

"Hey!" Beau's voice reverberated against the study walls as he pointed a finger in Joel's direction. "Don't you ever speak to her like that again."

Beau didn't give a shit what Joel thought of him, but he wasn't about to stand there and listen to him degrade Sadie.

"Baby, listen to me. I need you to go upstairs and gather your belongings. Can you do that quickly, please? Joel and I are going to have a nice little chat."

Sadie wiped her eyes and nodded her head. "Beau, please be careful. I don't trust him. He's drunk."

"I'm going to be fine. You run along. Get your stuff. You won't be coming back here again... understood?"

Sadie flew up the stairs and into her father's room. It was bare. Even his hospital bed was gone. She opened his top dresser drawer and found it empty. Finally, she checked his closet and found only empty hangers.

When she got to her room, it was apparent that Joel had gone through it with a fine-tooth comb. He wouldn't have found anything. Sadie wasn't as stupid as Joel thought she was. There were a few work files strewn about. She had completed an appraisal before she flew back to Nashville and hadn't had a chance to take into the office. Sadie quickly gathered the file and grabbed an oversized tote bag and stuffed it inside. On Sadie's nightstand were a stack of books and a few pieces of mail. She looked around the room again for anything that she wanted to take. In her closet were two storage boxes filled with family photos and documents, and she quickly carried those down to the bottom of the stairs, straining to hear the conversation in Joel's study. Sadie caught sight of Beau's backside in the doorway, and he turned and winked at her. It was all she needed to give her the strength to walk back up the stairs and gather the rest of her belongings.

Sadie grabbed a large suitcase from underneath her bed and opened up her closet. She ran her hands over the ballgowns, dozens of them hanging in her closet next to a white mink stole with a faux diamond broach and a floor-length Sabina sable fur. She didn't want them. Sadie didn't want most of the items hanging in her closet, but the furs were valuable. She worked her way through the rest of the closet, grabbing a couple of sweaters and a pair of trousers, workout clothes and pajamas. Most of the clothes that she loved were downstairs in the suitcase she brought home from Nashville or hanging up in Beau's loft closet, waiting for her return. Sadie didn't need nor did she want any reminders of the life she had with Joel, and she knew deep down that he would have a cleaning crew throw everything out as soon as she and Beau walked out the front door.

Sadie caught sight of herself in the mirror in the hallway outside of her bedroom. Her left eyebrow was crusted over in blood, and she reached back to feel the lump on the back of her skull. Her head still pounded, and she felt weak. Not once in all the years she was with Joel did he ever so much as raise his voice to her. Joel was always in control… confident and smooth. Guilt filled Sadie's soul as she turned to make her way downstairs.

"Beau, I'm ready."

He quickly turned and held out his hand for her, but she was afraid to walk towards him. Sadie didn't want to step foot in that study ever again, and then she remembered the ring.

Sadie walked into the study and marched past Beau to where Joel was sitting. He was slumped over in his wingback chair with his head in his hands. Whatever had transpired between Joel and Beau had broken him, although he didn't have a scratch on him, and Sadie was grateful for that. Joel was a shell of a man, and Sadie didn't even recognize him.

"I should keep this. Sell it on eBay, but I couldn't be bothered. I don't want it. It symbolizes everything that was so wrong about us for so long. I was wrong to lie to you, and I'll have to live with my decisions for the rest of my life, but what you did to me tonight was despicable… hurting my father and me out of nothing but sheer spite. I can't believe that I ever loved you." Sadie took the ring off her left hand and threw it in his lap.

Joel reached out for her and grabbed her by the wrist, and Beau took two steps forward. Joel quickly thought better of it and immediately let her go.

"Yes, Sadie… but you did love me, didn't you?"

Joel looked up at Sadie with tears in his eyes, and she turned and walked over to Beau.

"Did he tell you where my dad is?" Sadie asked. Beau shook his head up and down and handed her a business card.

"He's in West Seattle. We need to go."

Beau grabbed Sadie's hand, and they made their way towards her things in the foyer. As they began to gather up her belongings, Joel shouted out.

"Sadie!"

She quickly turned and walked back towards him. Joel was barely standing, leaning heavily into the doorframe with his hands in his pockets.

"I'm sorry."

Sadie couldn't look him in the eye, and she turned and ran out the front door.

* * *

"Keep that bag of peas on the back of your head, please."

"It's cold."

"It will keep the swelling down. You've probably got a concussion. I wish you'd let me take you to urgent care," Beau demanded.

Sadie's head was still swimming – replaying the last hour in her mind. Beau's rental car was parked across the street when they exited the house in Magnolia. After they loaded Sadie's things into the trunk and Beau stopped off at QFC for the peas, he typed the address of the Providence facility in the GPS on the dash, and they headed for James.

"I'm fine, Beau... honestly. I just want to get over to West Seattle, okay."

There was an urgency in her voice, so Beau was okay with foregoing medical treatment for the time being. Instead, he wouldn't let her out of his sight.

"You mind telling me what you are doing here? Why didn't you say something? Who is with Patrick? You should be home with him." Sadie leaned her head back against the headrest and let out a muffled groan.

"Which question would you like me to answer first?"

Sadie turned her head and smiled.

"Beau, I am so fucking glad you are here. I mean, you're really here, right? My head... I'm still trying to process what just happened." Sadie felt the tears sting her eyes as she looked over at Beau.

"I'm here, baby. Are you mad?" Sadie shook her head from side to side and then stopped... stifling nausea that rose in her belly. "I had a bad feeling, Sadie Mae... and I just couldn't let you come back here alone. I knew you'd never agree with me flying to Seattle with you. So, I had to take matters into my own hands. When you mentioned that Joel would be gone, I figured I'd find you and your dad at the house tonight, and we'd all leave... together."

"And go where?" Sadie asked.

Beau let out a deep sigh and continued. "I made a few calls. I found a couple of places for your dad... short term care. Baby, I just wanted to get you out of that house tonight."

Sadie wanted to close her eyes, but it made her dizzy and turned her stomach.

"Beau, how did you get to Seattle? We said goodbye. I walked over to security, and when I turned around, you were gone."

Beau turned his head and chuckled. "I had to run back to the car for my backpack. My flight left 30 minutes after yours. Luckily, I was down at the other end of the airport. I changed my shirt... threw on a ballcap and my sunglasses... just in case."

Beau's story made Sadie laugh. Had she recognized him at the airport, she most likely would have tried to talk him out of the trip.

"I hurried as fast as I could, baby. The rental car was all ready for me when I landed. I typed in your address and drove there as fast as I could. Traffic sucks in this town."

Sadie started to cry again. Relief washed over her, but the guilt was still raw in her stomach. She couldn't get over the look on Joel's face when he came after her as he called her a whore and all those other degrading terms. Sadie would be haunted by the image of Joel's face when she left for a very long time.

"I'm so sorry, Beau. God... what have I done? Now, you are all caught up in this." Sadie put the peas in her lap and her head in her hands.

"Hey... don't you apologize to me! I'm the one that is sorry. Fuck, Sadie... when I think of what could have happened if I hadn't gotten there in time. If my flight had been delayed or canceled. It's my fault. I should never have allowed you to come back here alone."

"Now what?" Sadie asked. She wasn't entirely sure she wanted to hear his answer. She was afraid. Sadie had no idea what had transpired in that study and what Joel was capable of. She feared that Beau may have changed his mind and that what happened tonight might alter their future.

"Right now, I need to take you to your dad." Beau remained silent as they continued to head to West Seattle.

Sadie looked out her window – the lights of the city fading behind them as they crossed over the West Seattle Bridge. She tried to close her eyes and process her thoughts, but the events of the night played over and over again in her head.

"Sadie… I think we are here."

Beau pulled the rental car into the parking lot and found an empty spot. He put the car in park as Sadie opened her eyes.

The Providence facility stood near High Point, the highest point in all of Seattle. From the parking lot, Sadie could see downtown and the space needle across Elliott Bay. She grabbed her tote and dug around in her bag for her make-up case. She lowered the visor in the passenger seat and looked at herself in the mirror. The gash across her brow was crusted over, and the skin around her eye was bright red and swollen. Sadie opened her compact and patted some pressed powder over her nose and eye.

"I don't think it's going to make a difference. I just don't want… fuck… who am I kidding? He might not even recognize me… black eye or not."

Beau had opened up the passenger side door and was watching Sadie. He wanted to take her in his arms and kiss her lips, but something told him to hold back. Beau had only held her hand since they walked out of Joel's home. She was fragile, and he didn't want to smother her after her ordeal.

Sadie felt the tension between them as she exited the vehicle. She walked ahead of Beau, and although she wanted to look back and reach for him, she was afraid.

Breezing through the facility's entrance with the business card firmly in her hand, Sadie stepped up to the information desk and cleared her throat. She lifted her hand and smoothed her bangs across her forehead, hoping they covered up her darkening bruises.

"Good evening. I'm Sadie Morgan. My father, James Morgan, was brought here... yesterday, I believe. I was wondering if I could speak with the director, Ms. Blackmon."

Sadie looked down at the card and then up to the front desk clerk. She was a very young woman with pretty eyes. She had a diamond stud in her nose, and pink stripes throughout her jet-black hair.

"Rebecca Blackmon has already left for the night. She will be back in the morning. Would you like to leave her a message?"

"Yes... I mean, no. I'll just call her and leave her a voice mail. I'd like to see my father. Can you please tell me where his room is?"

"Ma'am, visiting hours are 8 a.m. to 8 p.m. daily. Breakfast begins at 7 a.m. You can see your father in the morning."

The receptionist quickly went back to typing on her computer. Sadie shook her head sideways, clutching the top of the information station as a wave of nausea ripped through her middle.

"I understand you have rules, but if I could just see his room and make sure that he is okay. I'll be on my way," Sadie said through gritted teeth.

"I can assure you that your father is okay. We run an excellent facility here. He's being well looked after."

Sadie let out a deep breath. If it weren't for her pounding head, she would have screamed.

"I don't doubt that you run a fine facility... but I really must insist. I need to see my father."

The pitch in Sadie's voice escalated, and Beau stepped towards her and placed his hand lightly on her shoulder.

"Sadie Mae... I'm sorry. We can come back in the morning. It's alright," Beau said calmly.

Sadie turned abruptly to face him. "No! It's not alright. None of this is alright. I want to see my father now... please!"

The desk clerk rose, and two orderlies approached from down the hall.

"Ma'am... I'm going to ask you to keep your voice down... or else I am going to have to call security."

Beau quickly turned Sadie away from the desk and grabbed her hands.

"Listen, you need to take a deep breath. James is safe. We found him. I need to get you into a hot bath and bed. Everything will look better after a good night's sleep. We'll be back here in the morning. I promise." Beau pleaded while Sadie defiantly shook her head.

"Beau, please do something."

Sadie knew that if anyone could charm the pants off someone, it would be Beau. His smile melted hearts... Sadie's heart for one. He turned to the desk clerk and smiled while Sadie stepped aside and watched.

"Lilly... right? That's a very pretty name. Listen... I apologize. Sadie is exhausted. She's just arrived from Nashville, and she only just found out an hour ago that her father was moved to this facility. She's stubborn as hell, and she loves him with all of her heart. Please... just allow her to hang outside his door. Have a brief peek at him. Honestly, she just wants to lay her eyes on him. If you let us do that, we won't bother you again. We'll leave quietly and come back in the morning for a proper visit, okay?"

One side of Beau's mouth curled up as he smiled.

Lilly looked like a deer caught in the headlights. Her eyes glazed over as her mouth turned upward into a faint smile. She reluctantly took her eyes off Beau and hit a few buttons on her computer.

"James Morgan... room 410... in building two. Take the elevators down this hall to the 4th floor."

"Thank you, Lilly. Much appreciated."

Beau turned to Sadie and grabbed her hand as they headed down the hallway towards the elevators.

* * *

"Where are we going?" Sadie asked as she climbed into the rental car. Beau typed an address into the GPS and pulled out of the parking lot. Sadie had accomplished her goal. She had seen her father, even if it was only for a few minutes.

"Downtown. The Westin Hotel."

"Beau… the Westin? No! How about the Red Roof Inn at the airport? You need to get back to Nashville tomorrow, right?"

Beau turned to Sadie and shook his head. "No. I've never been to Seattle before. I think I'm going to stick around for a few days. Get you settled. Update our plan."

Sadie let out a huff. They crashed and burned tonight. Retreated from the battlefield to lick their wounds. It was time to draw up a new battle plan.

"One night at the Westin. I'll go to Juliette and Geoff's tomorrow. I can stay with them for a while. Get back on my feet. Get back to work. Make sure that my dad is okay in that institution. Joel might be a prick, but at least he paid for my dad's rent through September."

Beau pursed his lips together and held his tongue. He knew that now was probably not a good time to tell her that he had made arrangements with Joel in the study to cover James's expenses. He wanted Joel out of Sadie's life for good.

"Baby, now that you have seen your father, there is something I want to ask you. I know now is probably not the best time, but what about Nashville, Sadie Mae? What about us?"

Suddenly Sadie felt unsure about everything – about Nashville and her father. Everything in her life had flipped upside down tonight.

"You still want us, Beau? You still want me? God, you must think I am some piece of work. What did Joel call me... a slut... a whore... a cunt?"

Beau slammed on the brakes and pulled into the Taco Time parking lot. He took in a long deep breath keeping his hands on the steering wheel.

"Sadie Mae... you are none of those things. Do you hear me? Those are just words. Words from a desperate and heartbroken man. Do you know what I tell Patrick when kids at school say bad things to him? Sticks and stones may break my bones, but names will never harm me."

Sadie couldn't help but smile at Beau's southern charm, but she had heard her own father utter those words a time or two.

"Listen, I know you are hurting, baby. We talked about how this might go down, and you knew that this might happen, but it's over now. You and me... we are just beginning. Nothing that happened tonight and nothing that anyone said changes anything about the way I feel about you." Sadie turned to Beau and smiled. "Baby... do you want a taco? God, I am absolutely starving!"

Beau looked out the window and up at the neon Taco Time sign. Sadie chuckled and then stopped. It made the pain in her head radiate.

"No beans, okay? You'll have gas all night."

Beau let out a deep belly laugh and grabbed for her, but Sadie winced and pulled away.

"Jesus... baby."

Sadie slowly slid her sweater down from her shoulders, and Beau saw the red swollen marks of Joel's hands upon her upper arms.

"Sticks and stones," Sadie said.

"Fucking bastard," Beau spat out, unable to control his emotions.

"Shhhh. It's over now. Why don't you go get us some tacos? I feel a hot bath in my future."

Beau turned to her, reaching out to cup her face. "Sadie Mae, would it be okay if I kissed you?"

Sadie's eyes welled up with fresh tears as Beau leaned into her, rubbing his nose against hers.

"I thought you'd never ask?"

Beau took his time and let his lips brush up against hers. He waited for her to part her mouth and let out a soft moan before he slowly let his tongue dive inside her... in the parking lot of a fast-food restaurant.

CHAPTER ELEVEN

"**H**oly fucking shit!"

Juliette stood on her front porch and surveyed Sadie's face. The skin around her left eye and down to her cheekbone was purple and a light shade of blue.

"Beau Walker, Juliette Robertson," Sadie said. Juliette couldn't take her eyes off Sadie's face. Her mouth hung open as she turned her attention to Beau.

"I'm so sorry," Juliette extended her hand to Beau. "It's so nice to finally meet you. Come inside. Geoff's picking up Liam from soccer, and Lola had a sleepover. I just made a pot of coffee."

Sadie and Beau had just come from seeing her dad and Sadie had spoken with the director of admissions. James was adjusting, and they were easing his transition with some medication. Her dad seemed groggy and lethargic, but he was showered and dressed when they arrived. All three of them drank coffee in the cafeteria before James got restless and asked Beau to take him back to his job site. James thought he was working on a construction project and was anxious to punch the clock. It made Sadie's day, though... introducing her dad to Beau. The two talked fishing, college football, and building – James enthralled that Beau was an architect.

"I can't believe it. I never thought in a million years that Joel would hurt you... physically. Sadie, he could have killed you," Juliette said, lowering her voice as she peered into the living room where Lola was watching television. Geoff, Liam, and Beau were out in the backyard kicking around the soccer ball as Sadie filled her friend in on the last 24 hours.

"It's over now. I don't want to go there. I just need to get my shit together. Decide what to do."

"You mean about Nashville and Beau?" Juliette turned to watch Sadie nod her head. "You're moving, aren't you?"

Sadie could hear the sadness in Juliette's voice as her eyes welled up with tears. Sadie turned and quickly walked to the open patio door – breathing in the scent of the Puget Sound.

"I love him. I love Patrick. I can't be apart from them. Believe it or not, after all this shit with Joel that I drug Beau into… I think he still loves me! Jules, you love Nashville. It's not like I'm never coming back to Seattle," Sadie said as she walked over to Juliette and hugged her tight.

"You know you can stay here as long as you need to… Beau too. Take your time, Sadie, okay?"

"But that's just it, Jules. I've wasted so much time. I don't want to waste another day. It's time I stood up for myself and for what I want. Not a life that someone else wants me to live. My dad wouldn't want that."

Juliette let out a deep sigh and pulled Sadie close.

"Hey, Beau's not leaving for a few days, and I want to show him around town. Do some fun things with him. Put the drama of last night behind us," Sadie said enthusiastically. Juliette was relieved to see a sparkle in Sadie's big brown eyes.

"Okay, what do you have in mind, Sadie?"

"How would Geoff and Liam feel about fishing?"

* * *

"So… Beau's Seattle bucket list, huh?" he asked. Beau had returned to the kitchen to check in on Sadie, and she shared her ideas for the list with him. All Beau cared about was seeing Sadie smile. The stress with Joel and her dad was evident in her eyes and her body language, especially when he touched her.

"Yes! I've got a whole line up for tomorrow, just the two of us, but this morning, it's just you and the boys."

Sadie looked deep into Beau's eyes and then stretched up on her tippy toes to give him a quick peck.

"Oh… sorry to interrupt," Juliette exclaimed as she walked back into the kitchen, catching Beau and Sadie's quick kiss.

"Geoff's out gathering the fishing gear for you guys. He's going to take you to a beautiful spot along the Snoqualmie River, Beau."

Juliette poured herself another cup of coffee and brought the mug to her lips. She leaned against the kitchen counter and took in Sadie and Beau. Juliette had never seen Sadie so happy despite the trauma of last night. She had also never seen a man look at a woman the way Beau looked at Sadie. There was no doubt that they were in love.

"Wow… I am totally into that. That sounds great," Beau responded.

"Okay, then. Jules and I are packing up a cooler. If you catch some fish, we've got something for dinner, and if not, we are making a back-up plan."

Lola piped in from the living room. "You forgot to tell Beau about the cupcakes. Sadie and I are making vanilla cupcakes with chocolate frosting."

"Lola, that's my favorite. I'm looking forward to it. Don't worry about a back-up plan. I got you girls covered," Beau said with a wink, taking the cooler from Sadie's hands.

"Alright, then. Let's get the first item on Beau's Seattle bucket list ticked off."

* * *

The girls spent the day shopping and running errands, and Sadie was happy for the distraction. She hoped that Beau was lost somewhere along the river, erasing the memories of last night from his brain.

"So only two fish, huh?" Juliette barked with her hands on her hips. The boys had been gone since late morning and into the early afternoon and had just arrived back home. Sadie, Juliette, and Lola were in the kitchen, organizing dinner and making cupcakes.

"Yes. Liam caught the first, and Beau caught the biggest," Geoff said.

"And you caught…?"

"Four rib eyes at Metropolitan Market," he sheepishly replied.

"Where are the boys?" Sadie asked, turning her attention away from the cupcakes that she and Lola were frosting.

"Beau and Liam are finishing cleaning the fish and Beau's teaching him how to make a smoker. The kid is the new president of the Seattle chapter of Beau's fan club," Geoff said, laughing. "Liam's got a crush on him… damn, I've got a crush on him."

Sadie, Lola, and Juliette all started giggling about the time that Beau walked into the kitchen.

"Ewwww! I smell fish guts," Lola screamed, dropping her frosting bag and running from the kitchen.

"Hey, did you have a fun afternoon?" Sadie asked. As Beau got closer to her, she too smelled the aroma of dead fish.

"The best! Did you get everything on my grocery list?" Beau asked.

"Yes, I did!"

"Thank you, baby!"

Beau leaned in for a kiss, but Sadie wrinkled her nose and placed her hand in the middle of his firm chest. Taking the hint, Beau stepped away and leaned against the kitchen counter.

"So, it's okay with you girls if the boys take the appetizer and first course?"

Beau was planning on smoking enough trout to make smoked trout pâté on garlic toast points and a trout salad with Washington apples and pecans.

"Beau, your menu sounds wonderful... but I have to tell you something. You stink!" Sadie exclaimed.

"I guess I could use a shower."

Sadie cupped Beau's ruddy cheeks in her hands and nodded her head.

"Whoa! You need a cold beer, first," Geoff exclaimed. Beau watched as his new friend threw the steaks in the refrigerator and took out two cold beers.

"This is from the 15 best Washington beers to drink before you die list. I'm going to start you out light, and we'll move our way up. Here is a Big Al Rat City Blonde. It's got subtle malt sweetness and a mild hoppy flavor. Cheers, man. Welcome to Seattle!"

Beau was humbled. Sadie talked about Juliette and Geoff, but Sadie had also filled Beau in on her sterile life with Joel. He was nervous about meeting her friends and genuinely fitting in.

"Thank you... both of you for hosting us and taking care of Sadie. I know she will be in good hands... safe when I head back to Nashville," Beau said, taking a long swig of beer.

"Let me take you downstairs. Show you where our room is. We'll be back," Sadie said with a wink at Juliette. She clutched Beau's hand as they headed for the stairs.

"You guys take your time. We will have happy hour on the patio around five." Juliette winked back at Sadie as she watched her lead Beau downstairs to the guest room.

Beau watched Sadie as she gathered her toiletry bag from her tote and walked into the bathroom. He sat on the edge of the bed and took a deep breath as he heard Sadie start the shower. Beau wanted to go to her, but he was unsure.

Sadie let the steam fill up the bathroom as the shower got hot. She approached Beau, and he stood up, kissing her gently and slowly while remaining cautious. Sadie pulled away and slid her jeans off her hips and lifted her t-shirt over her head. Beau couldn't help but notice the bruises on her upper arms, and it tore his gut open. She turned slowly, but Beau saw the corner of her mouth upturned.

"Can you unhook my bra?"

Sadie winced as Beau grabbed the clasp. It was smack dab in the middle of a series of bruises that ran down her spine. Sadie let her bra fall to the floor, and Beau put his hands on her hips and slid her lace panties off her hips, watching her walk naked to the bathroom and into the shower.

They hadn't made love since Nashville. Sadie was still mentally fragile and physically battered. He held her in bed last night while she fought sleep... waking up several times from nightmares. Beau cradled her delicate naked body next to his and gave her the comfort that she needed. He had barely slept a wink... wondering all night why he hadn't beat the shit out of Joel.

Beau desperately wanted her as they laid together and let the morning light fill up the hotel room, but he didn't want to hurt her – the pain of the bruises making her uncomfortable. It was a constant reminder of where Joel had repeatedly pushed her into the doorframe, and Beau felt the guilt at having not reached her in time.

In the guest shower at Juliette's, Beau still wasn't sure if Sadie was ready, but he slowly walked into the bathroom to join her. He stood at the edge of the shower and watched the water cascading down her hair and all over her body. There was no doubt that he needed a shower, but Beau needed Sadie as well, and he wasn't sure if he could resist her much longer. He pulled off his cargo shorts and underwear and discarded his black t-shirt and stood before her in the shower.

Beau took a step closer to her and watched her nipples hardened by his gentle touch. Sadie reached up, circled his neck with her arms, and drew him into a soft peck, laughing. It was her subtle way of letting him know that she was a willing participant. What started as an innocent kiss, turned into a deep hunger. Their lips melted into one as Sadie's tongue went in search of his. As she sucked on his bottom lip, a moan escaped from deep inside Beau's throat.

Suddenly, Beau grabbed Sadie's hips and pulled her close, and she felt him hardening against her belly.

"Turn around."

Sadie's voice was husky and demanding, and Beau did what he was told. He turned his back to her, and Sadie grabbed a washcloth and poured body wash onto it, gently gliding it over his shoulders first and then down his back. She stepped aside and let the hot water rinse the soap off before placing her lips against his skin and giving him little kisses down his spine.

Sadie walked around Beau to face him and placed her hand on his chest as he took two steps back into the water. He tipped his head back, wetting his hair, letting the water run down his face, neck, and chest. Sadie started washing Beau's front. His face was serious, and his eyes zoned in on Sadie's ample breasts. He could never get enough of her breasts. They were round and perfect, and all his and Beau leaned down into her, his mouth open and longing. He wanted them in his mouth to suck and nibble on, but Sadie threw her hand up.

"No!"

"Baby, please…" Beau responded.

"Shhhh… I want to take my time and take it slow… let you admire the view. I just want to wash you now."

Beau was instantly lost in her smile and in her need for control.

Sadie poured more body wash onto the washcloth and knelt, running her hand down the outside of Beau's muscular thigh to balance herself. She gently ran the soapy cloth down his leg and over the top of his foot and then carefully between his toes, which Beau wiggled for her.

"That tickles," Beau said. Sadie looked up and into his smoldering smoky eyes but not before stopping to admire his erection. She let out a snicker before continuing onto his other leg.

When Sadie finished the front of Beau's legs, she asked him to turn around, and she ran her hands up the back of each leg, scrubbing the washcloth over his firm calves up past the backs of his knees and over the firm cheeks of his ass.

She quickly rinsed him off and then carefully folded the washcloth and knelt on it, lifting her body up to cup Beau's backside... planting soft kisses over each cheek. Her hands moved around Beau's hips, hugging him tight as she turned her head, pressing it against him. Sadie ran her hands around until she found what she was searching for, slowing slightly to run her fingers through the mound of hair that surrounded him.

"Turn around, please," Sadie commanded, and Beau immediately complied.

After admiring the full length of his powerful physique, Sadie was desperate to taste him. She wanted him to lose control, relax into her, and finally feel his release. She grabbed him and guided him into her mouth, a moan escaping his lips. Sadie could feel him giving into her as he leaned against the shower wall to brace himself.

Feathery strokes of her tongue traced from his base to the tip... drawing circles around the head over and over again. As she absorbed the feel of him, Beau's body surged into her, and Sadie took him deeper inside her mouth. She reached up and grabbed Beau's ass, digging her fingertips gently into each cheek.

Beau was losing his grip... losing control as he called out... half-spoken profanities mixed in with grunts and moans and a light whisper of her name – his hands tangled in Sadie's hair. Beau was careful not to force him into her, and he let her remain in complete control. Her movements delicate and deliberate.

"Baby... that feels so good."

Sensing Beau's final surrender, Sadie flicked her tongue over the tip and placed her hands around the base... twisting and turning. Beau lifted his hands to his mouth to squelch a scream.

"Please don't stop... baby... oh god... I'm going to come."

Sadie could feel Beau's legs shaking with hers as he began to quiver and tense up in her mouth. She relaxed and continued to stroke his base when he exploded... showering himself down upon her mouth and chin, then over her chest.

"Fuck! Oh, god... baby."

Sadie let Beau savor the moment as he stepped back into the shower. Sadie abruptly stood, and Beau reached out for her, wrapping his arms around her and turning her towards the shower stream, so the last of the hot water flowed down upon her.

"I didn't hurt you, did I? I just... lost control." Beau's voice was barely a whisper. Sadie moaned as his lips brush across her cheek and down her neck then finally resting at the curve of her collarbone.

"Don't be silly. I love taking you in my mouth. God, you taste amazing, lover." Sadie looked up at him, and he could see her eyes were still on fire.

"I didn't want you to stop. Baby, when you do that to me... you are so incredible."

Sadie giggled and then grabbed for her washcloth. "Will you help me wash my hair before the water turns cold."

Sadie spun around, and Beau lathered up her hair, quickly... digging his fingers into her scalp to massage her.

Sadie was pleased with herself. Satisfying Beau like that gave her a warm afterglow. She loved seeing him so fulfilled by her and so happy.

Beau kissed Sadie's forehead and turned off the shower grabbing a thick bath towel, wrapping it carefully around her back and shoulders.

He quickly drew Sadie to the bed sitting on the edge and carefully drying her off, running the towel gingerly over her battered arms. Beau leaned forward, prepared to take her breast in his mouth when Sadie pulled away.

"We should get dressed… or else, we will be in here all night."

Beau looked up at her and caught her doe eyes looking back at him. He pulled Sadie close again, and as his lips brushed against hers, she let out a soft sigh.

"Baby, I didn't pack a lot. A few t-shirts. One button-down shirt. A pair of shorts and a pair of jeans."

Sadie left his embrace and tied her towel around her chest as Beau rifled through his backpack.

"Perfect! Juliette will be in a pair of Lululemon black leggings and a t-shirt, her signature outfit. Geoff will be in tan or black shorts and also a t-shirt. I think you can relate. Beau, these are my friends. Plain vanilla everyday people."

Beau watched as Sadie toweled off her hair and headed back into the bathroom.

"Baby, will you excuse me."

Beau quickly pulled on a pair of shorts and a gray t-shirt. His hair was wet, and his face and chest still flushed from his orgasm.

"I want to Facetime with Patrick. I told Hannah I would call about seven o'clock Nashville time."

Sadie had forgotten… caught up in the last 24 hours.

Patrick.

Beau was missing out on potential time with his son because of her and a pang of guilt shot through her stomach.

"Yes, of course. Beau, I am so sorry. With everything that has been going on, I totally forgot about... wait... I have some more photos... of Max. Let me grab my phone."

"I'll get them later. He loves what you've taken so far... it's just that... he doesn't know I am with you. Hannah and I thought, well. Not knowing what might transpire, we figured it was best to tell him that I had to go out of town for a few days. I'm going to see him when I get back."

"Yes... absolutely. I understand."

What Sadie meant to say was that she was trying to understand. How do you explain last night to a five-year-old child? You simply don't. You shelter children from the horror of last night. Sadie shuttered, wondering what Beau might have told Hannah about Seattle... about his fears about following her out west. Sadie wondered what the rest of Beau's family would think and if she was worthy of Beau and Patrick after what she put them through.

"What about George?" Sadie was just as concerned about the dog as she was Patrick.

"Mac and Mazie have George. It's all good, baby... I promise."

Sadie took a deep breath and smiled at Beau.

"I'll meet you upstairs, okay?"

Sadie nodded her head and then watched as Beau grabbed his phone and headed out the door.

* * *

"Okay... so how do y'all know each other?" Beau asked as the four adults sat on Juliette and Geoff's patio, watching the late August sun fall west across the sound.

Geoff and Juliette lived in one of the most beautiful places in all of Seattle, Beach Drive in West Seattle near Me-Kwa-Mooks Park. Their three-story house sat across the road from the water but with an unobstructed view of the Puget Sound and the Olympic mountains. The entry-level of their home had a large patio courtyard with a round teak table and several ruby red patio umbrellas. All year round, Geoff and Juliette had a front-row seat to the most spectacular sunsets in all of Seattle.

The house was modest, with Juliette's office and photography studio, including a darkroom in the basement, along with laundry and the guest bedroom and shower where Sadie and Beau were staying. On the main level was a huge great room with a formal dining room, kitchen, and a family room, and upstairs were four additional bedrooms... one of which served as Geoff's office. As a partner in a law firm specializing in estate planning, Geoff worked long hours, but both he and Juliette had the luxury of working from home while the kids were still young.

"Sadie, you tell part one, and I'll tell part two," Juliette squealed.

Sadie shook her head and turned towards Beau just as Geoff handed him the second beer on the best Washington beers to drink before you die list, a Manny's Pale Ale. The girls topped off their glasses, savoring a caber-net before Sadie began the story.

"Juliette and I met the first day of middle school. She was posh... hung with the *in crowd*, and I was the girl from across the tracks. My dad and I went school clothes shopping at Goodwill," Sadie said as she shrugged her shoulders and took a sip of her wine.

"Hey... I still buy my jeans at Goodwill, Sadie, just saying."

Juliette clinked her glass next to Sadie's and reached out to affection-ately slap her upper leg.

"Anyway... some of Juliette's super-rich friends were bullying me, and she came to my rescue."

Beau caught the way that Sadie looked at Juliette. He knew that leav-ing Seattle was going to be hard on her. Juliette was more than just a friend, she was like Sadie's sister.

"Sadie just looked like a lost puppy dog that needed love… a haircut and some lip-gloss! I scooped her up and took her home, and the rest is history," Juliette said with a giggle.

"Hey… not so fast," Geoff interjected. "Beau asked about me as well."

Juliette rolled her eyes at her husband and continued. "Yes, so Sadie and I were friends all through high school. I went off to the University of Washington and met Geoff junior year. It was love at first sight!" Juliette said, swooning. She then clutched her throat and pretended to choke.

"We were together for two years and then ne dumped me. Geoff broke my heart," Juliette said as her voice grew heavy.

Geoff rolled his eyes and cut in. "In my defense… Juliette was wild. I tried to tame her. I couldn't. I wasn't man enough to handle her. I needed to leave her wild. I needed to sow my oats, then see what was left of me… you know, for her." Geoff smiled as he finished speaking and then took a swig of his beer.

"And you did just that, didn't you lover? Geoff went out and got himself engaged… within like three months of breaking up with me. Fuck! I thought I was going to die when I heard. And that was it… or so I thought."

Juliette looked over at Sadie and nodded, and it was then Sadie's turn to take back over the story.

"So, I hadn't moved in with Joel yet… and Juliette called me one night and asked me if I would look after her apartment for a few weeks in the summer. I think this was about two years after you guys broke up? Juliette was heading off to Beijing, China for the summer Olympics, and so she asked me to move into her place." Sadie took a sip of wine, and Juliette jumped back into telling the story.

"So… Sadie came over with a joint of killer weed and a bottle of rosé and basically moved in the night before I left for China. We were laughing… stoned off our ass and getting shitfaced on cheap wine. I am packing photographic materials and thousands of dollars in camera equipment all while eating Pringles for dinner. Then we heard a knock on my door."

Both girls laughed and then looked at Geoff who was taking the last sip of his beer.

"I hadn't laid eyes on him in almost two years. The last I heard anything about him... he was engaged. He didn't know if I was married, pregnant or even living in the same apartment."

"Hey, I looked at the mailboxes before I knocked, and I saw your name," Geoff smirked and began peeling the label off his beer bottle.

"But there he was... the love of my life, Geoff Robertson. He was standing in front of me on my doormat... looking like the cat that ate the canary. But I just knew."

Beau saw the tears in Juliette's eyes as she spoke. He thought of his own love story... the one he was creating with Sadie.

"So, Jules invites Geoff in. He eats the rest of our Pringles and finishes off the rest of our wine and the two of them had sex all night long. Fuck! I thought I was going to kill myself. You guys were so obnoxiously loud," Sadie said while laughing.

"And the next day, I left for China. Geoff woke up in my bed, and I was gone... Sadie?" Juliette turned towards Sadie, nodding her head.

"He fucking freaked out! Shit... did you hyperventilate, dude? Like didn't I almost call an ambulance?" Geoff shook his head from side to side. "It took me hours to get you out of the apartment, Geoff."

"You're so funny, Sadie. Beau... Sadie exaggerates. Watch yourself, okay?"

"Seriously, Beau... Geoff wrote me an e-mail every day while I was in China. Some serious sappy shit. Long, drawn-out dissertations of his feelings the last two years. How he loved me... never stopped. He wrote poems, and essays. Didn't you write a Broadway play about us?"

"No, Juliette... it was a musical!" Geoff announced.

The girls doubled over in laughter, and Sadie had to wipe tears from her eyes.

"I arrived back in Seattle, and Geoff was waiting in the international arrivals lounge with a dozen red roses and a diamond ring," Juliette said as she turned and smiled at her husband.

"I got down on one knee and proposed. Best thing I ever did."

Geoff leaned over and kissed Juliette on the lips, and Beau had no doubt that he meant every word.

"So… two weeks later, Jules and Geoff got married at the court-house in downtown Seattle, and I was their witness and best person! End of story," Sadie said, as all four of them clinked their glasses together before Juliette interjected.

"Well… seven and a half months later, Liam was born!" she said while blushing.

"Yes, but sweetheart… I proposed before we knew about the baby, right?"

"I thought it was a stomach virus from China. Ugh! I was sicker than a dog," Juliette said, burying her face in her hands.

"Guys, that's the best story. Cheers!" Beau tipped his beer back and finished it.

"Okay, who is ready for smoked trout?"

"And our third beer, Beau!"

"Heck ya!"

* * *

Beau watched Sadie fall asleep, as he gently curled his body next to hers. After dinner… cupcakes and copious amounts of wine, Beau finally took Sadie to bed. He had taken his time to please her, and when he was sure that she was ready, he finally succumbed and climaxed with her. Beau was just glad that he had something left to give her. A few minutes before he dozed off, he heard her softly snoring.

The next morning, they laid in each other's arms as the sun rose. It was Beau's last day in Seattle, and Sadie was prepared to make it extra special.

"Hey, you... how did you sleep?" Beau asked.

The bruising around Sadie's eye was lighter, and he brushed the bangs out of her eyes and kissed her lips before letting her respond.

"I slept well, No... um, bad dreams. Let's get going, okay? We have a big day planned. I'll fry us up some bacon. Geoff's at work and the kids are at camp. Juliette mentioned she would be in and out... so we have the house pretty much to ourselves."

Beau thought back to yesterday's shower and seriously thought of asking Sadie for a repeat performance, but he knew that she wanted to show him Seattle.

"You don't mind driving, do you? Geoff locked my car in the garage in the alley out back, and I forgot to ask for his key."

Beau nodded his head and reached out to cradle her in his arms. "Sure... but first... um...baby, we need to talk. I need to tell you something," Beau said as he pulled himself up in bed.

"I need coffee first, okay?"

Beau watched as Sadie pulled on a pair of sweatpants and his gray t-shirt. It didn't take her long to return with two mugs of coffee.

"Okay... I'm ready. Fire away!" Sadie smiled. Given what she had been through and knowing how Beau felt about her, she was ready for just about anything. She pulled the covers around her and turned to face Beau.

"I wired Joel $6,000 yesterday afternoon... on our way to the river... to pay for your dad's care."

"You what? Beau? Why?" Sadie set her mug on the bedside table and let Beau continue.

"I couldn't handle him controlling you anymore… holding anything over your head. I wanted it to end… yesterday. It needed to be over… for me, anyway. I'd never be able to move forward knowing that bastard still held strings to you… and James. He agreed to give me a voided check, and with that information, I wired him the money. It's over. You're free of him."

Beau took a sip of coffee and waited for Sadie's response. He watched as the weight seemed to fall off her shoulders, and a sparkle of light filled her eyes.

"I don't know what to say. Thank you. I'll pay you back… right away." Sadie suddenly seemed small, like an innocent child.

"If that's what you want, baby. I just don't want you worrying about it, okay?"

Sadie had the money, but she wanted to be cautious. She'd been adding up the moving costs and budgeting the best she could with her father's money. The charge for the West Seattle facility hadn't even been considered. She reached for Beau's hand and squeezed it.

"Okay, then. Let's get cleaned up. I want to take you to the top of the space needle."

Beau watched as Sadie leaped out of bed.

"But first, Beau… how about you and I take a quick shower?"

* * *

Beau looked over Sadie's shoulder and out onto the Puget Sound. They were sitting at a picnic table at Old Stove Brewing Company nestled inside Pike Place Market. Sadie had taken Beau on the big Ferris wheel along the waterfront and up to the top of the space needle where they had lunch at the Atmos Wine Bar. To end their day, they walked around her favorite farmer's market, Pike Place, and then stopped off for happy hour at the brewery and to try more local beer, which Beau couldn't get enough of.

"Beau… about Nashville."

He had been waiting… patiently for her to bring it up. He knew sooner or later that before the sun had set on their Seattle bucket list day, Sadie would have to talk about the timeline of their future.

"My conversation with the director yesterday… about my dad… it was good. I like the facility. I mean, it's old and doesn't have a lot of access to the outdoors, but they have outings… to parks, which will suit him. There is also a courtyard where he can putter… build his airplanes and birdhouses. He will be safe there. Well taken care of… until… we get a call from Tall Oaks Manor."

Beau let out a heavy sigh and smiled… the biggest smile that Sadie had ever seen on his face.

"You're coming home with me tomorrow, then?"

"Um… not that fast, I'm afraid. Listen, while you chatted with Patrick this morning, I called my boss and put in my two weeks' notice. It was the least that I could do. Work has been so generous with me… about my dad, especially when I've needed time off. My boss was upset. He begged me to stay on. The good news is, we are understaffed in compliance, and he's offered me a position as a reviewer, which I can do remotely in Nashville. I have to be able to pay some of my way. I also want to pay you back and get some money together for transferring my dad."

Beau listened intently and then nodded his head. He knew that Sadie would continue to fight him on any money that he offered up.

"I've got to take care of a few things here. For one, I have a brand-new leased vehicle. I need to find out how much it will cost to transport it across the country. It has to be less than breaking the lease and returning the vehicle, and since I don't have that many personal possessions, what I have will fit nicely in my trunk. That solves the issue of shipping anything back to Nashville."

Beau couldn't stop smiling, listening to Sadie's plan. She had it all figured out.

"How long then... until you come home?"

Sadie picked up her Streaker summer ale and brought it to her lips. The late summer sunshine picked up the gold and auburn in her hair, and Beau reached out and touched the soft strands that framed her face.

"Oh... see... that's the best part. I already booked my ticket."

"You what?" Beau exclaimed.

"I'll be back in Nashville, two weeks from tomorrow. Listen, I know it's a Saturday and if you have Patrick... don't worry about me... I can get an Uber from...."

Sadie didn't have a chance to get all her words out before Beau grabbed her and picked her up... spinning them around. She heard him faintly crying in her ear – the side of her face wet with his tears.

"Oh my god, Beau. Put me down! You're making a scene."

Beau continued to hold her tight, stifling his tears in Sadie's ear.

"I'm s'ited, Sadie Mae."

"I'm s'ited too, Beau."

CHAPTER TWELVE

"Something smells wonderful."

Beau walked into the loft and made a beeline for Sadie. She'd been back in Nashville less than a week, and Beau hadn't taken the smile off his face. Even when sleeping, Sadie swore that one side of his mouth was upturned.

Sadie was home to stay in Nashville, and despite having to leave her father behind, which Beau knew tore her heart open, she was now his, and he would move heaven and earth to reunite her with her father as soon as possible.

"Baby, I am so sorry I am late."

Beau dropped his messenger bag and blueprint tubes on the couch and took her in his arms. If Beau greeted Sadie like this every time he worked late, she would never complain.

"It's just tacos… pretty simple."

Beau kissed Sadie's neck. He then reached behind her, took her open beer bottle off the kitchen counter, and took a sneaky swig.

"You know I could get used to this, Sadie Mae."

"What? Stealing my beer?"

Sadie playfully swatted Beau's butt with a kitchen towel in an attempt to reclaim her beer.

"No! Sharing a beer... my dog... my son, but mostly... my bed!" Beau said with a chuckle. He brought the beer bottle to his lips again and took another long gulp.

"You are insatiable... you know that, right?" Beau nodded his head in response. "Man, I am one lucky girl."

With Sadie not working and Beau's flexible schedule, they had been spending late nights out on the patio drinking wine and talking and then inside the loft... all over the loft, making love night and day.

Sadie hit the ground running in Nashville, while slowly wrapping her mind around the fact that this was her new home – the loft, Beau, Patrick, and George.

The two weeks apart after Beau came home from Seattle had been productive for him too, preparing Patrick for the changes in their life and doing little things to make Sadie feel welcome. Beau even built a shelf in the bedroom closet for her to store more of her shoes, clothes, and personal items.

Since Sadie had officially moved in, Beau welcomed her personal and feminine touches, including buying a few house plants and new cushions for the outside patio furniture... not to mention, she was one hell of a cook.

"So, I have some news."

Sadie was thrilled to tell Beau that her ex-boss from Seattle had worked out all the details and e-mailed her dozens of files to audit. The pay sucked, but at least Sadie would be working, and she would have health insurance and benefits for the foreseeable future. Before she left Seattle, she managed to get enough hours to complete her land appraising certificate. Still, it would be weeks before the certificate was activated. With the land certification and the transfer of her appraiser's licenses to Tennessee, Sadie could find a much better and higher paying job.

"Baby, that's fantastic. I know how much you want to work and get some money saved up. This sounds perfect."

"Well, I am glad that you are pleased."

Beau continued to nod his approval. Although he would never tell Sadie, he didn't much care if she worked, and he was thrilled to have her around to help out with Patrick and George. He'd made subtle references to Lady Jane never working, but he was careful. Sadie was a modern and independent woman, and Beau wasn't out to change her.

"Um... so... I have some news too."

Since Beau had pretty much polished off Sadie's beer, he walked over to the refrigerator and grabbed another.

"I just found out that I need to fly to Memphis tomorrow. Sebastian wants me to pitch to a client in person. Our flight is at 7:30 in the morning, but I couldn't get a flight home until late evening."

Tomorrow was Wednesday. Beau's standing dinner date with Patrick, Hannah, and Ryan, and Sadie knew that Beau must be disappointed to miss a night with his son. He had mentioned to her that it might be time for Sadie's gradual initiation into the weekly dinners.

"Oh, okay... so no Wednesday night dinner with Patrick? I'll call Mazie... see if they want some company."

Sadie shrugged her shoulders and gave the taco meat a quick stir. She never wanted to be clingy, and she didn't want Beau thinking that she would be upset if he had to work late, travel, or even spend some one-on-one time with his son.

"Actually... I could use a favor, Sadie. See... Hannah and Ryan have concert tickets at Bridgestone Arena for tomorrow night. I totally forgot. She asked me weeks ago to take Patrick overnight. I don't want to let her down. So, can you keep an eye on him for a few hours until I get back?"

The way Beau was looking at Sadie made her question if he thought she could do it.

"Hannah will drop him off at five o'clock. There is a ton of stuff in the freezer that he can eat for dinner. I'll be home by nine at the latest. Just help him with bedtime, read him a story, and if he fights you on going to bed before I get home, just pop a DVD in, and he'll crash on the couch with George. Sound doable?"

Sadie's expression was blank as she shook her head up and down. It would be the first time that Sadie would be left alone with Patrick for longer than a quick walk with George or a run to the grocery store. Although Sadie and Patrick got along very well, even better than Sadie could have imagined this early in their relationship, she was still nervous about taking care of Patrick on her own.

"Hannah's okay with all this?" Sadie asked. She stepped away from the stove and grabbed Beau's beer.

"She's totally okay with it. I'm okay with it, and Patrick is okay with it, but Sadie Mae, are you okay with it?" Sadie hesitated and then smiled.

"Of course, Beau. I'll look after Patrick. I'm okay with it."

Beau had just entrusted Sadie with his most precious possession, and she was practically walking on air.

* * *

"You mind your manners, young man. You hear me?" Sadie clutched Patrick's hand tightly as Hannah waved goodbye and blew kisses from the car window.

"Sadie don't hesitate to text me… if something comes up, okay?" Hannah seemed fairly relaxed to be handing her son over to Sadie.

"Oh, we will be fine. Beau will be home in a few hours," Sadie calmly replied as both she and Patrick watched Hannah and Ryan pulled away from the loft.

"Let's go see what George is up to Patrick. He's been missing you."

Sadie kept a tight grip on Patrick's hand until they got inside the building and into the elevator.

"I'm hungry!" Patrick yelled out as he played with George on the living room floor. Sadie poured herself an iced tea and looked down at her checklist. Dinner was the first item at the top of the list.

"Okay, I've got a ton of suggestions for you. Your dad left the freezer full of all your favorites."

"Like what?"

"Well, he left some fresh frog legs and lizard eyeballs. I've already taken them out to defrost." Sadie said with a straight face. She watched as Patrick rolled around on the floor, making gagging noises.

"No, Sadie Mae! I don't want to eat that. Are you serious?"

"Ummm... well. I did see a package of moose brains and alligator toes. How does that sound?"

Sadie threw herself down on the floor next to Patrick and started tickling him. His laugh was infectious. She suddenly stopped when her cell phone rang.

"Patrick... it's your dad," she said, sliding her finger across her phone.

"Dad... dad... Sadie is going to feed me alligator toes and lizard eyeballs for dinner. Please tell her no, okay." Sadie couldn't help laughing, watching Patrick on the phone with his father. She could hear Beau's reassuring voice telling his son that Sadie was only teasing him. Patrick handed Sadie her phone and ran into his bedroom to put away his backpack and retrieve his Matchbox cars when Sadie heard Beau clear his throat.

"Alligator toes and lizard eyeballs, Sadie Mae?"

"Yum... two of my all-time favorites."

"How you two gettin' along?" Beau asked.

Sadie thought it was cute that Beau was checking in on them so soon. He knew that Patrick had only been in the loft with her alone for less than 10 minutes.

"So far, so good... but I'd better get going. Patrick's hungry, and I've got to get the lizard eyeballs in the saucepan," Sadie said with a chuckle.

Beau could see her standing there in the loft – tucking her hair behind her ear. She was most likely barefoot with a V-neck t-shirt on and that faded pair of jeans that made her ass look delicious. Sadie loved to turn the wireless music system on to Sirius XM – *The Highway* playing her new favorite country songs.

"I love you, baby... thank you."

"For what?"

"For loving my son and taking care of him. It's a lot to ask. You've never once batted an eyelash... about him."

Patrick tore out of his bedroom, Matchbox cars flying all over the loft floor. "Sadie Mae... tonight we are going to make the biggest car track, ever!"

"Hey, Beau... I've got to go. Patrick wants to set up his Matchbox track, and I seriously need to get dinner going."

"Okay. We are headed to the airport in 30 minutes. I'll text you from the gate."

With their conversation over, Sadie went back into the kitchen to tackle the second item on her list.

"Chef Patrick... I need your assistance, please. Let's start with a cocktail!"

Patrick didn't hesitate. He grabbed his stool and joined Sadie in the kitchen.

"How about a Beach Sunset?" Sadie asked.

Patrick's eyes were as big as saucers as Sadie opened up the refrigerator.

"Wow... what's that?"

"Well... it's orange juice, 7UP, a splash of grenadine and a cherry on top," Sadie exclaimed. "It's going to look just like the sky at sunset."

Patrick threw his hands in the air and danced around on his stool.

"Careful, okay."

Sadie gathered all the ingredients, including the blender and her, and Patrick made their cocktails and sipped them out of their superhero cups with fancy straws that Sadie picked up at the dollar store.

"Sadie, this is way better than dad's purple stinger."

Sadie high-fived herself. This parenting thing was a piece of cake... a breeze. She was actually enjoying herself and felt calm and in control.

"Okay... dinner. Dad left us with a choice of hot dogs, dinosaur chicken bites, or mac and cheese."

Sadie was grateful she had leftover taco meat to put on a bed of salad greens. She'd eaten more hot dogs since coming to Nashville than she'd ever had in her life.

"I want pizza!" Patrick yelled. He looked up at Sadie, who was holding the freezer door open, searching for frozen pizza.

"Buddy, I don't see any frozen pizza. I'm sorry," Sadie responded as Patrick hit the palm of his hand on his forehead.

"No, Sadie... it isn't in there. You find the picture on your phone, and they bring it right to the front door."

"Oh, you want a pizza delivered. Why not? Beau does it all the time." Sadie mumbled to herself. She was relieved. She would have them include a Caesar salad, and she wouldn't even have to prepare a thing.

"Can you wait that long... starvin' Marvin? It might take thirty minutes?" Patrick shook his head up and down and flopped down on the floor to start his racetrack as Sadie pulled up the app on her phone and ordered the pizza.

They sat out on the patio table and devoured dinner as the sun dipped low in the sky. Patrick ate two pieces and started on a third, which Sadie and George ultimately finished before resuming his cars and racetrack. After dinner, Sadie noticed that Patrick was unusually quiet. They played on the floor for a while, and then he asked her if he could put on a DVD of *Paw Patrol*, quickly losing interest in his toys. After they picked up the racetrack, Patrick climbed up on the couch with George, and they snuggled under a blanket while Sadie read a book.

"No shower tonight, but let's wash our face, brush our teeth and get our pajamas on, okay."

Patrick seemed disinterested in any of those activities, so Sadie had to be flexible with the bedtime countdown, just as Beau had warned her. She finally asked Patrick to help her set the alarm on her phone to the Batman theme song, and once the song came on, she told him it would be time for all superheroes to get ready for bed.

Sadie grabbed Patrick's pajamas out of his drawer, went into the downstairs bathroom, pulled out his stool, and let the water run warm in the sink as she grabbed a washcloth.

"Patrick... you ready? Let's wash up, and then we can have story time." Sadie listened but heard nothing from the boy.

She had just walked out of the bathroom when she noticed that Patrick was standing just outside his bedroom with his pajama bottoms on but no top. He looked up at her with tears in his eyes, took two steps towards her and opened up his mouth. Projectile vomit spilled out onto the wood floor as Sadie gasped.

"Oh... my god. Patrick!"

He bent over slightly before another forceful gush of vomit flew out of his mouth and onto the bottoms of Sadie's jeans. It splashed across the tops of her bare feet, and George jumped up from his dog bed to investigate and began licking the vomit off the floor.

"George... no! Stop it... bad dog!"

Sadie grabbed Patrick and ran into the bathroom. The look on his face broke her heart when he whispered in a raspy voice that he was sorry. Patrick heaved one more time, luckily into the toilet as Sadie held onto him for dear life. He clung to her as she flushed the toilet and sat down on his stool. They were both covered in sour barf.

"Oh, sweet boy. Let's get you cleaned up, okay?"

Sadie grabbed the warm washcloth and wiped off Patrick's face and chest, but she realized that he was entirely covered in vomit. The smell made her gag as she stripped off his pajama bottoms.

"Sit here, okay."

Sadie placed Patrick on his stepping stool and turned to start the shower.

"Do you still feel sick?"

Patrick looked up at her and shook his head from side to side. Sadie couldn't imagine that there would be anything left in his stomach, but she wanted to make sure.

Once the water was warm, she slipped off her jeans and held Patrick in her arms and walked them both into the shower. She set Patrick down, sat on the shower floor, grabbed the soap, and carefully lathered him up, washing his hair with calming lavender shampoo. Sadie's t-shirt, bra, and undies were soaking wet as she reached up to turn off the water and grab them both a towel.

"Can you walk into your room and go sit on your bed?"

Patrick shook his head, and once he was out of sight, Sadie took off her wet clothes and left them in a pile on the bathroom floor. She opened the dryer and pulled out a pair of Beau's sweatpants and an old t-shirt and quickly put them on.

"How are you doing?"

Sadie knelt in front of Patrick and dried him off, grabbing a clean pair of pajamas out of his drawer.

"I threw up."

Patrick still had tears in his eyes, and Sadie kissed the top of his forehead.

"It happens… no big deal. I'm just sorry that you don't feel well. Is there anything that I can do to make you feel better?"

Patrick thought for a moment before shaking his head up and down.

"When I am sick mama rubs my tummy and sings to me."

It sounded simple enough, but Sadie was no singer. She imagined that Hannah's voice sounded like a choir of heavenly angels compared to her voice – alley cat in heat.

"Okay, let's get you tucked in."

Sadie cradled Patrick in her arms and rocked him gently to sleep. She prayed that he would sleep through the night and not be sick again. There was no thought of cleaning up the mess. She'd deal with it later. For now, her only job was comforting the sick boy. Sadie took back everything she said about parenthood being a piece of cake… a breeze. Tonight, a hurricane blew through the loft and threw Sadie on her ass.

* * *

George jumped up from his dog bed as Beau quietly opened up the front door to the loft. He heard Sadie singing softly and tiptoed inside before letting out a loud gasp.

"What the fuck?"

Beau caught sight of Sadie – Patrick curled up tight against her in his bed. The smell of vomit filled the loft.

"Shhhh." Sadie put her finger up to her lips as Beau surveyed the carnage.

He watched as Sadie kissed Patrick's forehead and gently laid him down and pulled the covers around his body before slowly extricating herself from the bed.

Sadie stood before him a disheveled mess. She was holding Beau's sweatpants up from falling around her ankles. Sadie's hair was damp and pulled back away from her face, and as she drew closer to him, Beau caught her scent – sour and vile.

"Welcome home. How was Memphis?"

Sadie couldn't help but laugh, and Beau reached out and ran his hand down her arm.

"You look like shit, baby."

"Really? Projectile vomiting apparently does that to you."

Sadie bit her lip. She didn't want to disappoint him, but she just wanted to sit in a heap on the floor and cry.

"Beau, he was so sick. I felt so bad for him. I did the best I could."

Sadie fought back her tears. Perhaps she was too old and inexperienced for parenting. Sadie felt like a failure.

"What can I do?"

"Well… it appears that your dog has already started cleaning up. Shit, Beau… I think George ate some vomit."

"He's eaten worse. Let me clean up the floor, and you go get a shower. Did he throw up anyplace else?"

"No… just pretty much all over here." Sadie threw her arms open and laughed. She had never seen someone so small produce so much vomit.

"Shit, Sadie Mae… I am so sorry."

"No, it's my fault. Patrick begged for pizza, and I caved. It was probably too rich for him."

Beau saw the tears in her eyes, and it broke his heart. "Baby, that kid eats pizza once a week. He loves it. He did not get sick because you fed him pizza. He got sick because kids are germ incubators. He's just started school, and the flu is running rampant. Hey, at least he threw up on the wood floor. Last time it was in his bed, and it came out of both ends. When sheets are involved... it's nasty!"

"Oh, so he's done this before?" Sadie asked incredulously.

Beau just laughed and shook his head up and down. There was no need to fill Sadie in on all the disgusting tasks of a parent. He'd tried to focus on all the good the past few months. Perhaps he had done Sadie a disservice.

"Welcome to the puke palace."

Beau leaned in to kiss Sadie and caught another whiff of bile and sour pizza.

"Whoa... upstairs, Sadie Mae," Beau commanded as he pointed to the bedroom, and she turned and headed up the stairs.

"Hey... take your time, okay. Use that body wash I like, please. I'll help you wash your hair if you wait for me. Just give me a few minutes down here," Beau said with a wink.

Sadie didn't want to argue. It was still hands-off when Patrick was sleeping downstairs, but she figured after the night she had, that she just might take Beau up on his offer.

* * *

 "Put that track piece over there... next to the other side of the bridge."

Sadie heard Beau and Patrick playing downstairs. She quickly grabbed her robe and went to join them... anxious to see how Patrick was feeling. He had not come up to crawl into bed with them last night. No doubt the trauma knocking him out until dawn. Sadie was grateful. After she climbed the loft stairs and started the shower, Beau quickly cleaned the downstairs and put fresh batteries in an old baby monitor. He set the speaker on Patrick's bedside table before bringing the monitor upstairs into the shower to join Sadie.

"Sadie's up... Sadie's up!" Patrick squealed. George let out a loud bark as they both scrambled off the living room floor and made a beeline towards her.

"Dad... get Sadie some coffee, please. She had a rough night."

Patrick's comments made Beau and Sadie both laughed.

"Hey, you... how are you feeling this morning?" Sadie asked, ruffling Patrick's hair. The color was back in his cheeks, and he seemed his typical ball of energy.

"I feel all better now, but dad says no school today. Thank you for taking care of me. Dad... Sadie sang me a song about a blackbird... written by a bug and rubbed my tummy until I felt all better."

"You told me you don't sing. I heard your voice, baby. It was beautiful. You sang "Blackbird" almost as good as McCartney."

Beau handed Sadie a steaming mug of extra strong coffee, and she felt her cheeks get hot.

"Well... I only sing for the sick and infirmed. They are truly the only ones who appreciate my talent." Sadie said with a giggle.

"Hey... this is pretty exciting. I just got a text alert from American Auto Shipping. Guess what is arriving today?" Sadie held up her phone and did a little happy dance.

Sadie's car had been loaded onto a semi-trailer in the front of Juliette and Geoff's house four days ago. After a few stops to pick up and drop off other vehicles, Sadie's car would be at the loft in a few hours.

Later in the morning, when she finally got the alert that the driver was outside the loft, Beau, Patrick, and George all joined her downstairs.

"Whoa! That is so cool, Sadie Mae. Your car is inside that truck," Patrick said enthusiastically as he jumped up and down on the sidewalk.

"Yes. It came all the way from Seattle."

A burly looking man with a half-smoked cigar hanging out of his mouth stepped out of the semi.

"Sadie Morgan?"

"Yes, sir," she said with a nod.

"I need to see your receivables slip and your driver's license."

Sadie quickly handed the driver her form and license, and he checked off a few items on a stack of forms he had attached to a clipboard.

"Wait right here. We got an Audi A6 ahead of you."

The three watched as the driver's assistant, a tall skinny kid with a bald head and a goatee rolled up the back door of the semi-trailer and pulled out a large control panel, lowering a long ramp down the backend of the trailer. He pushed a few buttons, and the front end of a black Audi slowly pulled forward. Once it cleared the trailer door's opening, the assistant jumped up on the ramp, opened up the driver's side door, and started the engine. He drove the Audi down the ramp and half a block away and then came hustling back to remove Sadie's car from the trailer.

"Any chance you want to take that one," Beau said, pointing to the black Audi A6 Sedan with leather seats, a V6 engine, and a Bang and Olufsen 3D premium sound system.

"No way! I love my car, and besides, black cars are way too hot. Mine is pearl white." Sadie sounded like a small child describing her favorite toy.

"I like that one too, dad," Patrick agreed, jumping around and dancing the floss.

Sadie folded her arms across her chest and glared at the boys.

"I love my car."

"Baby, it's a Hyundai."

Sadie had heard enough. She turned with a huff and walked away.

"Suit yourself, boys. Just see if either one of you ever get a ride with me." George barked at Sadie's reply. "And that goes for you too, Georgie."

It was at that moment that the assistant tapped a button on the remote, and Sadie's car appeared at the top of the ramp. The Hyundai Elantra Sport was just that. A cute little sporty car with leather interior and a sunroof. The black front grill glistened in the sun as the assistant drove it off the ramp. Sadie jumped up and down and clapped her hands.

"I've missed you, Walter White!" Sadie exclaimed as Beau laughed and shook his head.

"Sadie Mae, you named your car, Walter White... like Walter White from *Breaking Bad*?"

"Um... yeah!"

Sadie giggled as she stepped towards her car.

"Wow, dad. Sadie has a cool car. Sadie, can I ride in your car, please?" Patrick ran after Sadie as the assistant handed her the fob.

"Oh, so now you want to know me, huh?" Sadie quickly turned and patted the top of Patrick's head.

"What do you think, Beau?"

He didn't want to admit it, but he liked Sadie's car, and as she climbed behind the wheel, he thought she looked pretty sexy.

"I say we all go for a ride. What do you think, Beau?"

"I think that sounds perfect... and I know just the place!"

* * *

Beau accelerated onto the freeway as the car roared to life. He turned to Sadie and smiled. He looked fucking hot, driving her car.

"Um, baby... you told me you drove a Hyundai," Beau said as he tapped the button on the sunroof, and a warm wind blew through the front seats.

"Be careful in sport mode. This thing can really corner. I used to cut loose on I-5 between Portland and Seattle. I took him up to 90 once."

"Him? You mean *Walter*." Beau said. He turned to Sadie and smiled – one corner of his mouth turning upward.

"Yes, Beau and stop making fun of me," Sadie replied as Patrick giggled in the back seat.

"You too, silly boy!"

Sadie turned around and grabbed ahold of Patrick's foot and gave it a squeeze.

"I suppose I should have an extra booster seat, huh?"

Sadie would have never imagined six months ago that she would have to learn how to install a booster seat.

"I'll take care of it," Beau said as he smiled at her.

"Where you boys taking me?"

Sadie turned on the satellite radio and pulled her favorite pair of sunglasses out of the car's sunglass holder. It was a beautiful day, and she was thrilled to see Nashville fading in the rearview mirror.

"Oh, out and about. We haven't been on an old country road, yet. Let's get lost, Sadie Mae!"

* * *

Arrington Vineyards was about an hour south of Nashville in the hills of Arrington, Tennessee, right in the center of Tennessee wine country. Owned by country music artist Kix Brooks, the winery was a well-known venue for weddings as well as the Music in the Vines concert events. Beau knew that Sadie loved wine, and she often talked of the wineries and tasting rooms that surrounded Seattle. Beau was on a quest to show Sadie that she wasn't losing some of her northwest hobbies, she was gaining a whole new wine region and experience.

They pulled off the freeway and hit the backroads. Soon, the landscape around them changed, and rolling green hills encircled them. Beau powered the sports car on tight turns making Sadie and Patrick giggle.

With the sunroof open, Sadie's hair flew around her face as the three of them sang along to songs pulsating from the radio.

"Wow, Beau. This part of Tennessee is beautiful."

Sadie couldn't get over the green hills as far as she could see. It was hard to believe that she was in Tennessee and not Washington State. The resemblance was amazing. Beau drove through the gates of the winery and up a small hill to the tasting room.

"Shall we go in… have a flight? Patrick can run around. This place sits on about 75 acres."

"Yes! That sounds amazing. It doesn't look too crowded either for a Thursday?"

"Then, a little day-drinking it is!" Beau triumphantly exclaimed as they walked hand in hand into the tasting room with Patrick and Max leading the way.

"Can I have some wine too?" Patrick yelled out as he ran up to the tasting room bar.

"No, you may not! How about something else, son?"

A tall, middle-aged brunette greeted them with a friendly wave. "Welcome in. Just the three of you?" Beau nodded his head in response. "Are you wine club members?"

"No, ma'am."

"Well, that's okay. Maybe I can convince you. My name is Bobbi, and I'll be showcasing our wines for you today. Where y'all from?"

As much as Sadie still wanted to say Seattle, she knew now that her life was in Nashville. She knew it would be a slow adjustment, and she still felt like she was visiting from another planet.

"Oh, we are from just… up the road… Nashville. I'm Sadie, and this is Beau and Patrick." Beau turned to Sadie and smiled.

"Excellent and welcome in. I have some sparkling grape juice for that young man right there and how about I start you two off with our 2017 sparkling rosé."

Bobbi filled a plastic glass with grape juice for Patrick, and Beau escorted him outside the large sliding barn door and out onto a picnic table with a bowl of goldfish and his color book and crayons.

"That should keep him occupied for five minutes," Beau said, causing all three of them to laugh.

"What do y'all think of the Sparkle?"

Sadie held the flute up to the sunlight and studied the color. "Wow… I love this! Strawberries on the nose with a hint of watermelon and lime on the palate."

Sadie closed her eyes as she took another sip. Bobbi seemed thrilled to have someone to talk wines with. The tasting room was empty, and Sadie was a captive audience.

"Next up is my all-time favorite, our 2017 Stag's White. Very similar to a pinot grigio. We use nine fruity grape varietals to make this white blend."

Sadie swirled her wine glass and brought it to her nose. "Ummmm… citrus and cantaloupe."

Beau chuckled. He smelled and tasted none of that until he heard Sadie's description.

"Exactly! Nice description, Sadie. This recently won a bronze medal at the International East Meets West Wine Competition. 97% of the grapes in this wine were grown right here in Tennessee." Sadie had no idea that wine and Tennessee went together.

"I think a bottle will be going home with us. What do you think?" Sadie said, turning to Beau. He was lost in her beauty and in her worldliness. Beau was a beer drinker and loved bourbon. He didn't know shit about wines, but he knew that Sadie was in heaven. His decision to bring her here was going to earn him lots of extra points.

"Let's try one more white wine, shall we?" Bobbi pulled another bottle from behind the bar as Sadie shook her head up and down.

"Have you been here before, Beau?" Sadie asked.

"Mmmmm... this is where Mac and Mazie got married. Right over there."

Beau pointed out through the tasting room door and out towards a farmhouse, further up the hill from the tasting room.

"You should go up there and check it out if you've not seen it before, it's stunning," Bobbi exclaimed as she topped off their glasses with a 2017 chardonnay. The dry white wine melted on Sadie's tongue.

"Okay, I've got two reds for you. The first is our 2016 Red Fox Blend, which primarily consists of Sangiovese grapes. It's a wonderful wine with pasta... anything Italian and grilled meats." Beau's eyes lit up at Bobbi's description.

"Now, we are talking," Beau said. He picked up his glass and downed his pour in one gulp. "Excellent."

"Bobbi, it looks like we have another one that might be heading back to Nashville with us."

All of a sudden, Patrick came back into the tasting room with his empty glass.

"Dad, I have to go to the bathroom."

Beau grabbed Patrick's hand and escorted him out of the room as Bobbi poured their last tasting.

"He's cute."

"Which one?" Sadie said, making both women laugh. "I think they are both pretty cute. I am very fortunate!"

Sadie felt extremely grateful at that moment to be at a place in her life where she had found the joy she had been missing.

"My boys are 23 and 18. Enjoy every minute. They grow up fast."

Sadie didn't feel the need to explain to Bobbi that Patrick wasn't her son. He sure felt like he was growing into being a part of her. She was grateful that Beau was patient and really made sure that Patrick felt included when they were all together, while still carving out time alone with his son. The more time Sadie spent with Patrick, the more she thought about what could have been... a child. That ship had sailed, though. It was the first time that Sadie felt like she wanted to have a child and be a mother. Beau was the perfect dad, and Sadie felt a deep sadness that they would never experience being parents with a child of their own.

"Since y'all are cute and so appreciative of the wines I am pouring today. I'm going to give you a little treat. This here is the 5th edition of Kix Brooks' very own private reserve. It was aged 18 months in French Oak barrels, and it's made with the best of our cabernet sauvignon grapes." Sadie watched Bobbi pour the dark crimson wine into a clean glass.

"Wow... get a load of that aroma! Cedar and blackberries with a hint of black pepper." Sadie took a sip and smiled just as another customer walked into the tasting room.

"Welcome in." Bobbi turned her attention away from Sadie and greeted the woman with a friendly wave. Sadie did a quick double-take and watched the tall blond approach the bar. She was a stunning woman with platinum blond hair that fell in loose rings down the middle of her back. She wore a dark plum suede jacket draped stylishly across her chest, paired with a tight pair of black stretchy jeans and three-inch stiletto pumps in the same shade as her jacket. She removed her sunglasses, and Sadie caught sight of her sparkling emerald eyes.

"Are you a wine club member?" Bobbi addressed her new customer as Sadie watched the blond pull her hair away from her face as she reached into her taupe Coach bag.

"Yes, I am here to pick up this quarter's wine club picks."

The woman had just pulled a slip of paper from her bag and handed it to Bobbi when Beau and Patrick returned.

"What did we miss?" Beau no sooner got those words out of his mouth when he surveyed the room. Standing in front of him and right next to Sadie was Mia.

"Beau!"

Sadie watched the blond woman's face light up as she took two steps towards Beau, shouting out his name. As she got closer to him, she bent over and placed her hands on her knees to address the little boy standing in front of his father.

"Hey, you must be Patrick. Your dad has told me a lot about you."

Mia extended her hand to the little boy, and Patrick reached out to her giving her hand a quick shake.

"Mia... um... this is Sadie Morgan... um, baby... this is Mia Quinn. Mia and I work together."

Sadie watched Beau thread his fingers through his hair and exhale deeply. Mia quickly turned around and looked at Sadie... eyeing her up and down. Sadie was grateful she had decided to change from shorts and a t-shirt into a V-neck boho maxi dress, which made her feel pretty sexy.

"Nice to meet you, Sadie." Mia didn't offer her hand... instead, she quickly turned her attention back to Beau as Bobbi reappeared at her side and handed over a tote bag with three bottles of wine.

"Are you a wine club member, Beau? I never took you for much of a wine drinker." Mia chuckled slightly and flipped her hair over her shoulder. Sadie had seen that move hundreds of times before, and it made her roll her eyes as she could feel her grip tighten on her wine glass.

"No. We are just out for a little drive in the country. Sadie is the wine connoisseur, and she's recently moved to Nashville... moved in with me." Beau caught himself stuttering as Mia nodded her head and kept her eyes fixated on him. Beau fidgeted nervously like a smoker who had recently quit cold turkey.

"Well… I've got a planning meeting down in Franklin. I was just so close I thought I'd swing in here and pick up my wine," Mia said, clutching the wine tote to her chest as she whipped her head around.

"Thank you, ma'am," Mia said to Bobbi and then turned back to Beau.

"I'll see you around, Beau. You guys take care."

Sensing the tension in the air, Bobbi headed back behind the bar and gave Sadie another generous pour of Kix Brooks's special edition. As Mia passed by Beau, she reached out and tousled Patrick's hair and continued to sashay out the tasting room door.

"Dad, can I go back outside?"

Beau nodded to Patrick and watched him head back to the picnic table before slowly returning to Sadie's side. He took the wine glass from her hand and drank its entire contents in one long gulp.

Sadie didn't know what to do about the green-eyed monster, and she wasn't referring to her feelings. It was pretty clear that Beau had a type… tall blondes with dazzling green eyes, and Sadie fought hard to understand what it was that Beau saw in her.

"So… that's Mia, huh?"

Sadie let out a giggle and affectionately leaned into Beau's shoulder. One side of his mouth turned up as he met her gaze nodding his head and looking at her like a kid coming in the front door 30 minutes after curfew.

"What do you say, Sadie Mae? Let's go find us some barbecue before taking Patrick home?"

Beau didn't know what else to do, so he grabbed Sadie by the waist and planted a kiss on her waiting lips. It was the kind of kiss that made a woman forget her own name, not to mention her boyfriend's ex. Mia didn't even cross Sadie's mind as she chased Patrick back to the car.

* * *

"So, it's a couple's baby shower?" Beau said as he ran his hand over Sadie's back, stopping at her ass as he gave it a gentle squeeze.

They had dropped Patrick back with Hannah after their wine tasting adventure giving Beau the time he needed to make sure that Sadie would never again need to worry about Mia.

Beau was a selfless lover. He didn't have an issue putting his pleasure aside to give Sadie what she needed. She was still dazed and mellowed as she rolled towards him and Beau ran his hand over the delicate inner face of her thigh.

"Yes, apparently… that's the new thing."

Sadie grabbed the invitation off the nightstand. It had come addressed to both of them a few days before Sadie went back to Seattle. At the time, she had no idea if she would be back in time for the shower, let alone Tucker's impending arrival in October.

"A bun in the oven and burgers on the smoker. Please join us for a backyard barbecue baby shower honoring soon-to-be-parents Mazie and Mac." Sadie held the blue invitation in her hands and read it out loud to Beau.

"It's just another excuse for Mac to smoke something and start drinking beer at dawn."

"Sounds like a fun afternoon if you ask me." Sadie rolled over towards Beau… her lips always finding something of pleasure.

"I've got a better idea for my Saturday afternoon."

Beau took the invitation out of Sadie's hands and pulled her on top of him. Her knees clamped around his naked hips, pressing hard against his arousal.

"And I have an even better one, Beau."

* * *

The following weekend, the Mackenzie's backyard was filled with family and friends and just about every shade of blue imaginable. Blue streamers, banners and balloons, and even blue solo cups decorated their home and backyard. Mazie had also asked everyone to dress in their favorite shade of blue.

"How you feelin', Mama?" Beau asked as he brought Mazie a cold glass of sweet tea and sat down beside her on the porch.

Mac had asked Beau and Sadie to help with the party set-up, and Beau arrived to help Mac with the smoker at half-past five this morning. Mazie couldn't do much, and in the late summer heat, she was resigned to sitting in a chair she could easily get in and out of with her feet elevated.

"Fucking miserable... excuse my French. All I care about is making it through this day and starting our babymoon tomorrow afternoon."

"Excuse me."

"Babymoon. You know our last hurrah before Tucker comes, and Mac's life totally changes," Mazie said, winking at Beau.

"Huh... babymoon... is it supposed to be like a honeymoon?" Beau looked at Mazie with a confused look on his face.

"Shit, I hope not. If Mac thinks that sex is part of this trip, then I am staying home! It's three days at a five-star resort and spa in the Chattahoochee National Forest. Mac can spend his days fishing, and I am getting every spa treatment on the menu. Gosh, I hope I can survive the car ride. I literally have to pee every 10 minutes. It's gonna take us eight hours to go 200 miles."

Sadie came out of the kitchen – dishtowel slung over her shoulder, looking dazzling in her dark indigo blue jean overall shorts with a light blue t-shirt underneath. She had tied her hair back with a royal blue bandana, and sapphire blue drop earrings hung from her ears that she and Mazie had found shopping in the Gulch.

"Okay… so the veggie platter is done. I've carved out the watermelon for the fruit salad, and those two tubs on the porch are filled with beer and wine."

Sadie plopped down in a chair next to Mazie and Beau. She had arrived 90 minutes before the official start of the party with George and Patrick to help Mazie's sister-in-law and her mom with some last-minute details.

"You two are amazing and wonderful friends… you know that? We could not have done this without you. I wished we had planned this party months ago, but with Mac's summer classes, it just wasn't possible." Mazie got tears in her eyes, and Sadie grabbed her hand.

"Shit! I can't stop crying. I look like an overripe blueberry in this dress. What was I thinking?"

"I think you look beautiful and I am so happy to be here," Sadie's voice caught. She adored Mazie, and she couldn't wait to see her, and Mac become parents. The girls looked over at Beau, who also had tears in his eyes and started to giggle.

"Dang allergies are bad this time of year. I'd better take George for a walk. Patrick needs to blow off some steam."

Beau gathered the dog and Patrick and took off through the side gate.

"So, Sadie… I'm sorry we haven't had much of a chance to talk… you know in private, but Beau told us about Seattle… your dad. My… how awful."

Sadie lowered her eyes and nodded her head. "Honestly, I don't know what I would have done had Beau not been there. I just never realized what Joel was capable of."

"The whole thing sounds like a scene from a movie."

"You got that right… a really bad horror movie," Sadie said, lowering her eyes.

"Hey, speaking of your dad… how is he?"

"Okay, I guess. The place in Seattle is an institution… a hospital. The only reassuring thing is that he is well taken care of and safe. He's got very little access to the outside other than a supervised walk around the patio garden. He has his good days and bad days. It just tears me up to think that he's in there because of me." Sadie leaned back in her chair and bit the outside of her lip.

"Oh, Sadie… don't think that. You are doing everything you can to get your dad moved out here. It's gonna happen. Soon, we all hope. Beau mentioned that you've taken on a part-time job, you're on the waiting list at Tall Oaks Manor, and you've got the most amazing man wrapped so tight around you." Mazie's giggle made Sadie giggle.

"That boy is head over heels for you, girl. He said the loft is nothing but smoking hot domestic bliss."

"Beau said that!"

"Yes, he did. He's so happy."

"I'm so happy too. I really am."

Sadie reached up to dab a stray tear that had fallen from her eye.

"Then, Sadie… enjoy it because it doesn't come around every day. You've got to grab it while you can. Everything about the two of you has been extraordinary," Mazie said as she leaned her belly forward in her chair and grabbed Sadie's face.

"You deserve this… you both do. Promise me that you won't regret it. No matter how hard it is with your dad right now. I feel it. I know that it's all going to work itself out."

Sadie's eyes continued to well up with tears, so Mazie joined her.

"Now, get your hot little ass off this porch and get back to work!"

* * *

The barbecue was a huge success, and everyone had a great time. Mazie hired a screen printer to assist each guest in making adorable onesies with graphic designs. Some choices read *Future Ladies Man, Wild One, and Locally Brewed*. Sadie made a light blue onesie with the design, *Sweet as a Peach* in honor of Tucker's Georgian parents.

As the evening was wrapping up and only a handful of guests remained, Sadie's cell phone buzzed in her overalls. She looked at her phone and shot Beau a serious glance before excusing herself out the side gate.

"Hello, this is Sadie Morgan."

"Hello, Miss Morgan… this is Maybelle Reed at Tall Oaks Manor."

"Yes… Miss Reed. How are you?"

"I'm well, thank you. I'm calling with some good news. We have an opening for your father."

"Oh… that's wonderful."

"His room will be ready on November 1st. We can coordinate his prescriptions and care plan with his current facility closer to his arrival date. Until then, we will require three months' rent 30 days prior to him moving in. We can coordinate all the details with Medicare and find out what his out of pocket expenses will be."

Sadie's heart skipped a beat, realizing that in seven weeks, she would need to come up with almost $15,000, not to mention the transportation costs. Sadie had reluctantly agreed to go with the charter flight company. It seemed like the easiest and best option. They would give her father a mild sedative, and he would most likely sleep on the plane for the entire flight. As much as Sadie would like to be on board with him, she couldn't justify the cost of her flying back to Seattle and then her ticket on the charter. He would be well looked after, and it wasn't really essential for her to tag along. Sadie was crunching the numbers, and James's cash reserves just wouldn't last that long and would only escalate as his mind further deteriorated. After Sadie had paid Beau back for James's care at the Providence facility, she re-worked the budget, which frightened her. Sadie would need to cover some of the burden of the relocation costs. She took in a deep breath and turned around when she heard the gate close behind her. Beau stood with a worried look on his face.

"Miss Reed, my father, won't have any furnishings. The brochure mentioned something about the possibility of having some furniture provided."

"Oh, absolutely. As you might expect, residents pass on, and they leave items behind... things their family no longer has a need for. I don't think it would be any problem at all to find James the things he needs. I think we might even have a radio or a TV. Don't worry about bringing anything other than personal items... pictures and things that have sentimental value. The rest, we can assist with."

"Oh, that is fantastic. Thank you," Sadie said with a deep sigh.

"I'll have the finance department give you a call next week. I was just so excited when I saw the opening come up on the computer today that I just had to call you. I am sorry to bother you on the weekend."

"No, Miss Reed. I am thrilled. Beau and I are very pleased to hear from you. Thank you," Sadie said, turning towards Beau to give him a thumbs up.

"Just give me a call if you have any questions. Good day, Miss Morgan."

When the call ended, Sadie burst into tears and dove into Beau's arms.

"Hey, now. I take it those are happy tears. This is good news?"

"They have a place for my dad. His room will be ready November 1st."

Sadie pulled away and looked up into Beau's eyes. He placed his hand under her chin, lifting her lips to his.

"This is all happening, Beau," Sadie said. She let out a big sigh as Beau brushed his lips against hers.

"Yes, baby. This is all really happening."

Beau wrapped his arms around her again and rested his chin on top of her head.

"Beau..."

"What, baby?"

"I really need to get a job!"

CHAPTER THIRTEEN

Sadie had just opened up her portfolio and resume when Beau and Patrick got back to the loft. It was Columbus Day, and Patrick didn't have school, so the boys took George for a walk before Beau got ready for work. It would be a busy day juggling their schedules.

"Okay, Patrick. Behave yourself and mind Sadie Mae, please. I'll be home by one o'clock, and that will give you enough time to get to your interview and knock em dead!"

Beau grabbed Sadie from behind and kissed her neck before grabbing his messenger bag and leaving the loft.

This interview was huge for Sadie. A real full-time job, making more than enough money to cover a portion of her father's out of pocket expenses at Tall Oaks Manor, and still have some leftover at the end of the month. Sadie needed this job. The benefits alone were icing on the cake. The free-lance job that her former boss in Seattle had given her would not be enough, long-term to bring her father out to Nashville and cover his care. Although his room was still not ready for another month, Sadie was hoping to have a paycheck in the bank before James arrived.

"Sadie, can I prepare for a meeting too?"

Patrick sat up on Beau's computer chair and spun around.

"Yes! You can be my assistant," Sadie proclaimed. She stapled a stack of writing paper together and handed Patrick a couple of felt tip markers, hoping to keep him entertained.

"How about you take the biggest desk in the office?"

Sadie laid the stack of paper on the kitchen table, and Patrick began scribbling and drawing. This kept him occupied for about eight minutes, and Sadie began to regret that Patrick had talked her into sugary cereal for breakfast instead of making eggs and toast, as Beau had suggested. The little boy was bouncing off the walls.

By ten o'clock, Sadie relented and handed Patrick her tablet. She knew that Hannah and Beau were pretty strict about screen time, but Sadie simply needed a break and for Patrick to quiet down. While her resume was complete and had already been submitted to the hiring manager, Sadie was still working on updating her portfolio. She was also asked to submit a sample appraisal that her interviewer, Chris Holland, had sent over to her only yesterday.

The educational games that Sadie had downloaded on her tablet did the trick, and Patrick was occupied until Sadie set a grilled cheese sandwich and a small cup of tomato soup on the kitchen table at 12:30.

"Where's the animal crackers?" Patrick barked at Sadie.

"After lunch, Patrick. Let's get some real food in your belly first." Patrick began swinging his legs… kicking his heels into the butt of his chair. He was on Sadie's last nerve.

"Young man. Mind your manners at the table, please. Your dad will be home any minute." Sadie pleaded. She could hear a slight drawl to her voice as she reprimanded Patrick. Sadie hoped and prayed that Beau would be home soon. She wanted him to take George and Patrick and get out from under her feet so that she could have a few minutes of peace and quiet to prepare for the interview of her life.

"I've had three bites of my sandwich. I want my animal crackers now, please," Patrick said, smiling at her with stringy cheese stuck to the sides of his cheeks. Sadie could feel herself beginning to cave.

"Okay, then. Count them out, please. Four cookies and not one more."

Sadie watched as Patrick jumped up from the table and ran to the pantry door.

"Um… Sadie, one fell on the floor, and George ate it. Does that count as one of my four cookies?" The kid negotiated just like his father, and it brought a smile to her face despite his antics.

Sadie stuffed her resume and her portfolio in her briefcase and set them on the kitchen counter. She checked her phone, but no messages from Beau. Sadie needed to change into her suit.

"No, Patrick… you still get your four cookies. Listen, I want you to bring me your bowl and plate, and let's load them in the dishwasher, and then I need to go upstairs and change my clothes.

"For your big meeting?"

"Yes, for my big meeting."

After Patrick brought Sadie his dishes and went back to playing games on Sadie's tablet, Sadie headed upstairs.

"Listen for your dad, okay. I'll be upstairs if you need anything."

Sadie grabbed her cream-colored knee-length pencil skirt with the thin black belt and pulled it over her hips and zipped up the back. She paired it with a black cap-sleeved chiffon blouse and matching cream jacket. She carefully slid her feet into a pair of smart-looking patent leather Mary Jane's and admired herself in the mirror. Sadie was pleased with the results. She freshened up her makeup and slipped on a pair of black onyx earrings. She looked classy, smart, and sophisticated.

Twenty minutes later, Beau was still not home, although he had texted Sadie to tell her that he was running late, but that he was on his way.

Sadie made her way downstairs to check in on Patrick, just about the time the battery on Sadie's tablet died, and Patrick had a complete meltdown.

"But I was in the middle of *Once Upon a Monster*. Plug it in, Sadie." Patrick's face was red with anger, and he stomped down hard on one foot and then the other. Sadie stood, staring down at the child.

"Patrick, you have lots of other toys to play with including a few new library books. Why don't you go get your cars and set up a track until your dad gets home? I know you guys are heading out to the park as soon as he gets back."

Sadie's words fell on deaf ears. Patrick started jumping up and down, and Sadie felt certain at any minute that smoke might billow from his ears and that his head might explode.

"Noooo!"

Patrick picked up the tablet and threw it to the ground. He immediately knew that he was in trouble, and he ran to the couch and plowed into the pillows. Sadie bent down to retrieve her tablet and set it on the kitchen counter. Patrick was a smart kid, and today he was testing Sadie to see how far he could push her.

"I want the rest of my animal crackers and grape juice."

Tears were forming in his eyes. Sadie felt bad for Patrick. He was obviously bored and not used to being cooped up inside all day. He was an energetic and athletic kid, and she realized that they should have made other arrangements for his care and well-being, today of all days.

"Okay then, I will get you a few more animal crackers and juice if you apologize for throwing my tablet to the ground. You know I am going to have to talk with your dad about this."

Patrick rubbed his eyes and shook his head. Sadie heard a muffled and unsympathetic, *I'm sorry* as she headed to the kitchen to get Patrick some cookies and juice.

Suddenly Patrick roared back to life. Running and jumping all over the loft. Sadie was relieved. A bit of expelled energy was good for him. She set his cookies and juice on the kitchen table and turned to gather her tote and briefcase.

"Hey, Patrick… enough okay. How about you sit down and eat your cookies and drink your juice." Patrick picked up two cookies off his plate, stuffed them into his mouth, and raced into his bedroom.

"No running with your mouth full, please."

Sadie suddenly remembered what Juliette had told her about the benefits of taking a pediatric first aid course. The last thing Sadie needed was Patrick choking on his animal crackers.

Sadie stood in the kitchen, ready to go as soon as Beau walked in the door. She looked down at her phone, making sure that she had the address of her interview plugged into her GPS when Patrick came running at her with a full glass of grape juice.

Everything happened in slow motion, but Sadie knew that she couldn't get out of the way fast enough. Patrick raced around the kitchen counter and plowed right into her, grape juice flying everywhere, splashing her in the face and drenching the front of her cream-colored skirt in dark purple liquid. Patrick froze as Sadie gasped in horror.

"Oh shit. Look what you've done, Patrick. Fuck! My skirt is ruined, and it's all your fault!"

Sadie knelt to Patrick's face and shouted at him. She immediately stood up and put her hand over her mouth as the little boy burst into tears.

"Sadie Mae!"

Sadie hadn't heard the front door open. She hadn't noticed that Beau had come home and was standing by the front door. As soon as Patrick saw his dad, he went screaming into Beau's arms.

"Hey… Patrick… son. It's okay. Calm down."

Sadie just stood there drenched in grape juice as Beau looked over at her. She watched him soothe his son's back as Patrick continued to sob. Sadie reached for a kitchen towel and began wiping the front of her skirt and then the floor, George hot on the trail... already licking the grape juice off the floor.

"You mind telling me what's going on?" Beau asked as Patrick continued to cling to his neck.

"He was running... with grape juice. It was an accident. I'm sorry."

Tears formed in Sadie's eyes. She'd never seen Beau look at her like that. She had screamed at his son, and worse yet, she had cursed at him. She could see that the little boy was traumatized.

Sadie let out a long sigh as the alarm on her wrist went off. She was going to be late for her interview if she didn't walk out the door right now, and there was no way that Sadie could walk out the door in her state – grape juice dripping from her bangs.

"Oh, Patrick. I am so sorry that I yelled at you."

Sadie walked briskly over to Beau and Patrick. The child still had a death grip around his father's neck. He turned his little head towards her and screamed at her.

"Go away! I don't like you! You are mean!"

Sadie bit her lip as Beau just shook his head at her.

"I'm so sorry," Sadie mumbled as she burst into tears and ran upstairs.

* * *

Sadie sat on the edge of the bed, lost in her own thoughts. She didn't care about the job interview anymore. None of that mattered right now. All she cared about was how Beau looked at her and how Patrick had shunned her. Would she ever get them back? They meant more to her than anything in the world. There would be other jobs and other opportunities. Sadie only wanted to make this right, but she had no idea what to do.

Just as she was about to take the grape stained clothes off, she heard Beau on the stairs. He slowly approached the bed, but Sadie couldn't look up. Her heart practically beat out of her chest with fear.

"Baby… you okay?"

Sadie shook her head from side to side as big tears rolled down her cheeks.

"Beau, I am *so* sorry. It was just an insane morning. He was… difficult, and I was pre-occupied. It was a bad mix. I tried, honestly… to make him happy. Take care of him. Today, I just didn't do a very good job. I lost my patience, and I lost control of the situation." Beau reached for Sadie's hand as he took a seat next to her.

"It happens. You think that I haven't lost control… lost my patience? It doesn't make me a bad parent… it makes me a better parent. You'll learn from your mistakes. Shit, Sadie… you are already terrific with him. He loves you."

"Yes, well… not so much anymore," Sadie said through quivering lips. She looked up and into Beau's eyes, and he felt his heart break.

"He's fine. He's having a timeout and reading in his bedroom. He knows better than to run around with food or liquids. He really wants to tell you he is sorry about your skirt. Whenever you are ready."

Sadie leaned her head against Beau's shoulder. If anyone should be apologizing, it should be her.

"Beau… I cursed at him. I yelled at him. That's not me. I don't do that." Sadie bit her lip, trying to stop crying.

"Baby, we all do that. I try and keep the F word out of it, but hey… whatever. He's heard it before. He's going to hear it a lot in his life and probably say it more than his old man wants to hear it, but he'll be fine." Beau rubbed Sadie's back just the way that she saw him comfort Patrick downstairs, and it touched her soul.

"Listen, I brought up your phone. You should call them... who did you say you were meeting with?"

"Um.... it's Cushmen and Wakeland. Chris Holland, is the office manager."

Beau quickly turned to Sadie and smiled.

"I think if you explain that you had an emergency but that you are on your way to your interview, it will be okay. Come on, Sadie Mae! Let's get you cleaned up and ready to go."

Fifteen minutes later, Sadie came running down the loft stairs in a gray skirt and a light pink top. Her hair was free of grape juice, and although she had freshened up her makeup, she knew that her eyes looked red and puffy.

"Look, all I can be is myself right. They either want me for the job, or they don't. I am just going to do my best. Give it everything I've got!"

Beau, Patrick, and George were all waiting for her by the front door. Patrick held onto Sadie's tote, and Beau had her briefcase.

"You got this, baby!"

Beau gave her a quick peck on the cheek, and then Sadie knelt down to Patrick.

"Patrick, will you please accept my apology for my behavior. I am so sorry that I yelled at you. It was wrong of me to use those words and lose my temper. I hope that you can forgive me and that we can still be friends, okay."

Patrick shook his head up and down. "I'm sorry I ruined your dress."

"It doesn't matter. Spills happen, right? Besides, I like this outfit better anyway."

"Me too!"

Sadie fought back fresh tears as Patrick wrapped his arms around her and gave her a big hug.

"Max wants a kiss too."

Sadie clutched the monkey against her chest and pressed a kiss to the top of his head.

"I'll see you this weekend, Patrick... okay... and I'll see *you* later."

Sadie kissed Beau one final time before walking out the door to her interview.

* * *

"Chris Holland's office, please... this is Beau Walker."

Beau sat down in his office chair and stared out onto the patio where George and Patrick played. He took a deep breath. If she ever found out about the phone call, she'd never forgive him.

"Walker... buddy... long time no chat. What can I do for you?" Beau's smile was broad, hearing his voice. Of all the luck in the world... Sadie's job interview was with Chris Holland, Beau's fraternity brother from Sigma Phi Epsilon. The memories of their frat house parties, beer pong tournaments, and tailgating before the Georgia bulldogs home football games filled his mind.

"Hey, Holls... I need a huge favor."

* * *

Sadie texted Beau when she was finished with her interview, but she didn't tell him what had taken place. She still couldn't believe it. Cushmen and Wakeland had offered Sadie a job that Sadie had accepted. She felt a pang of guilt, wondering if it was something that she should have discussed with Beau first, then decided to head home quickly and surprise him in person.

Chris Holland told Sadie to take a few days to decide, but Sadie didn't need the time. She told them that as soon as the state of Tennessee processed her licenses and registration, she would be ready to start.

"Hey..." Sadie called out as she closed the front door to the loft. George galloped towards her, and she reached down to pat him on the head. She scanned the loft for Beau.

"Where's Beaufart... huh, Georgie?"

"I heard that," Beau responded, and Sadie let out a laugh. "I'm upstairs... putting away the laundry." Beau appeared at the top of the stairs and quickly made his way down to her.

"Well..."

Beau already knew her answer. He knew that Sadie got the job. Chris told him that he would hire her, especially given Beau's glowing recommendation. Chris mentioned that they had quite a few applicants for this recent job posting, but he felt inclined to honor Beau's favor. It didn't hurt that Beau sang Sadie's praises on the phone to Chris and gave him a quick rundown of her situation. He initially defined himself as her close friend and character reference, but Chris figured it out.

"She's... *the one*, huh?" Chris asked, and Beau knew that there was no sense in lying.

"Listen... Holls, if for whatever reason... she doesn't get hired, I'll understand. I know you'll do the right thing. It's just that... I don't think that you will be disappointed. It would mean a lot to her... to me."

"You owe me one, brother. Falcons/Saints tickets, Thanksgiving Day? 50-yard line!"

"I'll see what I can do."

* * *

Beau could see the excitement in Sadie's eyes, and he knew how hard she had prepared for the interview. If she lost out on her opportunity because of his irresponsibility, he'd never be able to live with himself. He had to make it right, and he seemed justified in doing so.

"I got the job, Beau. Can you believe it? I got the job."

Sadie did a little happy dance – her smile lighting up the entire loft.

"What? Baby... you got the job?"

Beau lifted her into his arms and spun her around – George barking and nipping at their feet.

"Sadie Mae, I am so proud of you. I knew that you could do it, baby. I knew they would love you."

Beau hugged her close to him, trying to suppress his desire to tell her the truth. Sadie was proud and independent, and he knew that she would not appreciate Beau's meddling. It would be foolish to tell her now and spoil her joy. It was all for the best.

"Can you believe it? Chris... the office manager who I'll be reporting too loved my portfolio. He said they were looking for someone to appraise land as well as some of their larger building acquisitions. He told me that he thought that I would be a great fit. Oh, they have flexible working hours, so I can work from home if I want too... um, they have two office locations in Nashville, great benefits, amazing salary. Beau, this blows away all my expectations," Sadie said, beaming like a lighthouse in the darkness of night.

"Let's celebrate!"

"Oh, Beau... I'm so excited, but I don't want to go out tonight. Can we just stay in?"

"Baby, please... that's all I had in mind."

Beau winked at her as he pulled a bottle of champagne out of the refrigerator and set it on the kitchen counter.

"Wow! Someone was very optimistic."

Beau's stomach lurched. After he ended his call with Chris and took Patrick home, he stopped off at the farmer's market for a bottle of champagne along with steaks, artichokes, and those butter pecan cookies that Sadie loved.

"I just knew you'd get the job, or at the very least, a second interview. I mean, come on... you are Sadie Mae Morgan."

Hearing Beau's words and knowing how proud he was made Sadie's day. She was so excited she jumped into his arms, wrapping her legs around his waist. Beau cradled her ass in his strong hands as Sadie clung to his neck. He shuffled out of the kitchen and made a beeline for the loft stairs.

"Where are you taking me, Beauford Walker?"

"Into my bed," he said as Sadie's lips brushed over his ear. "Oops... almost forgot."

Beau quickly spun them around and grabbed the champagne off the kitchen counter before taking them upstairs.

* * *

"Baby, please come back to me."

Beau swirled the ice cube in his Belle Meade bourbon and leaned forward in his patio chair.

After Beau and Sadie had made love and taken a shower, they sat together on the patio. Beau watched the joy on Sadie's face as she texted Juliette and Mazie the good news. He knew one friend's heart would be broken in two, while the others would be broken open with joy.

"I'm here... sorry."

Sadie leaned into him for a kiss and weaved her tongue inside Beau's mouth. He reached for her, running his hands up her legs and under her skirt. The first weeks of October were upon them, and the air was cooler as the sun dipped down earlier in the western sky.

"When do you start work?"

"Well, I can't officially appraise anything until Cushmen and Wakeland get updated copies of my license and registrations, including the land certificate. I'm having lunch with HR on Friday. Wow! I still can't believe it." Sadie took another sip of her champagne and let the bubbles flow throughout her entire body.

"Beau... things are going to be different. I mean with me working. Our schedules. Are you okay with all this?"

Beau nodded his approval. All he wanted was for Sadie to be happy. He would do anything even if it meant lying to her.

"It's all going to be just fine, baby. I promise."

Beau brought the bourbon to his lips and took a sip, letting the thoughts of a confession escape his mind.

* * *

Beau slid the white envelope across the balcony table at Acme Feed and Seed and smiled. Sadie had been in Nashville for five weeks, and he had planned a happy hour get together to celebrate not only her move to Nashville but also her new job. Beau wanted to give her the envelope before everyone arrived.

"Um, what's this?" Sadie exclaimed.

"Just a little something," Beau replied.

The way Beau looked across the table at her, Sadie knew he was up to something. Only one side of his mouth was turned up.

"A little something, what exactly? It isn't my birthday. It's not our anniversary."

"We have an anniversary?" Beau exclaimed. His facial expressions suddenly became serious.

"Yes, Beau... we have an anniversary," Sadie said with a giggle.

"Is it when you came to Nashville... and if so... which time? The first time... the second time or the third time?" Beau asked.

"No, Beau! You mean you don't know what day our anniversary is?"

"Ummmm..."

Beau leaned back in his chair and ran his hand through his hair. He brought his blonde ale to his lips slowly. Beau was stalling for time.

"Baby, are you gonna help me out here?"

Sadie just laughed, and Beau realized that she was just stringing him along.

"I think our anniversary should be our first date," Sadie exclaimed.

"Perfect! Our first date?"

"Oh, Beau... our first date. Don't you remember?"

Sadie furrowed her brows and quickly sat back in her chair. It was fun watching Beau squirm in his seat.

"Baby, do you mean the brewpub... my loft, and then your hotel room?"

Sadie just shook her head and laughed. Beau did have a point. If their first date was technically the night they met, then their anniversary would revolve around when they first had sex. Something about that felt wrong, but right at the same time.

"No... Martin's... the ribs?" Sadie's eyes glazed over with the thought. Beau remembered many things about that night, and the ribs weren't one of them.

"I still keep going back to the first time we laid eyes on each other, baby. Do you remember that feeling?" Beau said as he leaned forward and grabbed for her hands. "I think about that moment a lot. Not a day goes by that I don't think about that afternoon and how all the stars lined up. If one little thing had changed, then we wouldn't be sitting here together. If that's not an anniversary... a reason to remember and celebrate, then I don't know what is."

Hearing Beau's sweet description brought tears to Sadie's eyes.

"Now... are you gonna open the damn envelope or not?" Beau barked as Sadie tore the envelope open.

Inside were two airplane vouchers and a brochure for a resort in South Carolina, the Montage Palmetto Bluff, nestled along the scenic May River in South Carolina's Lowcountry between Hilton Head Island and Savannah, Georgia.

"Oh, my God!" Sadie exclaimed. She quickly flipped through the brochure for the spa, which included such treatments entitled Carolina Kur Experience and Palmetto Body Restore. They ranged from body wraps and soaks to stone massages and body masques with May River mud.

"Are you sending me away?"

"No, baby! I'm coming with you?" Beau said.

"Seriously? Like you would be interested in the hair and scalp renewal and the foot reflexology?" Sadie couldn't take her eyes off the brochure.

"No! I'm going to be out on the river... charter fishing while you spend your days at the spa."

Beau laughed as he watched her. His plan to take her away was brilliant.

"Beau, this is... wow. This place looks very..." Sadie didn't want to say it. She looked up at Beau and laid the envelope back on the table.

"What brought all this about?"

"It's our daddymoon?"

"Our what?" Sadie responded with her mouth hanging open.

"Daddymoon... you know, before your dad arrives. Mac and Mazie gave me the idea. They went on their babymoon. Apparently, it's very trendy, you know, for the expecting parents. Time together before the baby comes. Well, I got to thinking that with your dad coming and all the stress of his travel, your new job... our crazy life with Patrick, I just thought that you and I could go away for a few days to celebrate. Baby, the last three months feels like three years, and I don't mean that negatively."

Sadie couldn't argue with Beau's reasoning. Between the drama with Joel, her officially moving to Nashville and getting a job... getting to know

Patrick and becoming part of Beau's life… it felt like enough to cram into a year and not just a few months.

"Do you think that we can get away next week… like for my birthday?"

Sadie blushed as she threw her hands up in front of her mouth.

"Oh my God, Beau… your birthday is next week? I am so sorry. I didn't know. I should be planning something for you not the other way around," Sadie said, as her cheeks flushed pink with embarrassment. "Yes, Beau. I think this is an amazing idea, and I can't wait to see South Carolina!"

CHAPTER FOURTEEN

The American Airlines Airbus flew east first to Charlotte, North Carolina, landing in Hilton Head Island in the mid-afternoon. Beau told Sadie that South Carolina's Lowcountry was the most pleasant in October, with average temperatures in the high 70's with little rain. Defined by three historic rivers and set amid 20,000 acres, the Palmetto Bluff was secluded and pristine and was one of the wildest and most beautiful places in all of South Carolina. It didn't hurt that the Montage Palmetto Bluff resort was a five-star luxury complex.

In the Uber ride to the resort, Sadie read down through the sample itinerary the resort e-mailed them once Beau confirmed the booking of their stay. They held on tight to each other's hand – Beau peering over Sadie's shoulder at the itinerary.

"Oh my... did you know that we can roast a s'more over at the River House firepit?" Sadie looked up at Beau – her big doe eyes wide with excitement.

"Beau... they have a biscuit bar! An entire bar full of biscuits. We have to go tomorrow for breakfast, okay? Oh, and the intro to stand up paddleboarding class starts at nine."

Beau was hoping to be devouring something other than biscuit tomorrow morning. He had fantasies that perhaps Sadie wouldn't even want to get out of bed... let alone dress tomorrow.

"Promise, you'll remind me that we need to reserve our bikes to cruise out to the conservatory tomorrow afternoon, just after lunch at Fore and Aft. Their fish tacos look amazing!"

"Baby..."

Sadie paused and put the brochure down, looking up and into Beau's eyes. He would do just about anything to make her happy, including running all around the resort keeping to the schedule if he had too.

"I'm just s'ited, Beau."

* * *

Beau wished he would have taken a picture of Sadie's face when she walked into the River View Cottage suite. Their one-bedroom cottage with waterfront views and a screened-in shabby-chic porch was going to be a perfect place to enjoy the Carolina sunset over the May River. It was easy for Sadie to see why it was named one of the world's most romantic hotels. Her smile said it all.

"Welcome, Mr. and Mrs. Walker. Please let us know if there is anything we can do to make your stay more memorable."

Beau looked at Sadie, and Sadie turned away and blushed.

Mrs. Walker.

"You'll find complimentary bourbon milk jam and vanilla salted shortbread cookies on your bedside tables... and Mr. Walker, we have the 2016 Raymond reserve selection chardonnay in the ice bucket on the porch that you requested, as well, sir."

Beau handed the bellboy a wad of dollar bills as he exited the room. It hadn't dawned on Sadie that Beau had traveled like this before. Beau was a throw-the-fishing-rod-in-the-back-of-the-pick-up-truck-and-take-off-down-an-old-dirt-road kind of guy.

Sadie looked around the cottage. The room was soothing in creams, yellows, and blues with a king-sized bed, cut out in a small room off the patio. Dark wood furniture and inviting sofas and chairs made up the rest of the living area. Sadie pulled out her phone and connected the Bluetooth speaker to her vacation playlist... some of her favorite downtempo/deep house songs, which Beau affectionately described as their occasional love making music. Beau knew immediately what Sadie was in the mood for.

"Would you care for some wine on the porch?" Beau pushed the French doors open and let the warm breeze flow into their cottage. "Our dinner reservations aren't until 7:30."

"Perfect! I thought you'd never ask. Can I unpack a few things first?"

Sadie just wanted to see the rest of the cottage, and the bathroom was stunning. All white with the exception of the black marble floor. Sadie's mouth dropped open when she saw the freestanding tub with a separate rainfall-fixture shower, just big enough for any extracurricular activities they might want to indulge in. She picked up the small cosmetic bag of complimentary toiletries from Gilchrist and Soames. The rosemary mint body lotion smelled amazing.

Sadie quietly and quickly slipped out of her clothes and stood in the bathroom doorway.

"Beau... why don't you bring the wine into the bedroom, okay."

* * *

They headed out on the May River just before sunset. It was the first time that Sadie had ever been in a kayak. Joel had never been much of an adventurous traveler and preferred to keep his activities cultural... or rather dull, as Sadie recalled. If it involved fine art or classical music, Sadie hoped she never had to endure it again. The fact that Beau was up for anything made the idea of this vacation with him so exciting. Ten minutes after they paddled out into the river and turned themselves towards the setting sun, Sadie spotted fins. They tried to keep up with an entertaining pod of Atlantic bottlenose dolphins for the next 30 minutes but lost them in the fading light of day. It was one of the most memorable experiences of Sadie's life.

Before their first dinner, Beau and Sadie headed out to the inn's central gathering point, the crowded, wood-paneled old-school Octagon Bar. They were pleasantly entertained by a jazz trio while sipping cocktails under the stars.

"Ummmm… how does this sound… a blackberry vanilla mule with house-infused blackberry vodka, lime, and ginger beer."

Beau looked across the table and reached for Sadie's hand. The moonlight radiated off her toned bare shoulders – her creamy tan skin a stunning complement to her off white strapless jumpsuit.

"Absolutely God awful!" Beau exclaimed. He gave her a look that made her laugh deep from within.

"Not one sip, Beau Walker… okay?"

"I can promise you!"

The tuxedo-clad waiter appeared and took their orders – Sadie's blackberry concoction and Beau's River Dog pilsner with a shot of Four Roses single barrel bourbon.

"Is this place, okay?"

The waiter pulled out Sadie's chair as they took a small table by an outdoor fireplace an hour later at Buffalos, a bistro specializing in south Italian cuisine with picturesque views of the river. They walked over to the restaurant hand in hand after their round of drinks.

"You're kidding me, right? You know me… next to ribs, I can eat my weight in pasta."

Beau and Sadie split an heirloom tomato salad with burrata cheese, pickled shallots and arugula, and a huge slab of Saul's lasagna. It was the perfect meal for two people, and it paired nicely with a bottle of Italian red wine from Nebbiolo, which they corked to take back and finish on the porch.

"Can I buy dinner... please?" The check came, and Sadie snatched it up quickly in her hand, and Beau shot her a warning look.

"Baby, this was my idea... the daddymoon. Hand it over, please." Beau held his hand out across the table, and Sadie swatted it away.

"No! Besides... it's your birthday. I am so lame, Beau... I didn't even get you a present."

"Um... that thing you did in the cottage before we left to go kayaking was the best birthday present a man could ever... and I mean *ever* hope to receive."

Sadie's face turned an adorable shade of pink as she batted her long eyelashes at him.

"I'm still not giving you the check, Beau."

Sadie quickly reached into her purse to retrieve her wallet as the waiter returned to clear their bill.

"What are you going to tell your family, huh? They are going to ask you what I got you for your birthday." Beau simply shook his head and laughed.

"Good point, Sadie Mae. Thank you very much, then... for dinner."

Beau's cell phone vibrated in his back pocket as they prepared to walk back to the cottage. He pulled his phone out and looked at the screen. It was a text from Mac. Simultaneously, Sadie's phone also vibrated, and she quickly pulled her phone out of her purse. It was a text from Mazie.

"What's going on?"

Beau and Sadie opened their texts at the same time – Sadie squealing in delight.

"Oh my God, Beau... Tucker is here!" Sadie shouted.

Mac and Mazie had sent a few adorable pictures, one taken just a few moments after they wrapped the 9-pound, 3-ounce baby, in a blue blanket, and placed him in his mother's arms.

"Tucker just wanted to wish Uncle Beau a very happy birthday!"

Sadie and Beau's text messages were identical, and Sadie got big tears in her eyes, as did Beau.

"Tuck and I are going to share the same birthday... how about that?" Beau said, genuinely thrilled with the news.

Mazie texted that she was exhausted but doing well and that her labor started last night, and after 26 hours, Tucker had been born at 6:45, just a few hours ago.

"Wow, Sadie! I can't wait to meet the little guy. I'll text them, and maybe if they are up for visitors, we can stop by on our way home on Sunday."

Sadie nodded her head in approval as she clutched Beau's hand tight. "Perfect... now off to the firepit to roast a s'more. We've got to keep to the schedule, Beau."

* * *

"So, tell me more about your yachting adventure?"

Mazie sat Indian style on the couch in her living room with Tucker swaddled tightly in her arms. Sadie found it hard to concentrate on her stories of their romantic weekend in South Carolina with the cooing baby in Mazie's arms.

"Oh, it was so amazing. The yacht was called *Grace,* and it pulled into the dock, and the captains brought us on board and served us mimosas. It was so out of this world."

Sadie suddenly realized that her stories about their vacation probably paled in comparison to Mazie's story of giving birth... to another human being.

Mazie caught Sadie... her lapse in her stories and her visible curiosity with Tucker. Sadie couldn't take her eyes off the baby.

"Would you like to hold him?"

"Oh, um… sure… yes!" Sadie said, giggling. She had held Liam and Lola, but not another baby since. Infants scared the shit out of her. "But… Mazie. I'm not as good as all of you."

Sadie had watched Beau scoop Tucker out of Mazie's arms like a pro. He rocked the infant in his arms and got this look on his face that Sadie had never seen before. It made her want to cry immediately and for so many reasons that she had never contemplated.

"You think we got this down pat… um, we don't. Mac almost dropped him this morning, lifting him out of his bassinette. It was 2 a.m. in the dark. First, he kicked the side of the bassinette… traumatizing the poor little guy, and if that didn't do it, Mac then let out a blood-curdling scream because he stubbed his big toe on the bedframe handing Tucker over to me. Lucky for me, my brother taught me how to catch a football, otherwise." Mazie finished with a deep sigh, and Sadie tried hard not to laugh.

"Fuck, I still don't know if he's getting enough to eat, and my milk has come in so my breasts are so engorged that I can't even move without wanting to cry. If negative sleep is possible, then that's all I've had since Thursday night." Sadie nodded her head as Mazie continued.

"I'm still having contractions when he nurses, and I am bleeding like I am having my worst period ever. Mac just stands around with his hands in his pockets, asking me if I want a sandwich."

Mazie paused and then looked over at Sadie and burst into tears.

"Here… shit. Take him!"

Mazie thrust Tucker into Sadie's arms, where he slept peacefully for the next 30 minutes while Mazie showered and ate.

* * *

"You're very quiet, Sadie Mae. You okay?"

Sadie had come downstairs after unpacking her suitcase upstairs in the loft and sat down next to Beau, who was engrossed in the Georgia football game he taped.

"Don't you know who won already?" Sadie asked, lying down next to Beau. She put her head on his thigh and threw her feet over the back of the couch. They'd lay like this almost every night for hours. Beau watching football and Sadie reading. He loved it when she closed her eyes, and he could watch her – study her features or run his hand through her hair.

"Tucker sure is cute... holding him was... um."

Sadie let out a small sigh and turned towards the TV, which Beau had temporarily paused. He didn't know what to say. Sadie's words hung in the air like a fine mist rolling off a lake at dawn.

Beau then knew that this was the one thing that he couldn't give her, and it killed him inside.

CHAPTER FIFTEEN

Sadie stared out onto the patio and watched the rain trickle down the sides of the pumpkins that they had carved with Patrick for Halloween. The clouds hung low over the Nashville skyline as a gust of wind swirled the leaves around that had accumulated on the patio.

"Anything?" Beau stoked the fire that he had built them at dawn. The Indian summer had finally ended, and it was cold enough for Beau to make Sadie a fire. He hoped that it would not only take the chill off the room but also calm her nerves. After Beau had started the fire, he carried Sadie downstairs and laid her down on a soft blanket. He kissed the delicate inner face of her thighs until the fervor of her response made him plunge inside her... making them both soar to the sky.

Sadie looked at her phone for the hundredth time in five minutes, shaking her head at Beau. Angel Med Flight had promised Sadie that they would be in constant contact, keeping her informed with the step by step process of James' transfer from Seattle to Nashville. They were due at the Providence facility in West Seattle at dawn to transport him to Boeing Field for the early morning departure. It would be late evening before Beau and Sadie met him at the small regional airport just outside of Nashville.

"You know, Sadie Mae... these people do this every day. It's all going to go smoothly. Your dad is going to be here before you know it."

Beau kissed her lips and wrapped his arms tight around her. Without him, she wouldn't have made it through the day. Sadie wouldn't have been able to make it through anything without Beau. He was her rock... her constant companion... her partner.

"I know. Honestly, I'm fine. I just want this all to be over with, you know. This is the last piece of the puzzle. I just want to see my dad."

With the light fading quickly in the sky, Beau and Sadie watched the plane land in a steady downpour and slowly pull towards the hangar. Sadie had tracked the flight all day, and she even received a call from the nurse on board when they landed in Colorado Springs for a fuel pit stop. The nurse told Sadie that her dad was resting comfortably and had been a perfect traveler.

The medical transport ambulance Tall Oaks Manor had arranged pulled up next to the plane, and two paramedics climbed out of the vehicle and waited for the doors to open. Sadie and Beau watched the staircase descend as the paramedics jumped on board. A few minutes later, James' gurney was carefully maneuvered down the stairs, and the security guard inside the lobby nodded that it was okay for Sadie to head outside and greet him.

"Hi, dad... how was your trip?" Sadie held her umbrella high above his face and stretched on her tiptoes to kiss her father on the cheek. He nodded his head but was unable to speak – a large oxygen mask covering his mouth and nose. Sadie looked at the nurse with concern, but the nurse just shook her head.

"Nothing to worry about. Just a precaution. He's still very groggy, and he will probably be a bit more alert by the time he arrives at the facility," she said. The nurse caringly reached out to pat James' leg. "Nice chatting with you, James. You take care, okay."

James lifted a frail hand and gave the nurse a friendly wave goodbye.

"Dad... Beau and I will be right behind your ambulance, okay. We are taking you to Tall Oaks Manor. You are going to love it. We've got your room all set up, okay."

Sadie and Beau had spent the last few days decorating James' room. Tall Oaks Manor supplied the medical bed, and Sadie and Beau scavenged around a storage unit for other items. They found a small desk and a chair that Sadie placed in front of the large picture window in his room. It would be a perfect place for him to work on his airplanes if he couldn't get outside. They found two mismatched oversized chairs and a small end table to place between them. James could sit and read the paper if he wished, and there would be a place for company to sit when visiting. His kitchen was amended since he was not allowed any cooking privileges, so Sadie had dozens of pictures framed and placed them on the empty countertops, including updated pictures of her with Beau and Patrick. She filled in the rest of the space with several varieties of house plants, and they bought two model airplanes and three birdhouse kits, which would keep him busy as he adjusted to his new life in Tennessee.

Beau and Sadie pulled into the driveway of Tall Oaks Manor right behind the ambulance, and Sadie was pleased to see Maybelle Reed waiting at the door to greet her newest resident.

"Good evening, Miss Morgan. I wanted to welcome James personally. I heard that he had a very uneventful journey."

The director reached out and took ahold of Sadie's hands, sensing in her eyes that despite her father arriving in Nashville, her adjustment was still in transition.

James was unloaded from the ambulance, and he was alert enough to reach up and remove the oxygen max.

"Hi, dad. Welcome to Nashville," Sadie said. James looked at her with concern on his face and shook his head back and forth.

"Nashville, Tennessee? Skookum… what on earth are you talking about?"

Miss Reed quickly stepped in, and James was wheeled inside the facility.

"Miss Morgan, I understand that you want to be here to greet your father and get him acclimated, but that's where we step in. James needs to be cleaned up... a shower and some clean clothes. He needs a full assessment by our medical staff which... believe it or not, has already begun. He's had a long day, and he needs a bite to eat and some fluids."

Beau grabbed Sadie's shoulders as she took in all of Miss Reed's words.

"Okay. So maybe we should come back in the morning, then?"

Sadie turned around and looked at Beau. He could see the disappointment in her eyes, but he knew she was resigned in knowing that her father was safe and that he was finally home with them.

"Why don't you call in the morning and check in. It might be a few days for James to get settled. That's all normal. The staff has both your numbers and if there is something that we feel you should be made aware of, I promise you that someone will be in touch immediately."

Sadie shook her head and let her shoulders drop, and she and Beau got back into the Jeep and went back to the loft.

* * *

"Nashville? Why I'll be. She did it!" James exclaimed. Sadie looked deep in his eyes and shook her head.

After a few restless days adjusting to his new life at Tall Oaks Manor, Sadie and Beau drove out to have dinner with her dad and try as best they could to explain his move, even though Sadie had done this before... several times.

"What are you talking about, dad? Who did it?"

"Your mother! She finally made it to Nashville. I was wondering what brought us all here. She always said that she would take that notebook of hers and make us all rich! I never believed her. Your mother, sapphire is a songwriter. What do you know?"

Sadie looked over at Beau and shrugged her shoulders. She watched as James continued to lay out the pieces to his model airplane, and Sadie let his comments dissolve in the air.

"Dad... Beau and I are going to go now. Are you okay with that? Someone is going to come and get you in a minute. They are having an ice cream social tonight, and I think a movie... oh yes... it's *Rio Bravo.*"

Sadie glanced at the calendar and social schedule that she taped to the front of one of the kitchen cabinets.

"John Wayne... excellent. I'll be just fine, skookum," James said with a wink.

"Listen, young man. I need to have a word with my daughter... alone... in private," James barked out. Sadie quickly glanced over at Beau as James sat forward in his chair with his arms crossed at his chest.

"Yes, sir. Sadie, I'll be right outside, okay?"

Sadie smiled and nodded and watched Beau leave James's room. "Dad... what's this about?"

"That boy! What do you know about him? I'm not sure I like him. He's quite... touchy-feely."

Her father's comments made Sadie giggle. Beau had always been quite restrained around James, and Sadie couldn't even recall Beau so much as holding her hand this evening.

"What happened with that other fella? I can't remember his name... it doesn't matter. I never liked him, anyway," James confessed. It was a relief to Sadie that James didn't have any lasting memories of Joel or an apparent longing for Seattle.

"Dad... Beau and I are... well, Beau is my boyfriend. I love him. He's one of the good ones, dad... honest." Sadie reached out and touched her dad's arm, looking into his eyes.

"I know it's been hard without your mother around but, we've done okay. Don't you think?" James asked.

"Yes, Dad... we've done just fine. You've been a great father... the best!"

"Sadie... there is only one thing a boy like that wants from a girl like you, and I can see where this is going. So, it's time."

"Time for what?" Sadie responded.

"Time that you and I have the talk."

Sadie bit the inside of her lip to squelch her laughter, but her dad caught on.

"Now you listen to me, young lady. As of right this minute, you are grounded. You are not allowed to see that young man unless I am present. I don't want him in this apartment without my permission... understood?"

Sadie now fought back the tears. "Yes, sir."

James was lost again in his model airplane and in 1985.

"Listen, dad... I've got homework to do, okay. I best be going," Sadie said as she dabbed her eyes with a Kleenex. "I'll see you soon, okay. I love you."

Sadie knew there was nothing more she could do and no way to reach him and bring him back. She quickly stood, kissed her dad on the cheek, and walked out of his room.

"Sadie Mae... is everything okay?" Beau could see the tears in Sadie's eyes as she walked out of her father's room and closed the door behind her.

"Ummmm... not exactly. As of this minute, I am grounded, and you're not allowed over unless supervised."

Sadie wiped her tears again as Beau grabbed her hand, and they both started laughing.

CHAPTER SIXTEEN

"I'm taking Mama over to Whole Foods and then to Trader Joe's. You sure you girls don't want to tag along?"

Both Sadie and Presley shook their heads. It was the morning before Thanksgiving, and they had been given the task of preparing the dining room at Broadfield House. Presley had already popped the cork on a bottle of champagne, and Sadie was arranging fresh cut flowers to stuff into hollowed-out pumpkins for the centerpiece. When they were finished with the decorations, Presley was making a chocolate pecan pie, and Sadie was making a pumpkin cheesecake. If Beau and Lady Jane were lucky, between the traffic and the crowds… they'd be home before dinner tomorrow.

Beau and Sadie had arrived yesterday afternoon, and Hannah, Ryan, and Patrick were already in Atlanta. It was Beau's year with Patrick for dinner, and he was excited to share his first Thanksgiving with Sadie and his family, even though he knew she was struggling with her decision to not spend Thanksgiving near her dad. James continued to slip away… more and more each day, and as much as Sadie would have loved to have shared Thanksgiving with him… truth be told, there was a high likelihood that James wouldn't know Thanksgiving from just another Thursday.

An hour after Beau and Lady Jane had left, the doorbell rang at Broadfield House.

"Sadie Mae, can you get the front door... someone just rang the gate about a delivery." Presley had her hands full of table linens, so Sadie ran for the front door.

"Afternoon, ma'am. I've got a pickup for a Beau or Jane Walker." A young man stood on the front porch in an A1 Express Delivery uniform with a baseball cap on his head.

"Oh, I'm terribly sorry. They've gone out. Last-minute grocery store run for tomorrow... Thanksgiving," Sadie said, smiling at the annoyed-looking courier.

"Any chance you might be able to call them? This place is well out of my way, and I don't want to have to come back. I haven't even taken my turkey out of the freezer yet."

Sadie felt sorry for the young man. She didn't have the heart to tell him that the bird wouldn't be thawed out in time to cook tomorrow.

"Yes... hang on. Let me call them," Sadie replied as she pulled her phone from her pocket and rang Beau's phone.

"Butterball hotline, Beau speaking."

"Very funny."

"What's up, Sadie Mae?"

"Well, there is a delivery driver here... with A1 Express. Something about picking up an item. He's kind of put out that you are not here. What's going on, Beau?"

"Shit! I totally forgot. Hang on a minute."

Beau covered the phone with his hand, so all Sadie heard was Beau's muffled voice.

"Baby, can you go into the downstairs living room. You know the one with the desk by the window. On the desk is a large manila envelope. All you need to do is hand it to the courier, okay. It's just some work stuff that I forgot to take care of. Thanks for your help. We are on our way home. See you soon... I love you."

"Yes, sure. I love you too," Sadie replied as the line went dead.

Immediately, Sadie ran to the desk in the formal living room, where Beau told her the envelope was. She snatched it off the table and went running back to the front door. She got to the entryway, and a gust of wind blew through the front door, and the envelope went flying from her hand, its contents spilling out wildly in the wind.

"Oh shit… sorry… hang on."

The courier shifted from one foot to the next foot, clearly irritated.

Sadie retrieved the envelope and looked around the floor for its contents. She picked up the tickets next. Held together with a paperclip were two tickets to the Atlanta Falcons and New Orleans Saints football game on Thanksgiving Day. Even Sadie, who didn't care much for football, knew about this game. It was all Beau had talked about for weeks.

Sadie was puzzled by the tickets and wondered why Beau hadn't mentioned them to her and also why he told her that the envelope was a work issue when clearly it had nothing to do with Beau's job.

Sadie stuffed the tickets back inside the envelope and was just about to hand them to the courier when she spotted the note in Beau's handwriting. It had blown closer to the door, and she bent down and grabbed it.

Holls –

Thank you again, buddy, for the favor.

I'm glad to hear that Sadie is working out for you.

Much appreciated and enjoy the game.

Beau

Sadie gasp as she read and re-read the note. Who was Holls, and what was the favor that Beau was referring too? Sadie had heard that name before… and then it dawned on her. She heard co-workers referring to her supervisor, Chris Holland, as Holls. It was his nickname.

There had to be some mistake.

If Beau knew Chris Holland, why hadn't he told her, and why hadn't Chris ever mentioned it? They must have known each other fairly well since Beau had affectionately called him buddy.

As Sadie stood in the open doorway, it hit her. Beau got Sadie her job. Beau had called Chris Holland and asked for a favor. Beau asked Chris Holland to give Sadie her job in exchange for two football tickets.

"Ummmm… ma'am. I really can't wait here any longer. I need to pick up your item or leave."

Sadie looked down at the note and the tickets in her hand.

Lying bastard.

"I'm sorry to have wasted your time," Sadie said as she shut the door in the courier's face.

* * *

"Hey y'all, we're back. Man, the stores are zoos. People fighting over stuffing and pre-made pumpkin pies."

Beau placed four bags on the kitchen counter and glanced over at Presley, who was rolling out pie dough. Lady Jane had already plopped down on a chair in the solarium and kicked off her heels.

"Hey, squirt… where's Sadie Mae?" Beau asked, and Presley shot him a look.

"Ummmm… she's upstairs. Beau, something is going on. She told me she wasn't feeling well, but I am fairly certain that I heard her crying on her way up to your room. I called in on her, but she said she was okay and that she didn't want to be disturbed."

Beau took the stairs two at a time, confident that it had to be about Sadie's dad. He quietly opened up the door of their bedroom, unsure what state he would find her in but desperate to see if she was okay and what, if any, issues James was dealing with.

"Sadie… baby…"

He knew Sadie was unsure of leaving her father alone on Thanksgiving – their first Thanksgiving in Tennessee. Beau told her that he could make arrangements for her to do both, lunch with James and dinner with the family in Atlanta, but Sadie declined. She told him that he had been more than generous, and now that her dad was in Nashville, she could no longer accept any more money from him. She had to be strong and take care of her and James on her own.

"Presley said that you…"

Beau found Sadie sitting next to her suitcase, the lid open, and the contents full. Next to the suitcase sat the manila envelope and on top were the football tickets and his handwritten note.

"Oh, fuck! Baby… listen. Let me explain."

Sadie locked eyes with Beau. Hers were red-rimmed from tears and blazing with a kind of look that shook Beau to his core.

"So… it's true. This note. These tickets. They belong to you," Sadie's voice broke as she looked up at Beau. His expression was blank, and his silence said it all.

"Fuck, I thought for sure that it must be a mistake, you know. That it couldn't be true. I was imagining it… over-reacting. But it's true." Sadie put her head down as tears fell onto the bedroom floor.

"You fucking paid off my boss with football tickets so that he would hire me… give me a job. Why, Beau… why would you do that? Was it because you didn't think that I was smart enough to get the job on my own? Poor… stupid, Sadie."

Beau slowly walked towards her, and Sadie jumped from the bed.

"Don't come near me, Beau. Get away from me. I'm getting the fuck out of here and away from you."

Sadie quickly pulled her phone from her back pocket and tapped the Uber app ordering a car that would arrive in five minutes.

"Sadie, please! You have to let me explain. It's all my fault. I fucked up. I know I did," Beau said as he brought his hands to his lips, quickly formulating his next words, but Sadie beat him to it.

"The envelope. It flew out of my hands. The flap wasn't closed. I had no idea."

Beau looked at Sadie, who was staring off into space. He wasn't even sure if she was talking to him. She looked like she was in shock.

"The wind came through the front door, and everything just scattered about. I didn't snoop, honestly. I wouldn't have done that. Stuff just fell out. The tickets and the note just fell onto the ground. I saw your handwriting. I was interested in the tickets because you've been talking about that game for weeks. I was just curious... that's all."

Beau tried once again to walk closer to her. He reached the edge of the bed, and Sadie snapped back to life, shutting the lid on her suitcase, and pulling the zipper closed.

"You told me on the phone that it was work stuff. You fucking lied to me. You knew what was in that envelope. You've had this worked out for quite a while... with Chris. What a fool I am. You both did this all behind my back. What am I... some joke between you and your good buddy, Chris?"

Beau couldn't look at her. He placed his hand on his hips and stared at the floor.

"When were you going to tell me that you knew each other? At our company Christmas party or was it going to be your little secret?"

A dull ache filled Beau's stomach as he listened to her. This was all his fault.

"I can't believe this. I just don't understand why you would do this unless you didn't think that I could get a job without you. Is that it? My fucking super-rich boyfriend had to buy me a job?"

"No, that's not it at all," Beau said as he looked up and into her eyes, shaking his head.

"You disgust me, Beau. I can't believe that you did this to me. I can't believe that I was so stupid to fall for this. I should have known. All that talk about the money, not meaning anything to you. Who are you fucking kidding?"

Beau knew she was right. As much as he hated to admit it, Beau used his privilege and his wealth when he knew it benefited those he loved.

"Fuck, I turned my entire life upside down and not only my life, but my dad's life as well. I left my job and my friends… Seattle. I lied for you. And Joel… well, I fucked him up pretty good, didn't I? You must be so pleased with yourself. God, you are just like him."

Beau felt the bile rise in his throat as Sadie's phone chimed. Her Uber was arriving, and she pulled her suitcase off her bed and grabbed her black leather tote.

"Where are you going? What am I going to tell Patrick? Tomorrow is Thanksgiving. He's looking forward to seeing you… sharing our first Thanksgiving together as a family with Mama and Presley. Baby, please."

Sadie couldn't look at him. She had to get out of the house and get away from Beau Walker.

"Please apologize for me, but for fuck's sake, tell them the truth, Beau. See how they feel about what you did. Can you at least do that for me?"

Sadie didn't wait for Beau's answer. She carried her suitcase down the stairs and out the front door and into the backseat of her waiting Uber.

* * *

Mazie was sitting on her couch with the TV on mute when her phone chimed with a text. Tucker was sucking on her left breast, although he was half asleep, and Mac was out in the kitchen prepping for Thanksgiving dinner.

Hey, Maze…you home?

Sadie, I'm going to be home for the next 18 years…. wassup?

I'm standing outside on your front porch.

"Mac!" Mazie yelled at the top of her lungs, and Tucker squirmed in her arms. "Sweetheart, Sadie Mae's outside. Can you let her in, please?"

Sadie didn't know where else to go. She didn't want to go back to the loft, and when she called around for a hotel room, they were all booked, given it was Thanksgiving eve.

When she left Broadfield House, the Uber driver had taken her to the greyhound bus depot in downtown Atlanta, and she got the last seat on the bus, which departed at 5:15 and arrived at 9:30. Mac and Mazie were the only ones she knew who would help her.

Mac ran to the front door and welcomed Sadie inside. She left her suitcase out on the porch. She didn't want to impose and thought she would test the waters and perhaps ask if she might be able to crash on their couch for the night. Sadie needed some sleep. She would spend Thanksgiving with James at Tall Oaks Manor as soon as she returned to the loft and retrieved her car.

"Sadie Mae… why aren't you at Broadfield House with Beau? What's going on?" Mazie asked.

Sadie took two steps inside and burst into tears. So much for playing it subtlety.

"Oh, sweet Jesus. Mac will you get us some wine, please and then come and get your son off my boob and go change him."

"I'm so sorry… Mazie to bother you like this… it's just that… I don't have any… place… else… to… go!" Sadie gasped for air and continued sobbing.

"Sadie Mae… it's okay, sweetie. What happened? Did something happen with you and Beau?"

Sadie could only shake her head up and down.

"Fucking bastard!" Mazie huffed.

Mac suddenly reappeared with two solo cups filled with wine, and Mazie held their son out to him.

"Take him and get lost for a bit… okay?"

Mac shot Mazie a concerned look as he scooped up Tucker and retreated to the nursery.

"Okay, can you start from the beginning, please," Mazie said, as she took a deep breath and a sip of her wine.

"I think it's over, Mazie… Beau and I."

"Oh… okay then… start at the end, and I'll catch up."

* * *

Mazie threw a quilt over Sadie and took the wine glass from her hand. She had simply cried, talked, and drank herself to sleep. Mazie shook her head and contemplated pumping and dumping and grabbing her keys and driving to Atlanta and killing Beau with her bare hands.

Before Sadie passed out, Mazie got the entire story, Sadie's side of the story, but she cautioned her against making any more snap decisions.

"Sadie… you asked him to explain himself, right," Mazie asked. Sadie contemplated her answer. She looked up at Mazie and took another sip of wine.

"Explain what, exactly. The note was in his handwriting, and the tickets were for Chris Holland, my boss. What more is there to say."

Mazie didn't want to say it out loud, but Beau's situation didn't look so good. "Look… men are stupid when it comes to love… matters of the heart. Listen, Beau's one of the smartest guys I know… in business… with his son… but with relationships, he's clueless. You should have heard him after you went back to Seattle in June. I'm fairly certain that Beau Walker planned this whole thing out with his dick."

Sadie choked on her wine and managed a laugh.

"Look, I have no idea what he was thinking, but don't you want to know, Sadie Mae? Don't you want to give him the chance to hear his explanation before you chuck this all away?"

Sadie started to cry again as Mazie took in a deep breath. She hoped that she was talking sense to her friend, but Sadie's attitude was unwavering.

"I just feel like he bought me off… like I am his possession. Oh fuck, Mazie… it's just like Joel. He didn't love me, not really, but he had to have me and control me. I had to be his and no one else's. He bought me with clothes and trips and a life that I would never have been able to have for myself. I thought Beau was different. He told me he was different. He told me that the money didn't mean anything to him. That's a lie, and you and I both know it."

Mazie knew that Sadie had a point, and what Beau did was wrong… very wrong, but she wasn't sure if she could just walk away without talking it through. Mazie knew that there was another side to the story, and she was prepared to find out… beat it out of Beau if she had too.

* * *

The sunrise filtered through the backyard as Beau reached over the fence and opened up the gate. Mac was sound asleep in a lawn chair next to the smoker… his beer in a cozy between his legs. Beau reached the porch and kicked Mac's foot startling him awake.

"Beau… man, what's going on?"

Mac had heard the girls talking and knew that it wasn't good. When Mazie had finally come to bed at half-past one, she was fuming.

"I know she's here… Sadie Mae. Mazie texted me last night. She told me that I better make it right, or else," Beau said with a laugh. He grabbed Mac's beer and took a long swig.

Stacy Brady

"I'm not so sure it's safe for you to go in there. Sadie was pretty upset. She cried all night. Mazie is mad as hell, Beau. What the fuck did you do? Did you cheat on her with Mia?"

Beau defiantly shook his head back and forth. "No way, man. I'd never do that to her. I love her. Does Mazie think that?"

"I don't know. Look, I wasn't invited to the Beau bash session last night. I had to take Tucker and chill out in the bedroom. I was asked to provide the wine… that's all. The girls talked all night long. Your ass is so fucked, dude!"

"Is she awake?" Beau asked, and Mac nodded his head.

"I think so. Tucker was up at five o'clock, and I came out to start the smoker. I put him back to bed about an hour later. When I heard the shower start about seven, I just assumed it was Sadie getting up. What are you going to do?"

"Fuck, Mac. I wish I knew."

* * *

"Ain't no sunshine when he's gone. It's not warm when he's away. Ain't no sunshine when he's gone… and he's always gone too long. Anytime he goes away."

Beau came through the back door and crept quietly into the kitchen. He paused when he heard her voice and caught sight of her through the porthole window between the kitchen and living room. Tucker was in Sadie's arms, and she was pacing the floor and rocking him. It was the most beautiful thing Beau had ever seen.

"Wonder this time where he's gone. Wonder if he's gone to stay. Ain't no sunshine when he's gone… And this house just ain't no home. Anytime he goes away."

Sadie wore a form-fitting cream V-neck cashmere sweater, a tan suede skirt, and brown riding boots. She was no doubt dressed for the

286

holiday. Sadie had an animated smile on her face as she looked down at the baby in her arms... softly singing to him. She had pulled her hair back away from her face and out of Tucker's exploring hands. Beau liked the way it looked, and he couldn't take his eyes off her. Sadie looked at peace, when... in fact, Beau knew that it couldn't be farther from the truth.

He let his mind wander as he watched her. He could see her – belly swelling with their child. Her hair growing long and thick, and her eyes sparkling with joy. He often thought of how it could have been if Sadie were Patrick's mother. Beau wasn't sure if he even wanted another child until he saw Sadie holding Tucker. He chuckled to himself, took a step forward, and opened his mouth.

"And I know, I know, I know, I know, I know, I know, I know, I know, I know. Hey, I oughtta leave young thing alone... but ain't no sunshine when she's gone."

Beau appeared in the doorway and continued Sadie's song. She spun around – a shocked expression on her face.

"Beau! What are you doing here?" Sadie exclaimed as Tucker squirmed in her arms.

"You're my girl. I came for you. I came to make it right."

Sadie simply shook her head. "It was a mistake for you to come. You shouldn't have left Atlanta. It's Thanksgiving."

In his eyes, Sadie saw sincere regret and remorse. Beau looked like he hadn't slept all night.

"I didn't like the way we left things. It wasn't right. I've been worried sick. All of us, Sadie Mae... Mama and Presley too."

"Yes, but you told them. You told them why I left and why I had to leave Atlanta?"

Before Sadie could get another word out, Tucker threw his arms up and let out an ear-piercing wail. Sadie trying desperately to soothe him.

"Sorry... hey now, little man," Mazie said as she came running out of the bedroom. She grabbed her son, giving Beau the evil eye when she entered the room. "Good morning, Beauford. Happy Thanksgiving."

"Mazelle... Happy Thanksgiving to you too."

Mazie didn't even register a smile when she addressed Beau.

"He's just hungry. He loved your singing, Sadie Mae. Didn't you, big boy?"

Tucker cooed in his mother's arms as Mazie ripped her nursing bra off her shoulder and latched her boob onto Tucker's quivering mouth.

"Oh, hey now... you two go right on ahead with your conversation. Tucker and I are just going back to bed. Don't mind us."

Mazie raised her hand and shooed Sadie and Beau, and Sadie quickly turned and walked to the front door. She stepped out onto the front porch, and Beau followed.

"Mazie told me you took a greyhound bus back to Nashville. Sadie Mae... why on earth? Baby, I was so afraid that something bad happened to you."

Sadie felt guilty. She knew it was wrong to have left Broadfield House so suddenly. She was impulsive, and she hated herself. Mazie was right. Sadie hadn't given Beau a chance.

"I told Prez as soon as you left... Mama too. They know everything. Needless to say, I'm not real popular at Broadfield House. Baby, we all want you to come back to Atlanta. You need to hear me out."

Sadie folded her arms across her chest. She wanted to run to him and bury herself in his cream-colored fisherman's sweater. They both looked ready to walk hand in hand in the Macy's Thanksgiving Day Parade.

"Beau, I honestly don't think that it's going to matter much. I know what you did, and I don't think I can forgive you."

With that, Sadie heard a rap at the window. Mazie tapped the glass with her hand and wagged her finger at Sadie. She had promised Mazie that she would hear Beau out... one of them would hear Beau out, and Sadie knew that she wasn't giving him a fair chance.

"I want you to come back to Broadfield House. Don't be mad, but Mama organized a jet. It leaves in an hour. We can talk on the plane... work everything out," Beau pleaded.

Sadie was stunned as she let Beau's words sink in. Sadie stood her ground, and defiantly shook her head.

"No, Beau! I made other plans. My dad needs me. It wasn't right of me to leave him. It's his first Thanksgiving in Nashville. I wasn't thinking. I got caught up in myself... in us. It's not fair. I just can't leave him alone. I'm sorry. I should have realized sooner that it was a mistake." Beau turned away and sighed. "I'm going to spend the day at Tall Oaks Manor and then come back here for dinner. Mac and Mazie invited me."

Mazie threw the curtains open, and Sadie could hear her screaming no from inside.

"Sounds like Mazie thinks otherwise."

Beau's comment broke the tension, and they both let out a chuckle.

"She's just trying to be a friend," Sadie said.

"Well, I think you should listen to her. She's one smart cookie. Even keeled and levelheaded."

Sadie shot Beau a look of warning.

"Oh, and I am not. Is that what you're saying?"

Beau took his hands out of his pockets and ran them through his hair. He was not winning the battle.

"No, that's not what I am saying. It's just that... I think you have it wrong, Sadie Mae."

Sadie turned her back to Beau and leaned up against the porch railing.

"So, let me get this straight... all of a sudden, this is all my fault. I've got it all wrong. I'm flying off the handle... out of control?"

"No, baby. Listen to me. I'm sorry. What I did was wrong. I used my name... my connection to Chris to get you a second chance. Sadie, it's all my fault that you were late for that interview. I acted irresponsibly. I left you with too much on your plate that day, with Patrick, and I knew better. I lost track of time. I should have come right home, but I didn't. I just got caught up in myself and work. When I walked in on you and Patrick and the grape juice and the meltdown... it was all my fault. Sadie, I didn't buy your job. I never once offered up those tickets for your job... that's not what happened."

Sadie turned around and reached back for the porch railing. Beau was hopeful that she was softening a bit.

"Go on..."

"It's true. I called Holls. When you told me, it was Chris Holland that you were meeting with, I took a chance and called him. Chris and I went to Georgia together. We were fraternity brothers. We see each other around... alumni events here in town. I usually run into him at a football game every year. His mama and my mama are on Junior League together. I called him and asked him for a favor. I wanted that job for you, and I was afraid that if you were late to your interview that they would decline your meeting. You know, first impressions are everything, and being 45 minutes late to a job interview is suicide. I thought that if Chris could hear it from me... that it was my fault that you were late and that we had had an emergency, then he'd continue with the interview."

"I see..."

"I explained your situation to him. I told him that you had just moved to Nashville. I gave him some background on your dad... and I told him how much this job would mean to you and what a great appraiser you are... good with numbers... attention to detail. I told him that I was your character reference."

"You told him that you were sleeping with me."

"No, Sadie Mae I did not, but he's not stupid. He figured it out. He asked me if you were *the one*… and I told him yes."

Beau saw the look in Sadie's eyes and the way her lips curled up slightly.

"Then why did you bribe him with the tickets?"

"Sadie Mae, I swear on Patrick's life that I did not offer up any football tickets. Chris said it in passing as a joke at the end of our conversation. Nothing else was ever said. I swear to you. He held the cards. I know he wouldn't have hired you if he didn't think that you were the best person for the job."

"And you expect me to believe that, Beau. I saw the note… in your handwriting."

"Yes, it's true. I wrote the note, but the tickets were not mine. The tickets came from Mama. She won them at an auction at the country club a few months ago, and she asked me if I wanted them, but since the game was on Thanksgiving, I declined. She told me that she would give them away. That's why she had them." Sadie felt sick in the pit of her stomach. Now Lady Jane was involved.

"Look, I ran into Chris last week at an alumni lunch. Mama had told me his dad was sick with cancer. I wanted to share some things with him… give him some comfort. Sadie Mae… he couldn't stop talking about you. How wonderful you are and what an amazing job you are doing. You are way out meeting their expectations. They love your work. Chris thanked me again… for the introduction and told me that he was glad that I had called him. He told me that he had made the right choice in hiring you. Baby, that was you. That had nothing to do with me."

"I don't understand then… about the tickets."

"Chris never once asked me about the tickets. He never once said I owed him anything. I think he knew… that it wasn't appropriate. Apparently, my mama and his mama got to talking. He mentioned something to his mama about wanting to take his dad to the game… you know in case it was his last chance. She knew that Lady Jane had won those tickets. I had no idea she promised those tickets to the Hollands. She told me the night we arrived in Atlanta. She told me that a courier was coming to the house to pick them up."

Beau watched Sadie's face soften a bit. "I told Mama the conflict of interest. Shit, baby… Mama didn't know Chris was your boss. She just thought you both worked for the same company. When you called me to tell me about the courier, I panicked. It had all gotten way out of hand. I should have told you that I knew Chris. I should have told you about the tickets. Man, Mama feels horrible. Honestly, it all just snowballed out of control, and I didn't know what to do."

"So, you just kept lying. Jesus, Beau… you shouldn't have lied. If you had just told me the truth… about knowing Chris… and your phone call. I wouldn't have been happy about it. I probably would have confronted Chris… maybe resigned, but you kept that from me."

Beau took a step forward. He wanted to be done with the conversation and hold Sadie in his arms and get them back to Atlanta. As Beau stepped forward, Sadie stepped back.

"Beau, please. You need to get going… back to Atlanta, and I need to get back to the loft and get my car. I need to head out to Tall Oaks Manor."

Beau couldn't believe what he was hearing. He shook his head and continued to walk towards her.

"Baby, please. Sadie… I love you."

Sadie dropped her head. She couldn't look him in the eye. "I'm not sure if that is enough. I need some time. Please try and understand, but I just can't go back to Atlanta. I think we need some time apart."

Sadie threw her arms to her side and abruptly headed for the Mackenzie's front door.

"Baby, please…"

"Goodbye, Beau."

As Sadie reached the front door, she looked over her shoulder and watched Beau walk down the front steps and out to his waiting car.

* * *

Sadie walked to the parking lot at Tall Oaks Manor and pulled her phone from the bottom of her tote as she unlocked her car. She hadn't looked at her phone since she left town to head to her dad. All she could see in her mind was Beau walking off the porch... out of her life and back to Atlanta. She deeply regretted her decision, but it was too late now. No calls and no texts... and no Beau. Sadie fought back the tears, but it was no use. She sat in her car, feeling sorry for herself and tried to cry it all out.

The rain was falling steadily, and the sky was turning dark. Sadie would have just enough time to drive back to Nashville and make it to Mac and Mazie's for dinner at five. She didn't want to go back there, and she was tempted to return to the loft and crawl up into their bed, but it made her stomach hurt. All she could picture in her mind was the last time she made love to Beau in the loft. They were both so excited about the holidays for the first time in years. Their joy pulsating through their souls as their bodies came together.

Sadie's visit with her father had not gone as planned. James was having a bad day and seemed agitated the longer she visited with him. Sadie encouraged him to work on his latest model airplane as she sipped watered down coffee and observed him in a comfy chair by the fireplace in the recreation center. She looked around at the other residents, celebrating the holiday with their families – her father oblivious to the fact that it was Thanksgiving. Finally, as the afternoon arrived, he became even more upset... a condition known as sundowners. James suddenly realized that it was Thanksgiving, and he couldn't locate his daughter. He kept telling Sadie that his daughter had been left home alone even though Sadie repeatedly told her father that she was right there with him.

Today, Sadie's father was living in 1977, and he was frantic to find his eight-year-old daughter. When the staff was unable to reason with him, they gave him a mild sedative and escorted him back to his room. Sadie stayed with him until he fell asleep, knowing that he would most likely miss Thanksgiving dinner entirely.

Sadie wanted to call Beau, but she knew that the family was sitting down to dinner. She would call him as soon as she got back to Mac and Mazie's... the wheels inside her head turning. Sadie would drive to Atlanta tomorrow. She could be there mid-day for a feast of leftovers and for what Beau called a college football smorgasbord. Sadie laughed at the thought even when she knew that Lady Jane and Presley had already roped her into a marathon black Friday shopping session.

God, she was so foolish. It had all been a really big misunderstanding. She should be so lucky to have someone who cared about her the way Beau did. He would move heaven and earth for her, and Sadie realized in her heart that he already had.

The windshield wipers worked overtime as Sadie, through her tears, tried to concentrate on the country road ahead of her. The drive into Nashville from Tall Oaks Manor was beautiful, and the leaves on the trees had already turned and had begun to fall, coating the road.

The more Sadie drove and tried to clear her mind, the more foolish she felt. Beau was right. Not only had Chris Holland repeatedly praised her work but so had several others at Cushmen and Wakeland. Sadie knew deep down in her heart that this was her doing and not Beau's. He was right. Had he not placed that call to Chris, they would have probably not met with her.

"Oh, what have you done, Sadie Mae. You've gone and made it all worse."

She cried harder, thinking about the look in Beau's eyes when he walked towards her on the porch, and then she remembered what he said. How Beau Walker confessed to her that she was *the one*.

Sadie took her eyes off the road for just a brief second to reach into her purse for the packet of Kleenex. When she looked back up and came around the bend, she saw the deer in the middle of the road and slammed on her brakes.

The crash seemed like it took forever as Sadie felt the adrenaline course through her entire body. In swerving to avoid the deer, the car hydroplaned, and she couldn't do anything as the car skimmed along the surface of the water. Braking wouldn't help. It was like a slow fall off a precipice, and Sadie saw her life flash before her eyes.

Beau.

The seatbelt tugged around her middle as she tried to gain control of the vehicle, but it was no use. The tires hit the gravel at the edge of the road, and the car spun out of control. Sadie braced for impact, and her body lurched forward as the seatbelt constricted her movement.

Sadie heard the explosion of the airbag as her face and upper body made contact. She felt her lungs contract, knocking the wind out of her, and in the distance, she could hear herself screaming… followed by the crushing sound of glass shattering and metal twisting. Suddenly, everything just stopped, and all she heard was the sound of the rain beating down on the car roof and the drops falling softly in her hair.

Sadie felt disorientated as she drifted in and out of consciousness – the taste of blood in her mouth. Her eyelids fluttered, and her body shivered. She was cold, and she reached for him, but a pain radiated in her arm.

Beau.

For a moment, Sadie thought she was in bed in the loft, and then darkness fell over her again. Had it not been for the cold and the pain radiating throughout her body, she would have sworn she was in bed with Beau. Sadie opened her mouth and called out his name over and over again.

As the rain continued to fall, Sadie drifted back into consciousness and opened her eyes. As she focused, she saw the blue lights and heard the wail of sirens.

Then, in a moment, it was all gone.

CHAPTER SEVENTEEN

"**D**o you want pie, fartface?"

Beau shook his head sideways at Presley. He was slumped on the couch and had been staring at the same piece of fuzz on the carpet for almost two hours.

"I'll eat his piece, then."

Patrick jumped up from behind the couch in the solarium, where he had set up his Matchbox racetrack, and plopped down on the couch next to Beau.

"Just a small piece for him, please."

Lady Jane looked across the room at her son and followed Presley into the kitchen.

They all tried, for Patrick's sake, but Thanksgiving was a real downer, not to mention that Lady Jane and Presley had lost their back-up cook. With Beau being gone most of the morning and Patrick arriving at noon, the girls hustled to get a simple meal prepared. Luckily, a few of Lady Jane's friends and two of Presley's co-workers added bodies to the quiet dining room. Everyone had been so excited to meet Sadie Mae, and Beau had to grit his teeth every time he had to explain that she stayed behind in Nashville to care for her father.

No actually... Sadie Mae isn't here because I am a lying sack of shit, and I've gone and fucked up the greatest love of my life. Please pass the peas.

Beau pulled his phone out of his back pocket for the 300th time, and then he remembered what she said about giving her space. He had fucked it up so bad now he didn't know what to do, and he wasn't about to go taking any more advice from Lady Jane or Presley. Their plan to rescue Sadie and bring her back to Atlanta had failed miserably. Just as he was about to put his phone away, he got a text from Mazie.

Have you heard from Sadie Mae?

No!

She was due back here for dinner at 5.

Beau looked at his watch. Nashville was one hour behind. It was almost six o'clock there, and she was an hour late. That wasn't like Sadie.

She's probably just enjoying the time with her dad.

She asked for space. I've got to respect that.

If she texts me, I'll let you know. You do the same, ok?

Ok!

"Patrick, I've got your pie."

The little boy hopped up and ran for the kitchen where Lady Jane had set a small slice of chocolate pecan pie. Patrick picked up the Ready Whip and covered his entire plate in the white foam. With Patrick occupied, Presley joined Beau on the couch.

"Was that a text from Sadie Mae?" Presley asked. Beau let out a pained laugh and shook his head. Presley's heart ached for him. She knew all too well how Beau felt.

"I don't know what I am going to do, Prez... without her." Beau's eyes welled up with tears. "I screwed this up, and now I don't think she's ever going to forgive me."

"Don't go there. She'll come around. I know she will. She loves you."

Beau wished he had Presley's positive attitude and optimism.

"Beau, I know she said she wanted space, but be careful, okay."

Presley ran her hands down the front of her wool crepe pants. She had asked Andrew for space once... to focus on her nursing degree and look where it got her. If only things had been different for her and Andrew, then perhaps it would be her rubbing her hands over her pregnant belly and not Andrew's wife.

"Just let her clear her head, and I bet you, she will call."

Presley leaned into Beau and squeezed his arm as Beau's phone began to vibrate with a call. He pulled the phone from his back pocket and stared at the screen.

Sadie.

"Oh, my God... see, I told you!" Presley squealed as Beau jumped up from the couch and slid his finger across the screen.

"Sadie... baby?"

There was silence, and then someone clearing their throat. Beau pulled the phone away from his ear and looked at the screen again. It was definitely an incoming call from Sadie's number. He loved it when she called him. Her glowing face popped up on his phone screen. He had cropped Patrick out of the picture on his phone, but he had a full shot with the two of them framed on his desk at work. They were so happy that day... right after she moved to Nashville. They had taken that drive to Arrington, and her cheeks were pink from the wine that she drank at the vineyard. She had chased Patrick back towards the car and caught up to him and picked him up and twirled him around, and they both laughed uncontrollably. Beau captured their joy in a photo at that moment.

"Hello, excuse me. Is this Beau?" A young male voice cut through the silence.

"Yes, who is this and why are you calling me on my girlfriend's phone?"

A million thoughts raced through Beau's mind, but the one that sliced him open was the vision of Sadie's mouth on another man. That little moan she made when her seeking tongue found what it was looking for. Her soft hands kneading the back of his head. Sadie's delicate hands through his hair. Would her pain and disappointment cause her to stray?

"Oh, so you are Sadie Morgan's boyfriend, excellent."

Beau tried to remain calm, but a fire burned in the pit of his stomach. He could see her... tangled in this guy's sheets with that satisfied smile on her face. Her cheeks flushed from her last orgasm... still trying to catch her breath.

God, no wonder she didn't go to Mac and Mazie's for dinner.

"Who the fuck is this?"

Beau just wanted this conversation to be over with. Was she lying there listening in? What was this kid... because the guy on the other end of the line sounded like a kid... going to tell him? How Sadie loved it when he took her nipples in his mouth. The way she cried out in anticipation whenever his fingers brushed the opening between her legs or how Sadie arched her back and then dug her fingernails into his lower back right after he took her to ecstasy.

"Excuse me, sir, I am so terribly sorry. This is Eddie."

Bile rose up in Beau's throat.

Eddie. I'll kill the motherfucker.

"So, Eddie. What in the fuck can I do for you?"

"I'm an emergency room nurse at Vanderbilt University Medical Center. Beau, your number was listed on Sadie's phone as her emergency contact. I'm sorry, but she was in a motor vehicle accident earlier this evening, and she's been calling out for you since she was brought in here."

Beau opened his mouth to let out a scream, but nothing came out.

* * *

"Morgan! Sadie… she was brought in here about an hour ago."

Mazie flew into the Vanderbilt University Medical Center emergency room, screaming at the receptionist. The ER was packed. Thanksgiving was a busy night at the hospital. After Beau had called her to give her what little details he had, Mazie grabbed the baby and Mac, and they took off for the hospital. Thank God the hospital was exactly one mile from their front door.

"Are you family?"

"Huh?"

"Family?"

"Why… yes, ma'am. I am her sister," Mazie replied.

"Mazelle Maureen!" Mac shouted. Mazie whipped her head around and hissed at him.

"And this is her brother-in-law."

"Just one moment, please. You might want to take a seat," the receptionist said, pointing to the seating area behind her.

"Yes, thank you."

Mazie turned towards Mac as he set the baby carrier down. The only open chair in the waiting area was next to a guy who had his right hand wrapped up in a blood-soaked towel.

"Happy Thanksgiving!" Mac nervously said to the guy as he took a seat next to him.

"Oh gosh, Mac. Beau is calling again! Stay here, and if the reception-ist comes back, I'll be right over by the vending machines."

Mazie slid her finger across the face of her phone. "Beau… we just got here."

"Oh, thank God. How is she?"

"Ummmm... I don't know. The receptionist told us to take a seat. The ER is really busy. As soon as I speak to a doctor, I'll let you know," Mazie said. She heard Beau let out a deep sigh.

"Listen, I'm at the airport. We are waiting for the pilot. I've got Presley with me, and Mama's looking after Patrick. Assuming we take off soon, I should be there in about an hour. Maze, she's got a broken..." Beau couldn't get arm fully out of his mouth before he sputtered.

"Beau... Mac, Tucker and I are here. I'll text you as soon as I hear anything, okay?"

All Mazie heard on the other end of the line was Beau sniffling.

"Please! Mazie, make sure you tell her that I love her."

"Yup... will do."

Mazie needed the call to end before she completely lost it. She turned around to Mac just as a nurse with a clipboard in her hand shouted out.

"Sadie Morgan!"

Mazie stuffed her phone in her back pocket and took off running to the nurses' side.

"As family, I'll need you to sign this consent for service form. Miss Morgan is drifting in and out of consciousness. She has a possible broken left arm, and the doctor wants a head CT scan."

The nurse shoved the forms into Mazie's hands as Mac shook his head. Mazie didn't give a shit. They were Sadie's family. She had no one. Beau had asked Mazie to take care of her, and Mazie was prepared to do just that... even if her lawyer-to-be husband objected.

"Give her a pink cast, please. She'll love that," Mazie said as the nurse nodded back at her. "When can I see her?"

"Do you know who Beau is?" the nurse asked. "She's been in and out of consciousness, but she keeps calling out for him."

"Yes, ma'am. Beau is her boyfriend. He is on his way."

"It's crowded back there, but I'll take you back for a minute."

Mazie swiftly turned and smiled at Mac, kissed her infant son on the forehead, and followed the nurse to Sadie.

* * *

Mazie was not entirely prepared when the nurse abruptly pulled back the curtain, exposing Sadie on the gurney. She was almost unrecognizable. Her hair was wet and smoothed back from her forehead and there were ruby red abrasions on both cheeks and her chin. On her forehead, near her hairline, was a gash which had been closed with a butterfly bandage. Her eyes were red and swollen shut, and Sadie's left arm was heavily bandaged and folded tightly across her chest, held in place by a dark navy-blue sling.

"Oh, dear. Sadie Mae?" Sadie followed the sound of Mazie's voice and turned her head slightly.

"Beau..."

It was barely audible, but Mazie watched as Sadie parted her lips to let out a raspy reply.

"Darling, he is on his way. You hang in there... you hear me?"

Mazie reached down and squeezed Sadie's hand, but Sadie was out again, and her hand fell limp in Mazie's.

"She's stable but serious. We need to rule out any head injuries... brain bleeding."

Mazie's knees buckled, and she let out a gasp as the nurse continued speaking.

"I'll send the doctor out to meet y'all. He can give you an update on her condition. The x-ray shows her left arm is a clean break. She's lucky there. Miss Morgan won't need surgery, just a cast for about eight weeks. We need to take her upstairs for more tests. We will keep you posted."

Mazie stepped away from Sadie's side as they wheeled her down the hall and out of sight.

* * *

The emergency room was still buzzing when Beau and Presley flew through the door. Mazie was gently rocking Tucker, and he seemed content nursing despite the chaos that surrounded them. Mac spotted them and whistled loudly, and Beau and Presley rushed to their side.

"Can I see her?" Beau asked, slightly out of breath as if he had run all the way to Nashville from Atlanta.

"No. She's upstairs, Beau. They are running a CT scan of her head. They need to rule out…"

Mazie stopped and looked at Presley and started crying. Mac scooped up the baby and a cloth diaper and laid his son over his shoulder and gently patted his back.

"Beau, let me talk with the charge nurse and see if I can get an update," Presley said, grabbing Beau's hand and giving it a quick squeeze. "I'll be right back."

Beau watched as his sister kissed the top of Mazie's head before heading up to the reception desk.

"Good thing you brought her. She'll be a good advocate for Sadie. Fuck, Beau! I signed the consent forms. I didn't know what else to do. They wanted to scan her brain. I hope I did right by her. I hope I did the right thing."

Beau knelt down to Mazie. "I take it, Perry Mason, over there did not approve?" He chuckled and then turned his gaze to Mac, who was still burping Tucker. "It's all gonna be fine, Mazie. She's going to be fine."

Beau caught sight of his sister, having an in-depth conversation with a nurse, and he rose and hurried to them.

"This is my brother, Beau Walker… Sadie's boyfriend. Beau, this is Sandra… she is the charge nurse on duty," Presley said. Beau extended his hand and gave Sandra a firm handshake.

"I was just explaining to your sister that Miss Morgan is stable but serious. She's upstairs waiting for a head CT. This is routine for most car accident patients. The doctor wants to rule out bleeding, a brain injury, or a skull fracture."

Beau shook his head, trying to take it all in.

"Her x-rays show a fracture of her left arm. Closed, not compound."

Beau furrowed his brow and looked over at Presley.

"It just means the bone is not sticking out," Presley clarified, reaching for Beau's hand to squeeze it tight.

"We'll get a look at the arm and the rest of her body with a full CT scan. We need to make sure that Miss Morgan doesn't have any internal injuries that may require surgery. I will say that in our initial examination, we do not suspect any internal damage. Airbags do an amazing job." The nurse smiled and excused herself, adding that she would keep them posted and let Beau know when he could see Sadie.

"You okay?" Presley turned towards Beau and asked. She reached up and placed her hands on his shoulders. Beau paused as he looked down at his shoes and shook his head sideways.

"I'm gonna call Mama and give her an update. I'll be right back."

Beau quickly returned to Mazie, and she stood to greet him, wrapping her arms tight around him as Beau updated her and Mac on Sadie's condition.

"Why don't you guys head home. I'll text you with an update. Come back in the morning if you want. This ER is no place for that little guy."

Beau reached out and ran his hand down Tucker's little back remembering back to the days when Patrick was that tiny.

Mazie embraced Beau again… and whispered in his ear. "You want Mac to stay?" She pulled away, and Beau shook his head.

"No. I got Prez. We are good. I'll text you, okay?"

Mazie turned away from Beau before she started to cry again and grabbed the baby carrier and walked towards the exit.

"You hang in there, buddy," Mac said. He reached out and grabbed Beau's shoulder and squeezed it.

As he watched his friends walk out of the ER, Beau turned and slumped into a chair and silently began to weep.

* * *

Sadie's eyes fluttered. She didn't know where she was, but her first thought was of her father. Her eyes opened long enough to see that her left arm was in a pink cast before she shut them tight again.

"What's going on?"

Sadie heard her voice, but it didn't sound like the words were coming out of her mouth. Her throat was dry, and pain radiated throughout her entire body.

"Sadie?"

A voice filled her head, and she opened her eyes again and stared straight into his dark, slate-gray eyes.

"Oh my God, baby..." he whispered.

"I'll go get the nurse." A soft female voice spoke.

Sadie's mind swam in confusion. The voices made her head pound to the rhythm of her beating heart. Sadie opened her mouth, but no more words formed, only a sickening moan.

"Sadie Mae, I am right here. Baby, please just squeeze my hand, okay." Beau clutched Sadie's hand, but she didn't reciprocate.

He hadn't left her bedside since they brought her up from the ER six hours ago. Beau sat next to her and held her hand... only leaving her side when Presley insisted that he take a walk or grab a coffee. It was five in the morning, and Sadie was finally waking up.

Beau stood, afraid to squeeze Sadie's hand any harder. His eyes darted back and forth between Sadie and the door, anxiously waiting for the nurse. Beau gently leaned over her and kissed her cheek, and she immediately cried out. It wasn't a cry of agony but a cry of fear, and he watched as her whole body shook in terror.

"Well, who do we have here?"

Another voice filled Sadie's head as she fluttered her eyes and opened them again. This time, a large black woman came into view.

"Can you tell me your name, darlin'?" Sadie shook her head up and down. Her name filled her head, but little else. Places, memories, and all those voices were mixed up like someone threw clothes in a dryer and tumbled everything on high.

"Sadie Morgan."

Sadie barely got the words out as she opened her eyes wider and caught a glimpse of the woman. She was a nurse with a stethoscope around her neck, and she held a white light that she shined in Sadie's eyes.

"I'm April Williams. It's nice to meet you. Do you know where you are?"

Sadie shook her head sideways, desperately trying to piece it all together, but she couldn't.

"Seattle…?"

"Oh, I've always wanted to go to Seattle. I've never been west of the Mississippi. Well, except that time I went to Memphis and walked over the bridge, but I don't think that counts, right? You know you can stand on that bridge and have one foot in Tennessee and one foot in Arkansas. Imagine that?!"

April had a friendly and reassuring smile, and Sadie squinted at her and registered a faint grin. The nurse grabbed the remote for Sadie's bed and raised her head slightly.

"How's that? Better?"

"Yes, I think."

Sadie tried to see beyond April, but her eyes were blurry. She needed her glasses. In the distance, two figures were silhouetted – backlit from the overhead fluorescent hallway lights.

"I'm going to call your doctor. He's going to be quite pleased that you are awake. How much pain are you in? Can you look at this picture and let me know? Which one of these emojis best describes your pain level?"

Sadie stared down at the plastic picture and looked up at April. She was in a hospital room. She must have fallen and broken her arm, but she couldn't remember all the details. She shut her eyes again and began to cry.

"Baby, please don't cry." Beau walked back to her bedside and shot an angry look towards the nurse. "Can you give her something! Can't you see that she is in pain."

His voice was angry, and Sadie shook her head. She was frightened, but she didn't know why.

"Beau, please," Presley pleaded. Beau's sister reached for his arm, trying to calm him. She pulled him back and away from Sadie's bed. "Let the nurse assess her, okay." Beau relented, turning towards his sister with a nod of his head.

The whispers made Sadie uneasy. She turned her head towards the voices once again. Her sight was still fuzzy, and she couldn't make out their faces, so she blinked again. Sadie focused her attention on the picture the nurse held in front of her. She pointed to the angry face and then closed her eyes. She wanted all the people near her to just disappear and all the voices to quit talking.

"Right in the middle. Safe choice. I'll be right back."

Nurse April closed the curtain around her and left Sadie's bedside as a silence fell over the room.

Sadie let out a deep breath and let the images fill her mind. She was trying hard to remember every little detail.

Her suitcase was heavy as she lugged it down the stairs. The house was dark, but she had tiptoed into her father's room and kissed his forehead. Philomena said that he would be fine. Joel's study door was closed, but the light was on. She didn't bother knocking. The markets were closing in Tokyo. He wouldn't be pleased with the disturbance.

Sadie next remembered the heat. It was so humid that she hit the buttons on the air conditioning unit on the wall and sat on the end of the bed. The room was enormous and smelled like lavender and citrus. Sadie was in a hotel room in Nashville.

She opened her eyes and smiled. She remembered as she turned her head and found his familiar eyes.

"Hey there, baby."

His voice was so beautiful. It was the most beautiful thing that Sadie had ever heard. So strong and so sexy. She opened up her mouth, and a faint giggle escaped her lips. She was just about ready to speak when he leaned into her and brushed his lips near her ear, and Sadie screamed out.

"Baby! Oh God... I am so sorry. Did I hurt you?" Sadie realized that he was holding her hand and squeezing it, and she felt sick to her stomach.

"No! Let me go..." Sadie shook her hand loose and closed her eyes again. She wanted to wake up. This was all a dream... a nightmare. She felt the tears streaming down her face as she cried out.

"Sadie! Baby... please open your eyes. It's going to be okay. I understand. You've been through a lot, and I am so very sorry. You were in an accident. Coming back from Tall Oaks Manor. Everything is going to be fine."

His voice was calming, and Sadie shook her head up and down in response, and when she opened her eyes again to look at him, she remembered... but nothing made sense. Nothing he had said to her made any logical sense.

"Beau... right?"

Sadie watched his eyes fill with tears as she looked up at him.

"Aren't you that guy I met in that brewpub in Nashville?"

CHAPTER EIGHTEEN

"I'm sorry, can you repeat that?"

Beau's eyes were brimming with tears as he clutched Presley's hand. They sat next to one another in a small room down the hall from where Sadie lay resting.

"Transient global amnesia. I believe Miss Morgan is experiencing a temporary loss of memory. In severe cases, difficulty forming new memories may occur. We won't know anything for a few more days. We need to run more tests. This traumatic amnesia is a direct result of a hard blow to the head. It's not uncommon in car accident victims... however, you did mention that Miss Morgan had experienced another recent head trauma. A physical assault."

The doctor shuffled through Sadie's file, and Beau's mind was filled with the image of Joel's hands on Sadie's shoulders repeatedly slamming her into the doorframe.

"Beau, the good news is that her second CT scan looks clean. There is no brain hemorrhage."

Thank God for Presley. How lucky was Beau to have an emergency room nurse for a sister? She hadn't batted an eyelash when the call came in that Sadie had been in an accident, and Beau was grateful she flew back to Nashville with him. She was vital to his understanding and acceptance of Sadie's situation. Without her, he would be lost.

"There is another avenue to discuss. I wouldn't normally bring it up with car accident victims, but Miss Morgan's scans all look very clean." The doctor squirmed uncomfortably in his chair. "It's called dissociative amnesia. It's a type of disorder that involves an inability to recall important personal information. It's a sort of blocking out of events caused mainly from stress."

Beau took in the doctor's words and leaned forward in his chair.

"Like if Sadie was upset by something?" Beau asked.

"Exactly. You mentioned she has been under a lot of stress lately. The assault, plus her recent move to Nashville, and her father is ill with Alzheimer's disease."

"And we just had a fight," Beau said through gritted teeth. He let out a held breath and buried his head in his hands.

"Beau, don't. Please don't go there," Presley said as she reached her arm around Beau's shoulder. He released and began to weep softly.

"I did this to her. This is all my fault. Son of a bitch!" Beau shot up from his chair and walked towards the window... wiping his eyes clean of tears. He could see a faint line of pink in the sky. The sun would be up shortly. A throng of employees were making their way across the parking lot, ready to start their shifts. Beau could see steam rising from their mouths. He could feel the chill in his bones.

"Mr. Walker... it's highly unlikely that a verbal argument would have caused this type of episode. We just need to give it time. Miss Morgan needs rest. Based on her test results, I am extremely optimistic that she will be feeling better in no time. I would caution you, though... it's probably best that she remains calm... not upset by... anything or anyone."

"Well, I'm not going to leave her here alone," Beau said tersely.

"No. I understand. But I believe your presence may be causing her added stress. Right now, Miss Morgan has no recollection of you or your family other than a brief memory of meeting you. You may want to reconsider."

The doctor quickly stood and handed Presley his business card. "I'm available for questions. If you need to reach me."

"Thank you," Beau squawked, never bothering to turn from the window.

"I'll check in on her later. If her condition changes, I'll let you know." The doctor turned quickly and exited the room.

Beau pulled his phone from his back pocket and tapped his Google app. "Dissociative amnesia." He spoke the words slowly into his phone.

"No, Beau... please. You don't want to do that," Presley shouted out. She quickly approached Beau, ready to grab the phone from his hands, if necessary.

"The fuck I do. I want to know everything there is to know about this."

"Beau, please... trust me... better yet, ask me. Please don't go snooping around the Internet. It's dangerous, and it's gonna fill your head with a bunch of nonsense."

Beau knew that Presley was right, but he felt so lost.

"What am I going to do, Prez. I don't know what to do?"

Presley grabbed Beau's hands and looked deep into his eyes. "Well, we are going to make a plan. I think you need to go home. Get a few hours of sleep. Take a hot shower."

Beau looked at her and just shook his head. "No! I can't leave her," he shouted.

"Listen, I am used to being up all night... working 12 plus hours. Let me stay with her. Right now, I'm just a stranger to her."

Presley caught herself before she lost it. She needed to be strong for Beau. Strong for Sadie. Presley needed to be nurse Walker now and remove her personal connection from the situation.

"Give Mama a call, please. She wants to hear your voice," she instructed her brother as he reached out for her and hugged her tight.

"I'll call Mazie too. I don't know what to tell her. She's going to be so... ummmm... and shit... Juliette. It's the middle of the night in Seattle."

"Go, Beaufart! Go home. Make your calls. I'll text you every hour, and I will only call you if necessary."

Beau walked past Sadie's room on his way out of the hospital, but her eyes were closed. He watched her chest rise and fall and prayed that she was sleeping soundly, dreaming of him and their new life together. Beau put his fingers to his lips and blew her a kiss. One from him and one from Patrick.

I love you, baby.

When he got back to the loft, Beau walked straight upstairs and into a hot shower. He closed his eyes and let the hot water flow down his back. He turned, instinctively looking for her... wishing she would reappear before him, but he shook his head and tried to let the memories fade.

"Well... good morning, Sadie Mae. What can I do for you?" Beau had turned around in the shower and wiped the water from his eyes. Sadie stood before him... completely naked.

"I'm just checking out your shower," she giggled out as she sauntered towards him... placing her hands on his chest and pushing him back further into the water. Beau watched the water as it lightly cascaded down her breasts, completely in a trance. Sadie's kiss was smoldering, and Beau wanted to reach back and turn the water temperature down. He felt his whole-body aflame.

"What do you think then?" Beau asked. He let his hands run the length of her body... stopping to cup the cheeks of her ass.

"About what?"

Sadie brought her hips closer to his and felt his growing erection. She looked up… deep into his eyes, and he no longer had any desire for them to continue talking.

Beau shook his head, and she was gone. He realized that he was standing alone in his shower. The memory of their first shower in the loft burned into his mind and seared the backs of his eyeballs. He reached for a washcloth, and body wash. It smelled like rose petals and vanilla, and he brought the bottle up to his nose and took in a deep breath.

Sadie.

The bottle landed with a thud on the shower tiles as Beau bent at the waist and sobbed.

* * *

Sadie woke from a deep sleep. When she opened her eyes, a beautiful blond woman was sitting next to her bed. The hospital room was bathed in bright light with the sun streaming through the window.

"Hello."

The blond woman had a calming voice, and she rose and took a few steps closer to Sadie.

"Hello," Sadie replied.

"My name is Presley Walker. I'm a nurse. I'm here to help you and aid in your recovery. How are you feeling, Sadie?"

Sadie took a deep breath. Her mind was still uncertain, and she tried hard to remember the events of the past few days, but Sadie had no idea what day it was.

"Confused. I'm in Nashville, still… right?"

"Yes. You are at Vanderbilt University Medical Center. Do you know how you got here?" Presley asked.

Sadie shook her head sideways. She didn't have a fucking clue, but she had read about things happening to women who traveled alone. Men in bars slipping drugs into drinks and then kidnapping and raping them. Sadie shut her eyes and began to cry.

"Was I raped?" Sadie asked. She opened her eyes and looked at Presley.

"No! Oh God, no… Sadie. You were in a car accident."

Sadie slammed her eyes shut again and threw her head back into the pillow. She tried to remember as she brought her hand to her face and rubbed her eyes.

"Why can't I remember?" Sadie mumbled.

Presley pulled her chair closer to Sadie's bed and sat down.

"You will. I promise you, you are going to remember, but you've bumped your head, and it's going to take time and rest… lots of rest. You are safe, that's all that matters. You are being treated by some of the best doctors and nurses in the state of Tennessee."

"Thank you… ummmm…" Sadie had forgotten her name.

"Presley. Presley Walker."

"Presley. Yes… thank you."

"My mama loved Elvis."

Sadie remembered their argument. Her mother was standing in the living room of their tiny apartment in Seattle as her father took the dusty sheet off the painting. If that's what you called it.

"No, Jim. It's not gonna happen. Look, I loved him too, but he's dead now. It's morbid to have that man's face in our living room," Sadie's mom argued, stomping her foot down and crossing her arms over her chest.

Jim wasn't listening. Sadie's father knelt on the floor next to the painting and ran his hands over it, as if in a trance.

"Elenore. Come feel this. It's velvet!"

Sadie's mom threw her dishtowel down on the ground and plodded down the hallway. There was no way she was going to have a velvet painting of Elvis Presley hanging in her living room.

"What do you think, skookum?"

Sadie's father had several go-to nicknames for her. Skookum and sapphire were two of her favorites. Skookum was short for skookum chuck a Chinook Indian jargon term, which meant strong or powerful. Her father heard the term when he was fishing the coastal inlets in British Columbia as a young boy. Sadie's grandfather was Canadian, and James spent every summer near the Sechelt Inlet, a fjord along the Sunshine Coast.

Sadie knelt next to her father and watched him look at the painting. His idol, Elvis, had been dead for almost a month, and he had slowly been working his way through his entire album collection… playing a different album from *the king* nightly.

"Do you think she's going to let me keep it? What luck, huh? Another member of our construction crew found it in the attic, and the old lady we are working for didn't want it… no one did. Those young kids I work with now are into disco. Imagine that?"

Sadie didn't want to tell her father that she had asked her mom if she could save up her allowance and buy the *Saturday Night Fever* soundtrack.

"I'm going out. I'll be back later."

Sadie jumped off the floor and ran towards her mother. Elenore stood in the hallway in tight bell-bottom jeans and a macramé halter top. She had a leather headband tied around her forehead, and her ears were adorned with turquoise feather earrings. She had her guitar in one hand and her song notebook in the other.

"What about dinner, mommy? We haven't finished it." Sadie's eyes stung with tears, but she knew that never worked on her mother.

"You guys can finish it off. Pot roast is in the oven. It will be ready in 30 minutes."

Lacking further emotion, Sadie's mom strolled to the front door.

"You'd better not hang that thing while I am gone," Sadie's mom protested, pointing a ridged finger at her husband.

"Nora..."

Sadie's mom turned and slammed the door on her way out.

After four days and nights without a trace of Sadie's mother, James hung the painting in the living room above the couch. It would be the first thing she would see if and when she came home.

* * *

"Presley... what's wrong?"

Beau picked up his phone on the first ring. He had laid it across his chest as he fell into bed after his shower.

Beau had been gone for almost five hours, and Presley thought she ought to update him on her most recent conversation with Sadie. The nurse had come into Sadie's room to bath her and change her hospital gown. Presley took the opportunity to make a few phone calls and then take time for a bathroom and food break.

"The good news is she is more alert. They are bathing her, and she's asked for some lunch. Beau, these are all good things. She needs sustenance... water. It will aid in the healing. Also, her pain has subsided. This means they will ween her off the narcotics, which I think will have a direct link with her head clearing." Presley paused and brought a forkful of salad to her mouth.

Beau listened intently to Presley's update and then let out his held breath. For the first time in almost 24 hours, he felt hopeful.

"But she still doesn't remember anything, right?" he asked.

"Beau... I'm afraid Sadie Mae has had very little memory recall. She thinks she just arrived in Nashville. It was so heartbreaking. She thought she had been slipped something in her drink. Sadie Mae thought she might have been sexually assaulted."

"Fuck, by me… she thinks I could have done that to her, right?"

Beau sat up and threw his legs over the side of the bed. He stood and paced the loft bedroom.

This was a fucking nightmare.

"No, she never said that. She's just confused. She had no recollection of driving. Sadie Mae told me she didn't rent a car when she came to Nashville. She asked me if someone was going to go get her suitcase from the JW Marriott."

Presley didn't want to tell Beau, but she knew that she had to.

"Beau, she asked about Joel. She wanted to know if the hospital has tried to contact him. I didn't know what to say, but she mentioned that he might be out of town on business. I think we may have bought some time."

"Fuck! Over my dead body is she allowed to call him. Do not give her access to her phone… any phone. I'm coming back. I'll be there in 30 minutes. You need a break anyway," Beau huffed. He launched himself out of bed, reaching for a clean pair of jeans and a shirt.

Presley had to tell him. She knew that it would kill him, but she had to tell him about the rest of her conversation with Sadie. The good parts and the bad.

* * *

"Is Beau still here?"

Presley sat up straight in her chair. She felt a glimmer of hope at Sadie's question.

"No, he's gone home. He needed to rest and take a shower."

"I wanted to thank him… I mean, I am assuming that whatever happened to me… after we met… he brought me here?"

Sadie looked at Presley, searching for something in her face before lowering her eyes and shaking her head. "No, that's not what happened, is it?" Sadie answered her own question.

She remembered his eyes and something else, but the memory was so distant... deep within her brain. She pounded her fist on the bed.

"Sadie, do you remember something... about Beau?"

Sadie smiled at the memory. It was just a flash, but it came to her clear as the blue sky outside.

"George," she replied.

"Yes, Sadie! That's Beau's dog. He has a dog named George," Presley said fighting back tears.

"Presley... why would I know that Beau has a dog? Why do I remember that Beau's dog is named George?"

Presley stood and walked to Sadie's bedside and filled her water glass... handing her the plastic cup with a straw.

"I should know you, shouldn't I? But I don't," Sadie asked.

Presley couldn't deceive her any longer. She shook her head up and down as Sadie began to weep.

"I think I'd like to be alone for a while. I can't take it. You're all looking at me. I don't know you. I don't know, Beau. I'm sorry. Please just leave me alone! I want you all to just go and stay away from me!" Sadie shouted.

Tears rolled down Presley's face as Sadie watched her walk back to her chair and grab her sweater and purse.

"The nurse will be in shortly... to bathe you... and bring you some lunch. Perhaps we can talk later if you feel like it."

Sadie closed her eyes tight as Presley left the room and went to phone Beau.

* * *

"Miss Morgan. My name is Grace Gulliksen. I'm a staff psychiatrist. Everyone just calls me Dr. GG. Would it be alright if we talked?"

After her conversation with Presley ended abruptly, Sadie bathed, ate a bit of lunch and requested a book from the hospital library. She had just propped herself up in a chair by the window when the doctor came in to introduce herself.

"Sure... I guess."

Dr. GG looked to be in her early sixties with a kind face and safe eyes. Her hair was cut severely short... almost spiky on top and was pure white. Sadie noticed that her left ear was pierced about a dozen times, and she was amused by her fashion choice – a pair of khaki pants with Birkenstocks and a brightly colored top with fuchsia and yellow wild birds adorning a front pocket. Inside the pocket, Sadie saw a pair of purple reading glasses, which Dr. GG pulled out as she scanned Sadie's file.

"So, it appears you were in a car accident... near Somerset Farms on Thanksgiving Day?"

Sadie looked up at the doctor with a shocked expression on her face. "Did you say Thanksgiving Day? No... that can't be right. That would mean that I have been in Nashville... five months. Is that right?" Sadie asked. She sat up a bit taller in her chair, waiting for the doctor's response.

"Miss Morgan..."

Sadie interrupted her. "Sadie... please... just call me Sadie."

"Why don't we take this slow, Sadie, and you tell me everything you remember, okay?" Dr. GG asked.

Sadie nodded her head and turned towards the window. "He has a white English bulldog... named George, who pees on the floor."

Sadie chuckled under her breath as the doctor scribbled down some notes.

"Dr. GG... am I going crazy because if I am not going crazy, then how do I know that, and why can't I remember anything else?"

* * *

Mazie fidgeted in her seat as the doctor entered the room and extended her hand.

"Mrs. Mackenzie... Mr. Walker... it's nice to meet you both. I am Dr. Grace Gulliksen... please call me Dr. GG. I am Miss Morgan's psychiatrist."

Mazie cleared her throat and looked over at Beau. She had to make this quick. Mac was at home with Tucker, and the baby was going through his first growth spurt. He had to eat constantly.

"As Miss Morgan's sister... since you signed the HIPPA consent, I thought you would like to be brought up to speed."

Mazie nodded and shot Beau a look of warning. They were in deep, and Mac had already cautioned her about taking this thing too far.

"Does Sadie know... that you are talking to me?" Mazie asked. She let out a held breath and sat back straight in her chair.

"Miss Morgan and I only just scratched the surface of her family history... enough for me to know that she does not have a sister if this is what you are worried about. Listen, I understand that this is a delicate situation. You two are obviously important to her... otherwise, you would never have been in the situation to sign the consent in the first place. Am I right?" Both Mazie and Beau nodded, and Mazie took in a deep breath.

"Look, I think we all want the same results here... for Miss Morgan to get her memory back. I think that she will... *eventually.*"

It was the way that Dr. GG stressed eventually that made Beau shuffle in his chair.

"We had a productive session yesterday afternoon," the doctor continued.

"Productive in what way?" Beau asked. He sat forward with a half-smile on his face.

"Mr. Walker, Sadie is slowly remembering things… although very, very brief memories are surfacing. She seems to have some very clear memories of a dog. I believe it is your dog, George, which she described as an English bulldog, am I correct?"

"Yes! Sadie loves that dog."

The doctor chuckled at Beau's response. "That's good! Remembering George and that love is an excellent step."

"What else?" Beau quickly asked. The optimism in his voice was infectious, and Mazie reached over and squeezed his shoulder.

"Miss Morgan clearly recalls coming to Nashville in June… leaving Seattle. She remembers her hotel room and the purpose of her trip… a work conference. She vaguely remembers walking into the brewpub. She's described your eyes. She knows your first name, and she mentioned that you are an environmental architect. Miss Morgan hesitated when I asked her anything else. I sensed that she felt threatened in some way."

"Threatened? By me? That's ridiculous." Beau stood up in his chair, raising his voice.

"Beau… please," Mazie said, grabbing his hand in an attempt to calm him.

"Mr. Walker… I'm simply trying to explain some of Sadie's feelings when we talked. It was only our first meeting. She's agreed to talk to me again today. I think we are making good progress."

Beau sat back down and let all of the air he had been holding in escape his lungs. His chest felt heavy and burned like a hot fire. He laid his head in his hands and moaned in frustration.

"Would it be okay… if I saw her?" Mazie asked with tears in her eyes. She didn't know what she would say to Sadie, and she certainly didn't want to scare her.

"In my professional opinion, I do not believe that it is in Miss Morgan's best interest for visitors. I've allowed Mr. Walker's sister because she is a nurse, and Sadie seems somewhat comfortable with their visits.

"Presley has to leave soon... head back to Atlanta," Beau said. He hated to see her go, but he knew that she had to get back to the hospital... and her life.

Beau and Mazie had asked for a consult with Dr. GG to discuss Sadie's condition leaving Presley in Sadie's room. They had been hopeful that perhaps Sadie would want to see them... remember them in some way, but that was not the case.

"Thank you, Dr. GG... very much for your time. Please reach out if there is anything that I can do," Mazie said as she stood to leave. "Beau, I should go. Tucker is gonna be screaming his head off any minute. I want to see her... hug her... tell her I lo..." Mazie stopped talking and sat back down and laid her head on Beau's shoulder.

"Me too, Maze... me too."

Dr. GG quietly slipped out of the room, leaving Beau and Mazie in shared despair.

CHAPTER NINETEEN

Sadie pushed the IV stand out in front of her and took a few steps. This was her third walk around the fifth floor since dawn. She was bored and restless and also still very confused. They had served her waffles this morning for breakfast, and a memory flashed into her head.

Patrick.

She didn't want to talk with the psychiatrist, and she knew that Presley Walker was gone. Sadie had not meant to be rude to her, but the pictures upset her, and she became angry. When Presley left her room last night, she told her that she would be returning to Atlanta as she said her goodbyes.

* * *

"Can I show you something, Sadie Mae?" Presley asked.

Sadie turned her head sharply and let out a huff. Presley pulled her phone out of her purse and scrolled through a few photos. Sadie glanced towards the hospital corridor. She thought she saw Beau and a dark-haired woman outside her door a few minutes ago, and she felt on edge.

"It's just Sadie," she scoffed. "No one uses my middle name. It should have been Maeve after my grandmother, but my mother misunderstood my father and put Mae on my birth certificate. They always laughed about it," Sadie finished, shrugging her shoulders at Presley.

"Yes… I'm sorry, Sadie."

Presley knew that she was probably crossing a line. Still, it had been two and a half days, and Sadie had not made any more progress other than remembering Beau's dog. Sadie had an extended therapy session with a psychiatrist and was being taken off all painkillers. It was frightening to think that the hospital was talking about releasing her, and Sadie had mentioned to the doctor that she was eager to return to Seattle and to Joel despite being told that her dad lived in Nashville now.

"This picture was taken in August, at this little café in Atlanta. That's me… my mama, Lady Jane Walker, and you."

Sadie grabbed the phone out of Presley's hand and stared at the image.

"You can swipe left, the next few are funny."

There were several photos of Sadie and Presley laughing… hanging on one another and snapping selfies like the Kardashians.

"Were we trying on clothes?" Sadie asked.

Presley shook her head up and down. "Uh-huh. Mama took us shopping. We drank a few mimosas that day." Sadie looked up and into Presley's eyes, but still nothing. "More champagne than orange juice, I reckon."

"I'm sorry. I just don't remember."

Sadie shoved the phone back at Presley. It was pointless. Sadie felt nothing looking at those photos. It was like looking at her face on a stranger's body.

"Keep going, if you'd like. There are more," Presley pleaded as Sadie reluctantly pulled the phone back and swiped her finger across the screen.

The next few images made her stomach turn. Sadie almost didn't recognize herself. Her smile was radiant, but so was his. The first picture was of Sadie looking at the camera, but Beau looking at her. He had his arm tight around her waist. His shoulders were broad, and his tight jeans hung low on his hips. Sadie felt something at that moment… a memory on the edge of her brain. His touch. Sadie held the phone closer to her face and willed herself to remember. All she saw in his deep grey eyes was love. She could feel it buried somewhere deep in her soul. She shook her head and swallowed hard, but there was nothing. Sadie remembered nothing.

"It's like I am looking at a stranger, even though I know that it is me. I've never seen that dress before. It's beautiful."

Presley nodded and smiled, trying desperately to hold back her tears. "Mama picked it out for you. Sadie, you looked so beautiful that night. We had dinner at the country club... and."

Sadie's eyes turned dark, and she stared at Presley with her mouth open. "Country club... I don't understand. Do you know Joel, my boyfriend? Was Joel with me?" Sadie screamed as Presley vehemently shook her head sideways.

"No, Sadie... and Joel isn't your boyfriend... my brother Beau is."

Sadie tossed Presley's phone at her. She was Beau's sister, and now Sadie knew her real motive for spending time with her.

"Get out! I don't know you! I live in Seattle. My boyfriend is Joel Lewis. He's an international banker. We live in Magnolia. I don't know your brother... Beau. I met him... briefly at a brewpub in Nashville... in June! This has all been some mistake. I just want to go back home. Please... just go!"

Presley had never seen Sadie so upset. Her shouting brought the nurse from down the hall.

"Is there a problem, Miss Morgan?"

Sadie shook her head and folded her arms across her chest. "No. There is no problem. Ms. Walker was just leaving."

Presley felt defeated, and more than anything, she felt like she had let Beau down. She knew that it was best for Sadie if she left her alone.

"Sadie, I have to return to Atlanta. I did not mean to upset you. I wish the very best for you, and I hope that you are feeling better soon."

Sadie could tell that Presley was crying as she gathered her purse and coat. She turned back towards Sadie when she reached the door and put her hand up and waved goodbye.

"Alright, Miss Morgan. Let's get you something to eat."

* * *

As Sadie continued walking around the fifth floor, she shook her head, trying to rid the memories of yesterday and Presley's visit from her mind. All she saw was that white lace dress... the dotted mesh sleeves... Beau's hands on her waist... his eyes on her body. She pushed the IV stand out in front of her and stopped in front of the nurses' station.

"Good afternoon, Miss Morgan. You're out and about today."

Sadie's day nurse was quite young and way too perky for Sadie's current attitude.

"I'd like to talk to my doctor about going home... back to Seattle. The psychiatrist said that I should be released soon." Sadie put her hands on the nurses' station to steady herself. Her mind was still a jumbled mess, but she didn't want to let on.

"Oh, probably not today, Miss Morgan. Maybe later in the week... besides, you don't want to miss out on all the fun today."

Sadie shook her head and let out a chuckle at the nurse's comment. "Fun... I'm in a hospital. This place is not fun, sorry... no offense."

The nurse shook her head. "None taken, ma'am. It's just that it's manic Monday around here. The activity director has the new schedule out with all the activities for patients. The first Monday of the month is always my favorite. It's karaoke day!" Her enthusiasm made Sadie laugh... a real giggle and not something she felt like faking.

"You've got to be joking... karaoke?"

"Sure... why not? It's Nashville, right. Music city! Hey, even some of the nurses join in. We all have a really fun day. You should go check it out. It's just down the hall. Listen! Oh my, I can hear them now."

Sadie abruptly turned to follow the noise pushing the IV stand ahead of her. "Well, I only sing for the sick and infirmed."

The words caught in her throat. Sadie smelled the vomit and saw the sweet face of a child as the memory passed through her mind at warp speed.

Sadie closed her eyes and held on tight to the IV stand. It was Liam. It had to be Liam she saw in her mind... only Sadie knew that it wasn't Liam. It was a little boy named Patrick... Beau's son. Sadie opened her eyes and smiled, but that feeling was over all too quickly, and she shook her head and continued down the hall.

Sadie rounded the corner and heard the singing... if that's what you called it. Everyone was laughing inside the activities room, but Sadie felt miserable. The new memory played repeatedly in her mind, and the more she saw the images of the little boy's sweet face, the more Sadie wanted to run screaming down the hall. She honestly thought that maybe she was going crazy. Perhaps a little karaoke was just what she needed. What else did she have to do? She was trapped – a prisoner in her own mind.

As Sadie got closer, she strained to hear the first words of the song. She knew it, even though she wasn't a big country music fan. Sadie began to hum along with the music and found herself mouthing the first verse of the song as she continued to walk down the hospital corridor.

Last night, I got served, a little bit too much of that poison baby.

Last night, I did things I'm not proud of, and I got a little crazy.

Last night, I met a guy on the dance floor, and I let him call me 'baby'.

Sadie wheeled the IV inside the entrance to the activities room. A dozen people were milling about, including her doctor and several other staff members. Sadie's eyes found the other car accident victim. A young man with a broken right leg and next to him was an elderly gentleman who broke a hip walking his dog on Thanksgiving day. Sadie laughed to herself, thinking that this was all they had to cheer them up. Bad karaoke with amateurs singing sharp and off-key... and Nashville was supposed to be such a hotbed for talent.

And I don't even know his last name.

My momma would be so ashamed.

It started out, "hey cutie, where you from?"

Then it turned into, "oh no! what have I done?"

And I don't even know his last name.

Sadie suddenly felt dizzy, and the room began to spin. She felt like someone had turned her upside down and given her a shake. She grabbed for the doorframe to steady herself.

"Beau... stop it... put me down!"

Sadie remembered. She heard her voice in her head and felt his hands on her body... lifting her up and twirling her around.

"No, I will not, Sadie Mae. Oh, God... baby. I LOVE YOU!" Beau shouted at the top of his lungs in the middle of the Piedmont Country Club dance floor. He caught the eye of Lady Jane, who had a smile but with a concerted look on her face.

"Beauford... Patrick... Walker! You are making a scene. Your mama is going to be so upset. Stop!" Sadie demanded.

Beau continued to spin her around, whispering in her ear until Sadie was dizzy. "You're moving to Nashville! I love you, Sadie Mae. I love you... I love you."

"I love you too, Beau... but please stop."

Beau gently put Sadie down in the middle of the dancefloor, and all eyes locked on them.

"Baby, we are going to have the best life. I promise you," Beau said as he cupped Sadie's face in his strong hands, brushing a stray tear off her cheek with his thumb.

The memory faded quickly, but Sadie remembered. She remembered the night she finally told Beau that she wanted to move to Nashville and start their life together.

Sadie clutched the IV stand and stood by the entryway of the activities room and listened to the nurses' aid sing *her* Carrie Underwood song. Everything flashed in her mind like the lighting in the sky the night they ate barbecue at Martin's.

Sadie remembered Beau's lips and their first kiss. His hands cupping her face as she sat on the kitchen stool in his loft... the taste of cognac in his mouth and Beau's soft moans making her heart flutter.

The memories came fast and furious and filled her mind, one right after the other. Sadie remembered Beau pushing her back onto the hotel room bed. His hot breath in her ear and the way he groaned as they came together that first time. She felt herself clutching his hand as they walked through the Tennessee State History Museum... then sitting in the beer garden at Martin's Barbecue. Sadie's eyes welled with tears as the memory of Beau pleading with her at the airport flashed through her mind. She heard his voice in her head... telling her that he loved her for the first time, as she wiped the tears from her cheeks. Sadie saw Mazie on her back porch, Beau's hand in the small of her back as he introduced her to his best friends. She closed her eyes tight and then laughed out loud when she recalled Beau winking at her when Patrick pulled his Batman pajamas out of the box... his sweet scent as he cuddled next to her while she read him a story. Their trip to Atlanta flashed before her next. Sadie remembered the butterflies in her stomach when she met Lady Jane and her belly aching from all the laughs that she and Presley shared. Sadie remembered Beau hugging her tight against his body after Joel assaulted her... smoothing her hair and whispering words of comfort in her ear. The memories filled her mind of lathering up Beau's body in the shower at Juliette's and him making love to her over and over again in the days following her move to Nashville.

"Oh, my God!"

Sadie spun around and smiled, throwing her good hand to her mouth. "I remember! Shit! I remember everything. Beau?"

Sadie started to run, and the IV stand pulled tight against her arm. Sadie's day nurse came up behind her and placed her hand upon her shoulder, grabbing the IV stand before Sadie toppled it over.

"Fuck! Do you know where my phone is? I really need my phone!"

"Is everything alright, Miss Morgan?" the nurse asked.

"Yes! Everything is fine. Where is my phone?" Sadie steadied herself, but her legs and feet did a little dance.

"Perhaps I should call for your doctor, Miss Morgan?"

"No… no… I'm good. I'm excellent! I just need my phone. I need to call Beau. I remember… everything!" she shouted.

Sadie suddenly didn't think anyone would believe her. She was frightened, and the nurse stared back at her with a stoic expression on her face.

"Let me take you back to your room. Let's see if we can page your doctor."

Sadie defiantly shook her head. "Please… can you please call him. He must be out of his mind. He thinks I don't love him, but I do. I never stopped and I never will. Oh, please… call Beau."

* * *

Beau opened his eyes and turned his head. It took him a few seconds to remember, and his smile quickly faded. Sadie wasn't in the loft. She wasn't in bed next to him. He reached out and grabbed her pillow and pulled it close to him. Her scent was everywhere.

It made no sense to stay at home today. There was nothing he could do. He took Presley to the airport last night and then came home and drank four beers. It was unlikely Sadie would call him… need him. It was just Beau and George. He couldn't even care for his son. Patrick understood, but it broke his heart.

"Daddy is still sick, son… both Sadie Mae and I, but I promise we will see you soon."

Hannah was understanding and agreed that Beau needed some time to clear his head and decide what and how he was going to put one foot in front of the other and move forward… possibly without Sadie in his life.

* * *

"Shit, man. I was not expecting to see you today. What are you doing here?" Sebastian asked, looking up from the drafting table as Beau sauntered like a zombie to his desk.

"Hey, man. I just needed to get away from the loft."

Beau took his messenger bag off his shoulder and tucked a couple of blueprint tubes behind his desk. He flopped lifelessly in his chair, and it spun around like a dingy set adrift in the ocean.

"What's the latest? How's Sadie Mae?" Sebastian asked.

Beau shook his head and grunted. He didn't think he could speak, and he began to wonder if coming to work was such a good idea. He contemplated just getting up and walking out, but instead, he reached over and booted up his laptop.

"Listen, Beau… Torrie and I want you to come over tonight and bring Patrick. I'll throw something on the grill. You can talk… or not. It's *Monday Night Football*? What do you say?" Sebastian asked.

All Beau saw was Sadie.

* * *

"What should I wear? Beau… come up here and help me get dressed, please."

Beau took the bedroom stairs two at a time. He never thought twice when Sadie called him up to the bedroom.

"Isn't the goal to take your clothes off... not put them on?" Beau queried.

Sadie had laid out a few outfits on the bed, George panting at her heels. She had on Beau's lucky Georgia Bulldogs 1980 national championship t-shirt and a ruby red thong. Red was Beau's new favorite color. The t-shirt was so old and had been worn so often by Beau growing up that it had shrunk up and only came to just about the middle of Sadie's ass.

"I'm just excited to meet Sebastian and Torrie, that's all. I don't know what to wear. Help me, please?"

Beau just laughed and grabbed the end of the t-shirt and pulled it over her head. "First off. This t-shirt is sacred. It's gotta come off, baby. We haven't won a national championship since 1980," Beau said, making Sadie giggle.

She didn't know much about football or superstitions. Still, she made a mental note to steer clear of any Georgia paraphernalia in Beau's closet.

"Second... you look good naked... so anything you wear is only going to make you that more beautiful, okay?"

Convinced he had set her mind straight, Beau wrapped his arms around her and kissed her letting his fingers run along her spine, pulling her close to him. Sadie could feel the beating of his heart against her chest.

"God... you are good. You are really fucking good, Beau Walker."

Pleased with himself, Beau smiled and nodded his head before brushing his lips against hers.

As the memory played in his mind, Beau continued to smile and shake his head, sitting at his desk at work.

"So... is that a yes, Beau? I see you shaking your head. You'll come for *Monday Night Football*?" Sebastian asked again. He had hope in his eyes watching his friend smile, but he could tell that Beau was lost in thought.

"Ummmm..."

Beau was quickly brought back to life. The memory left his mind, only to be replaced with another one... he knew that for sure. He couldn't escape her. He would have to fucking move... change his name and quit his job... alienate his friends and fuck over his family. Sadie was everywhere. She was all over the loft, all over his life, and all over his mind.

"Beau..."

Sebastian had walked into his cubicle and perched himself on the edge of Beau's desk. Beau looked up and nodded his head.

"Let's go to yoga today. Okay, man?"

Sebastian shook his head. "Yea... sounds good."

* * *

After yoga, Beau contemplated going home and working a while from the loft, but he knew that was a mistake. The more he thought about Sebastian's offer for dinner and football, the more he realized that being in the loft alone, was not in his best interest. He showered on the third floor of his office, and as he was dressing, he heard his phone vibrating at the bottom of his gym bag.

"Beau Walker..."

Beau recognized the number for the hospital, and his heart skipped a beat. They couldn't keep her there much longer even though Beau pleaded with the doctors.

"Mr. Walker. This is Ally Edwards. I am Miss Morgan's nurse. Sir... Miss Morgan has asked... well, I guess what I should say is that it is more of a demand, really."

Joel. Beau knew that this call was about Joel. Another one of Sadie's demands that they give up her phone so that she could call Joel. Beau didn't know what she would say to him or what Joel's reaction might be, but as hard as it was for him to contemplate, Beau knew that it was out of his hands.

"It's okay... nurse Edwards. Give her the phone. I can't do anything about it. Sadie is going to make up her mind on her own, and I won't be able to stop her... as much as I'd like too. I need to move forward. Let her make the call. It's okay."

Beau was just about to slide his finger over his phone to end the call when the nurse screamed out.

"Wait... Mr. Walker... Sadie only wanted her phone to call you. She's remembered. Mr. Walker, I think you should get to the hospital as soon as possible, sir. Miss Morgan remembers you."

* * *

Sadie kept one eye on her hospital room door and the other on Mazie. The baby cooed and kicked his little feet, wedged tightly in the crook of Sadie's good arm. Mazie's eyes were wide, and her expressions exaggerated. She hadn't taken a breath since she sat down 15 minutes ago.

"And then... they told me I had to sign this consent form. I didn't know what to do, Sadie Mae. Beau made me promise to look after you until he got here, but it was Thanksgiving, and they had to find a pilot to fly the jet, and he thought it might be hours until he got back to Nashville. Mac was so pissed. All he could think about was how he was going to have to bail me out of jail! Like they would ever arrest me. I mean, we had no idea about your memory. Did I mention how horrible you looked?" Mazie asked, taking in a deep breath. She reached up and pulled her high ponytail tight and winked at Sadie.

All Sadie could do was chuckle as she let Mazie continue. Her stories were more for Mazie and her healing then they were for Sadie.

She heard the footsteps... coming faster and growing louder as they approached her room. He was running to her. The sound of his cowboy boots echoed sharply through the hospital corridor.

Mazie never stopped talking as Beau skidded into Sadie's hospital room. Sadie looked up and chuckled, but Beau's expression was cautious and blank. He didn't know the extent of her memory, other than Sadie's nurse asking him to come to the hospital as soon as possible. Beau was hoping for a few good memories... perhaps beyond their first meeting. He stood with his hands on his hips, bent slightly to catch his breath.

"Beau... it's about time you showed up. Poor Sadie Mae here has been waiting for you."

Mazie jumped up and scooped Tucker out of Sadie's arm. She shoved him down the front of the Baby Bjorn and grabbed the diaper bag.

"I'll be back later. I'll give you two some alone time. Okay?"

Mazie stepped up to Beau and planted a kiss on his unshaven cheek. "Scoot... she's not going to bite. Get on over there," Mazie whispered, pointing to Sadie and winking. She disappeared quickly, blowing Sadie a kiss as her and Tucker left the room.

"Hi," Beau said. It was the first thing that popped into his mind after four and a half days.

"Well, hi... yourself," Sadie responded. She picked up her cast-less hand and gave Beau a friendly wave.

Beau stared back at her like a scared child. He had a few days' worth of stubble and that God-awful patch of hair below his lower lip had returned. He had dark bags under each eye, and he looked utterly exhausted. Sadie could only imagine. All she could think about was how she would feel if Beau had no memory of her. Sadie knew that she would want to lie down and die.

"I'm Beau... Walker... you remember me?" Beau cautiously asked.

Sadie shook her head up and down, but Beau remained frozen, having not moved from where he stopped after sliding through the door.

"Can you come here, please?" Sadie lifted her finger, motioning for Beau to come to her. He looked down at his feet as if willing them to move to her and slowly threaded his fingers through his hair. Beau took small steps towards her and then stopped at the end of her hospital bed.

"Beauford Patrick Walker… can you please come here… all the way here," Sadie said as she patted a place next to her left hip. It took him a second to process what she had just said… his full name, but certainly Mazie, could have given her that information before he arrived.

Beau rounded the edge of Sadie's bed, looking deep into her eyes… searching for her… hoping to recapture her heart and her soul. He gently sat down on the edge of the bed, but with his body turned towards the window and away from her. She reached out for his arm, but he remained rigid.

"Beau…"

Sadie's voice was barely a whisper, and he closed his eyes and took in a deep breath.

"When I get out of here… the first place I would like you to take me is to Martin's, okay? Upstairs to the beer garden with the picnic tables and the twinkle lights… only this time, I want my own damn ribs… no more of this sharing stuff, okay?"

Sadie could see him nodding his head and smiling slightly. Beau turned to her slowly with tears falling down each cheek.

"You remember?"

"Yes, Beau… I remember every little thing. I don't know how or where I was. It's a strange feeling, let me tell you, but I remember," she said, letting out a long sigh.

"I'll be honest… I'm fuzzy on Thanksgiving Day. My doctor said that part is normal and to be expected. I remember seeing my dad. Oh boy… what a shitty day at Tall Oaks Manor, but we can talk about that later. It was raining and starting to get dark. I wanted to text you… call you. I wanted to apologize. I had decided that I was going to drive to Atlanta the next morning. I was just trying to get to Mac and Mazie's for dinner."

"Sadie Mae… were you texting and driving?" Beau asked.

"No… I don't think so. I wouldn't do that. The leaves were falling… the roads were slick. I was driving Walter too fast, I think. I don't remember the accident. I might never remember. It was just an accident."

Beau put his hands on each side of him and pushed down on the thick mattress… twisting around, partway to face her.

"Beau… I want to apologize to you. I over-reacted. I was wrong. You've been nothing but kind and supportive… so patient and understanding since we met. I should have given you a chance. I should have let you explain and been a bit more reasonable in regards to your call to Chris. I know you were just trying to fix things… make it better. I am so sorry."

Beau looked up and into Sadie's eyes. "Sadie, I lied to you. If anyone is wrong, it's me. This is all on me. Your accident… everything. It all could have been prevented." Beau pulled back a bit. Sadie didn't blame him. Beau was cautious.

"Yes… you hid the truth… not the best move. In the future, we both know the standards, right?" Sadie said as she leaned closer to him. She wanted nothing more than to touch him. She felt like she had been waiting for years.

"Beau, you can't take the blame for my accident. It was no one's fault. It just happened. Look, I'm going to be just fine. I remember all of yesterday… and today, okay… new memories. My doctor is very pleased. Aside from a few hours… on Thanksgiving day… I remember everything."

Sadie's lips lifted upward as Beau reached for her hand.

"Everything?" he asked. Beau wanted to know, and he wanted to be sure.

"Beau… would it be okay… if I kissed you?"

Before Beau had a chance to answer, Sadie reached up and cupped her hand around his cheek and pulled him close to her.

"Have you ever made out with a woman in a pink cast before?" Sadie asked with a giggle.

Beau shook his head sideways. He stared into her eyes like it was the first time he had ever seen her before.

"Well, I think you are about to."

Beau was certain that he saw a flash of lightning and heard a crack of thunder when Sadie brushed her lips against his. A fire lit in the pit of his stomach – a flame he knew would never be extinguished. He loved this woman… heart, and soul with every fiber of his being.

"I've missed you, Sadie Mae."

Sadie's kiss turned aggressive, and she parted her lips to let a soft moan escape.

"I want to go home, Beau. Will you take me home?" Sadie breathlessly pleaded.

Beau's tongue sought hers in a way he had never sought it before. There was a longing in the way he reached out towards her, and in the way, he held her close. Sadie knew for certain that she would never let him go again… she would never let any of them go again. For so long, she had yearned for it, and now she knew that she could never bear to lose it… lose the thing that made her feel so complete.

CHAPTER TWENTY

"Oh, Beau... God, I want this to be special, okay... mmmm... that's it! Oh yes! That's... no, ummmm... wait!"

"Wait?"

"Okay... just move a little to the right... yes, just like that... maybe a little more... that's so good."

"Sadie Mae... is that my right or your right?"

"Oh, I think it's my right. Yes! I think that is it. Right there! Now stop!"

"Stop?"

"Yes, Beau! Stop for just a second."

"Baby, I can't hold on much longer."

"Shoosh! I just want to make sure... you know. Oh, yes! I think that's it... right here."

"Here?"

"No, Beau! Are you even paying attention! Look at where my hands are! Yes... this might be it!"

"Baby, are you about done?"

"Beau, stop! Your talking is messing up my concentration. This is important to me. I want it to be special."

"Sadie Mae, can we please be done with this? God, I am getting tired, baby."

"Let me think about it for a minute."

"Baby, please! What is there to think about? It's not like you've never done this before. I'm ready. Let's finish."

Sadie watched as Beau let go and then gasped as the Christmas tree toppled over, narrowly missing George and landing with a thud in the middle of the loft.

"Well, now… we are going to have to start all over again!" Sadie said with a giggle, watching as Beau rolled over onto his back in the middle of the loft.

"Beauford Walker… please get up and help me. We are gonna have a full house in a few hours. Patrick will be here at three o'clock, and I want this place looking like Santa Claus just threw up."

"Baby, I'm gonna throw up," Beau said, letting out a long groan – kisses from George wetting his cheek.

"I warned you… remember? I sat right there on that stool and told you that I loved Christmas."

Beau wanted to weep. Sadie remembered everything with vivid details. Her memory was even better than his, and her recovery continued to amaze him. Her resilience and her determination… her passion and her capacity to live was evident in everything she said or did since the accident. Sadie was different, no doubt. She had a clear vision of what gratitude felt like and how it breathed and lived and wove its precious fibers around the lives of people every day.

"Sadie Mae… you asked me not to get you started on Christmas. Lord have mercy, I sure wish I had."

"Oh… hush up!"

"Knock knock… y'all decent in there?" Lady Jane came through the front door of the loft in perfectly pressed jeans, leopard suede mules, and a tan sweater. "Oh… my," she exclaimed, eyeing her son flat on his back beside the disheveled tree.

"We are having a bit of difficulty with the tree," Sadie said as she greeted Lady Jane with a good old southern bear hug.

"Hey, Mama..."

Beau sat up, trying to determine how best to proceed and gauging Sadie's level of irritation with him.

"I am so glad you are here, Lady Jane. Having one arm sucks!" Sadie said, while waving her pink cast in the air.

"I smell turkey. That's a good thing."

"Yes, we managed to get the bird in the oven an hour ago. With a bit of luck, dinner should be served around 5:30. Everyone except Patrick, Hannah, and Ryan will be here at four o'clock."

Beau brought Sadie home from the hospital the day after her memory resurfaced. The doctor saw no reason why she couldn't go home, and with her memories intact, there was no reason to keep her any longer. He protested her release, but it fell on deaf ears. Sadie knew that he was still scared, and she tried to be patient every time he looked at her – deep into her eyes as if she had left him again.

"Baby...?"

"Yes, Beau."

He exhaled loudly and shook his head. He had crawled into her hospital bed and fell asleep for hours after the doctor cleared her to be released the following morning. Beau never left her side. It felt like it had all been a bad dream... a nightmare, but Sadie knew just what to do. She quickly started in on a story... a memory... something funny that Patrick had told her... until she felt his heartbeat return to normal... heard his breathing slow so that he knew in his heart that she had returned.

Sadie promised Beau that she would rest and take her recovery slowly and follow all of the doctor's recommendations, but she had other ideas.

"What the fuck? No... absolutely not!" Beau cried out. He had carried Sadie up to the loft and tucked her into bed, George struggling up the stairs behind them. Sadie begged and pleaded with Beau and gave him that smile and then giggled like a small child.

"You can't say no to a Thanksgiving do-over! We can totally pull this off this coming Sunday?"

"Baby, that's five days away. I think this is a bad idea. You are supposed to be on bed rest, remember?"

"Bed rest? Beau... the doctor said take it easy. He said light exercise, eat well, and get plenty of sleep. I think you are taking this too far. I'm fine."

Beau knew that there was no point in saying no, so he finally agreed to her Thanksgiving dinner party and watched as she spent the next few days planning the whole thing out.

* * *

"Baby, where is your sling?"

Beau finally pulled himself out from under the Christmas tree and up off the floor... scowling at Sadie.

"I don't know," Sadie said with a shrug. "I think it's upstairs. I'm good. I don't really need it. My shoulder is fine."

Sadie twirled her left arm around in circles and winked at him.

Beau knew that physically, Sadie was fine. He had found out that morning when he had come back from walking George and climbed the stairs... finding the bedroom bathed in candlelight. Her invitation was Beau's salvation as she lifted back the covers, exposing her naked body. He came to her, and she let his hands explore her longingly.

"I want to give you more pleasure than you have ever felt before. I love you so much, baby."

Beau was tender as he gathered her body closer to his... until Sadie molded complete with him.

"Go slow," Sadie murmured. "I need you to please me for a very... very long time."

* * *

Beau finally wrestled the tree upright and spun it around to face her, and Sadie quickly glanced at it and gave him a thumbs up. Her attention was needed elsewhere.

"It's fine, Beau… really. I'm over it!"

Suddenly the intercom buzzed, and Sadie ran for the door.

"Oh, dear God, now what?" Beau shouted. Sadie glared at Beau as she pressed the button on the wall, opening the door downstairs for the delivery man.

"Amazon!"

"What on earth did you order, Sadie Mae?"

"Christmas… Beauford! I ordered Christmas. Now you'd better help the poor man. I think he's got more than he can handle alone."

Beau let out a loud snarl as he walked to the front door and out to the elevator.

"Okay, Sadie Mae… what can I do to help?"

Lady Jane was standing in the living room with her hands on her hips, pleasantly amused by her son and Sadie.

"Food is pretty much taken care of. We are doing the turkey and some light hors d'oeuvres. We've got beer, wine, champagne, plus whatever your son has in his liquor arsenal. Ummmm… Mac and Mazie are bringing rolls and smoked cheddar mac and cheese. Sebastian and Torrie are bringing Indian collard greens, Chris Holland and his date are bringing sweet potato casserole, and Hannah, Ryan, and Patrick are bringing the stuffing.

"Don't forget the chocolate pecan pie!" Lady Jane exclaimed.

Sadie still couldn't believe that Presley was flying in on a private plane with a chocolate pecan pie on her lap. She wanted to ask Beau what the cost would have been to fly them all back and forth between Atlanta and Nashville, but she didn't dare. It wasn't any of her business.

"I just need y'all to start decorating! I've got enough stuff in those boxes to cover this entire loft!" Sadie said, jumping up and down. She clapped her hand against her pink cast as Beau led the UPS man inside the loft.

Three hours later, the loft looked like Santa's workshop. Beau still couldn't believe all the details that Sadie thought of including Rudolph the Red-Nosed Reindeer sheets for Patrick's bed and towels for the downstairs bathroom with blue and white snowflakes. He thought the patio's seven-foot blow-up snowman was a bit much, but he found an extension cord, plugged it in, hit the switch, and watched the thing inflate in two minutes.

The star of the show was the tree, and Beau insisted that it be real – a Norway blue spruce. Sadie gasp when Beau brought it through the front door on Friday night. He wanted to take her deep into the Tennessee woods, but he knew she was tired, and if she didn't rest, he was pulling the plug on Sunday's Thanksgiving do-over. Sadie relented and stayed in bed with George all day binge-watching *Hallmark's* Christmas movie marathon.

The spruce was nearly eight feet tall and was so dark in color that Sadie honestly could see the blue tint in the needles. The way it sparkled after Beau strung it with almost 1,000 lights made Sadie teary.

"So, only the lights?" Beau asked her. He hadn't fully grasped Sadie's vision.

"Yes, this is Thanksgiving dinner with a twist. It's Thanksmas! Everyone is required to grab a cocktail and help decorate the tree. That's why we are only doing the lights for now."

Sadie radiated energy, and Beau was hoping that she wouldn't wear herself down before the party began.

Fifteen minutes before Patrick was due to arrive, Sadie walked down the loft stairs. Her dress just about brought Beau to his knees. He knew that Lady Jane had bought it for her. His mama had good taste, and she knew just what suited Sadie. The petite pleated ruffle sheath dress in candy apple red fit Sadie like a glove. It had crisp pleats along the bustline and romantic ruffles along the jewel neck, with a keyhole back... but it was the shoes that Sadie loved the most. She didn't think she would ever take off the black suede sandals, and she told Beau that she would be sleeping in them. They wrapped around her ankles with a knotted wide ribbon, and she soared in the stiletto heel.

Beau brought his hands to his face, biting his upper lip. The left corner of his mouth curled up, right on cue, and Sadie saw the tears in his eyes.

"The cast clashes with my dress, but I don't care. I feel like the heroine in one of those treacle Christmas movies."

Beau enveloped her in his strong arms, never uttering a word. His mouth sought out her neck, and she felt his tears wet on her cheek.

"Well, Sadie Mae... I think you look just stunning," Lady Jane exclaimed as she watched Sadie quickly pull away from Beau and make a beeline for her. Lady Jane stood before her in a striking long black skirt with a silver knotted belt that hung down to her knees and a white silk lace blouse.

"Thank you, Lady Jane. This dress is amazing... and these shoes. I'm never taking them off!" Sadie did a little twirl, and George jumped up from his dog bed to join her.

"I've got something else for you... if you don't mind."

Sadie watched as Lady Jane reached into her pocket and pulled out a pair of diamond teardrop earrings.

"I'd like you to have these. It would mean a lot to me."

Sadie reached out and touched the earrings in Lady Jane's palm. They looked vintage, and Sadie guessed that the pear-shaped earrings had to be at least two carats each.

"Oh, ma'am... they are so lovely, but I just can't." Sadie mumbled.

"Please, I insist. Patrick gave them to me the day Beau was born. They symbolized a new beginning for us."

Lady Jane placed the earrings in Sadie's palm and closed her hand around them. Sadie discarded the earrings in her ears and replaced them with the diamonds.

"You and Beau have been given a new beginning. That's something precious. It deserves a special gift."

Sadie caught sight of the earrings – their reflection sparkling in the patio door as she reached out to embrace Lady Jane.

"Beau…"

"Beautiful, baby… just beautiful. Ummmm, Presley just texted me… wheels down. She will be here in 20 minutes."

Beau was interrupted by the sound of the intercom buzzing. "I think that's Hannah, Ryan, and Patrick. I told them they could get here a few minutes early," Beau said.

"Well, then… I guess we are ready for Thanksmas!" Sadie said as she jumped up and down for nothing other than pure joy.

* * *

"Welcome back, Sadie!"

Several of her co-workers, including Chris Holland, jumped out of her cubicle to surprise her on her first day back to work. Sadie had told Chris at Thanksmas dinner that she was ready to come back as soon as possible, but Beau stepped in.

"Not until the doctor clears you. Sadie Mae, you are supposed to be resting!" Sadie pulled Chris aside and asked him if he could e-mail her some files. She wanted to get back into the swing of things and get her life back. The following day, Sadie's doctor cleared her to return to work.

"Aww… thanks, everyone. You shouldn't have gone to the fuss." Sadie said, spotting the tray of pecan cookies from the Nashville Farmer's Market. "On second thought… who is ready for cookies and sweet tea?"

Sadie sat down at her desk and booted up her computer. She was excited about getting back to work. Everything was returning to normal, and she suddenly felt like today was the first day of her new life.

"Hey, Sadie... so can we have a quick chat?"

Sadie spun around in her chair. Chris Holland stood next to her desk with a serious look on his face, and Sadie got a sick feeling in the pit of her stomach. They were going to let her go... it was no wonder. Between Beau's phone call... the favor and the misunderstanding with the football tickets... not to mention her two-week absence from work and a debilitating cast that would be on until the middle of January. Sadie knew they didn't have much of a choice.

Even though they had chatted when Sadie called and invited Chris for Thanksmas and cleared the air, she knew that it was probably for the best and that she should consider finding another place of employment. She was just surprised that someone from human resources wasn't with him.

"Sure... ummmm, what's up?"

"Well, first of all, I want to thank you for Sunday... Thanksmas. It was a blast. Thank you for including me and for being so understanding about Beau and me. My part too. I should have told you right off the bat that we knew one another. But that's not why I wanted to chat with you."

Sadie bit the inside of her cheek. She didn't want to cry. She would find another job. Everything was going to be okay. Chris was a good guy, and this wasn't entirely his fault.

"It's okay, Chris. I understand... about my job. I'll resign if that makes things easier," Sadie said as her eyes fell to the floor.

"Resign? Huh? Sadie... gosh no. I don't want you to leave. I'm just hoping that once your cast is removed that you can take on a junior appraiser. I'd like to offer you a promotion. I'd like you to set up a training program. Sorry, I'm getting way ahead of myself."

Sadie bit down a bit harder on the inside of her mouth and then smiled. "A promotion? You mean you are not going to let me go?" Sadie asked. She watched as Chris smiled and then shook his head.

"Sadie, I need to start over again. Listen, I came in here to give you this. It's a voice activated-dictation system. IT will be here to install it on your laptop and phone shortly. I thought since you can only type with one hand that it might come in handy. After the first of the year, we can talk about the training program. But I am serious. I like your style and your work ethic. I think that you would be a great trainer. I'd love for you to give it some thought, okay?" Sadie emphatically nodded her head and couldn't wait to share the news with Beau.

"Okay, so now that we have that out of the way… can we have a personal chat?"

Chris stepped into Sadie's cubical and pulled up a chair and sat down.

"Sure… what is on your mind?"

"Well… Beau's sister, actually."

"Presley?"

"Yes! Sadie is Presley dating… ummmm, I mean, is she seeing anyone?" Sadie raised her eyebrows at Chris, whose face had reddened.

"What about Taylor?"

Chris had brought a date to Thanksmas, and Sadie thought the girl was very nice and that they made a cute couple.

"Oh, we met on-line. It's not a good match, unfortunately. She's looking for casual, and I am kinda looking for something more. We went out a few times. Thanksmas was our last date."

"Oh, Chris. I am so sorry."

"Naw… don't be. Your dinner party was probably the best thing that has happened to me in a long time. I've only seen Presley a few times… the last time was at a Georgia football game… gosh like twelve years ago, but now."

Sadie nodded her head. She remembered how Chris seemed to be paying particular attention to Beau's sister at Thanksmas, and now it all made sense.

"Sadie, I was wondering what you would think if I asked Beau... you know if I could call his sister?"

Sadie couldn't help but laugh. What was it about Southern men?

"Ummmm, Chris... so you want to ask for Beau's permission... if it would be okay if you asked Presley out on a date?"

"Yes... do you think he would be okay with that?"

Sadie tried not to laugh as she nodded her head. "Yes, Chris... and I think Presley is going to be thrilled with your call."

* * *

"Baby, this is absolutely the last night with the snowman, right?"

Sadie leaned into Beau and nuzzled her face into his neck. It was New Year's Eve, and tomorrow Christmas was going to be boxed away, and Sadie and Beau would be starting the first day of the new year together.

"Ahhhh, I'm going to miss him. He's become like a part of the family, Beau," Sadie said, gazing out towards the patio. "You wanna make out? We have like eleven minutes before the new year!"

Beau laughed and laid Sadie down on the couch. "Sadie Mae, we have an hour and eleven minutes until the new year."

"Yes, I know Nashville time, but I've always celebrated the east coast countdown... you know from Times Square. That way, we don't have to stay up until midnight."

Beau couldn't argue with her west coast logic. Sadie had a good point, and he knew that she had to be as exhausted as he was. They had Patrick for the second half of his Christmas break from noon on Christmas morning until noon yesterday. They hadn't even gotten out of bed until ten o'clock this morning, and Sadie had stayed in her pajamas all day. Beau told her he would take her out to dinner and then dancing, if she wanted, but Sadie was content to spend New Year's Eve at the loft with Beau and George making crab cakes and drinking sparkling rosé from Arrington Vineyards.

Sadie's phone vibrated, and she squirmed away from Beau and reached out towards the coffee table to grab it.

"It's another text from Presley! Oh, my God... look how adorable they look!" Sadie squealed in delight as picture after picture had begun to arrive in her text feed. Presley looked amazing in a silver strapless dress cut just above the knee... her hair curled into big rings, cascading down to her clavicle. Her eyes were smoky charcoal, and her lips a pale beige, making her eyes sparkled like two diamonds.

Presley had told Sadie that she was falling hard for Chris, and she was very excited to be his date for New Year's Eve. She was also nervous because he had asked her if she wanted to spend the night at the hotel where the New Year's Eve ball was being held. Sadie knew that Presley and Chris were sharing a bed for the first time tonight.

"It's almost midnight in Atlanta. Presley promised to send me a kissy photo too," Sadie squealed.

Beau grunted and rolled his eyes. He had heard too much tonight already. The kissy photo of his sister and Chris Holland just might send him over the edge.

"So, let me get this straight. They are at a party in a hotel in downtown Atlanta," Beau asked.

"Yes, the champagne ball."

"Smooth operator," Beau said sarcastically.

"What's that supposed to mean, Beau Walker?"

"I mean... how convenient. Get my sister drunk off her ass on champagne, and then he only has to take her upstairs."

"I think she is a very willing participant, Beau. Don't be like that. She's happy... very happy. She's falling in love... they are falling in love.

This is amazing. What did you tell me on Christmas Day... about how much you thought that they made a nice-looking couple?"

Chris had confided a lot to Sadie in the weeks since he and Presley had started dating, and he too told Sadie that he was falling hard for Presley. With his father ailing, Chris spent almost every weekend in Atlanta, giving him ample opportunities to see Presley. For their first date, Chris took Presley to the Georgia Aquarium, a stunning backdrop to a romantic evening of music, tapas, and cocktails called *Sips Under the Sea*. Right after their first date, Chris asked Presley if she had plans for New Year's Eve, and she gladly accepted.

"No one is ever going to be good enough for my sister. Anyway... he lives in Nashville, and she lives in Atlanta. I mean, I just don't see this thing working out."

Sadie quickly sat up and shook her head. "Beau... have you lost your mind? Look at us. Look at what we made possible this year. You know what got us through... me and you and love! L-O-V-E. They'll figure it out. He'll move to Atlanta, or she'll move to Nashville. They are young and smart and successful. I mean, how difficult could it be, huh?!"

Beau had heard enough. He pushed Sadie back down on the couch and brushed his lips against hers.

"Hush up, baby... you are cutting into our make out time. Just let me kiss you until the new year."

"Here or in New York?"

"I'll let you decide, okay?"

CHAPTER TWENTY-ONE

"Slow down, son."

The little boy went running along the fresh cut meadow and out towards a duck pond lined with benches. The March breeze was warm, and the spring air smelled like the magnolias that were blooming along the path. Wildflowers circled the pond and a family of goslings trailed obediently behind their mother.

"I see him. Across the pond. He's sanding one of his birdhouses."

Sadie was nervous. Although Beau had been out to Tall Oaks Manor with Sadie many times, today was the first day that Patrick had come along. Sadie had no idea how her father would react to the precocious child. She hoped that this wasn't a mistake, but she was confident in Beau's decision to introduce Patrick to Sadie's father. The little boy had been asking, and it only seemed fair.

"Do you think he will like this?" Beau asked, holding the model airplane in his hand. He had taken Patrick to the toy store that morning while Sadie was getting ready, and the little boy had picked out the P-40B Tiger Shark.

"What's not to like? It has a shark mouth on the nose of the plane. I don't think he's ever put that one together before. I think he will love it."

Patrick had circled back around and ran into Sadie's arms as Beau tucked the box under his arm. "Which one is your dad, Sadie Mae?" Sadie patted down Patrick's hair and knelt beside him.

"See the man sitting across the pond... in the red plaid shirt and the glasses. That's James."

"Okay!" Patrick shouted as he took off, running as fast as he could across the mowed grass.

"Patrick!" Sadie yelled out and started after him, but Beau grabbed her hand, pulling her back.

"Baby, it's going to be fine. He's good, right? We talked about this."

"It's just that I don't want him to get hurt... Patrick, not my dad. I'm just afraid... you know that my dad might say something to him."

Sadie turned her head and looked across the pond. Patrick had already taken a seat next to James, and the two of them were engaged in a conversation. James had already placed his birdhouse on Patrick's lap and given him a small piece of sandpaper.

"See... just look at them," Beau said as he turned Sadie around and grabbed her waist, pulling her close to him. He gently kissed her neck until she giggled – the spring sun bathing them both in a loving warmth.

They stood in complete bliss, watching Patrick and James for a few minutes. Patrick looked up and out across the pond and waved to Beau and Sadie... which prompted James to wave as well, although Sadie figured he had no idea who he was waving too.

Although James had settled in nicely at Tall Oaks Manor, his memories were fading... more and more with each visit, and his cognitive skills were rapidly slowing. What used to be days to put together a birdhouse or an airplane now took weeks. Sadie would find the pieces scattered about haphazardly – uncompleted projects littering his room.

Sadie could never be sure if James would recognize her when she visited, and he never remembered Beau. Sadie re-introduced the love of her life to her father every time they visited, and it crushed her heart every time. Beau never cared. He and James always talked about construction, college football, and fishing, and in return, he learned a lot about Sadie. James always told a funny story or two about his little girl, even if he didn't realize that she was sitting directly across the table from him, a grown woman.

It was just last weekend... Beau and Sadie had driven out to Tall Oaks Manor when Beau worked up his courage. He knew it was the right thing to do. He had to ask James. Beau just hoped that it was a good day.

The three of them had found a picnic table in the sunshine. It was the first weekend of spring, and Sadie packed a basket full of her father's favorite things... deviled ham sandwiches, homemade potato salad, and snickerdoodles still warm from the oven. When she realized that she had forgotten the thermos of lemonade, Beau saw his opportunity.

"Shoot... boys, I am sorry. Let me run inside and get us all something to drink. Don't wait for me. Go on ahead and dig in."

Sadie quickly ran back to the cafeteria inside the manor's main hall, and Beau cleared his throat.

"James, sir... I want you to know that I am in love with your daughter. I ummmm... love her very much, sir... and I would like to take care of her for the rest of her life." Beau looked into James's eyes and saw a faint glimmer.

"You love my daughter, Sadie?"

"Yes, sir... very, very much. I'd like to ask you, sir... if I might have her hand in marriage."

James took a bite of his sandwich and wiped his mouth. The wait for him to swallow seemed like it took forever.

"She's quite young to be getting married," James muttered. Beau let out a tiny laugh. There was no sense trying to explain that Sadie was months away from turning 51. Beau was just grateful that James seemed to recognize Sadie today... as his daughter and not as a stranger.

"Yes, sir… but we are in love, and I'd like to take her as my wife."

James nodded his head up and down, and Beau looked up and watched Sadie walk towards them with bottles of water in her hands.

Beau didn't want her to find out, but he had a plan in case she did. They had no secrets anymore. He'd just play his cards and let the chips fall where they might. He had tucked the ring inside the front pocket of his jeans just in case.

"Well, if my daughter would like to marry you, then by all means… you have my blessing," James said as he took another bite out of his sandwich.

Beau let out a long-held breath and nodded back at James with a broad smile across his face. "Thank you, sir."

Beau finished just about the time that Sadie plopped down opposite him at the picnic table.

"Well… how's lunch? Neither one of you has hardly touched anything. I told you not to wait," Sadie said with a sigh.

"This young man and I were just talking," James said.

Beau felt his gut tighten. James was going to spill the beans, and Beau was going to have to think fast on his feet.

"Beau… dad. This young man is Beau."

"Yes, Beau… I know!" James barked defiantly.

Beau watched as Sadie's dad stuffed a spoonful of potato salad into his mouth, and nothing more was mentioned of their conversation.

* * *

"We should go join them… Patrick and James… don't you think?" Sadie asked.

Beau nibbled one last time on her neck until she squirmed free in his arms.

"I just can't take you anywhere, can I?" Sadie said as she turned and wrapped her arms around Beau's waist and kissed him full on the lips. "Save some for later, please."

Beau released her and nodded in response and then took Sadie's hand to lead her across the meadow to Patrick and James.

"Hey, dad. How are you today?" Sadie asked.

"Well... well ... look who is here. Skookum... and you brought my grandson!"

James patted the top of Patrick's head and winked at Beau. Sadie's mouth fell open. She didn't know what to say.

"Dad... this is Patrick, Beau's son. You remember Beau?"

James stood and extended his hand. "It's a pleasure to meet you."

Patrick set the birdhouse down next to James and jumped off the bench and lunged for Sadie.

"Sadie Mae... I have a grandpa... just like the other kids at school. I have a grandpa!"

Sadie looked up at Beau with tears in her eyes. She was speechless. She didn't know what to say to Patrick.

"Grandpa James... look what we brought you." Patrick's voice was full of excitement as he grabbed the model airplane out of Beau's hands and thrust it into James's lap.

"Well, look at what we have here. A P-40B Tiger Shark. Did you know, young man that they were flown by the Flying Tigers, known officially as the 1st American Volunteer Group and were a unit of the Chinese Air Force, recruited from U.S. aviators?"

Sadie let the tears fall down her cheeks as she watched her father talking to Patrick.

"Why don't you and I go put this thing together?" James said to Patrick, and the two of them raced off the bench and over to one of the empty picnic tables. Patrick reached up his tiny hand to grip James's arm... skipping merrily beside him.

"You okay, baby?"

Sadie silently shook her head and pulled a Kleenex out of her jacket pocket.

"Ummmm... grandpa? Are you okay with that, Beau? Patrick calling my dad... grandpa?" Sadie asked. Beau simply nodded his head and took her hand.

"Look at that kid! It's Christmas Day to him. Sadie, I had no idea that Patrick had any desire to have a grandpa. Hannah's estranged from her family, and my dad is gone. Poor kid. He's never said anything to me about other kids at school having a grandpa."

"We should tell him, Beau. He's going to be heartbroken... if we come out here next time, and my dad doesn't remember him."

"I agree. We'll talk about it tonight, okay? He's probably not going to understand, but we will do our best. That's all we can do."

Beau gathered Sadie in his arms and whispered in her ear. "Now, baby... I'd love to go see how they are coming along with the airplane, so why don't you go and get us some sweet tea and cookies."

CHAPTER TWENTY-TWO

"**S**adie Mae... are you ready?"

Patrick's sweet voice carried up into the bedroom of the loft. His antics made Sadie laugh. Although she didn't want a big fuss for her birthday, she knew how much the little boy had been looking forward to it. Since he couldn't spend Sadie's actual birthday with her, they planned to celebrate the weekend after, and she knew that the boys were planning a special day for her.

She had been relegated to the bedroom Saturday afternoon, and she heard the boys whispering downstairs. They asked Sadie to be ready at four o'clock, wear a dress (which was Beau's request), and that she could only come downstairs when escorted. Amidst the hushed conversation Beau had with the 5-year-old, Sadie didn't have a hard time figuring out or smelling that Beau was cooking her favorite meal... grilled shrimp and his (Lady Jane's) famous cheesy grits, not to mention the unmistakable scent of chocolate cake.

Patrick yelled at George to behave and sit at the staircase and then called up for her. It was time for the party to begin, and Sadie appeared at the top of the stairs in a strapless navy-blue floral dress that hit her just above the knee. Patrick climbed the stairs, and Sadie hooked her arm under his, and he led her down to where Beau was waiting with a bouquet of sunflowers.

"Wow... you boys have been busy. Thank you, Beau... they are beautiful!"

Sadie reached out and took the flowers grabbing Beau by the waist and kissing him on the lips.

"You look amazing, Sadie Mae."

Beau grabbed the back of Sadie's thigh, but he didn't dare do anything other than kiss her with Patrick in the same room. Beau's returned kiss made Sadie's knees buckle.

Nashville suited her. Her skin was bronzed from the late spring sunshine, and her hair a bit lighter in color and longer. Beau loved how her messy locks sexily brushed over her shoulders. Her body was fit and tone... not only from chasing Patrick around, but also keeping Beau satisfied in bed.

"Yuck... stop kissing! Sadie, come on!" Patrick yelled as he grabbed her by the hand. Sadie quickly followed him towards the patio, George galloping behind them.

"Oh, wait!" Patrick exclaimed, stopping dead in his tracks. "You are supposed to close your eyes, Sadie... or else you'll see your present."

"Okay... eyes closed. Lead the way, buddy."

Beau watched as Patrick carefully led Sadie out through the patio door.

"Okay, Sadie... you sit here," Patrick instructed like a drill Sargent, and Sadie reached behind her to feel for the chair and quickly took a seat.

"Eyes closed," Patrick barked.

"Hey, son... not so bossy, okay?"

Beau tried not to laugh but watching his son's interactions with Sadie warmed his soul. They were inseparable, and Beau hated to admit it, but he caught himself a little jealous a time or two of his young Romeo. Patrick always wanted Sadie to read him a bedtime story, and it was Sadie that Patrick wanted to sit next to at the booth of the local diner when they ate pancakes on Saturday morning. If Patrick climbed the stairs to the bedroom, it was always Sadie's side of the bed he went to when the thunder woke him up, or Max needed another goodnight kiss.

"Sorry, dad. I'm just so s'ited," he giggled.

"Me too, Patrick. I'm s'ited too," Sadie replied.

"Okay, you can open your eyes now, Sadie Mae."

Patrick was standing about three inches from Sadie's face… grinning from ear to ear.

"Yay! I got a 5-year-old boy for my birthday. You. Are. The. Best. Present. EVER!" Sadie said in her best caricature voice. She reached out and tickled Patrick until he squirmed free.

"No… not me, Sadie Mae. Look behind you."

Sadie quickly turned to find a stainless-steel gas patio heater decorated with about 25 bows.

"Patrick wanted to wrap it up, but I told him that it was probably not going to work," Beau said as he watched Sadie leap up from her chair and ruffled Patrick's hair.

"I love it! Thank you, boys. We can sit out here all year long, now… and I can look for my stars every night."

Sadie felt her eyes prick with tears… her heart busting open with an abundance of love so profound that it left her speechless.

Beau and Patrick excused themselves back into the kitchen as Sadie re-took her seat, George at her feet pantinng.

"Time for drinks!" Patrick exclaimed as he appeared with his Batman glass filled with a purple stinger. Beau was right behind him and brought out Sadie's Wonder Woman mug filled with chardonnay.

"Sorry… about the stemware. Patrick insisted," Beau exclaimed as they clinked their glasses together and all shouted cheers.

"I love you both very much, and you shouldn't have gone to all this trouble," Sadie said.

Patrick began to giggle and dance... his purple concoction sloshing from his cup. Beau cautiously reached out and took the drink from his son before he spilled the entire contents on Sadie.

"Can I ask her now... dad... please? Can I ask her now?"

Patrick walked over to Beau, who was standing at the other end of the patio table, hands deep in the pockets of his dark cobalt blue jeans, watching Sadie. His tanned skin made his V-neck white T-shirt blaze in the spring sunshine. She returned his observation and saw nothing by love in his hazel gray eyes.

"Yes... son. Go on ahead. Just like we practiced, okay?"

Sadie knew that Patrick had been practicing a poem about Tennessee for school, but he seemed too excited for it to be about that. He turned and ran towards Sadie at full speed, and she threw her arms up as the little boy pounced on her lap.

"What is it, Patrick? What's got you so excited? What do you want to ask me, buddy?"

The little boy just looked into Sadie's eyes and melted her heart.

"Remember, Patrick... just like we practiced," Beau pleaded as he gave his son an affectionate look.

"What are you boys up too?" Sadie asked. She let out an adorable giggled and shrugged her shoulders as Patrick ran back to Beau. Sadie watched as Beau knelt to his son and whispered in his ear.

"Remember this part... right. You need to be careful... very careful, okay?"

Patrick nodded as Beau reached into his back pocket and removed the small velvet box and placed it in his son's hands. Patrick carefully tucked it behind his back and slowly returned to Sadie.

"Ummmm... Sadie Mae. I was wondering something..."

The little boy hopped from one foot to the other, and Beau wondered if he was going to have to intercede. He turned back towards his father, and Beau nodded his head.

"I would like to ask you to marry us?"

Patrick quickly pulled the box from behind his back and carefully opened it as Sadie let out a squeal.

The ring glistened in the early May sun as Sadie stared down at it. Before her eyes was an antique art deco ring with an old mine cut two-carat diamond, centered in white gold. Sadie reached for the box and held it in her hands as she began to sob.

"Oh, dad... she's crying. She's upset." Patrick's lower lip began to quiver as he took a step back from Sadie.

"It's okay, son... remember we talked about this," Beau said. Sensing Patrick's disappointment, Sadie reached out for him and grabbed his arm.

"Come here... beautiful boy."

Sadie took him in her arms and hugged him tightly. "I'm not upset. I'm happy. You make me very happy, okay?"

Patrick's lower lip puffed out as he nodded his head.

"Yes, I'll marry you and I'll marry your daddy, too."

Patrick pulled away from her and ran back to his father. Beau placed his hand on top of the boy's head and gave him a loving pat. His son's tears replaced with a full grin.

"Dad... she said, yes!" Patrick shouted.

Sadie jumped from her chair and ran into Beau's arms. He picked her up like a feather and twirled her around – Patrick jumping up and down and George barking. Beau set Sadie down and ran his hands down the length of her body before falling to one knee.

"Sadie Mae Morgan... will you please do me the honor of being my wife?"

Sadie leaned forward and kissed Beau on the lips then whispered into his ear the words he had been waiting to hear.

"Beauford Patrick Walker, I would love to marry you, and it would be an honor to be your wife."

Beau took the ring from the box and ceremoniously slid it on Sadie's finger.

After more hugs and kisses and a quick walk across the street for George's nightly deposit, Beau and Patrick served an incredible meal of Caesar salad, shrimp and grits, and parmesan biscuits, although Patrick opted for a grilled hot dog which seemed perfect to Sadie.

* * *

"One more story… please."

Beau had taken Patrick for a shower, put him in clean superhero pajamas, and deposited him into his bed where Sadie was waiting – a stack of books on her lap. The little boy snuggled close to her, and she leaned in to kiss his wet bubble gum scented hair.

"Patrick…"

Beau heard his son's pleas and called out. He was desperate to get Sadie… his new fiancé all to himself.

"It's okay. It's my birthday party, and I think one more story is perfectly fine, Beau."

They were both in luck as Patrick fell asleep before Sadie finished the story. She tucked the covers around the little boy and quickly dashed out to the patio to meet Beau and George.

"I grabbed your sweater, baby."

Beau had turned the new patio heater on, and they sat outside and sipped on cabernet in real wine glasses.

"Sadie…"

Beau had caught her staring up at the stars and then down to her ring. The lights of Nashville made the stars hard to spot, and the sky had long since darkened past her favorite shade, but Sadie felt the tears stinging her eyes as she stared at the ring glistening on her hand.

"The ring was my great-grandmothers. If you don't like it… we can get you something else, okay?" Beau cautiously asked.

Sadie smiled and shook her head sideways. The tears overwhelmed her. They came from deep inside and filled her eyes until overflowing.

"Baby… you're crying."

Beau reached out for her hand and rubbed his thumb over her knuckles.

"I'm good… it's all good. No, Beau… it's perfect, actually!"

Beau crawled out of his chair and got down on his knees in front of her. He grabbed for her face and kissed her hard – silencing her tears.

"The ring is amazing. Thank you. Lady Jane is okay with this?"

Sadie's stomach tightened as Beau shook his head from side to side.

"The ring is a Walker ring… not a Broadfield. Hard to believe, huh?! But to answer your questions… yes, Lady Jane and Presley are thrilled… over the moon!" Beau didn't think he'd ever seen Sadie's smile any bigger.

"I asked him, Sadie… your dad. A few weeks ago. Remember that first warm day of spring… the picnic lunch? Well, I told him that I loved you and that I wanted to take care of you for the rest of your life. I asked him for your hand, and he gave me his blessing."

Sadie's eyes overflowed with tears once again, hearing Beau's words.

"All I want to do is make you happy… every day for the rest of my life, Sadie Mae."

Sadie had no idea that Beau would ever ask her father in his condition, but she thought back to their very first meeting at the brewpub. Beau was a true southern gentleman.

"Oh, Beau... you do make me happy. Every day!" Sadie exclaimed.

Beau stood and kissed her soft lips and then sat back down across from her, leaning forward in his chair, elbows on his thighs.

"When do you want to get married?" he asked as Sadie chuckled. Beau was almost as adorable as Patrick. His longing eyes anxiously waiting for her response.

"Tomorrow?" Sadie said, laughing.

"Tomorrow... really... you'd marry me tomorrow?"

Sadie emphatically shook her head up and down, her cheeks flushing pink.

"I am assuming that we need to get a license... so maybe tomorrow won't work, but I see no reason to wait. God, Beau.... I don't want to wait, okay.... not another day."

Sadie dashed out of her chair and plopped herself down on Beau's lap.

"I don't want to wait either, Sadie Mae. Baby, I love you so much."

Beau's kisses on Sadie's neck made her desperately want more... so she let Beau reach under her dress and run his hands up the inside of her thigh.

"Is it too early to go to bed?" Sadie asked. She didn't wait for Beau's answer as she rose from his lap and grabbed his hand. As they turned to head back inside, Beau's cell phone shook the patio table.

"Who could this be?" Beau said as he picked up his phone. It was Tall Oaks Manor, and Beau let out a deep sigh. "Sadie, I think this might be about your dad."

Beau quickly slid his finger across the screen and lifted the phone to his ear. Sadie had no idea where her cellphone was. The last time she remembered having it was upstairs before the evening's festivities had begun.

"Beau Walker..."

Sadie stood next to Beau as she listened to the one-sided conversation. "Yes! Miss Morgan is right here with me. I see. Okay… how long ago? Oh… dear God."

Beau ran his hand through his hair and looked over at Sadie, shaking his head from side to side. Sadie closed her eyes, and she instantly knew.

"Yes, ma'am. I understand. We will be right there. Thank you for calling."

Beau turned to set his phone down on the table and took her in his arms, and she silently began to cry.

"They think it was a stroke… about an hour ago. He went to lie down after dinner, and it happened in his sleep. He didn't suffer, baby… but he's gone now."

Sadie tried to let the words sink in. It was the happiest day of her life in more ways than one. The pain of losing her father had already occurred… years ago. She would selfishly mourn him, but he was long gone, and in a way, he was already dead to her. This would start her healing. Sadie's tears were for their memories and her past – a part of her that no one knew. A door had just closed, never to be opened again.

"Let me get Patrick. I'll get a blanket and carry him to the car," Beau said as Sadie wiped the tears from her eyes.

"No, Beau. I don't want you dragging him out of bed… it's late. He won't understand, and he will be scared."

"Sadie… I think you should go and say goodbye."

Beau suddenly remembered the day his father passed away and how grateful he had been to have not driven away from Broadfield House that night to go back to Athens.

"No… it's okay. Last weekend… you know I felt something in my heart. It felt like a goodbye. He was so happy with Patrick… he remembered you for the first time… called you by your name. He knew I was happy… we were happy, and he touched my arm, and I knew… he looked me in the eyes, and I knew right then. He was at peace. I was at peace. That was our goodbye, Beau."

Sadie wrapped her arms tight around his waist and softly laid her head against his broad chest. "I just want to be here with you. Wake up in your arms with our little boy tomorrow morning and start planning our life together. Okay?"

"Okay, baby. Are you sure?" Beau asked.

"Yes, I am sure."

Beau went inside to check on Patrick, and Sadie made a couple of phone calls. She felt like she should let him know, so she texted Joel and told him that James had passed away. It took him three days to respond to her, and his reply was a curt, *I'm sorry for your loss.* She no longer cared, and she finally felt free.

George was waiting for Sadie at the patio door when she finally came inside. She put him to bed and climbed the stairs and found her two boys sleeping soundly. Sadie let out a deep sigh when she finally snuggled in next to Beau – Patrick sideways on her side of the bed.

That night, Sadie slept the best that she had slept in years. She was free of anxiety about her father and excited for her future with Beau and Patrick. Deep in the night, Sadie dreamt of her father. She heard his voice calling her name as he climbed into an old rowboat and took off down a lazy river, fishing pole in hand. He looked over his shoulder to smile and wave back at her as the boat rounded the bend out of sight.

CHAPTER TWENTY-THREE

Sadie dabbed her eyes with a tissue and let out a deep breath. The May sunshine filled up the solarium, and she could hear the songbirds chirping at the birdfeeder that Lady Jane had hanging off the patio awning.

"Sadie Mae… it's time to go, baby," Beau called out. He stood in the doorway of Broadfield House's solarium and watched her quietly sitting on the sofa. "Presley and Mama are helping Patrick into the car."

Beau walked over and placed his hand upon her shoulder and gave it a firm squeeze. Sadie had not been able to let go of the silver urn since the funeral director handed it to her. It was all she had left of her father.

"Do you want me to take that?" Beau asked as Sadie stood shaking her head sideways. She clutched the urn tight as her eyes began to well again with fresh tears.

"No, thank you. I want to hang onto it for the ride."

Sadie felt Beau's hand in the middle of her back as he gently walked her through the house and out onto the front porch.

"It's going to be a beautiful drive. You're gonna love this spot, Sadie. Beau's picked out the best place for James," Lady Jane said as she met Beau and Sadie on the bottom step of the porch. "We've got Patrick all snug in the booster. Why don't you ride up front with Beau?"

"Thank you, ma'am."

Sadie gave Lady Jane a faint smile as she walked to the front seat of the car and opened the door.

"No!" Patrick shouted from the backseat. "I want Sadie to sit next to me." Patrick began to squirm and kick his feet against the back of the driver's seat.

"Enough, young man," Beau said as he leaned into the backseat to reprimand the child.

"I want to sit next to grandpa and Sadie Mae," Patrick said with a hush.

Patrick still didn't fully understand how Sadie's father fit into the urn, and he had been asking all morning when the two of them were going to finish the latest model airplane.

"You take the front seat, Lady Jane. Presley and I... and dad... will keep Patrick company here in the back."

Lady Jane squeezed Sadie's arm, and Presley slid in next to her as Lady Jane closed the back-passenger door. Patrick reached for Sadie when he saw her dab her tears with her handkerchief.

"Is grandpa going to ride on your lap the whole way, Sadie... because he can ride on my lap too." Patrick's sweet words made Sadie chuckle.

"Promise you'll hold on tight?" Sadie asked as Patrick nodded his head. Sadie smiled and gently placed the urn between his legs. He wrapped his arms tight around the silver canister and hugged it.

"I love you, grandpa."

Sadie choked on her tears as Presley reached out to grab her hand.

"Ummmm... Jesus, Sadie. That thing has a lid, right?" Beau exclaimed as he turned around in the driver's seat. Patrick had the widest grin imaginable, and Beau saw Sadie's smile return for the first time since they received the call that her father had died eleven days ago.

"It's all right. He's a big boy. We will be just fine."

Beau nodded and turned to start the Jeep and they made their way down the driveway.

"I'm sorry to have messed up your plans, Prez," Sadie spoke. She leaned her head on Beau's sister's shoulder and let out a sigh.

Chris was arriving later from Nashville in a U-Haul. They had signed the papers four weeks ago on a bungalow near Piedmont Park in the Virginia Highland neighborhood of northeast Atlanta. The house was perfect and a combination of classic southern charm and modern luxury with a chef's kitchen, spa-inspired bathrooms, gleaming hardwoods, a huge backyard, and a rocking chair swing on the front porch. Only Beau knew that tomorrow night, when all the boxes were unloaded from the U-Haul and Chris and Presley prepared to spend their first night in their new home, that Chris would be getting down on one knee. Beau had given his blessing in Nashville two weeks before... just days before Beau got down on one knee and proposed to Sadie.

"Don't be silly. This is where I want to be... with family," Presley said as she wrapped her arm around Sadie's shoulder and squeezed her tight. "Besides... I kind of got out of all the heavy lifting," Presley said with a wink as she cupped her hand over her tiny baby bump.

The drive through rural Georgia was breath-taking. Rolling hills with fields and pastures and babbling brooks that divided small one street-light towns. Sadie peered out the window as the greenery floated by... massive oak and pecan trees and tall grass as far as she could see. It reminded her so much of the Pacific Northwest that she had to remind herself that she was in Georgia.

Sadie had let Beau plan the scattering of her father's ashes, and he told her that he would be taking them about thirty minutes northeast of Broadfield House. He had a special place in mind, but he didn't want to tell her. Beau wanted to show her. The land had been in the family for decades, and it was his, he just never knew what to do with it until now. It was their future now... Beau, Sadie, and Patrick's.

Beau had been working on the plans for years, but in light of recent events, he changed course. Beau feverously worked well into the night the past week, trying to create the perfect house for the three of them. It would be a place where they could spend holidays and summers, and after Patrick grew up and went away to college, Beau and Sadie could spend more time there. Her father would be on the property, his ashes scattered near a grove of trees on the creek's bank. Beau envisioned the most beautiful memorial garden near the trees with a bench where Sadie could sit and be with her father whenever she wanted. The drawings and plans were tucked away in the back of the Jeep.

As the car slowed, Lady Jane helped with the directions. "The Mackey's share this same road. Just past that grove of hickory is the lane to the property... stay to the right."

Beau took the road slowly. The late spring rains had washed away the gravel creating huge potholes. He barely recognized the place. It had been years since he surveyed the land, but now he was excited to plan their future and create a long-lasting legacy for his family.

"Wow, Beau look. It's fairly overgrown, you know... it's gonna be a lot of work," Lady Jane chimed in as she leaned forward in her seat and gazed out the window.

"I know Mama. Thank you."

"But... oh, Sadie... those trees in the fall. They are so beautiful."

Lady Jane reached out and tapped Sadie's hand, which was resting on the side of the driver's seat. Sadie quickly glanced back at Patrick, who was sound asleep, still clutching the silver urn as the car slowly made its way down the rough road.

"Beau... where are we?" Sadie asked. She unfastened her seatbelt and leaned forward.

"Welcome to Coal Mountain, Georgia, Sadie Mae," Beau exclaimed.

The overgrown brush and tree branches snapped against the side of the car, and Sadie looked back at Patrick, who remained fast asleep.

"Do you remember the first time we came here, Beaufart?" Presley asked as she also unfastened her seatbelt and leaned forward.

"Daddy took us fishing, and you fell into the creek... soaking wet, and we had to leave. I never even got a line in the water."

Beau looked into the rearview mirror at his sister with a smile on his face.

"He wouldn't talk to me for three days. I was barely as old as Patrick is now. I didn't think you were ever going to forgive me, Beau."

"Now, wherever Presley goes... we make her take a change of clothes," Beau said with a laugh. He loved teasing his sister. It made Sadie jealous to not have close family or a sibling, especially on a day like today.

Beau pulled the car up into a clearing, where the grass had been cut recently. "I'm glad to see the boys did as they were told."

Beau hired the Mackey's oldest son and a friend to clear a patch of grass down to the creek. He pulled the Jeep forward and turned off the engine.

"Okay... everybody we are here. Let's get out and go exploring."

"Um... really... we are here. Okay?" Sadie cautiously replied. She began having some immediate trepidations. She wasn't sure if she could let go. Let her dad go today. His final resting place was going to be Coal Mountain, Georgia. Suddenly it all felt very wrong.

"Beau... um... can I have a quick word with you," Sadie whispered as Lady Jane and Presley exited the vehicle.

"You kids go on. Prez and I will stay with Patrick until he wakes up. I packed a cooler with some sweet tea and cookies. You go on now."

"Thanks, Mama." Beau jumped out of the Jeep and ran around the back for the plans, hiding them under an old blanket. "Come on, baby."

Beau took Sadie by the hand and led her down the mowed grass path towards the creek. They took two steps, and Sadie's black pumps got stuck in the soft ground.

"Wait a second... sorry! Baby, your gonna need your boots. I am just so excited. I wasn't thinking straight."

Sadie smiled up at Beau and walked back to the Jeep to put on her black cowboy boots.

"You're lucky they go with my dress."

Sadie hadn't wanted a big fuss for her dad, but she knew that he would be okay with the small ceremony at the funeral home earlier that morning – James' ashes still warm when the funeral director set them in her lap. They all sang "Amazing Grace" and "Nearer, My God, to Thee", and the preacher gave a service, especially for woodworkers, as if Sadie knew there was such a thing.

Lady Jane had taken Sadie shopping and bought her the most gorgeous black A-line dress which fit her snug through the middle and cut her right at the knee. She paired the dress with a vintage pearl bracelet with a glass cameo clasp that she had picked up a few weeks ago, at a flea market shopping with Mazie. Sadie leaned against the Jeep to put her boots on... about the time that Patrick began to rustle in the backseat.

"Let me out! I want to go s'ploring," Patrick squealed. Sadie opened up the driver's side back seat and undid Patrick's seatbelt. He clung tight to Sadie's neck as she pulled him out of the car, and he whispered in her ear.

"Where's grandpa?"

"He's in the back with us, Patrick," Lady Jane yelled out as she unfolded a couple of camping chairs and set up the iced tea and cookies, placing the urn with James's ashes in one of the empty chairs.

Sadie looked back at Beau. His hands were on his hips, and Sadie could tell that he was trying very hard to remain patient. He looked so good in his jeans and boots – a light blue button-down shirt paired with a dark navy-blue blazer. His Wranglers fit tight over his back end. Sadie still had a hard time believing that he was her fiancé. That he loved her as he did. Even on a day like today as she was letting go, the universe had opened itself wide open and had given her so much more.

"You stay here with grandpa... keep an eye on him, okay. Dad and I will be right back, and then we will all go exploring. Don't eat all the cookies, buddy."

Sadie set Patrick down on Presley's lap and ran back to Beau, who placed his arms around her waist and pulled her close.

"Are you ready, baby?" Beau asked, and Sadie nodded her head. Beau held her hand as they silently walked down to the creek.

As they got closer to the bank, Sadie felt a cool breeze off the water. The morning rain made the fresh-cut grass smell sweet, and Sadie spotted wildflowers just coming up along the creek bank. She still wasn't sure about dumping her father off here and leaving, but Sadie trusted Beau, and she had, after all, asked him to plan out his final resting place. Since Sadie didn't have any idea what to do with her father's ashes and she couldn't stand for him to remain trapped in an urn for the rest of eternity, she really needed Beau's guidance. It was just that something about this place seemed wrong.

"Beau, I've been thinking. Maybe I should take my dad back to Seattle. I know the military cemetery would take him. In a way, he would be home, I guess. Oh, God, I am not really sure anymore." Sadie buried her head in her hands and began to cry. "This is all so much... today. I know I need to let him go, and it's just that... shit... I'm standing in a field in Coal Mountain, Georgia. Beau... why am I standing in a field in Coal Mountain, Georgia?"

Sadie snorted her tears – half laughing and half crying. She wiped her eyes and turned from Beau, staring out onto such beauty that she started re-thinking her previous comments.

"This is mine... my land... our land... you and me and Patrick. It's about 70 acres." Beau came up behind Sadie and grabbed her by the waist with one arm and extended the other arm out in front of her. "So… as far as you can see, due south… about 2 miles." Beau grabbed her waist tighter and spun her around, and Sadie let out a squeal.

"Look out that way, baby… east, about one mile to the fence line on the road we came in on. The other side is the Mackey land and then right over that creek north and through that grove of hickory to the edge of the creek again… that's about a mile. If you look west, out past the tall grass, it goes another half mile."

Beau let go of Sadie's waist and turned her towards him, cupping her face. Sadie's expression hadn't changed, and Beau could tell that she was confused and frightened.

"Baby, the reason I brought you here to Coal Mountain, Georgia, is because I think your father would have loved it. The trees… wildflowers… fish in the creek… so many songbirds, they drive you crazy. This place is very special. I'm gonna make it even better. Can I show you?"

Beau quickly pulled away and laid a blanket down on the ground, and Sadie dropped to her knees. She watched as Beau took the plans out of the blueprint tube and unrolled them in front of her. On the plans… embossed in gold at the top were the words *Beau loves Sadie* inside a big heart.

"This is the house… cabin… Mama says your gonna want to call it a cottage, but that's fine by me. It's not going to be big… three bedrooms… ours will be the biggest," Beau said with a wink as he continued. "I've still got to design a closet big enough for all your boots."

He watched as Sadie started to cry again, but Beau knew those tears… those were tears of joy and love.

"Listen, the house isn't all that finished yet… maybe in my mind. I've been working more on the outside. Shit… I started this a long time ago. It was going to be a fishing cabin for Patrick and me, but now… I think I could get used to the idea of calling it a cottage," Beau said with a chuckle.

"I just want you to be happy. I want you to have joy and be at peace. Sadie Mae, I promised your dad that I would take care of you… that means doing right by him as well."

Sadie reached up and touched Beau's cheek and looked deep into his eyes.

"See that spot right on the other side of the creek… right up against that grove of trees, that's where the house goes. The kitchen… great room facing east/west… wrap around porch… plenty of room to watch the stars." Beau's description made Sadie giggle.

"Do you see it, baby? Close your eyes and tell me you see it."

Sadie nodded her head and closed her eyes. "I see it, Beau… I do," Sadie said as she opened her eyes and smiled.

"Okay, so right off the front porch is the garden… leading down to the creek. Not sure how formal we can make it… lots of deer around. I'm thinking some kind of fence but see this design… I did something similar for a cancer center a few years ago. It's a garden labyrinth… a pathway to healing. I added a bench for you and these large fieldstone steps. I'm going to build a little bluestone wall right there… see where the trees slope up. In between the stone steps, I'll plant some grass sod, and I'll fill it in with tiny pebbles. Sadie Mae… you can come here anytime you want… be with your dad… alone… quietly. You can listen to the birds and hear the creek. All the things your dad loved. I think he'd be real pleased to know that this was his final resting place."

Sadie stood up and looked around again. She could see it in her mind… the house, the garden… Patrick running around with George… the sun going down and the stars lighting up the Georgia sky. Sadie turned back to look at Beau and realized that he was waiting for a definitive reaction. She closed her eyes tight and began to cry. As big tears fell from her face, Beau jumped up from the blanket and embraced her tight as her crying turned into deep sobs.

"It's okay, baby... I understand. It's too soon. I get it. I'm fine... honestly. Let me take you home, okay. Let's go back to Broadfield House and then Nashville tomorrow."

Sadie pulled away and shook her head, trying hard to stop crying. "No! Beau... that's not... that's not it at all." Her eyes were overflowing with tears, but Sadie's smile was wide.

"I'm sorry, Beau... I am *so* sorry. It's beautiful. It's the most beautiful thing I've ever... not yet seen with my own eyes." Sadie let out a big laugh and wiped her nose on her handkerchief.

"Your plans for the house and the garden. God... my dad would love it, you were right. This is the most beautiful place. I'm not sure that I am worthy of this... my dad and me, but if it's what you want, then yes, Beau. Yes, to all of it!"

Sadie jumped into Beau's arms, and he twirled them around and let out a loud whoop. In the distance, Patrick, Lady Jane, and Presley began walking towards them as Beau put Sadie back on the ground and gave her a long deep kiss. He still made her knees buckle.

"Are you going to tell them?" Sadie asked as she reached down for Beau's hand.

"We will tell them together, okay?"

* * *

Three weeks later, in the back garden of Broadfield House, Sadie Mae Morgan married Beaufort Patrick Walker in front of a handful of close friends and family.

Her father's ashes sat in the front row.

The End

NOTE FROM THE AUTHOR

Thank you, dear reader, for sticking with this story until the end. I hope you enjoyed the story of Beau and Sadie as much as I enjoyed creating these two characters. I left a piece of my heart and soul on every page and to put it out to the universe for others to read was a big emotional step for me. While I know that it is not perfect, I am still excited to bring this part of the creative process to a close and share it with you. Thank you for allowing me the opportunity. I am extremely grateful.

I'd love to hear your thoughts, opinions or questions so please feel free to send a comment through the Tennessee Dreams website or via e-mail.

Next up is First Sight the story of Noah and Addison.

Love,

Stacy

ACKNOWLEDGEMENTS

Ain't No Sunshine
Words and Music by Bill Withers
Copyright (c) 1971 INTERIOR MUSIC CORP.
Copyright Renewed
All Rights Controlled and Administered by SONGS OF UNIVERSAL, INC.
All Rights Reserved Used by Permission *Reprinted by Permission of Hal Leonard LLC*

Last Name Words and Music by Luke Laird, Hillary Lindsey and Carrie Underwood
Copyright (c) 2007 by Universal Music - MGB Songs, Laird Road Music, BMG Gold Songs, Raylene Music and Carrie-Okie Music
All Rights for Laird Road Music Administered by Universal Music - MGB Songs
All Rights for BMG Gold Songs Administered by BMG Rights Management (US) LLC
All Rights for Raylene Music Administered by BPJ Administration, P.O. Box 218061, Nashville, TN 37221-8061
International Copyright Secured
All Rights Reserved *Reprinted by Permission of Hal Leonard LLC*